PRINCIPLES OF

PHARMACOVIGILANCE

For

All those interested in Drug Safety

Dr. S. B. Bhise

M. Pharm., Ph.D.

Ex. Principal, Govt. College of Pharmacy,

Karad / Aurangabad &

Managing Director, KLK Consultants, Pune

NIRALI PRAKASHAN
ADVANCEMENT OF KNOWLEDGE

N1619

PRINCIPLES OF PHARMACOVIGILANCE   ISBN 978-93-86084-89-7

First Edition : September 2016

© : Authors

Published By :

NIRALI PRAKASHAN

Abhyudaya Pragati, 1312, Shivaji Nagar

Off J.M. Road, PUNE – 411005

Tel - (020) 25512336/37/39, Fax - (020) 25511379

Email : niralipune@pragationline.com

➤ DISTRIBUTION CENTRES

PUNE

Nirali Prakashan : 119, Budhwar Peth, Jogeshwari Mandir Lane, Pune 411002, Maharashtra
Tel : (020) 2445 2044, 66022708, Fax : (020) 2445 1538
Email : bookorder@pragationline.com, niralilocal@pragationline.com

Nirali Prakashan : S. No. 28/27, Dhyari, Near Pari Company, Pune 411041
Tel : (020) 24690204 Fax : (020) 24690316
Email : dhyari@pragationline.com, bookorder@pragationline.com

MUMBAI

Nirali Prakashan : 385, S.V.P. Road, Rasdhara Co-op. Hsg. Society Ltd.,
Girgaum, Mumbai 400004, Maharashtra
Tel : (022) 2385 6339 / 2386 9976, Fax : (022) 2386 9976
Email : niralimumbai@pragationline.com

➤ DISTRIBUTION BRANCHES

JALGAON

Nirali Prakashan : 34, V. V. Golani Market, Navi Peth, Jalgaon 425001,
Maharashtra, Tel : (0257) 222 0395, Mob : 94234 91860

KOLHAPUR

Nirali Prakashan : New Mahadvar Road, Kedar Plaza, 1st Floor Opp. IDBI Bank
Kolhapur 416 012, Maharashtra. Mob : 9850046155

NAGPUR

Pratibha Book Distributors : Above Maratha Mandir, Shop No. 3, First Floor,
Rani Jhanshi Square, Sitabuldi, Nagpur 440012, Maharashtra
Tel : (0712) 254 7129

DELHI

Nirali Prakashan : 4593/21, Basement, Aggarwal Lane 15, Ansari Road, Daryaganj
Near Times of India Building, New Delhi 110002 Mob : 08505972553

BENGALURU

Pragati Book House : House No. 1, Sanjeevappa Lane, Avenue Road Cross,
Opp. Rice Church, Bengaluru – 560002.
Tel : (080) 64513344, 64513355,Mob : 9880582331, 9845021552
Email:bharatsavla@yahoo.com

CHENNAI

Pragati Books : 9/1, Montieth Road, Behind Taas Mahal, Egmore,
Chennai 600008 Tamil Nadu, Tel : (044) 6518 3535,
Mob : 94440 01782 / 98450 21552 / 98805 82331,
Email : bharatsavla@yahoo.com

niralipune@pragationline.com | www.pragationline.com

Also find us on f www.facebook.com/niralibooks

Acknowledgement

I am extremely thankful to Dr. R. B. Navale, Associate Professor, GCOP Aurangabad for editing the content. I am specially thankful to Manjiri, my better half in supporting me on all fronts related to the book.

I am thankful to Dr. S. B. Bumrela for designing cover page for the book.

I am very thankful to Mrs Manasi Pingle, for improving critical details in the content. Support from Prof. S. B. Gokhale and Mr. Jignesh Furia has been a source of inspiration for me.

Dr. S. B. Bhise

■■■

Preface

Pharmacovigilance is an emerging area for employment in recent years. Background of drugs is an advantage for anybody who wants to make a career in pharmacovigilance. Hence, pharmacists are well-suited to exploit the opportunity. The job potential is both local as well as global. Opportunities are enormous; only one has to make commitment for the career.

Hence, first book in the series on Principles of Pharmacovigilance is presented here. It will be followed by another book on Regulatory Aspects of Pharmacovigilance. The future books will depend on demand of stakeholders.

I have tried the contents of the book more informative and inclusive; however for an everchanging field like Pharmacovigilance, updates are probably a daily affair. I have attempted to make the content inclusive; however comments are welcome.

I appeal to all budding pharmacists, teachers and newcomers in the field to go through the contents and communicate constructive criticism to develop the book in coming editions.

September 2016   **Dr. S. B. Bhise**

■■■

Curriculum

1. **Introduction to Adverse Drug Reactions**
   1.1 Definitions and classification of ADRs
   1.2 Detection and reporting
   1.3 Causality assessment
   1.4 Severity and seriousness assessment
   1.5 Predictability and preventability assessment
   1.6 Management of adverse drug reactions
2. **Introduction to Pharmacovigilance**
   2.1 History and development of pharmacovigilance
   2.2 Importance of safety monitoring / Why pharmacovigilance?
3. **National and International Scenario**
   3.1 Pharmacovigilance in India
   3.2 Pharmacovigilance: global perspective
   3.3 WHO international drug monitoring programme
4. **Basic Terminologies used in Pharmacovigilance**
   4.1 Terminologies of adverse medication related events
   4.2 Regulatory terminologies
5. **Information Resources in Pharmacovigilance**
   5.1 Basic drug information resources
   5.2 Specialised resources for ADRs
   5.3 Critical evaluation of medication safety literature
6. **Establishing Pharmacovigilance Programme**
   6.1 Establishing in a hospital
   6.2 Establishment and operation of drug safety department in industry
   6.3 Establishing a national programme
   6.4 SOPs – Types, designing, maintenance and training
   6.5 Roles and responsibilities in pharmacovigilance
      6.5.1 Licence Partners,
      6.5.2 Contract Research Organisations (CROs) and
      6.5.3 Market Authorisation Holders (MAH)
7. **Pharmacovigilance Methods**
   7.1 Passive surveillance – Spontaneous reports and case series
   7.2 Stimulated reporting
   7.3 Active surveillance – Sentinel sites, drug event monitoring and registries
   7.4 Comparative observational studies – Cross-sectional study, case control study and cohort study
   7.5 Targeted clinical investigations
   7.6 Vaccine safety surveillance

■■■

Contents

■■■

Chapter 1...

Introduction to Adverse Drug Reactions

Contents ...

In the standard textbooks of pharmacology it is mentioned that consuming a drug is equivalent to consuming a risk. It is only when the benefit(s) associated with drug(s) are more than the risk(s), that the consumption of a drug is justified. Thus, it is the benefit vs risk ratio of the drug which decides whether a drug is to be taken or not. The next question is how to measure risks and how to measure the benefits. Due to individualization of drugs to patients, it is the clinical judgment of the physician to identify what will benefit the patient. At the same time, risk associated with the drug(s) can be ascertained by observations related to pharmacovigilance. The studies related to pharmacovigilance indicate what are possible risks associated with the drug. Every drug can be associated with possible adverse reactions, intended or unintended. The only exception to this generality is the case of drug(s) which are given in case of deficiency of specific components like vitamins or minerals. It is the study of possible adverse reactions of drugs which constitutes the essential content of Pharmacovigilance. This takes us to the definition of Pharmacovigilance.

Pharmacovigilance is a science which deals with adverse reactions to drugs. Although this meaning of the term Pharmacovigilance offers broad understanding about it, technical definition of few related terms are in place. Some important terms are defined here. Glossary of all terms is included in the Appendix.

1.1 DEFINITIONS AND CLASSIFICATION OF ADVERSE DRUG REACTIONS

1.1.1 Definitions

- **Absolute Risk**

  Risk in a population of exposed persons is the probability of an event affecting members of a particular population (e.g. 1 in 1,000). Absolute risk can be measured over time (incidence) or at a given time (prevalence).

- **Adverse Event (AE)**

  Any untoward medical occurrence that may occur during treatment with a pharmaceutical product, but which does not necessarily have a causal relationship with the treatment.

- **Adverse Drug Reaction (ADR)**

  A response to a medical product, which is noxious and unintended, and which occurs for doses normally used in Human beings for the prophylaxis, diagnosis, or therapy of disease, or for the modification of a physiological function.

- **Attributable Risk**

  Difference between the risk in an exposed population (absolute risk) and the risk in an unexposed population (reference risk) is called attributable risk. Attributable risk is the result of an absolute comparison between outcome frequency measurements, such as incidence.

- **Effectiveness Vs. Risk**

  The balance between the rates of effectiveness of a medicine versus the risk of harm is a quantitative assessment of the merit of a medicine used in routine clinical practice. Comparative information between therapies is most useful. This is more useful than the efficacy and hazard predictions from pre-marketing information that is limited and based on selected subjects.

- **Pharmacovigilance**

  The science and activities related to the detection, assessment, understanding and prevention of adverse effects or any other drug-related problem.

- **Relative Risk**

  Relative risk is defined as, 'ratio of the risk in an exposed population (absolute risk) and the risk in an unexposed population (reference risk)'. Relative risk is the result of a relative comparison between outcome frequency measurements, e.g. incidences.

- **Risk**

  The probability of harm being caused; the probability (chance, odds) of an occurrence.

1.1.2 Classification of ADRs

The adverse reactions to drugs can be are classified on the basis of effects as given below:

Type A Effects:

These are the effects which are due to (exaggerated) pharmacological effects. Type A effects tend to be fairly common, dose related (i.e. more frequent or severe with higher doses) and may often be avoided by using doses which are appropriate to the individual patient. Such effects can usually be reproduced and studied experimentally and are often already identified before marketing. e.g. dryness of mouth caused by Atropine.

Interactions between drugs, especially pharmacokinetic interactions, may often be classified as Type A effects, although they are restricted to a defined sub-population of patients (i.e. the users of the interacting drug).

Type B Effects:

These occur characteristically in only a minority of patients and display little or no dose relationship. They are generally rare and unpredictable, and may be serious and are notoriously difficult to study. Type B effects are either immunological or non-immunological and occur only in patients, with - often unknown - predisposing conditions. Immunological reactions may range from rashes, anaphylaxis, vasculitis, inflammatory organ injury, to highly specific autoimmune syndromes. Also non-immunological type B effects occur in a minority of predisposed, *intolerant* patients, because of an inborn error of metabolism or acquired deficiency in a certain enzyme, resulting in an abnormal metabolic pathway or accumulation of a toxic metabolite. e.g. chloramphenicol-induced aplastic anaemia and isoniazid-induced hepatitis.

Type C Effects:

These effects refer to situations where the use of a drug, often for unknown reasons, increases the frequency of a disease. Type C effects may be both serious and common (and include malignant tumours) and may have pronounced effects on public health. Type C effects may be coincidental and often concern long term effects; there is often no suggestive time relationship and the connection may be very difficult to prove.

The adverse effects can also be classified on the basis of related cause. It is separately dealt in the section 1.3 related to causality assessment.

1.2 DETECTION AND REPORTING

1.2.1 Detection of ADRs

Since ADRs may act through the same physiological and pathological pathways as different diseases, they are difficult and sometimes impossible to distinguish. However, the following step-wise approach may be helpful in assessing possible drug-related ADRs:

1. Ensure that the medicine received is the medicine ordered and actually taken by the patient at the dose advised.

2. Verify that the onset of the suspected ADR was after the drug was taken, not before and discuss carefully the observation made by the patient.

3. Determine the time interval between the beginning of drug treatment and the onset of the event.

4. Evaluate the suspected ADR after discontinuing the drugs or reducing the dose and monitor the patient's status. If appropriate, restart the drug treatment and monitor recurrence of any adverse events.

5. Analyse the alternative causes (other than the drug) that could on their own have caused the reaction.

6. Use relevant up-to-date literature and personal experience as a health professional on drugs and their ADRs and verify if there are previous conclusive reports on this reaction. The National Pharmacovigilance Centre and Drug Information Centres are very important resources for obtaining information on ADR. The manufacturer of the drug can also be a resource to consult.

7. Report any suspected ADR to the person nominated for ADR reporting in the hospital or directly to the National ADR Centre.

1.2.2 Reporting of ADRs

Within India, regulatory authorities have designed a format in which reports of adverse reactions are to be made. The form has been given in the appendix. There are specific instructions for filling up the form. Due to these instructions ambiguities in filling up the form are minimized. A similar form designed by USFDA is also available. The form by any regulatory authorities includes basic information about the patient, details about the suspected adverse reaction, details about all medications given to the patient, relevant laboratory data, and information about seriousness of the event is presented. Advice about what constitutes a serious adverse reaction, who can report, where the information is to be sent and what happens to the information is documented.

1.3 CAUSALITY ASSESSMENT

While reporting any adverse reaction, it is necessary to establish causal relation between the suspected drug and the observed effect. It is also possible that one of the disease process, interaction of the drug on disease process or even lack of effect of a drug exacerbating the disease process may be involved in the observed effect. In order to understand all such events, there is classification of adverse reactions based on causality. It is given below.

Table 1.1

Causality term	Assessment criteria
Certain	• Event or laboratory test abnormality, with plausible time relationship to drug intake. • Cannot be explained by disease or other drugs. • Response to withdrawal plausible (pharmacologically, pathologically). • Event definitive pharmacologically or phenomenologically (i.e. an objective and specific medical disorder or a recognized pharmacological phenomenon). • Rechallenge satisfactory, if necessary.
Probable/ Likely	• Event or laboratory test abnormality, with reasonable time relationship to drug intake. • Unlikely to be attributed to disease or other drugs. • Response to withdrawal clinically reasonable. • Rechallenge not required.
Possible	• Event or laboratory test abnormality, with reasonable time relationship to drug intake. • Could also be explained by disease or other drugs. • Information on drug withdrawal may be lacking or unclear.
Unlikely	• Event or laboratory test abnormality, with a time to drug intake that makes a relationship improbable (but not impossible). • Disease or other drugs provide plausible explanations.
Conditional/ Unclassified	• Event or laboratory test abnormality. • More data for proper assessment needed. • Additional data under examination.
Unassessable/ Unclassifiable	• Report suggesting an adverse reaction. • Cannot be judged because information is insufficient or contradictory. • Data cannot be supplemented or verified.

It is necessary to understand limitations of causality assessment. Following table provides it.

Table 1.2

What causality assessment can do	What causality assessment cannot do
Decrease disagreement between assessors.	Give accurate quantitative measurement of relationship likelihood.
Classify relationship likelihood.	Distinguish valid from invalid cases.
Mark individual case reports.	Prove the connection between drug and event.
Improvement of scientific evaluation; Educational.	Quantify the contribution of a drug to the development of an adverse event.
	Change uncertainty into certainty.

1.4 SEVERITY AND SERIOUSNESS ASSESSMENT

Severity and/or seriousness of an ADR is assessed by following guidelines:

Report all Serious Adverse Reactions:

A reaction is serious when the patient outcome is any one of the following:

- death
- life-threatening (real risk of dying)
- hospitalization (initial or prolonged)
- disability (significant, persistent or permanent)
- congenital anomaly
- required intervention to prevent permanent impairment or damage

All Suspected and Unsuspected Serious Adverse Reactions (SUSARs) should be expeditiously reported to the regulatory authorities as per their rule. USFDA provides following guidelines for how quick the information of a serious ADR should be communicated to the regulatory authorities.

Reporting Time Frames:

1. **Fatal or Life-threatening unexpected ADRs:** Certain ADRs may be sufficiently alarming so as to require very rapid notification to regulators in countries where the medicinal product or indication, formulation, or population for the medicinal product are still not approved for marketing, because such reports may lead to consideration of suspension of, or other limitations to a clinical investigation program. Fatal or life-threatening, unexpected ADRs occurring in clinical investigations qualify for very rapid reporting. Regulatory agencies should be notified (e.g. by telephone, facsimile transmission, or in writing) as soon as possible but no later than 7 calendar days after first knowledge by the sponsor that a case qualifies, followed by as complete a report as possible within 8 additional calendar days. This report should include an assessment of the importance and implication of the findings, including relevant previous experience with the same or similar medicinal products.

2. **All Other Serious, Unexpected ADRs:** Serious, unexpected reactions (ADRs) that are not fatal or life-threatening must be filed as soon as possible but not later than 15 calendar days after first knowledge by the sponsor that the case meets the minimum criteria for expedited reporting.

3. **Minimum Criteria for Reporting Information:** Final description and evaluation of a case report may not be available within the required time frames for reporting outlined above. Nevertheless, for regulatory purposes, initial reports should be submitted within the prescribed time as long as any one of the following minimum criteria are met:

- an identifiable patient;
- a suspect medicinal product;
- an identifiable reporting source; and
- an event or outcome that can be identified as serious and unexpected, and for which, in clinical investigation cases, there is a reasonable suspected causal relationship.

Follow-up information should be actively sought and submitted as it becomes available.

1.5 PREDICTABILITY AND PREVENTABILITY ASSESSMENT

Established drugs are responsible for the greatest burden of drug-induced morbidity and mortality. Therefore rational and appropriate prescribing is of key importance. The risk of some ADRs can be mitigated or eliminated by avoiding use of the drug or by taking suitable precautions in those patients with contra-indications or cautions for drug use. For example, the MHRA stated that more than 50% of reports they received of patients who had seizures associated with bupropion had predisposing factors for seizures, such as a past history of seizures or other drugs known to reduce the seizure threshold. In those in whom drug use is necessary, the appropriate use of concomitant treatments to protect against ADRs may be needed, such as proton pump inhibitors with NSAIDs. However, despite precautions being taken to avoid ADRs, not all cases are preventable. The use of a prescribed drug is an acceptance that harm may be caused to an individual patient even if the desired effect is more likely.

Monitoring of therapy through drug or biochemical testing provides an opportunity to prevent ADRs e.g. in the case of hyperkalaemia associated with the use of spironolactone in heart failure, practitioners may feel that initial frequent monitoring of potassium levels will detect those patients who are likely to develop hyperkalaemia. However, a significant proportion of cases occur more than three months after treatment has started. The optimal monitoring frequency may, therefore, be difficult to elucidate.

Impaired renal or hepatic function — either because of declining physiological function or natural individual variation in response — can increase the risk of ADRs. Due regard should be taken of the individual characteristics of drug responses to these disease states in order to chose the most appropriate drug and dose. The elderly are more prone to having adverse reactions, but this can be related to their generally higher levels of comorbidities, polypharmacy, and to declines in physiological function, rather than to chronological age itself. The young may beat higher risk of ADRs because of differences in drug metabolism and elimination, and end-organ response. Chloramphenicol, digoxin and ototoxic antibiotics such as streptomycin are examples of drugs that have a higher risk of toxicity in the first weeks of life. Older children and young adults may also be more susceptible to ADRs; a classic example of this in young people is the heightened risk of metoclopramide producing extrapyramidal effects. Children may have an increased risk of ADRs linked to the heightened possibility of dosing errors combined with a relative lack of evidence for safety and efficacy. Women may be more susceptible to several ADRs. Ethnicity has also been linked to susceptibility to ADRs. Examples include the increased risk of angioedema with the use of ACE inhibitors in black patients, and the increased propensity of white and black patients to experience central nervous system ADRs associated with mefloquine in comparison with patients of Chinese or Japanese origin. However, race or ethnicity can be argued to be a poor marker for the biochemical genotype of a patient.

Pharmacogenomics, the study of genes that influence individuals' responses to drugs, has yet to deliver on an appreciable scale the reduction in ADRs that many predicted. However, examples of severe ADRs exist that can be avoided with knowledge of a patient's genetic susceptibility.

The Food and Drug Administration (FDA) advised of an increased risk of severe skin reactions (such as toxic epidermal necrolysis and Stevens–Johnson syndrome) associated with carbamazepine in South East Asian populations (including those from China, Thailand, Malaysia, Indonesia, the Philippines, and Taiwan, and to a lesser extent Indians and the Japanese). The presence of Human Leukocyte Antigen (HLA) allele, HLA-B*1502, for which genetic testing is already available, indicates an increased risk of skin reactions. Carbamazepine is best avoided in this group of patients. Advice to patients on the correct use of their medication, and early warning signs of severe reactions can help mitigate the worst outcomes of drug therapy. Examples include warnings of mouth swelling with ACE inhibitors (angioedema), unusual bruising or bleeding with sulfasalazine (blood disorders), or signs and symptoms of liver failure with anti-tuberculosis treatment. However, many ADRs are not preventable because of the intrinsic nature of the drugs concerned or the continued difficulties in assessing the risk/balance in the use of medicines.

1.6 MANAGEMENT OF ADVERSE DRUG REACTIONS

Treatment of ADRs is dependent on the type of reaction, the severity of the reaction, and the risk–benefit of continuation of therapy. Some drugs may need to be continued despite the presence of an adverse reaction; for example, anti-epileptics despite some symptoms of drowsiness. Other reactions may respond to a dose reduction, such as digoxin toxicity. Others will require the withdrawal of drug therapy.

Some mild ADRs may be indicative of a more severe reaction to come. A mild rash in a woman taking strontium ranelate may later progress to a Drug Rash with Eosinophilia and Systemic Symptoms (DRESS), which has proved fatal in some cases. Immediate drug withdrawal in such cases is warranted and treatment should not be re-started. In other cases staged withdrawals may be required because of the risk of withdrawal reactions.

Thus, the consulting/practising physician in discussion with clinical pharmacists can take appropriate action based on known facts in the literature about management of ADRs in the concerned patients. The issue relates more to synthesis of knowledge based on available information.

■■■

Chapter 2...

Introduction to Pharmacovigilance

Contents ...

Pharmacovigilance is the science and activities related to the detection, assessment, understanding and prevention of adverse effects or any other possible drug-related problems. Spontaneous reporting of adverse events and adverse drug reactions is the commonest method utilized for generating safety data. Adverse drug reactions account for 2.1% of hospital admissions, with 39.3% of them being life-threatening. Safety data generated from clinical trials is incapable of identifying infrequent or late-onset adverse drug reactions. When a new drug is marketed, only limited information regarding its safety in children is available. Currently, several new drugs are being launched in India almost simultaneously as in the world market. Hence, even minimal post-marketing safety data is unavailable. The types of diseases and co-morbid conditions (*e.g.*, malnutrition, anemia and infestations) in Indian children, diverse genetic composition, and concomitant use of drugs belonging to alternative medicine could result in unforeseeable adverse drug reactions. Hence, it is mandatory that our country should have an active pharmacovigilance network.

2.1 HISTORY AND DEVELOPMENT OF PHARMACOVIGILANCE

If we trace back to History of Drug Development, then 1934 to 1960 can be rightly called as the period of drug explosion. The Second World War during 1934 to 1942 was a catalyst for the event. Penicillin was invented and developed during this period. Penicillin saved a lot of lives of wounded patients during Second World War by preventing bacterial infections and their consequences. Large scale production of drugs became a necessity and industrial production of drugs became a need. The need was accompanied with its own consequences. The first disaster of large-scale production of Sulphanilamide happened when Diethylene glycol was used to solubilize Sulphanilamide and consumption of the product killed 107 people who consumed it. The event was further followed by launching of

Thalidomide in Europe in 1956. Although Thalidomide was widely acclaimed to be a safe antiemetic and sedative drug even for pregnant mothers initially, it was observed that a large number of deformed babies were born, primarily in Germany, during 1959 to 1961. Both these events triggered a lot of rethinking about safety of drugs and a new science was found to be originating after 1960s. In 1962, USA promulgated a law stating that it is the manufacturer's responsibility to prove safety and efficacy of the drug before getting marketing authorization. In 1963, a committee on Safety of drugs was established in UK. In 1964, a system of "Yellow Cards" was established in UK to trace reporting safety of drugs by all users of drugs. By 1964-65, National Adverse Drugs Reaction-reporting system was initiated in countries like UK, Australia, New ZeaLand, Canada, West Germany and Sweden.

In 1978, WHO Centre for monitoring adverse reactions of drugs was shifted from Geneva to Uppsala in Sweden. This was the beginning of Pharmacovigilance. From then, the WHO-supported Uppsala monitoring Centre has spearheaded many activities of Pharmacovigilance all over the world.

From 1986 to 2010, the system is getting a stronghold in India. Now, Pharmacovigilance is a recognized entity at least in Public sector hospitals in India and is getting gradual acceptance in private sector hospitals also. Although acceptance of the system is slow in India, world over Pharmacovigilance has got a strong footing. By April 1998, 48 countries had voluntarily participated in WHO program on monitoring of Adverse Reactions to drugs. Now, by 2016, 123 countries had joined the programme. A close scrutiny of adverse reactions to drugs helps the regulator in many ways. Collection of sizable reports of a mild adverse reaction to a drug can help in publishing adequate caution while consuming the drug. It can be a good indicator to prescribers during further use of drugs. Report of a severe adverse reaction can further help adding a necessary contraindication to the use of a drug. It is to be noted that, observation of a new adverse reaction by trying the drug in a larger population is not a fault of the manufacturer. It is because of the fact that, before marketing permission to a drug, it might be tried only in about 5,000 patients. After marketing permission, the drug is administered to millions of patients; therefore a rare adverse reaction may be observed only when large number of patients are administered with the drug. A careful monitoring and documentation during administration is extremely essential when large number of patients receive the drug. Pharmacovigilance essentially works for the very purpose. It is worth noting that, corrective actions has been taken by both the regulatory authorities and Manufactures leading to withdrawal of 172 drugs during 1950 to 2013 (Table 2.1). The list is illustrative only.

Table 2.1: Drugs withdrawn (1950-2013) due to reasons of safety

Sr. No.	Withdrawn Year	Drug name	Country	Remarks
1.	1950s-1960s	Lysergic acid diethylamide (LSD)		Marketed as a psychiatric drug; withdrawn after it became widely used recreationally. Now illegal in most of the world.
2.	1960	Thenalidine	Canada, UK, US	Neutropenia
3.	1961	Thalidomide	Germany	Withdrawn because of risk of teratogenicity; returned to market for use in leprosy and multiple myeloma under FDA orphan drug rules.
4.	1962	Triparanol	France, US	Cataracts, alopecia, ichthyosis.
5.	1963	Bunamiodyl	Canada, UK, US	Nephropathy.
6.	1963	Dantron	Canada, UK, US	Genotoxicity. withdrawn from general use in UK but permitted in terminal patients.
7.	1963	Ethyl carbamate	Canada, UK, US,	Carcinogenicity.
8.	1964	Benziodarone	France, UK	Jaundice.
9.	1964	Butamben (Efocaine) (Butoforme)	US	Dermatologic toxicity; psychiatric Reactions.
10.	1964	Dithiazanine iodide	France, US	Cardiovascular and metabolic reaction.
11.	1964	Iodinated casein strophantin	US	Metabolic reaction.
12.	1964	Iproniazid	Canada	Interactions with food products containing tyrosine.
13.	1965	Metofoline	US	Unspecific experimental toxicity.
14.	1965	Pronethalol	UK	Animal carcinogenicity.
15.	1965	Xenazoic acid	France	Hepatotoxicity.
16.	1966	Phenoxypropazine	UK	Hepatotoxicity, drug intereaction.
17.	1967	Bithionol	US	Dermatologic toxicity.
18.	1968	Ibufenac	UK	Hepatotoxicity, jaundice.
19.	1969	Anagestone acetate	Germany	Animal carcinogenicity.
20.	1969	Chlorphentermine	Germany	Cardiovascular Toxicity.
21.	1969	Cloforex	Germany	Cardiovascular toxicity.

contd. ...

Sr. No.	Withdrawn Year	Drug name	Country	Remarks
22.	1970	Amoproxan	France	Dermatologic and ophthalmic toxicity.
23.	1970	Chlormadinone (Chlormenadione)	UK, US	Animal Carcinogenicity.
24.	1970	Diethylstilbestrol	USA	Risk of teratogenicity
25.	1970	Dihydrostreptomycin	US	Neuropsychiatric reaction.
26.	1970	Fenclozic acid	UK, US	Jaundice, elevated hepatic enzymes.
27.	1971	Diacetoxydiphenolisatin	Australia	Hepatotoxicity.
28.	1971	Triacetyldiphenolisatin	Australia	Hepatotoxicity.
29.	1972	Dimazole (Diamthazole)	France, US	Neuropsychiatric reaction.
30.	1973	Clioquinol	France, Germany, UK, US	Neurotoxicity.
31.	1974	Nialamide	UK, US	Hepatotoxicity, drug interaction.
32.	1975	Dipyrone (Metamizole)	UK, US, Others	Agranulocytosis, anaphylactic reactions.
33.	1975	Mebanazine	UK	Hepatotoxicity, drug intereaction.
34.	1975	Phenacetin	Canada	An ingredient in "A.P.C." tablet; withdrawn because of risk of cancer and kidney disease. Germany, Denmark, UK, US, others. Reason: nephropathy.
35.	1976	Azaribine	US	Thromboembolism.
36.	1976	Oxeladin	Canada, UK, US (1976)	Carcinogenicity.
37.	1976	Pifoxime (=Pixifenide)	France	Neuropsychiatric reaction.
38.	1977	Phenformin and Buformin	France, Germany, US	Severe lactic acidosis.
39.	1978	Buformin	Germany	Metabolic toxicity.
40.	1979	Alclofenac	UK	Vasculitis, Rash.
41.	1979	Methapyrilene	Germany, UK, US	Animal carcinogenicity.
42.	1979	Pyrovalerone	France	Abuse.
43.	1980	Amobarbital	Norway	Self poisoning.
44.	1980	Cyclobarbital	Norway	Self poisoning.
45.	1980	Pentobarbital	Norway	Self poisoning.

contd. ...

Sr. No.	Withdrawn Year	Drug name	Country	Remarks
46.	1980	Ticrynafen (Tienilic acid)	Germany, France, UK, US, others	Liver toxicity and death.
47.	1981-1986	Nomifensine	France, Germany, Spain, UK, US, others	Hemolytic Anemia, hepatotoxicity, serious hypersensitive reactions.
48.	1982	Benoxaprofen	Germany, Spain, UK, US	Liver and kidney failure; gastro-intestinal bleeding; ulcers.
49.	1982	Clomacron	UK	Hepatotoxicity.
50.	1982	Methandrostenolone	France, Germany, UK, US, others	Off-label abuse.
51.	1982	Pentylenetetrazol	–	Withdrawn for inability to produce effective convulsive therapy, and for causing seizures.
52.	1983	Dimethylamylamine (DMAA)	US	Voluntarily withdrawn from market by Lily. Reintroduced as a dietary supplement in 2006; and in 2013 the FDA started work to ban it due to cardiovascular problems.
53.	1983	Indoprofen	Germany, Spain, UK	Animal carcinogenicity, gastrointestinal toxicity.
54.	1983	Isoxicam	France, Germany, Spain, others	Stevens johnson syndrome.
55.	1983	Propanidid	UK	Allergy.
56.	1983	Zimelidine	Worldwide	Risk of Guillain-Barré syndrome, hypersensitivity reaction, hepatotoxicity. Banned worldwide.
57.	1983	Zomepirac	UK, Germany, Spain, US	Anaphylactic reactions and non-fatal allergic reactions, renal failure.
58.	1984	Althesin (= Alphaxolone amineptine + Alphadolone)	France, Germany, UK	Anaphylaxis.
59.	1984	Antrafenine	France	Unspecific experimental toxicity.
60.	1984	Fenclofenac	UK	Cutaneous reactions; animal carcinogenicity.

contd. ...

Sr. No.	Withdrawn Year	Drug name	Country	Remarks
61.	1984	Feprazone	Germany, UK	Cutaneous reaction, multiorgan toxicity.
62.	1984	Glafenine	France, Germany	Anaphylaxis.
63.	1984	Isaxonine phosphate	France	Hepatotoxicity.
64.	1984	Methaqualone	South Africa(1971), India (1984), United Nations (1971-1988)	Withdrawn because of risk of addiction and overdose.
65.	1984	Nitrefazole	Germany	Hepatic and hematological toxicity.
66.	1984-1985	Oxyphenbutazone	UK, US, Germany, France, Canada	Bone marrow suppression, Steven Johnson Syndrome.
67.	1985	Cianidanol	France, Germany, Spain, Sweden	Hemolytic Anemia.
68.	1985	Indalpine	France	Agranulocytosis.
69.	1985	Perhexilene	UK, Spain	Neurologic and hepatic toxicity.
70.	1985	Phenylbutazone	Germany	Off-label abuse, hematologic toxicity.
71.	1985	Suloctidyl	Germany, France, Spain	Hepatotoxicity.
72.	1986	β-ethoxy-lacetanilanide	Germany	Renal toxicity, animal carcinogenicity.
73.	1986	Bucetin	Germany	Renal toxicity.
74.	1986	Canrenone	Germany	Animal Carcinogenicity.
75.	1986	Difemerine	Germany	Multi-Organ toxicities.
76.	1986	Sulfamethoxypyridazine	UK	Dermatologic and hematologic reactions.
77.	1986-1987	Suprofen	UK, Spain, US	Flank pain, decreased kidney function.
78.	1987	Clometacin	France	Hepatotoxicity.
79.	1987	Cyclofenil	France	Hepatotoxicity.
80.	1987	Muzolimine	France, Germany, European Union	Polyneuropathy.
81.	1987	Vincamine	Germany	Hematologic toxicity.
82.	1988	Cinepazide	Spain	Agranulocytosis.
83.	1988	Nikethamide	Multiple markets	CNS Stimulation.
84.	1988	Prenylamine	Canada, France, Germany, UK, US, others	Cardiac arrythmia and death.

contd. ...

Sr. No.	Withdrawn Year	Drug name	Country	Remarks
85.	1988	Sulfacarbamide	Germany	Dermatologic, hematologic and hepatic reactions.
86.	1988	Sulfamethoxydiazine	Germany	Unknown.
87.	1989	Broazolam	UK	Animal carcinogenicity.
88.	1989	Etretinate	France	Withdrawn US (1999). Risk for birth defects.
89.	1989	Exifone	France	Hepatotoxicity.
90.	1989	L-tryptophan	Germany, UK	Eosinophilic myalgia syndrome. Still sold in the US
91.	1989	Proglumide	Germany	Respiratory reaction.
92.	1990	Dilevalol	UK	Hepatotoxicity.
93.	1990	Dinoprostone	UK	Uterine hypotonus, fetal distress.
94.	1990	Fenoterol	New Zealand	Asthma mortality.
95.	1990	Metipranolol	UK, others	Uveitis.
96.	1990	Pirprofen	France, Germany, Spain	Liver toxicity.
97.	1991	Encainide	UK, US	Ventricular arrhythmias.
98.	1991	Fipexide	France	Hepatotoxicity.
99.	1991	Flunitrazepam	France	Abuse.
100.	1991	Terodiline (Micturin)	Germany, UK, Spain, others	Prolonged QT interval, ventricular tachycardia and arrhythmia.
101.	1991	Triazolam	France, Netherlands, Finland, Argentina, UK others	Psychiatric adverse drug reactions, amnesia.
102.	1992	Benzarone	Germany	Hepatitis.
103.	1992	Temafloxacin	Germany, UK, US, others	Low blood sugar; hemolytic anemia; kidney, liver dysfunction; allergic reactions
104.	1992	Temafloxacin	US	Allergic reactions and cases of hemolytic anemia, leading to three patient deaths.
105.	1993	Bendazac	Spain	Hepatotoxicity.
106.	1993	Flosequinan (Manoplax)	UK, US	Increased mortality at higher doses; increased hospitalizations.
107.	1993	Ketorolac	France, Germany,	Hemorrhage, renal failure.

			others	

contd. ...

Sr. No.	Withdrawn Year	Drug name	Country	Remarks
108.	1993	Moxisylyte	France	Necrotic hepatitis.
109.	1993	Remoxipride	UK, others	Aplastic anemia.
110.	1993	Sorivudine	Japan	Drug interaction and deaths.
111.	1993	Thiobutabarbitone	Germany	Renal insufficiency.
112.	1995	Alpidem (Ananxyl)	Worldwide	Not approved in the US, withdrawn in France in 1994 and the rest of the market in 1995 because of rare but serious hepatotoxicity.
113.	1996	Chlormezanone (Trancopal)	European Union, US, South Africa, Japan	Hepatotoxicity; Steven-Johnson Syndrome; Toxic Epidermal Necrolysis.
114.	1996	Minaprine	France	Convulsions.
115.	1996	Tolrestat (Alredase)	Argentina, Canada, Italy, others	Severe hepatotoxicity
116.	1997	Dexfenfluramine	European Union, UK, US	Cardiac valvular disease.
117.	1997	Fenfluramine	European Union, UK, US, India, South Africa, others	Cardiac valvular disease, pulmonary hypertension, cardiac fibrosis.
118.	1997	Pemoline (Cylert)	Canada, UK	Withdrawn from US in 2005. Reason: hepatotoxicity.
119.	1997	Phenolphthalein	US	Carcinogenicity.
120.	1997-1998	Terfenadine (Seldane, Triludan)	France, South Africa, Oman, others, US	Prolonged QT interval; ventricular tachycardia
121.	1998	Bromfenac	US	Severe hepatitis and liver failure (some requiring transplantation).
122.	1998	Ebrotidine	Spain	Hepatotoxicity.
123.	1998	Mibefradil	European Union, Malaysia, US, others	Fatal arrhythmia, drug interactions.
124.	1998	Proxibarbal	Spain, France, Italy, Portugal, Turkey	Immunoallergic, thrombocytopenia.
125.	1998	Sertindole	European Union	Arrhythmia and sudden cardiac death.
126.	1998	Tolcapone (Tasmar)	European Union,	Hepatotoxicity

			Canada, Australia	

contd. ...

Sr. No.	Withdrawn Year	Drug name	Country	Remarks
127.	1999	Amineptine (Survector)	France, US	Hepatotoxicity, dermatological side effects, and abuse potential.
128.	1999	Aminopyrine	France, Thailand	Risk of agranulocytosis; severe acne.
129.	1999	Astemizole (Hismanal)	US, Malaysia, Multiple Nonspecified Markets	Fatal arrhythmia.
130.	1999	Grepafloxacin (Raxar)	Withdrawn Germany, UK, US others	Cardiac repolarization; QT interval prolongation.
131.	1999	Levamisole (Ergamisol)	US	Still used as veterinary drug and as a human antihelminthic in many markets; listed on the WHO List of Essential Medicines. In humans, it was used to treat melanoma before it was withdrawn for agranulocytosis.
132.	1999	Oxyphenisatin (Phenisatin)	Australia, France, Germany, UK, US	Hepatotoxicity.
133.	1999	Temazepam (Restoril, Euhypnos, Normison, Remestan, Tenox, Norkotral)	Sweden, Norway	Diversion, abuse, and a relatively high rate of overdose deaths in comparison to other drugs of its group. This drug continues to be available in most of the world including the US, but under strict controls.
134.	1999-2001	Trovafloxacin (Trovan)	European Union, US	Withdrawn because of risk of liver failure
135	2000	Alosetron (Lotronex)	US	Serious gastrointestinal adverse events; ischemic colitis; severe constipation. Reintroduced 2002 on a restricted basis.
136.	2000	Cisapride (Propulsid)	US	Risk of fatal cardiac

				arrhythmias.

contd. ...

Sr. No.	Withdrawn Year	Drug name	Country	Remarks
137.	2000	Phenylpropanolamine (Propagest,Dexatrim)	Canada, US	Hemorrhagic stroke.
138.	2000	Troglitazone (Rezulin)	US, Germany	Hepatotoxicity
139.	2001	Ardeparin (Normiflo)	US	Not for reasons of safety or efficacy.
140.	2001	Cerivastatin (Baycol, Lipobay)	US	Risk of rhabdomyolysis
141.	2001	Rapacuronium (Raplon)	US, multiple markets	Withdrawn in many countries because of risk of fatal bronchospasm.
142.	2001	Sparfloxacin	US	QT prolongation and phototoxicity.
143.	2002	Kava Kava	Germany	Hepatotoxicity.
144.	2003	Levomethadyl acetate	US	Cardiac arrhythmias and cardiac arrest.
145.	2004	Bezitramide	Netherlands	Fatal overdose.
146.	2004	Co-proxamol (Distalgesic)	UK	Overdose dangers.
147.	2004	Dofetilide	Germany	Drug interactions, prolonged QT.
148.	2004	Rofecoxib (Vioxx)	Worldwide	Withdrawn by MAH. Risk of myocardial infarction and stroke.
149.	2004	Valdecoxib (Bextra)	US	Risk of heart attack and stroke.
150.	2005	Adderall XR	Canada	Risk of stroke. The ban was later lifted because the death rate among those taking Adderall XR was determined to be no greater than those not taking Adderall.
151.	2005	Hydromorphone (Palladone, extended release version)		High risk of accidental overdose when extended release version (Palladone) administered with alcohol. Standard hydromorphone is sold in most of the world including the US
152.	2005–2006	Natalizumab (Tysabri)	US	Voluntarily withdrawn from US market because of risk of Progressive Multifocal Leukoence-

				phalopathy (PML). Returned to market July, 2006.

contd. ...

Sr. No.	Withdrawn Year	Drug name	Country	Remarks
153.	2005	Thioridazine (Melleril)	Germany, UK	Withdrawn worldwide due to severe cardiac arrhythmias
154.	2006	Alatrofloxacin	Worldwide	Liver toxicity; serious liver injury leading to liver transplant; death.
155.	2006	Gatifloxacin	US	Increased risk of dysglycemia.
156.	2006	Ximelagatran (Exanta)	Germany	Hepatotoxicity
157.	2007	Clobutinol	Germany	Ventricular arrhythmia, QT-prolongation.
158.	2007–2008	Lumiracoxib (Prexige)	Worldwide	Liver damage.
159.	2007	Nefazodone	US, Canada, others	Branded version withdrawn by originator in several countries in 2007 for hepatotoxicity. Generic versions available.
160.	2007	Pergolide (Permax)	US	Risk for heart valve damage.
161.	2007	Tegaserod (Zelnorm)	US	Risk for heart attack, stroke, and unstable angina. Was available through a restricted access program until April 2008.
162.	2008	Aprotinin (Trasylol)	US	Increased risk of death.
163.	2008	Rimonabant (Acomplia)	Worldwide	Risk of severe depression and suicide.
164.	2009	Efalizumab (Raptiva)	Germany	Withdrawn because of increased risk of progressive multifocal leukoencephalopathy.
165.	2010	Gemtuzumab ozogamicin (Mylotarg)	US	No improvement in clinical benefit; risk for death.
166.	2010	Ozogamicin	US	No improvement in clinical benefit; risk for death; veno-occlusive disease.
167.	2010	Propoxyphene (Darvocet/Darvon)	Worldwide	Increased risk of heart attacks and stroke.
168.	2010	Rosiglitazone	Europe	Risk of heart attacks and

		(Avandia)		death. This drug continues to be available in the US.

contd. ...

Sr. No.	Withdrawn Year	Drug name	Country	Remarks
169.	2010	Sibutramine (Reductil/ Meridia)	Australia, Canada, China, the European Union (EU), Hong Kong, India, Mexico, New Zealand, the Philippines, Thailand, the United Kingdom, and the United States.	Increased risk of heart attack and stroke.
170.	2010	Sitaxentan	Germany	Hepatotoxicity.
171.	2011	Drotrecogin alfa (Xigris)	Worldwide	Lack of efficacy as shown by PROWESS-SHOCK study.
172.	2013	Tetrazepam	European Union	Serious cutaneous reactions.

2.2 IMPORTANCE OF SAFETY MONITORING / WHY PHARMACOVIGILANCE?

The biggest advantage of monitoring and recording all events in pharmacovigilance is to the prospective users as a guideline. When a pharmacovigilance report is recorded, all readers are cautioned that under such prevailing circumstances as reported in the content, there is every possibility that the adverse reaction may be repeated. Thus, deliberate recurrence can be minimized. Of course, individuality of the patient, in terms of genomic content and predisposing factors is extremely vital. Any new report of adverse reaction points out to a new reality. In fact, post-marketing surveillance of a drug is a learning curve for investigators as well as sponsors. A new observation can add to precautions being taken to clinical use of a drug. A new clinical observation, if serious enough, may add to contraindication to use of a drug. There are events where repeated observation of a serious adverse reaction in a large number of patients can even lead to withdrawal of a drug.

Pharmacovigilance benefits everybody. The patients are protected from unsafe drugs; doctors and pharmaceutical industry keep their reputations intact and drug regulators receive pertinent data that helps them to take regulatory decisions. In India, although, Indian Council of Medical Research and Drugs Controller General of India began establishing Adverse Drug Reaction centers in 1980s, these activities remained confined to a few institutions and practicing doctors have either remained largely unaware of these activities or they have not shown interest in promoting these activities.

The key messages of the National program on Pharmacovigilance are as follows:

- The National Pharmacovigilance Program has been launched to improve the current state of functioning of pharmacovigilance activities. Its basic purpose is to analyze adverse drug reaction data for making regulatory decisions regarding drugs marketed in India.

- Not only doctors but other healthcare providers, *viz.*, pharmacists and nurses can now actively participate in the program. They should start reporting adverse events to help ensure that people in our country receive safe drugs.

It is expected that with the involvement of all related stakeholders, Pharmacovigilance program will help in reducing the cost of damages caused by drugs to minimal level. It will also try to prevent drug-related damages if appropriate care is taken by physicians on the basis of feedback from the pharmacovigilance program.

■■■

Chapter 3...

National and International Scenario

Contents ...

Having got a glimpse of what pharmacovigilance is, it is right to know what is Indian and global scenario about implementation of the program of Pharmacovigilance. Since the World Health Organization has taken a leadership role in the program, a separate section on activities of WHO in relation to Pharmacovigilance is also included.

3.1 PHARMACOVIGILANCE IN INDIA

The Central Drugs Standard Control Organisation (CDSCO), New Delhi, under the aegis of Ministry of Health & Family Welfare, Government of India has initiated a nation-wide pharmacovigilance programme in July, 2010, with All India Institute of Medical Sciences (AIIMS), New Delhi as the National Co-ordinating Centre (NCC) for monitoring Adverse Drug Reactions (ADR) in the country to safe-guard Public Health. In year 2010, 22 ADR Monitoring Centres (AMCs) including AIIMS, New Delhi had been set up under this Programme. To ensure implementation of this programme in a more effective way, the National Co-ordinating Centre was then shifted from the All India Institute of Medical Sciences (AIIMS), New Delhi to the Indian Pharmacopoeia Commission (IPC), Ghaziabad, (U.P.) in April, 2011.

The scope and objectives of the program are indicated below:

- To create a nation-wide system for patient safety reporting.

- To identify and analyse new signals from the reported cases.

- To analyse the benefit - risk ratio of marketed medications.

- To generate evidence based information on safety of medicines.

- To support regulatory agencies in the decision-making process on use of medications.

- To communicate the safety information on use of medicines to various stakeholders to minimise the risk.

- To emerge as a national centre of excellence for pharmacovigilance activities.

- To collaborate with other national centres for the exchange of information and data management.

- To provide training and consultancy support to other national pharmacovigilance centres across globe.

- To promote rational use of medicine.

Under the aegis of CDSCO, with AIIMS as the main co-ordinating centre, the Indian Pharmacopeia Commission is implementing the program in an effective manner. Four regional centres have been established in northern, southern, eastern and western areas of India. All medical colleges, both public and private, have been persuaded to establish and develop ADR monitoring centres. Till April 2014, 154 Adverse Reaction Monitoring centres have been established and 6300 Individual Case Study Reports (ICSRs) of elderly patient records have been reported to the National Centre from July 2011 to March 2014.

Functions of Pharmacovigilance System:

Following are the functions of a national pharmacovigilance system:

1. To create a nation-wide system for patient safety reporting.
2. To identify and analyse the new signal (ADR) from the reported cases.
3. To analyse the benefit-risk ratio of marketed medications.
4. To generate the evidence based information on safety of medicines.
5. To support regulatory agencies in the decision-making process on use of medications.
6. To communicate the safety information on use of medicines to various stakeholders to minimise the risk.
7. To emerge as a national centre of excellence for Pharmacovigilance activities.
8. To collaborate with other national centres for the exchange of information and data management.
9. To provide training and consultancy support to other National Pharmacovigilance Centres located across globe.

Requirements of a National Pharmacovigilance System:

Following are the requirements of a national pharmacovigilance system:

Pharmacovigilance activities may be undertaken by several organizations, individuals and agencies. The Pharmacovigilance programme of India fulfils the minimum requirements that should be present in any functional national pharmacovigilance system as per WHO, which include the following components of a functional pharmacovigilance system:

1. A national pharmacovigilance centre with designated staff (at least one full time), stable basic funding, clear mandates, well defined structures and roles, and collaborating with the WHO Programme for International Drug Monitoring (The National Co-ordinating Centre for PvPI, being the Indian Pharmacopoeia Commission, Ghaziabad, under Ministry of Health & Family Welfare, Government of India).

2. The existence of a national spontaneous reporting system with a national individual case safety report (ICSR) form i.e. an adverse drug reaction (ADR) reporting form.

3. A national database or system for collating and managing ADR reports (Vigibase database and Vigiflow software for PvPI).

4. A national ADR or pharmacovigilance advisory committee able to provide technical assistance on causality assessment, risk assessment, risk management, case investigation and wherever necessary, crisis management including crisis communication (Steering Committee provides technical assistance in PvPI).

5. A clear strategy for routine and crisis communications.

3.2 PHARMACOVIGILANCE: GLOBAL PERSPECTIVE

Pharmacovigilance is a globally accepted strategy to monitor adverse reactions to drugs. ICH has published guidelines about pharmacovigilance which are relevant to USA, Europe and Japan. In addition, there are separate European (EU), American (USFDA), and CIOMS guidelines for working of pharmacovigilance in their own regions. Australian system for reporting Adverse Drug Reactions also exist. All these systems will be discussed in detail in the book on regulatory aspects. The WHO system of reporting ADRs is discussed separately because of leadership role played by WHO in the Pharmacovigilance program.

The creation of the International Society of Pharmacoepidemiology (ISPE) in 1984 and of The European Society of Pharmacovigilance (ESoP – later ISoP – the International Society of Pharmacovigilance) in 1992, marked the introduction of pharmacovigilance formally into the research and academic world. It has an increasing integration into clinical practice. Specialist medical journals have appeared, and a number of countries have implemented active surveillance systems to complement conventional methods of drug monitoring.

Examples of such systems are:

- Prescription event monitoring systems (PEM) in New Zealand and the United Kingdom.
- Record linkage systems in the United States of America and Canada.
- Case control studies in the United States of America.

Pharmacovigilance activities have also evolved as a regulatory activity. In the early 1980s, in close collaboration with the WHO, the Council for International Organizations of Medical Sciences (CIOMS) launched its programme on drug development and use. CIOMS provided a forum for policy makers, pharmaceutical manufacturers, government officials and academics to make recommendations on the communication of safety information between regulators and the pharmaceutical industry. The adoption of many of the recommendations of CIOMS by the International Conference on Harmonization (ICH) in the 1990s has a notable impact on international drug regulation.

Widening Horizons:

Within the last decade, there has been a growing awareness that the scope of pharmacovigilance has extended beyond the strict confines of detecting new signals of safety concerns. Globalization, consumerism, the explosion in free trade and communication across borders, and increasing use of the Internet have resulted in a sea change in access to all medicinal products and information on them. These changes have given rise to new kinds of safety concerns such as:

- Illegal sale of medicines and drugs of abuse over the Internet.
- Increasing self-medication practices.
- Irrational and potentially unsafe drug donation practices.
- Widespread manufacture and sale of counterfeit and substandard medicines.
- Increasing use of traditional medicines outside the confines of the traditional culture of use.
- Increasing use of traditional medicines and herbal medicines with other medicines with potential for adverse interactions.

There is a need for a reconsideration of pharmacovigilance practice in the light of the lack of clear definition of boundaries between:

- Food,
- Medicines (including traditional medicines, herbal medicines and 'natural products'),
- Medical devices, and
- Cosmetics.

Increasing public expectations of safety in relation to all of these, add another dimension of pressure for change. National pharmacovigilance centres are in no position to address all these safety concerns on their own, but they are especially able to detect and anticipate impact of such problems on the safety of patients. Through strong links with the national drug regulatory authority as well as to other countries, National Centres are in a position to influence decision-making on drug and other health-related policies.

3.3 WHO INTERNATIONAL DRUG MONITORING PROGRAMME

The Sixteenth World Health Assembly (1963) adopted a resolution (WHA 16.36) that reaffirmed the need for early action in regard to rapid dissemination of information on adverse drug reactions and led, later, to creation of the WHO Pilot Research Project for International Drug Monitoring in 1968. The purpose of this was to develop a system, applicable internationally, for detecting previously unknown or poorly understood adverse effects of medicines. A WHO technical report is based on a consultation meeting held in 1971.

From these beginnings emerged the practice and science of pharmacovigilance. Systems were developed in member States for the collection of individual case histories of ADRs and evaluation of them. The collection of international ADR reports in a central database, has served the important function of contributing to the work of national drug regulatory authorities, improve the safety profile of medicines, and help avoid further disasters.

The initiative for setting up WHO international program on monitoring of adverse reactions was taken in 1968 to monitor adverse reactions to drugs which otherwise cannot be monitored with reports of clinical trials alone. Initially, the idea was only to create a database based on information from national centres. India joined the program in 1998. Till then 48 countries have agreed to participate in the program. Now, by 2016, 123 countries had joined the programmed. WHO headquarters in Geneva is responsible for monitoring the program. Operational aspects are managed by Swedish Foundation named the WHO collaborating centre for International Drug Monitoring, according to an agreement signed between WHO and Sweden in 1978. The centre is now known as Uppsala Monitoring centre (UMC). Budget for the centre is provided by Swedish Government.

Aims of Pharmacovigilance:

Major aims of pharmacovigilance are:

1. Early detection of hitherto unknown adverse reactions and interactions.
2. Detection of increase in frequency of (known) adverse reactions.
3. Identification of risk factors and possible mechanisms underlying adverse reactions.
4. Estimation of quantitative aspects of benefit/risk analysis and dissemination of information needed to improve drug prescribing and regulation.

The ultimate goals of pharmacovigilance are:

- The rational and safe use of medical drugs.
- The assessment and communication of the risks and benefits of drugs on the market.
- Educating and informing the patients.

■■■

Chapter 4...

Basic Terminologies used in Pharmacovigilance

Contents ...

There are various terminologies used in pharmacovigilance. Many of them have been included in the Appendix. Few more are included here.

4.1 TERMINOLOGIES OF ADVERSE MEDICATION RELATED EVENTS

Terminologies which are used in adverse medication-related events are:

- Adverse event(s)/Adverse experience (AE)
- Adverse Drug Reaction (ADR)

Unlisted / Unexpected Adverse Drug Reaction:

An adverse reaction, the nature or severity of which is not consistent with the applicable product information (e.g., Investigator's Brochure for an unapproved investigational medicinal product and prescribing information / Summary of Product Characteristics (SmPC) for marketed products).

Listed / Expected Adverse Drug Reaction:

An ADR whose nature, severity, specificity, and outcome are consistent with the information in the CCSI. (See section 4.2)

Challenge:

Administration of a suspect product by any route.

- **Positive challenge:**

  Drugs under consideration given deliberately.

- **Negative challenge:**

  Drugs under consideration avoided willfully.

Dechallenge:

Withdrawal of a suspect product from a patient's therapeutic regimen.

- **Positive Dechallenge:**

  Partial or complete disappearance of an adverse experience after withdrawal of the suspect product.

- **Negative Dechallenge:**

  Continued presence of an adverse experience after withdrawal of the suspect product.

Rechallenge:

Reintroduction of a suspect product suspected of having caused an adverse experience following a positive dechallenge.

- **Positive Rechallenge:**

  Reoccurrence of similar signs and symptoms upon reintroduction of the suspect product.

- **Negative Rechallenge:**

  Failure of the product, when reintroduced, to produce signs or symptoms similar to those observed when the suspect product was previously introduced.

4.2 REGULATORY TERMINOLOGIES

Company Core Data Sheet (CCDS):

- A document prepared by the Marketing Authorization Holder (MAH) containing in addition to safety information, material relating to indications, dosing, pharmacology and other information concerning the product.

Company Core Safety Information (CCSI):

- All relevant safety information contained in the Company Core Data Sheet prepared by the Marketing Authorization Holder (MAH) and which the Marketing Authorization Holder (MAH) requires to be listed in all countries where the company markets the product, except when the local authority specifically requires a modification.

- It is the reference safety information (RSI) by which listed and unlisted drugs are determined for the purpose of periodic reporting for marketed products, but not by which expected and unexpected are determined for expedited reporting.

Summary of Product Characteristics (SPC):

- Basis of information for health professionals on how to use the medicinal product safely and effectively.

International Birth Date (IBD):

- The date of the first marketing authorization for a medicinal product granted to the Marketing Authorization Holder (MAH) in any country of the world.

Data Lock Point (DLP):

- The date designated as the cut-off date for data to be included in a Periodic Safety Update Report.

Individual Case Safety Report (ICSR):

- A document providing the most complete information related to an individual case at a certain point of time.
- An individual case is the information provided by a primary source to describe suspected adverse reaction(s) related to the administration of one or more medicinal products to an individual patient at a particular point of time.

Periodic Safety Update Report (PSUR):

- Periodic summary of safety information for regulators, including any changes in the risk-benefit relationship for an approved drug, prepared by the Marketing Authorization Holder (MAH).

Unexpected Adverse Reaction:

- An ADR whose nature, severity, specificity, or outcome is not consistent with the Summary of Product Characteristics (SPC).
- It includes class-related reactions which are mentioned in the SPC but which are not specifically described as occurring with this product.

Unlisted Adverse Reaction:

- An ADR that is not specifically included as a suspected adverse effect in the Company Core Safety Information (CCSI). This includes an adverse reaction whose nature, severity, specificity, or outcome is not consistent with the CCSI.
- It also includes class-related reactions which are mentioned in the CCSI but which are described as occurring with this product.

Medication Errors (ME):

- They could occur during prescribing, transcribing, dispensing, administering a drug. Examples of medication errors include, misreading or miswriting a prescription.
- Not all medication errors lead to adverse outcomes.
- Medication errors are more common than adverse events, but result in harmless than 1% of the time. About 25% of adverse events are due to medication errors.

Risk Management Plan: It shall contain characterization of the safety profile and an identification of the risks of the medicinal product and depicts all measures and interventions to prevent or minimize those risks and ascertains the effectiveness of the mentioned measures and interventions. The post-authorization obligations imposed as a condition of the marketing authorization are also documented in the risk management plan.

Post-Authorization Safety Studies: These studies are non-interventional type and are initiated, managed or financed by the marketing authorization holder under obligations imposed by a National Competent Authority, the Agency or the Commission and involve the collection of data from patients or healthcare professionals.

Pharmacovigilance System Master File (PSMF):

It is a detailed description of the Pharmacovigilance (PV) system used by the marketing authorization holder with respect to one or more authorized medicinal products.

Qualified Person for Pharmacovigilance (QPPV):

An individual is identified by (MAH), who should be appropriately qualified, with documented experience in all aspects of pharmacovigilance in order to fulfill the responsibilities and tasks of the post. If the QPPV is not medically qualified, then access to medically qualified person should be available. The name and 24-hour contact details of the QPPV should be notified to the Competent Authorities of the member states.

4.3 THE ROLE AND RESPONSIBILITIES OF THE QUALIFIED PERSON RESPONSIBLE FOR PHARMACOVIGILANCE

QPPV is responsible for

- Establishing and maintaining of the marketing authorisation holder's pharmacovigilance system; and therefore shall have sufficient authority to influence the performance of the quality system and pharmacovigilance activities; and to promote, maintain and improve compliance with the legal requirements.

In relation to above-mentioned general responsibility, specific additional responsibilities of QPPV in EU are as follows:

- Having an overview of medicinal product safety profiles and any emerging safety concerns.
- Having awareness of any conditions or obligations adopted as part of the marketing authorizations and other commitments relating to safety or the safe use of the products.
- Having awareness of risk minimization measures.
- Being aware of and having sufficient authority over the content of risk management plans.
- Being involved in the review and sign-off of protocols of post-authorisation safety studies conducted in the EU or pursuant to a risk management plan agreed in the EU.

- Having awareness of post-authorisation safety studies requested by a competent authority including the results of such studies.

- Ensuring conduct of pharmacovigilance and submission of all pharmacovigilance related documents in accordance with the legal requirements and Good Pharmacovigilance Practices (GVP).

- Ensuring the necessary quality, including the correctness and completeness, of pharmacovigilance data submitted to the competent authorities in member states and the agency.

- Ensuring a full and prompt response to any request from the competent authorities in member states and from the agency for the provision of additional information necessary for the benefit risk evaluation of a medicinal product.

- Providing any other information relevant to the benefit-risk evaluation to the competent authorities in the member states and the agency.

- Providing input into the preparation of regulatory action in response to emerging safety concerns (e.g. variations, urgent safety restrictions and communication to patients and healthcare professionals).

- Acting as a single pharmacovigilance contact point for the competent authorities in member states and the agency on 24 hour basis and also as a contact point for pharmacovigilance inspections.

Thus, QPPV has oversight over the functioning of the system in all relevant aspects, including its quality system (e.g. SOPs, contractual arrangements, database operations, compliance data regarding quality, completeness and timeliness of expedited reporting and submission of periodic update reports, audit reports and training of personnel in relation to pharmacovigilance). Specifically for the adverse reaction database, if applicable, the QPPV should be aware of the validation status of the database, including any failures that occurred during validation and the corrective actions that have been taken to address the failures. The QPPV should also be informed of significant changes that are made to the database, which could have impact on pharmacovigilance activities.

The QPPV may delegate specific tasks, under supervision, to appropriately qualified and trained individuals, acting as safety experts for certain products. Such delegation should be documented.

Thus, QPPV is the key person in maintaining pharmacovigilance system; therefore every individual entering in the career of pharmacovigilance should have long-term aim of becoming QPPV by appropriate experience in related responsibilities.

4.4 RESPONSIBILITIES OF THE MARKETING AUTHORISATION HOLDER (MAH) IN RELATION TO THE QUALIFIED PERSON RESPONSIBLE FOR PHARMACOVIGILANCE

The MAH should adequately support the QPPV and ensure that there are appropriate processes, resources, communication mechanisms and access to all sources of relevant information in place for the fulfilment of the QPPV's responsibilities and tasks.

The Marketing Authorisation Holder should ensure that there is full documentation covering to all procedures and activities of the QPPV and that mechanisms are in place to ensure that the QPPV may receive or seek all relevant information. The MAH should also implement mechanisms for the QPPV to be kept informed of emerging safety concerns and any other information relating to the evaluation of the risk-benefit balance. This should include information from ongoing or completed clinical trials and other studies the MAH is aware of, and which may be relevant to the safety of the medicinal product, as well as information from sources other than the specific MAH, e.g. from those with whom the MAH has contractual arrangements.

The MAH should ensure that the QPPV has sufficient authority:

- to implement changes to the MAH's pharmacovigilance system in order to promote, maintain and improve compliance; and
- to provide input into Risk Management Plans (see Chapter I.3) and into the preparation of regulatory action in response to emerging safety concerns (e.g. variations, urgent safety restrictions, and, as appropriate, communication to Patients and Healthcare Professionals).

The MAH should assess risks with potential impact on the pharmacovigilance system and plan for business contingency, including back-up procedures (e.g. in case of non-availability of personnel, adverse reaction database failure, failure of other hardware or software with impact on electronic reporting and data analysis).

4.5 DETAILED DESCRIPTION OF PHARMACOVIGILANCE SYSTEM (DDPS)

DDPS should include the following elements:

- Details of QPPV.
- Details of the Organization.
- Documented procedures for all activities related to pharmacovigilance.

DDPS should indicate the processes for which written procedures are available. A list and copies of the global and EEA procedures should be available within two working days on request by the competent authorities.

All Marketing Authorisation Holders are required to have an appropriate system of pharmacovigilance in place. The detailed description of the pharmacovigilance system should include the following elements, as applicable, and be set out in a structured manner consistent with this list. Additional important elements pertinent to a specific situation, should be added.

Qualified Person Responsible for Pharmacovigilance (QPPV):

- The name of the QPPV, should be located in the EEA. The business address and contact details should be provided in the Marketing Authorisation Application form. Companies might, for example, use a 24-hour telephone number through which the QPPV or their back-up can be reached, diverting it to the appropriate person according to availability.
- A summary Curriculum Vitae of the QPPV with the key information relevant to their role (main qualifications, training and experience) should be given.
- A summary of the job description of the QPPV should be given.
- A description of the back-up procedure to apply in the absence of the QPPV should be clarified.

Organisation:

- Identification and location of the company units or other organisations where the principal EEA and global pharmacovigilance activities are undertaken (in particular, those sites where the main databases are located, where Individual Case Safety Reports (ICSRs) are collated and reported and where PSURs (Periodic Safety Update Reports) are prepared and processed for reporting to the Competent Authorities). Identification of affiliates may be made in a general sense, rather than affiliate-by-affiliate.
- Identification of the point(s) in the Community at which pharmacovigilance data are accessible (to include access to ICSRs, PSURs and the global pharmacovigilance data).
- High-level organisation chart(s) providing an overview of the global and EEA pharmacovigilance units and organisations (identified above) and, illustrating the relationships between them, with affiliate/parent companies and contractors. The chart(s) should show the main reporting relationships with management and clearly show the position of the EEA QPPV within the organisation. Individual names of people should not be included. Licensing partnerships are usually product-specific and should be indicated in a product-specific addendum in the application for that product, unless a partnership is a consistent feature of the company's organisation across most products.
- A brief summary of the pharmacovigilance activities undertaken by each of the organisations/units identified above.

- Flow diagrams indicating the flow of safety reports of different sources and types. These should indicate how reports/information are processed and reported from the source, to the point of receipt by the Competent Authorities. These should be limited to the major processes identified in Volume 9A.

Documented Procedures:

An essential element of any pharmacovigilance system is that there are clear, written procedures in place. The following list indicates topics that should usually be covered by these written procedures. The detailed description should indicate for which of these topics there are written procedures in place, but should not list the procedure titles per se. A procedure may cover one or more of the topics or one topic may have one or more procedures depending on its complexity and the organisation of the company. Care should be taken to ensure that, quality control in the various processes be reflected in the relevant procedures.

The procedures are listed below:

- The activities of the QPPV and the back-up procedure to apply in their absence;
- The collection, processing (including data entry and data management) quality control, coding, classification, medical review and reporting of ICSRs:
  - o Reports of different types:
    - ❖ Organised data collection schemes (solicited), unsolicited, clinical trials, literature.
    - ❖ The process should ensure that, reports from different sources are captured:
      - ▪ EEA and third countries, healthcare professionals, sales and marketing personnel, other marketing authorisation, holder personnel, competent authorities, compassionate use, patients, others;
- The follow-up of reports of missing information and information on the progress and outcome of the case(s);
- Detection of reports in duplicate.
- Expedited reporting.
- Electronic reporting.
- Periodic Safety Update Reports (PSURs):
  - o The preparation, processing, quality control, review (including medical review) and reporting;
- Global pharmacovigilance activities applying to all products: Continuous monitoring of the safety profile of authorised medicinal products.
  - o Signal detection and review,
  - o Risk-benefit assessment;
  - o Reporting and communication notifying competent authority and healthcare professionals of changes to the risk benefit balance of product etc.

- Interaction between safety issues and product defects;
- Responses to requests for information from regulatory authorities;
- Handling of urgent safety restrictions and safety variations;
- Meeting commitments to Competent Authorities in relation to marketing authorisation.
- Global pharmacovigilance activities applying to all products (signal detection, evaluation, reporting, communication etc.)
- Management and use of database or other recording system.
- Internal audit of pharmacovigilance system.
- Archiving.

The detailed description of the pharmacovigilance should indicate the processes for which written procedures are available. A list and copies of the global and EEA procedures should be available within two working days on request by the competent Authorities. Any additional local procedures should be available to respond to specific request.

Databases:

A listing of the main databases used for pharmacovigilance purposes (e.g. compilation of safety reports, expedited/electronic reporting, signal detection, sharing and accessing global safety information) and brief functional descriptions of these should be provided including a statement regarding the validation status of the database systems.

A statement should be included regarding the compliance of the systems with the internationally agreed standards for electronic submission of adverse reaction reports as referred to in Part III.

A copy of the registration, of the QPPV, with the EudraVigilance system and identification of the process used for electronic reporting to the Competent Authorities.

There should be an indication of the responsibility for the operation of the databases and their location.

Contractual Arrangements with Other Persons or Organisations Involved in the Fulfilment of Pharmacovigilance Obligations:

Links with other organisations such as co-marketing agreements and contracting of pharmacovigilance activities should be outlined. The company should identify the major subcontracting arrangements, it has for the conduct of its pharmacovigilance activities and the main organisations to which it has subcontracted these (in particular where the role of the QPPV, the electronic reporting of ICSRs, the main databases, signal detection, or the compilation of PSURs is subcontracted).

A brief description of the nature of the agreements the company establishes with co-marketing partners and contractors for pharmacovigilance activities should be provided.

Co-licensing or co-marketing arrangements within the EEA should be identified and the distribution of the major responsibilities between the parties made clear.

Since co-licensing or co-marketing arrangements are mainly product-specific, any information on these may be provided in a product-specific addendum, in the applicable Marketing Authorisation Application. Likewise, if subcontracting is product-specific, this should be indicated in a product-specific addendum.

Training:

Staff should be appropriately trained for performing pharmacovigilance related activities. This includes not only staff within the pharmacovigilance units but also staff who may receive or process safety reports, such as sales personnel or clinical research staff. A brief description of the training system and information about where the training records, Curricula Vitae (CVs) and job descriptions are filed, should be provided.

Documentation:

Provide a brief description of the locations of the different types of pharmacovigilance source documents, including archiving arrangements. Reference can be made to the organisation charts provided under information on organisation.

Quality Management System:

Provide a brief description of the quality management system, making cross-reference to the elements provided under the above Sections. Particular emphasis should be placed on organisational roles and responsibilities for the activities and documentation, quality control and review, and for ensuring corrective and preventive action.

A brief description of the responsibilities for quality assurance auditing of the pharmacovigilance system, including auditing of sub-contractors, should be provided.

Supporting Documentation:

The MAH should ensure that the pharmacovigilance system is in place and documented.

An essential feature of a pharmacovigilance system is that it is clearly documented to ensure that the system functions properly, that the roles and responsibilities and required tasks are clear to all parties involved and that there is provision for proper control and, when needed, change of the system.

Documentation supporting the pharmacovigilance system (and its detailed description) may be required during the pre-authorisation period, or post-authorisation, for purposes such as assessment or inspection.

■■■

Chapter 5...

Information Resources in Pharmacovigilance

Contents ...

5.1 Basic Drug Information Resources

5.2 Specialised Resources for ADRs

5.3 Critical Evaluation of Medication Safety Literature

There are various resources for getting information related to pharmacovigilance of drugs. In the primary literature on investigations related to new drugs, as well as new reports on existing drugs, new observations related to the effects of drugs are recorded. In addition, there are specialized resources dedicated only to reporting of adverse reactions to drugs. Further to this, there is a need that the literature reporting adverse reactions to drugs be critically evaluated in order to establish a causal link between drug administration and observation of adverse effects. All these aspects are discussed below.

5.1 BASIC DRUG INFORMATION RESOURCES

The information resources can be classified into three types: Primary, Secondary and Tertiary resources.

- Primary resources are the scientific journals in which articles related to investigations of effects of drugs on Human beings or on experimental animals are described.

- Secondary resources are those in which review articles or abstracts based on primary resources are published.

- Tertiary resources are the monographs and books which are published based on primary or secondary resources.

- Few databases can also be counted as tertiary resources. List of these resources is presented here:

Electronic Journals in Clinical Pharmacology and Toxicology:

Major journals covering adverse reactions of drugs are mentioned below:

- Alimentary Pharmacology & Therapeutics

- American Journal of Medical Science

- Annual Review of Pharmacology and Toxicology

- Anti-Cancer Drugs
- Antimicrobial Agents and Chemotherapy
- Behavioural Pharmacology
- Biochemical Pharmacology
- Clinical and Experimental Pharmacology & Physiology
- Clinical Pharmacology and Therapeutics
- Drug Metabolism and Disposition
- Drug Safety
- European Journal of Clinical Pharmacology
- European Journal of Pharmaceutical Sciences
- European Journal of Pharmacology
- Experimental and Clinical Psychopharmacology
- Food and Chemical Toxicology
- General Pharmacology: The Vascular System
- International Immunopharmacology
- International Journal of Immunopharmacology
- International Journal of Pharmaceutics
- Investigational New Drugs
- Journal of ECT
- Journal of Pharmaceutical and Biomedical Analysis
- Journal of Pharmaceutical Sciences
- Journal of Pharmacological and Toxicological Methods
- Journal of Pharmacology and Experimental Therapeutics
- Molecular Pharmacology
- Naunyn-Schmiedeberg's Archives of Pharmacology
- Neuropharmacology
- Neuropsychopharmacology
- Neurotoxicology and Teratology
- Neurotoxicology
- Peptides
- Pharmacogenetics
- Pharmacological Research
- Pharmacological Reviews
- Pharmacology & Therapeutics
- Pharmacology & Toxicology
- Pharmacology, Biochemistry and Behaviour
- Progress in Neuro-psychopharmacology and Biological Psychiatry
- Psychopharmacology
- Steroids
- Therapeutic Drug Monitoring
- Toxicology and Applied Pharmacology
- Toxicology *in vitro*
- Toxicology

- Toxicon
- Trends in Pharmacological Sciences

This list is illustrative and not exhaustive.

Few of the most cited medical journals are British Medical Journal, Lancet, New England Journal of Medicine, Journal of American Medical Association etc.

Some of the important websites providing information on drugs are listed here.

1. **AIDS Clinical Trials Information Service:**

   (http://www.actis.org/rwscripts/rwisapi.dll/@actis) Federally and privately funded HIV/AIDS clinical trials information from the US Department of Health and Human Services.

2. **CenterWatch Drug Directories:**

   (http://www.centerwatch.com/patient/drugs/drugdirectories.html) This source calls itself "The information source for the clinical trials industry". The following three drug directories from this site are extremely helpful:

   (i)   Drugs Approved by the FDA:

   (http://www.centerwatch.com/patient/drugs/druglist.html) This section can be searched by year and a medical specialty, such as Cardiology.

   (ii)   Drugs Currently in Clinical Research:

   (http://www.centerwatch.com/patient/cwpipeline/default.asp) According to the company, this site contains: "A listing of 2,000 active drugs in Phase I - Phase III trials are profiled sometimes including NDA submissions and withdrawals. Each summary contains information about the new treatment: the branded and generic name of the new therapy, the company sponsoring the research, and the phase of the clinical trials". It can be searched by medical condition.

   (iii) Clinical Trials Results Database:

   (http://www.centerwatch.com/patient/results/default.asp) The information in this section dates back to May, 2000 and is updated weekly. It is pulled from published materials from medical conferences, journals and company reports. The clinical trial result summaries typically include the name and phase of the new therapy, the company sponsoring the research, a description of the trial design, and information on how well the drug has performed.

3. **Clinical Trials.gov:**

   (http://clinicaltrials.gov/) ClinicalTrials.gov provides patients, family members, health care professionals, and members of the public; easy access to information on clinical trials for a wide range of diseases and conditions - brought to us through a collaborative effort of NIH, NLM and the FDA.

4. **DrugTopics.com:**

   (http://www.drugtopics.com/be_core/d/index.jsp) The online news magazine for pharmacists.

5. **FDA - Food and Drug Administration - Main Site with News and More:**

   (http://www.fda.gov/) This site includes news, product reports, and safety alerts for all FDA-regulated products, from USA.

6. **FDA/Center for Drug Evaluation and Research (CDER):**

   (http://www.fda.gov/cder/) According to their Web site, CDER serves as a consumer watchdog in USA by evaluating new drugs before they can be sold. Their goal is to ensure that prescription and over-the-counter drugs (brand name and generic) work correctly and that their health benefits outweigh the known risks. Three sections of special interest on the site are:

   (i)   New and Generic Drug Approvals:

   (http://www.fda.gov/cder/approval/index.htm) This is an alphabetical listing of all prescription drugs approved during 1998 through 2001. It is updated on a daily basis and contains links to labels, approval letters and reviews.

   (ii)   FDA Drug Approvals List:

   (http://www.fda.gov/cder/da/da.htm) This is a reverse chronological listing of all drugs approved since September 1996. It is updated on a weekly basis.

   (iii) Electronic Orange Book - Approved Drug Products with Therapeutic Equivalence Evaluations

   (http://www.fda.gov/cder/ob/default.htm)   Allows   searching   by   Active Ingredient, Applicant Holder, Proprietary Name and Application Number.

7. **FDA Enforcement Report Index:**

   (http://www.fda.gov/opacom/Enforce.html) A weekly report that contains information on actions taken in connection with agency regulatory activities, from USA.

8. **FDA - MedWatch:**

   (http://www.fda.gov/medwatch/safety) The FDA safety information and adverse-event reporting program, from USA.

9. **The Institute for Safe Medication Practices:**

   (http://www.ismp.org/) A non-profit organization that works closely with health care practitioners and institutions, regulatory agencies, professional organizations, and the pharmaceutical industry to provide education about adverse-drug events and their prevention. The Institute provides an independent review of medication errors that have been voluntarily submitted by practitioners to a national Medication Errors Reporting Program (MERP) operated by the United States Pharmacopeia (USP) in the USA. Information from the reports may be used by USP to impact on drug standards. All information derived from the MERP is shared with the U.S. Food and Drug link. Administration (FDA) and the pharmaceutical companies whose products are mentioned in reports.

10. Mosby's GenRx Top 200 Most Prescribed Drugs (ranked by sales volume):

(http://www.genrx.com/genrxfree/Top_200_2000/Top_200_2000.html) includes information about each drug listed.

11. NIH Clinical Alerts and Advisories:

(http://www.nlm.nih.gov/databases/alerts/clinical_alerts.html) Clinical alerts are provided to expedite the release of findings from the NIH funded clinical trials where such release could significantly affect morbidity and mortality.

Few more Important Databases for Drug Information:

1. **Databases for Drug and Chemical Information Biological Abstracts (BIOSIS):**

   Nearly 6,000 international journals are monitored for inclusion, representing virtually every life science discipline such as agriculture, biochemistry, biotechnology, ecology, immunology, microbiology, neuroscience, pharmacology, public health and toxicology. This host is silverplatter.

2. **ChemID and ChemIDPlus:**

   This is developed by National Library of Medicine (NLM). A chemical dictionary file for over 340,000 compounds of biomedical and regulatory interest.

3. **EMBASE:**

   This is developed by Elsevier. An index of the biomedical literature with greater depth of indexing than MEDLINE, unique Western European journal coverage, and coverage of drug research. EMBASE searches are available upon request to the Health Sciences Librarians.

4. **MEDLINE:**

   This is developed by National Library of Medicine. Available to search through the PubMed, Ovid, and MDConsult search interfaces Coverage: 1966 to the present.

5. **Ovid MEDLINE Search Guide (PDF):**

   (http://www.med.virginia.edu/hs-library/info_serv/edserv/guides/7steps.pdf)

6. **More MEDLINE Search Tips (PDF):**

   (http://www.med.virginia.edu/hs-library/info_serv/edserv/guides/tips.pdf)

7. **PubMed Search Tutorial:**

   (http://www.nlm.nih.gov/bsd/pubmed_tutorial/m1001.html)

8. **PREMEDLINE:**

   This is developed by National Library of Medicine. The "in-process" database for MEDLINE, PREMEDLINE provides basic information and abstracts before a record is indexed with MeSH heading(s) and added to MEDLINE. New records are added daily* to PREMEDLINE. After MeSH terms, publication types, GenBank accession numbers, and other indexing data are incorporated into a PREMEDLINE record; the completed citation is added to MEDLINE.

   Completed PREMEDLINE records are added as citations to MEDLINE on a weekly basis.

9. **OLDMEDLINE:**

This is developed by National Library of Medicine. Contains citations published in the 1958 through 1965 *Cumulated Index Medicus* and covers the fields of medicine, pre-clinical sciences, and allied health sciences. OLDMEDLINE is only available through the NLM Gateway. Coverage: 1958-1965.

10. **MICROMEDEX:**

This is developed by Thompson Healthcare. Contains peer-reviewed full-text drug information. It is composed of several databases that can be searched separately or through an integrated index. These databases allow you to search for summaries and detailed monographs for drugs, alternative medicine, toxicological managements, reproductive risks, and acute/emergency care.

11. **Toxline:**

This is developed by National Library of Medicine (NLM). This database provides toxicological, pharmacological, biochemical and physiological effects of drugs and other chemicals.

12. **TOXNET:**

This is developed by National Library of Medicine (NLM). It consists of a computerized collection of data and reference files on toxicology, hazardous chemicals and related areas. The records are derived from about 16 secondary sources that do not require royalty charges based on usage. Entering free-text terms as they appear in titles, keywords, and abstracts of articles will retrieve citations. The portions of the database derived from MEDLINE, DART, and that portion of BIOSIS added since August 1985, may be searched using MeSH vocabulary. Chemical substances can be searched by entering their corresponding CAS Registry Numbers and/or synoyms. Coverage: 1975 to the present.

13. **Web of Science, aka Science Citation Index:**

This is developed by Institute for Scientific Information. It provides a citation index of more than 5,700 major journals covering 164 scientific disciplines, 1,700 social sciences journals, and 1,100 arts and humanities journals. Updated weekly. It finds papers that have cited a primary paper. Coverage: 1987 to the present, but includes cited references irrespective of their date of publication, offering access to older relevant literature.

14. **Search Guide (PDF):**

(http://www.med.virginia.edu/hs - library/info_serv/edserv/guides/wos.pdf)

15. **Others:**

Consider also the **Cochrane Library** that includes the **Cochrane Database of Systematic Reviews** and **Cochrane Controlled Trials Register**.

The Cochrane Database of Systematic Reviews includes reviews of health care interventions including adverse effect information. The Cochrane Controlled Trials register contains 300,000 reports of randomized controlled trials in health care. These products are updated quarterly, but the records have no expiration dates as they are continuously updated. Other important drug databases include.

Derwent Drug File, **International Pharmaceutical Abstracts** and **SEDBASE** (produced by Elsevier) and derived from *Meyler's Side Effects of Drugs* and other sources.)

In addition, few standard books which are most frequently used as reference books can be added. Few books are indicated in the References.

5.2 SPECIALISED RESOURCES FOR ADRs

Some of the international databases can be used for information related to adverse reactions to drugs. Selection of right key words depending on the purpose of search is very important. e.g. If an investigator is interested about safety of a drug in specific period of time, then he/she can put proper key words related to the expected safety parameter, mention the name of suspected drug, indicate the duration of period for search, if any, and search the data base to get desired citations from the database. From the available citations, publications of appropriate interest should be selected by the investigator and an appropriate report can be generated. An alternative manual search can be key words mentioned at the end of a book in index. The advantage with search from databases is its updating as fast as desired. Citations in the global literature which is just few months old can also be included if the search is done from right sources. Journals related to drug safety, and information from regulatory resources for a specific country or region can also be made. Global resources can provide full information.

5.3 CRITICAL EVALUATION OF MEDICATION SAFETY LITERATURE

Mere availability of information is not enough. In fact, huge information can now be made available through electronic resources. Critical evaluation of the literature is extremely important. For the purpose of evaluation, specific issue for which evaluation is being carried out should be clear in the minds of investigators. Evaluation of literature is based on whether it is primary, secondary or tertiary source. Tertiary sources provide background information on the topics and provide quick and overall access on the topic. The content has limitation of time. If a book is published one or two years back, then the latest information on the topic in last two years or more may not be available. In such cases, secondary literature can be an alternative resource. If the investigator is interested in knowing latest adverse reactions for a new drug, then searching an appropriate data base for last few months will be a good choice. If more current and in depth knowledge is needed, then consulting primary literature is advisable. The most important limitation about primary literature is that, it may be biased and needs critical evaluation. Entire secondary or tertiary literature depends on the sourcing primary literature and therefore, avoiding bias and critical evaluation of primary literature is important in assessing safety of medicinal products.

Bias in a clinical trial may occur due to one of the following causes:

- Prevalence
- Admission rate
- Non-response
- Membership
- Procedure of selection
- Procedure of treatment
- Recall
- Intensive measure
- Detection
- Compliance
- Selection
- Observer, and
- Interviewer

Validity and confounding variables are two more parameters which should be looked in critical evaluation of the primary literature source. Validity of a trial can be internal or external. In a randomized clinical trial if blinding is not done properly, then it is an internal error. If there are excessive dropouts, the fact should be reported with adequate explanation; otherwise it can be invalid due to internal reasons. External validity refers to how results of the investigation can be extended to wider population. In a trial of an antihypertensive drug, if along with hypertensive patients, if asthmatic patients are not included, then the results of the investigation cannot be extended to hypertensive patients with asthma. It can be an issue of external validity. Confounding variables can be the concomitant diseases in a patient or administration of other drugs; even type of food can be a confounding variable. Their presence can be adjusted during statistical analysis. In critical analysis of safety of a drug, all these factors should be considered.

■■■

Chapter 6...

Establishing Pharmacovigilance Programme

Contents ...

A new pharmacovigilance centre can start operating very quickly. The development of a pharmacovigilance system, however, from the first and uncertain stage to becoming an established and effective organisation, is a process that needs time, vision, dedication, expertise and continuity. The most promising location for a new pharmacovigilance centre may depend on the organisation and development of the healthcare system in the country and other local issues.

A governmental department (health authority, drug regulatory agency) can be a good host for a pharmacovigilance centre. However, any department in a hospital or academic environment, working in clinical pharmacology, clinical pharmacy, clinical toxicology or epidemiology, may be a suitable starting point for pharmacovigilance. The reporting of adverse drug reactions may start locally, perhaps in one hospital, then extend to other hospitals and family practices in the region, and progress step by step into a national activity. In some countries professional bodies such as the national medical association may be a good home for the centre.

When the centre is a country-wide organisation from the start, it should be remembered that much effort, especially in effective communications, will be needed before a substantial proportion of practitioners are contributing.

When a centre is a part of a larger organisation (for example, a poison control unit, a clinical pharmacology department, or a hospital pharmacy) providing administrative continuity, it can get going as long as there is one professional (e.g. a physician or pharmacist) available who is primarily responsible for pharmacovigilance.

Whatever the location of the centre, pharmacovigilance is closely linked to drug regulation. Governmental support is needed for national co-ordination. Pharmacovigilance is nobody's individual privilege. Good collaboration, co-ordination, communications and public relations are needed for coherent development and for the prevention of unnecessary competition or duplication.

6.1 ESTABLISHING IN A HOSPITAL

In India, a hospital is attached to every medical college; hence having established the National Program of Pharmacovigilance, CDSCO has invited Dept. of Pharmacology of every Medical college to establish a centre of Pharmacovigilance in each hospital attached to every medical college voluntarily. Only technical and administrative support is being be provided by CDSCO. A hospital can adopt the ADR reporting form which is accepted at national level. Training of hospital staff about reporting ADRs is needed. The most important aspect is a strong desire on part of the management to participate in the national activity. Adverse report about any drug should be promptly reported to a designated authority in the hospital. Validation of the ADR and establishing a causal relation between the suspected drug and the observed adverse effect is the most crucial aspect of an ADR centre in the hospital. This has to be done by an appropriately trained person from the hospital. A system of reporting any adverse event with any patient in a hospital has to be developed for the purpose. Nursing staff, Clinical Pharmacist, or the doctor attending the patient can initiate the first reporting. The reporting has to be done in the standard format. After scrutiny and validation, the report through appropriate channel can reach the WHO centre through national centre after necessary scrutiny. Even independent hospitals, not attached to medical colleges can initiate it on their own.

6.2 ESTABLISHMENT AND OPERATION OF DRUG SAFETY DEPARTMENT IN INDUSTRY

A hospital is a public place using several drugs as needed by various patients for different ailments. Similarly while implementing a national program, all drugs marketed in that country will have to be considered. Thus, a pharmacovigilance program at a hospital or at national level will have to consider all the drugs used in it. Unlike this situation, whenever a safety department of a pharmaceutical industry sets up a pharmacovigilance unit, their interest will be cantered around only on drugs being marketed by them. However, if the industry is marketing the drug all over the world, then the system of pharmacovigilance has to cater to global level with appropriate network.

A global pharmaceutical industry will have to set up a data capture facility of all possible adverse events related to their drugs, may be at a call centre. The next step is processing a case and their medical review to establish a causal relation to the drug of their interest. When several such reports are collected, depending on classification and severity aggregate safety reporting has to be done to the sponsor and the regulatory authorities. This will be followed by safety surveillance and a search for signal detection.

This will be followed by assessment of risk in comparison to benefit. Having completed the benefit-risk review, an advanced workflow starts. During the next stage, integration of a number of tactical solutions into a fully managed service will evolve. The next stage is dealing with a huge data capture on a global scale on continuing basis. This can happen with support from specially developed computer software. Collecting such a safety-related data for all products, every day, from every possible reporting source, processing the data and achieving it continuously is a huge task. Mere archiving is not enough; taking appropriate action in consultation with the regulatory authority a national level and global level is a tremendous task. It is at this place that several job opportunities are available for newcomers.

6.3 ESTABLISHING A NATIONAL PROGRAMME

Various decisions and activities need to be conducted during establishment of a national program of Pharmacovigilance. What has been happening in India for last few years regarding pharmacovigilance is a live example of the event. Important points are discussed below:

Basic Steps in Setting Up a Pharmacovigilance Centre:

Prepare a plan according to the points below for the establishment of the pharmacovigilance system.

1. Make contacts with the health authorities and with local, regional or national institutions and groups, working in clinical medicine, pharmacology and toxicology outlining the importance of the project and its purposes.
2. Design a reporting form and start collecting data by distributing it to hospital departments, family practitioners etc.
3. Produce printed material to inform health professionals about definitions, aims and methods of the pharmacovigilance system.
4. Create the centre: staff, accommodation, phone, word processor, database management capability, bibliography etc.
5. Take care of the education of pharmacovigilance staff with regard to
    *   data collection and verification
    *   interpreting and coding of adverse reaction descriptions.
    *   coding of drugs.
    *   case causality assessment.
    *   signal detection.
    *   risk management.

6. Establish a database (administrative system for the storage and retrieval of data).
7. Organise meetings in hospitals, academia and professional associations, explaining the principles and demands of pharmacovigilance and the importance of reporting.
8. Promote the importance of reporting adverse drug reactions through medical journals, other professional publications, and communication activities.
9. Maintain contacts with international institutions working in pharmacovigilance, e.g. the WHO Department of Essential Drugs and Medicines Policy (Geneva) and the Uppsala Monitoring Centre, Sweden).

6.4 SOPS – TYPES, DESIGNING, MAINTENANCE AND TRAINING

There are several activities and documents to be performed and maintained during pharmacovigilance of a drug. In order to maintain global uniformity, it is essential that the documentation be done uniformly. Hence, few Standard Operating Procedures (SOPs) have been developed. A document on "Guideline on Good Pharmacovigilance Practices" (GVP), developed by European Medicines Agency is a useful tool for developing quality practices in pharmacovigilance.

SOPs on following activities have been developed:
- Filing of ADR Forms,
- Process and Reporting of ADR,
- Causality Assessment,
- Quality Assurance,
- Roles and Responsibilities,
- Training of PvPI personnel,
- Communication in PvPI,
- Pharmacovigilance and Safety Reporting for Sponsored Clinical Trials,
- Spontaneous Reporting of Adverse Drug Reactions,
- Reporting of Adverse Event.

The above mentioned list is illustrative only. Depending on the actual need of operation, new SOPs may be developed as and when necessary.

A standard format for SOP is suggested here.

Title of the SOP: SOP for ------- (Name of the Activity: e.g. Reporting of Adverse Drug Reactions)

SOP Number: Version Number:

Effective Date: Review Date:

Author Name and Title of the person

Reviewer 1: Name and Title of the person

Reviewer 2: Name and Title of the person

Reviewer 3: Name and Title of the person

(The number of reviewers may be less or more than three depending on the actual situation.)

Authorisation:

Name and title of the person:

Signature:

Date:

Purpose and Objective:

In the first part, the purpose and objective(s) for which the SOP has been prepared should be clarified in telegraphic language.

In the second part, if there is any legal authorisation of the main activity under which a SOP has been prepared, the relevant part of legal citation should be endorsed.

Scope:

The area for which a SOP is applicable should be clarified. If a private hospital has developed the SOP, then it should be clarified that it is applicable in the hospital ...... (Name of the hospital). If a Chain of hospitals or if a state controlling several district hospitals has developed a SOP, then it should be clarified that the SOP is applicable to .... (Names of the sites).

If there are several individuals involved in the mechanism of operation, then the details of who will report to whom and how, should be clarified in accordance with the protocol.

Procedures laid down by the sponsor are most important, hence who is the sponsor and what are the things specified by the sponsor should be clarified.

If there are multiple sites, then the Chief Investigator (CI) is responsible for the entire operations of clinical trials; the responsibilities can be further delegated to Principal Investigator (PI) of each site.

The main SOP text consists of three columns in a table:

Sr. No.	Responsibility	Activity

Column two indicates the title of the person who is supposed to be responsible for the activity; e.g. The Chief Investigator/Principal Investigator/Study Monitor/Governance GCP Manager. Column three indicates details of how the specific activity is to be performed. In order to ensure that every time the activity is performed in similar manner, it is necessary that all possible finer details of the activity should be clarified in the SOP. Hence, it is essential that the SOP should be prepared and checked by the persons who are actually involved in the activity on the field.

Some of the SOPs available in the public domain are included in the Appendix 2.

6.5 ROLES AND RESPONSIBILITIES IN PHARMACOVIGILANCE

There can be three kinds of agencies involved in the implementation of the program of pharmacovigilance. Roles and responsibilities of each one of them are detailed here.

6.5.1 Licence Partners

The Marketing Authorization Holder (MAH) can delegate activities related to Pharmacovigilance to a co-marketer or a consultant. In turn, the co-marketer or the consultant can license the activities to one or more partners. In one kind of arrangement, licensor may not have commercial interest while in other cases licensor may do co-promotion or perform co-marketing in one or more countries. According to the kind of arrangement terms oflicensing can vary. Roles and responsibilities of Licenced partner depend on the details of the agreement between licensee and the licensor.

6.5.2 Contract Research Organisations (CROs)

Alternatively, MAH can appoint CROs for different kinds of activities related to Pharmacovigilance. CROs may have their own SOPs to conduct the activities; however integrity of the CRO can grow based on their conduct. In any case responsibility of correctness of data lies entirely on the MAH. Appointing credible CROs, who perform their job correctly, depends on appropriate selection. The best thing which MAH can do is to have strict monitoring on activities of CROs along with appropriate control on proper documentation. Roles and responsibilities of CROs will depend on the kind of agreement between MAH and the CRO.

6.5.3 Market Authorisation Holders (MAH)

It is to be emphasized that in any case, irrespective of kind of delegation of authorities, the entire responsibility of correctness of the data related to Pharmacovigilance lies only with MAH. In case, if it is proved later that incorrect data of pharmacovigilance is recorded, then the action will be taken on MAH only.

■■■

Chapter 7 ...

Pharmacovigilance Methods

Contents ...

All other medicinal products except for vaccines are to be administered to a selected population with a specific indication. Five types of methods are used to collect the data related to Pharmacovigilance. The methods are discussed below.

7.1 PASSIVE SURVEILLANCE –

SPONTANEOUS REPORTS AND CASE SERIES

Passive surveillance refers to collecting the pharmacovigilance data from conventional procedures of treatment. There are three types of data.

7.1.1 Spontaneous Reports

A spontaneous report is an unsolicited communication by healthcare professionals or consumers to a national pharmacovigilance center, pharmaceutical company, regulatory authority or other organization (e.g., WHO, Regional Centers) that describes one or more suspected adverse drug reactions in a patient who was given one or more medicinal products and that does not derive from a study or any organized data collection system where adverse event reporting is actively sought.

Spontaneous reports play a major role in the identification of signals of drug related problems once a drug is marketed. They can also provide important information on at-risk groups, risk factors, and clinical features of known serious adverse drug reactions.

All these cases – 'Individual Case Safety Reports' (ICSRs) – are entered on the safety database i.e. Vigibase, which are examined individually and in the aggregate for a product in order to identify clusters of reports that could represent a signal of a previously unknown adverse reaction or drug interaction or some change in the character of a known adverse reaction. It may also be possible to recognize a new risk factor for a reaction to a product, such as a sub-group of patients at particular risk. Vigibase is maintained internationally by Uppsala Monitoring Centre at Switzerland. The activity is supported by World Health Organization (WHO). Under-reporting of the events is the criticism on this activity; because it depends on proactive initiatives taken carefully by the concerned medical and allied professionals. If the concerned staff is not very alert in recording the events, then total reporting may be lower.

7.1.2 Case Series of Spontaneous Reports

Series of case reports can provide evidence of an association between a drug and an adverse event, but they are generally more useful for generating hypothesis than for verifying an association between drug exposure and outcome. There are certain distinct adverse events known to be associated frequently with drug therapy, such as anaphylaxis, aplastic anaemia, toxic epidermal necrolysis and Stevens Johnson syndrome. Hence, when events such as these are spontaneously reported, it is important that pharmacovigilance centres place emphasis on these reports for detailed and rapid follow-up. Case reports and series have a high sensitivity for detecting novelty and therefore remain one of the cornerstones of medical progress; they provide many new ideas in medicine.

7.1.3 Targeted Spontaneous Reporting

This is a variant of spontaneous reporting. It focuses on capturing adverse drug reactions in a well-defined group of patients on treatment. It also enables focus on a specific drug of interest in a specific population of interest or a specific adverse drug reaction. Health professionals in charge of the patients are sensitized to report specific safety concerns. The method is intended to ensure that patients are monitored and that adverse drug reactions are reported as a normal component of routine patient monitoring and standard of care. This focused approach has the same objectives and flow of information as for spontaneous reporting. The reporting requires no active measures to look for the particular syndromes.

7.2 STIMULATED REPORTING

Several methods have been used to encourage and facilitate reporting by health professionals in specific situations (e.g., in-hospital settings), for new products or for limited time periods. All health professionals including physicians, nurses and clinical pharmacists are encouraged to add the reporting adverse reactions to drugs actively. Such methods include on-line reporting of adverse events and systematic stimulation of reporting of adverse events based on a pre-designed case definition. Stimulated reporting can occur in certain situations, such as direct healthcare professional communication (DHPC), a publication in the press or questioning of healthcare professionals by company representatives, and adverse reaction reports arising from these situations are considered spontaneous reports, provided the report meets the definition above.

Although these methods have been shown to improve reporting, they are not devoid of the limitations of spontaneous reporting, especially selective reporting and incomplete information. It is expected that stimulated reporting will add to spontaneous reporting.

7.3 ACTIVE SURVEILLANCE – SENTINEL SITES, DRUG EVENT MONITORING AND REGISTRIES

Active surveillance, in contrast to spontaneous reporting, seeks to ascertain completely the number of adverse events via a continuous pre-organised process. An example of active surveillance is the follow-up of patients treated with a particular drug as in Cohort Event Monitoring. Patients who fill a prescription for this drug may be asked to complete a brief survey form and give permission for later contact.

Active surveillance requires substantially more time and resources and is therefore less commonly used in emergencies. But it is often more complete than passive surveillance. In general, it is more feasible to get comprehensive data on individual adverse event reports through an active surveillance system than through a spontaneous reporting system.

It is further subdivided into three categories.

7.3.1 Sentinel Sites

Active surveillance can also be achieved by reviewing medical records or interviewing patients and/or physicians in a sample of sentinel sites to ensure complete and accurate data on reported adverse events from these sites. The selected sites can provide information, such as data from specific patient sub-groups that would not be available in a spontaneous reporting system. Further, information on the use of a drug, such as abuse, can be targeted at selected sentinel sites. Sentinel surveillance requires more time and resources, but can often produce more detailed data on cases of illness. It may be the best type of surveillance if more intensive investigation of each case is necessary to collect the necessary data. Some of the major weaknesses of sentinel sites are problems with selection bias, small numbers of patients, and increased costs. Sentinel sites can be more relevant to confirming a specific adverse reaction suspected with an established drug or monitoring adverse reaction with a new drug. It involves active participation of patients as well as medical and associated staff along with supportive record.

7.3.2 Drug Event Monitoring

Drug event monitoring is a method of active pharmacovigilance surveillance. In drug event monitoring, patients might be identified from electronic prescription data or automated health insurance claims. A follow-up questionnaire can then be sent to each prescribing physician or patient at pre-specified intervals to obtain outcome information. Information on patient demographics, indication for treatment, duration of therapy, dosage, clinical events and reasons for discontinuation can be included in the questionnaire. Limitations of drug event monitoring can include poor physician and patient response rates and the unfocused nature of data collection, which can obscure important signals. In addition, maintenance of patient confidentiality might be a concern. Success of Drug event monitoring depends on active participation of medical staff supported with appropriate documentation by supporting staff. Active involvement of patients is absolutely essential; but motivation by medical staff goes long way in ensuring success of drug event monitoring.

A subset of drug event monitoring is to attempt for retrospective information about existing patients based on earlier collected information. It is termed as cohort event monitoring.

7.3.3 Cohort Event Monitoring (CEM)

A modification of drug event monitoring is cohort event monitoring (CEM), an active pharmacovigilance method promoted by the World Health Organization and other agencies. CEM is a method where information is collected, with focus on events, on all patients in a group being treated with a medicine or group of medicines. A pre-treatment questionnaire is filled at time of recruitment and post-treatment questionnaires are filled at times of follow up which may either be once e.g. for anti-malarials or life-long e.g. for antiretrovirals. (WHO forms for antimalarial/ antiretroviral drugs are available on net).

7.3.4 Registries

A patient registry is a list of patients presenting with the same characteristic(s). This characteristic can be pregnancy (pregnancy registry), a disease (disease registry) or a specific exposure (drug registry). Both type of registries, which only differ by the type of patient data of interest, can be collected with a battery of information using standardised questionnaires in a prospective fashion.

7.4 COMPARATIVE OBSERVATIONAL STUDIES – CROSS-SECTIONAL STUDY, CASE CONTROL STUDY AND COHORT STUDY

Traditional epidemiologic methods are a key component in the evaluation of adverse events. A number of observational study designs are useful in validating signals from spontaneous reports or case series. Major types of these designs are cross-sectional studies, case-control studies, and cohort studies (both retrospective and prospective).

7.4.1 Cross-Sectional Study

Data collected on a population of patients at a single point in time (or interval of time) regardless of exposure or disease status constitute a cross-sectional study. These types of studies are primarily used to gather data for surveys or for ecological analyses. The major drawback of cross-sectional studies is that the temporal relationship between exposure and outcome cannot be directly addressed. These studies are best used to examine the prevalence of a disease at one time point or to examine trends over time, when data for serial time points can be captured. These studies can also be used to examine the crude association between exposure and outcome in ecologic analyses. Cross-sectional studies are best utilized when exposures do not change over time. Fluorosis caused by continual leakage of fluorine in water can be an example.

7.4.2 Case-Control Study

In a case-control study, cases of disease (or events) are identified. Controls, or patients without the disease or event of interest, are then selected from the source population that gave rise to the cases. The controls should be selected in such a way that the prevalence of exposure among the controls represents the prevalence of exposure in the source population. The exposure status of the two groups is then compared using the odds ratio, which is an estimate of the relative risk of disease in the two groups.

7.4.3 Cohort Study

In a cohort study, a population-at-risk for the disease (or event) is followed over time for the occurrence of the disease (or event). Information on exposure status is known throughout the follow-up period for each patient. A patient might be exposed to a drug at one time during follow-up, but non-exposed at another time point. Since the population exposure during follow-up is known, incidence rates can be calculated. In many cohort studies involving drug exposure, comparison cohorts of interest are selected on the basis of drug use and followed over time. Cohort studies are useful when there is a need to know the incidence rates of adverse events in addition to the relative risks of adverse events. Multiple adverse events can also be investigated using the same data source in a cohort study. However, it can be difficult to recruit sufficient numbers of patients who are exposed to a drug of interest or to study very rare outcomes.

7.5 TARGETED CLINICAL INVESTIGATIONS

When significant risks are identified from pre-approval clinical trials, further clinical studies might be called for to evaluate the mechanism of action for the adverse reaction. In some instances, pharmacodynamic and pharmacokinetic studies might be conducted to determine whether a particular dosing instruction can put patients at an increased risk of adverse events. Genetic testing can also provide clues about which group of patients might be at an increased risk of adverse reactions. Furthermore, based on the pharmacological properties and the expected use of the drug in general practice, conducting specific studies to investigate potential drug-drug interactions and food-drug interactions might be called for. These studies can include population pharmacokinetic studies and drug concentration monitoring in patients and normal volunteers.

7.6 VACCINE SAFETY SURVEILLANCE

Vaccines are normally given to healthy individuals, especially young children, and often on a mandatory basis. In contrast to medicines, they are given to prevent a disease, and so the urgency of receiving them is somewhat lower. Vaccines have a complex composition, a short duration of exposure with a long-term response. The result is that there is lower acceptance of any potential risks. Because of the wide utilization of vaccines, a safety risk could have extensive consequences, and thus rapid evaluation is critical. Also because of their wide-spread use, temporal associations might be seen as causally related, making appropriate causality analysis is extremely important.

There are special considerations for Pharmacovigilance of vaccines, which include careful attention to manufacturing methods (including use of adjuvants, stabilizers, preservatives and residual material from the manufacturing process), batch-related adverse reactions, special attention to target groups and group-specific host factors. The variables include potential transmission of infectious agents, especially in live attenuated vaccines, and to vaccination schedules and route of administration (because of potential concomitant organisms that might produce an augmented effect). Expedited reporting of cases for lack of efficacy, the non-applicability of causality assessments as applied to medicines, and the potential for programmatic errors complicate reporting of intrinsic adverse reactions. All these aspects need a special surveillance for vaccines. In addition, any adverse reaction to a vaccine is viewed as a defect in production in public opinion because they are being given to healthy children.

■■■

Chapter 8...

Adverse Drug Reaction Reporting

Contents ...

Since the main objective of pharmacovigilance is the identification of information that may affect the safety of patients, once a potential risk is noted, it must be communicated to all stakeholders. According to regulations of International Conference on Harmonization (ICH E2A), all adverse drug reactions (ADRs) that are both serious and unexpected (SUSARs Suspected Unexpected Serious Adverse Reactions) are subject to expedited reporting. This applies to reports from spontaneous sources and from any type of clinical or epidemiological investigation, independent of design or purpose.

Initial reports should be submitted within the prescribed timeframe provided the following minimum criteria are met:

- an identifiable patient

- a suspect medicinal product

- an identifiable reporting source, and

- an event or outcome that can be identified as serious and unexpected, and for which, in clinical investigation cases, there is a reasonable suspected causal relationship.

During global clinical trials, a SUSAR that occurs in one country may require expedited reporting to regulatory authorities, institutional review boards/ethics committees, and investigators in all participating countries. This must be done in accordance with each country's local laws and regulations. Unfortunately, countries vary in their requirements as to the format and timeframe for the reporting of cases. In addition, reporting requirements are frequently changing at the country level.

8.1 INTRODUCTION TO REPORTING SYSTEMS

The culture of reporting is extremely important. It is to be emphasized that the purpose of reporting is primarily to sensitize all stakeholders of pharmacovigilance about intricacies involved in all types of adverse reactions to drugs under varying conditions. Since every participant in the process is working under varying conditions, and the patients are of different types, it is essential that the wide experiences should be shared at global level. Hence, every country decides its internal system of reporting as per infrastructure and globally they report as per internationally accepted protocol to Upssala monitoring centre. This helps in maintaining uniformity within the system.

In India, following things are important as general considerations while recording adverse reactions to drugs.

WHAT TO REPORT?

The National Pharmacovigilance Program (NPP) shall encourage reporting of all **suspected** drug related adverse events, including those suspected to have been caused by herbal, traditional or alternative remedies. The reporting of seemingly insignificant or common adverse reactions would be important since it may highlight a widespread prescribing problem.

The program particularly solicits reports of:

- All adverse events suspected to have been caused by new drugs and 'Drugs of current interest' (List to be published by CDSCO from time to time).

- All suspected drug interactions.

- Reactions to **any** other drugs which are suspected of significantly affecting a patient's management, including reactions suspected of causing:
    - death,
    - life-threatening event (real risk of dying),
    - hospitalisation (initial or prolonged),
    - disability (significant, persistent or permanent),
    - congenital anomaly,
    - required intervention to prevent permanent impairment or damage.

WHO CAN REPORT?

Any health care professionals (Doctors including Dentists, Nurses, and Pharmacists) may report suspected adverse drug events.

The program shall not accept reports from lay members of the public or anyone else who is not a health care professional.

WHERE TO REPORT?

After completion, the form shall be returned/forwarded to the same Pharmacovigilance Centre from where it was received.

Reporting can be done to any one of the country vide Pharmacovigilance Centres nearest to the reporter. (updated list of centres is available on net at www.cdsco.nic.in).

In case of doubt, the form may be sent to the National Pharmacovigilance Centre at: Central Drugs Standard Control Organisation, Directorate General of Health Services, Ministry of Health & Family Welfare, Nirman Bhawan, New Delhi 110 011.

The details regarding "What, Who and Where" about reporting can vary from country to country. Similarly regional and global instructions are available from WHO.

8.2 SPONTANEOUS REPORTING SYSTEM

Standard form to report spontaneous reports are available. Indian form is reproduced in the Appendix. The form includes details of patient, existing diseases, medications given including indigenous medications along with their composition, route of administration, quantity and other relevant details which can have causal relation to the adverse reactions. Carefully filled up forms are uploaded to the respective regulatory authorities.

In order to develop the system of reporting, three kinds of centres have been developed in India.

1. There are two Zonal Pharmacovigilance Centres (ZPC):

    (i) AIIMS, New Delhi for North and East and

    (ii) KEM, Mumbai for South and West.

2. Regional Pharmacovigilance Centres (RPC): Four regional centres. North, East, South and West. PGIMER, Chandigarh (North); PGIMER, Kolkata (East); JSSMC, Mysore (South); and SGSMC & KEM Hospital, Mumbai (West).

3. Peripheral Pharmacovigilance Centres (PPC): Teaching hospitals or any other leading medical institution is assigned as PPC. They are more in number.

Co-ordinators of each type of centre have been assigned specific responsibilities as indicated in the adjacent table.

Table 8.1: Centre's Co-ordinators' Responsibilities at different levels of programme

Sr. No.	Responsibilities	PPC	RPC	ZPC
1.	To collect ADE notifications.	✓	✓	✓
2.	To receive blank ADE forms and acknow-ledge receipt.	✓	✓	✓
3.	To fill or get filled the ADE forms (fill all mandatory data).	✓	✓	✓

contd. ...

Sr. No.	Responsibilities	PPC	RPC	ZPC
4.	To forward duly-filled ADE forms to next higher level center.	✓	✓	
5.	To maintain a log of all ADE notification forms (blank or filled) received and forwarded.	✓	✓	✓
6.	To identify, induce PPC / RPC (with concurrence of NPC), provide them with general technical support, co-ordinate and monitor their functioning.	✓	✓	
7.	To identify and deploy a pharmacologist for management of pharmacovigilance tasks.	✓	✓	
8.	To identify and deploy a data manager for data management under NPP.	✓		
9.	To carry out (or review) causality analysis of all ADE forms or review such analysis by the RPC.	Optional	✓	✓
10.	To forward all duly-filled ADE forms (those generated at the same center and those received from immediate lower-level center) as per pre-determined time line.	* Weekly (Monday)	* Every 15 days (alternate Monday)	* Only archiving
11.	To report all serious adverse events within two week days, subsequent to receipt of its notification at the center.	✓	✓	✓
12.	To forward periodic report to next higher center as per the MIS format (appendix I).	Every 15 days (1st & 15th of every month)	Monthly (1st of every month)	Monthly (1st of every month)
13.	To liaison with healthcare professionals in order to inculcate / foster the culture of ADE notification / reporting. 1. Acknowledge the co-operation by the notifier. 2. Share with notifier relevant feedback from higher centers.	✓	✓	✓
14.	To organize and attend training programs / interactive meetings for all lower level centers	✓	✓	✓

Management of the reporting system from each type of centre has also been specified.

Table 8.2: Management Information System Reports to be provided under the Programme

[PPC to RPC]	[RPC to ZPC]	[ZPC to NPC]
1. Period of the report	1. Period of the report	1. Period of the report
2. No. of notifications received in the preceding period.	2. No. of notifications received in the preceding period	2. No. of notifications received in the preceding period
3. No. of reports made	3. No. of reports made	3. No. of reports made
4. No. of serious (or suspected serious) AE reports (if any)	4. No. of serious (or suspected serious) AE reports (if any)	4. No. of serious (or suspected serious) AE reports (if any)
5. No. of serious (or suspected serious) AE reports forwarded within specified time	5. No. of serious (or suspected serious) AE reports forwarded within specified time	5. No. of serious (or suspected serious) AE reports forwarded within specified time
6. No. of serious (or suspected serious) AE reports not forwarded within specified time	6. No. of serious (or suspected serious) AE reports not forwarded within specified time	6. No. of serious (or suspected serious) AE reports not forwarded within specified time
7. Reasons for delay	7. Reasons for delay	7. Reasons for delay
8. Important happenings or developments (events that happened other than the way they should have happened or events that dint happen the way they should have happened)	8. Important happenings or developments (events that happened other than the way they should have happened or events that dint happen the way they should have happened)	8. Important happenings or developments (events that happened other than the way they should have happened or events that dint happen the way they should have happened)
9. Total No. of AE forms received	9. Total No. of AE forms received	9. Total No. of AE forms received
10. No. of AE forms in which causality assessments made	10. No. of AE forms in which causality assessments made	10. No. of AE forms in which causality assessments made
11. Any other observations	11. New PPC identified and recommended if any	11. No. of recommendations from RPC for new PPC

contd. ...

[PPC to RPC]	[RPC to ZPC]	[ZPC to NPC]
	12. No. of notifications/ reports received from each center	12. No. of AE forms received from RPC in which causality assessment has been made
	13. No. of reports inappropriately filled in by respective PPCs	13. No. of AE forms received from RPC in which causality assessment has been verified/reassessed (all SAEs and 10% of all remaining)
	14. Actions taken / recommended	14. No. of forms archived
	15. MONITORING activities done	15. MONITORING activities done
	16. Acknowledgments sent in time	
	17. CME awareness activities if any	
	Any other observations	

8.3 REPORTING TO REGULATORY AUTHORITIES

The reported adverse reactions need to be scrutinized in order to establish a causal relation between the drug and the event. Careful scrutiny of the form is desirable by the regulatory authorities. Since regulatory authorities are expected to take remedial actions based on the feedback from the field, their scrutiny is important. Comments from the medical experts of the panel are valuable. Quality of the information based on authenticity, completeness and even legibility is checked. Reporter's identity is clearly verified so that he/she can be contacted for any clarification.

8.4 GUIDELINES FOR REPORTING ADRs IN BIOMEDICAL LITERATURE

Whenever any report about adverse reactions of drugs is published, then all readers take it as a gospel truth and corrective actions by physicians at their own level or at regulatory level may be initiated. It is desirable that every such report should be complete in information and should provide the information in a uniform manner. Hence, there should be common guidelines at international level. In 1985, a conference of editors of medical journals took up the issue and generated a set of guidelines. Subsequently a working group supported by French group published another set of guidelines in 1997. Later Indian Society of Pharmacoepedemiology (ISoP) and Indian Society of Pharmacovigilance (ISoP) published elaborate details in the form of Guidelines for reporting ADRs in biomedical literature. A list of those guidelines is presented here.

Table 8.3: Guidelines for Reporting ADRs

Category	Information Required	Highly desirable	If relevant
Title	Consistent with the content of the report		
Patient Demographics	Age group, sex.	Exact age, weight.	Height, race and ethnicity, obstetrical status, body mass index, occupation.
Current health status	Disease or symptoms being treated with suspect drug.	Duration of illness.	Severity of disease/symptoms. Previous therapy of active disease.
Medical history	Medical history relevant to adverse event .	Prior exposure to drug product or class. Underlying risk factors.	Alcohol, tobacco, and substance abuse history, relevant social circumstances, family history, drugs taken by household members.
Physical examination	Abnormal physical or laboratory findings. For off-label use, documentation of the reason.	Baseline labora-tory findings with normal range of values of the laboratory.	Pertinent negative physical findings.
Patient disposition	Presence or absence of death, life threatening circumstances, hos-pitallization or prolon-ged hospitalization or significant disability.	Status several months after adverse event.	

contd. ...

Drug			
Identification	Suspected drug identified by generic name. Herbal products can be described by Latin binomial of herbal ingredients, plants part(s), and type of preparation (e.g. crude herb or extract). Proprietary name and name of producer for manufactured products.	Suspected brand name with strength/dosage unit. For herbal extracts, type and concentration of extraction solvent used. For herbal products, state whether or not the product(s) implicated are authorized or licensed, and whether or not sample(s) have been retained for analysis, and any results.	Product formulation. For manufactured herbal products, whether the product was standardized for which constituent(s) and concentration(s), and for extracts, the drug-extract ratio.
Dosage	Approximate dosage, duration of therapy.	Exact dosage, start and stop dates.	Serum or other fluid drug concentrations. Restart dates.
Administration		Route.	Patient adherence.
Drug-reaction interface	Therapy duration before the adverse event.	First dose-event interval, last dose-event interval.	Last dose-resolution interval.
Concomitant therapies	Assessment of potential contribution of concomitant therapies.	Description of concomitant therapies, including non-prescription, herbal or complementary medicines.	Start and stop doses of concomitant therapies.

If these guidelines are followed by authors, editors of Journals and reviewers, then reporting of adverse drug reactions will be so complete that new signals can be easily detected without any bias and the factual status of the drug will be known to each stakeholder in a transparent manner very easily.

■■■

Chapter 9...

Signal Detection, Risk Assessment and Management

Contents ...

A risk management system is a set of pharmacovigilance activities and interventions designed to identify, characterize, prevent and minimize risks relating to medicinal products, including the assessment of the effectiveness of those interventions. Any new drug can impose a risk. The risk may be inherent and unintentional. The real points to be considered are:

- How serious is the risk?
- How common is it?
- What are the consequences of continuing the drug in the market?
- Is the risk acceptable?
- Can the risk be made acceptable by limiting its use with some instructions or warnings?
- Is the risk serious enough to withdraw the drug?
- Is the risk causally related to the drug or is it an exacerbation of symptoms of underlying disease?
- Are there any confounding factors which are responsible for adverse reactions to drugs?
- How a new causal relation between a drug and its adverse reaction be identified?
- What is the importance of signal detection in pre and post marketing stages?
- How to prioritize the assessment of risk?
- How to manage the risk?

Answers to all these questions need serious investigations. Various regulatory authorities have intervened in these issues and few regulations have come into place. The issues are discussed below.

9.1 IDENTIFICATION OF NEW ADVERSE DRUG REACTIONS

Identification of a new observation of adverse reaction is a vital and important issue in Pharmacmacovigilance. In this context, a term called safety signal is used. It is defined as "information that arises from one or multiple sources (including observations or experiments), which suggests a new, potentially causal association, or a new aspect of a known association between an intervention [e.g., administration of a medicine] and an event or set of related events, either adverse or beneficial, that is judged to be of sufficient likelihood to justify verificatory action".

In this definition, mention of one or multiple sources is important. In every source, the types of patients are likely to be different in terms of genetic composition, variables regarding severity of disease, presence of confounding factors like organ failure, concomitant diseases etc. Inspite of these variables if the said event is repeated, then it is likely that there is a causal relation between the drug and the signal. Another important point to be noted is that the event may either be adverse or beneficial. Since it can also be beneficial, the word safety signal is justified.

There are few more comments which need elaboration with respect to the definition.

- "Information that arises from one or multiple sources": An earlier definition of a safety signal referred to "report(s) of an event," implying that adverse event reports are the primary, if not the only, source of safety signals. The CIOMS VIII definition acknowledged that new information relevant to drug safety may arise from other sources, such as clinical and non-clinical experiments and published articles on clinical study results.

- "suggests": A safety signal is not synonymous with a confirmed safety issue. The information must be suggestive of something new that would be worth further investigation, after which the suggested association may or may not be confirmed.

- "new": The concept of newness has always been an important part of safety signal detection. It should be noted that newness may be on emerging trends and changes in the specificity, severity, and/or rate of occurrence (frequency) of a previously known (thus may not be totally new) adverse drug reaction.

- "judged to be of sufficient likelihood to justify verificatory action": As discussed above (regarding the word "suggests"), a safety signal by the CIOMS VIII definition precedes further investigation ("verificatory action"), not at the conclusion of such investigation. Importantly, this definitional element emphasizes the crucial role of clinical and scientific judgment in determining whether or not a possible association rises to the level warranting further action.

Safety signals that warrant further investigation include, but are not limited to:

- New adverse events, not currently documented in the product label, especially if serious and in rare untreated populations.

- An apparent increase in the severity of an adverse event that is already included in the product label.

- Occurrence of serious adverse events known to be extremely rare in the general population.

- Previously unrecognized interactions with other medicines, dietary supplements, foods, or medical devices.

- Identification of a previously unrecognized at-risk population, such as populations with specific genetic or racial predisposition or coexisting medical conditions.

- Confusion about a product's name, labelling, packaging or use.

- Concerns arising from the way a product is used (e.g., adverse events seen at doses higher than normally prescribed, or in populations not recommended, in the label).

- Concerns arising from a failure to achieve a risk management goal.

A safety signal is to be identified based on data mining of several observations being noted continually. Thus it is a never-ending process in the history of a drug. The incidence of reporting may come down with passage of time. Once a signal is identified, then its frequency and the conditions under which it is repeated again is watched. Causal relation between the signal and administration of the drug is understood in the form of mechanism of action of the signal.

9.2 SIGNAL DETECTION IN PRE AND POST MARKETING PERIOD

One thing needs to be emphasized clearly. The number of patients and the controlled conditions under which the drug under investigation is administered keeps a lot of uncertainties which are cleared only in the post-marketing phase of the drug. During various phases of clinical trials, only about 5,000 patients are treated; while when marketing of a drug starts, a population of millions is being treated. This population can be global. Hence, genetic composition of the population is varied. Some of the adverse reactions are rare; may be one in millions or one in billions; such rare ADRs are detectable only when a large population is exposed to the drug. Thus, observation of a new ADR which was not detected in clinical trial phase but is observed only during marketing phase is not the fault of MAH. The general approach during post marketing phase of the drug should be of cautious optimism coupled with careful scrutiny. The post-marketing phase is for population study of the drug as against limited exposure during clinical phase.

Signal detection in pre and post-marketing stages may face three hypothetical situations as described below:

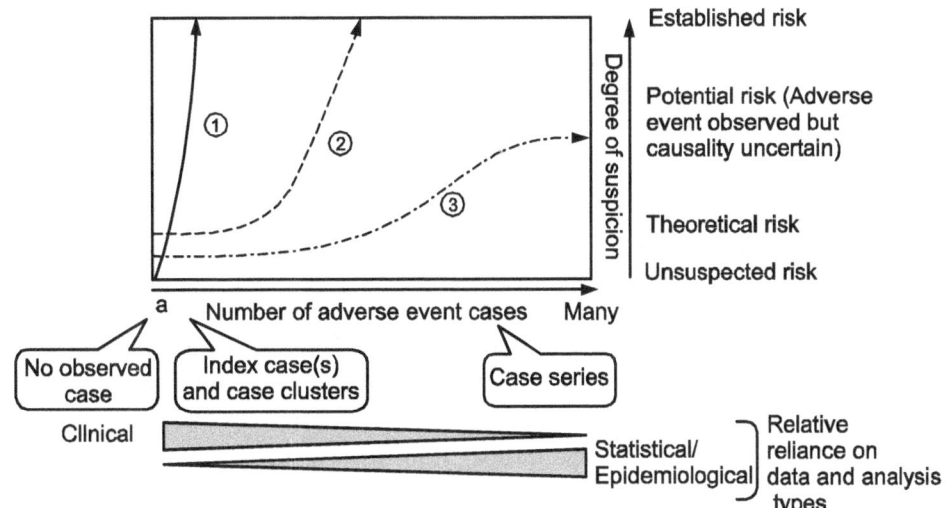

Note: This is figure is not based on actual data record, it is illustrative only.

Fig. 9.1: The natural history of safety signals (Hypothetical depiction)

Scenario 1:

Some suspicion about a safety risk exists at the time of starting a safety monitoring program. The suspicion could be theoretical based on the biological mechanism action of the drug or the risk associated with other drugs in the same therapeutic class or it may have been observed in animal studies. As the sample size of the clinical data (from clinical studies and post-market experience) grows, adverse event cases are reported. After a careful assessment of a case series, it is concluded that, this drug is very likely causally associated with a particular adverse event. The conclusion may result in risk communication actions (e.g., updating the prescribing information), and/or additional risk assessment activities (e.g., investigations in independent data sources).

Scenario 2:

At the beginning of clinical development, no anticipation exists for a particular type of safety risk. However, after just a small number of adverse event cases start to be reported, particularly some on rare conditions that have high drug attributability in general, a causal relationship between the drug and the adverse event is suspected. After further investigation, the level of suspicion reaches the point where risk communication actions, such as label change, are deemed necessary.

Scenario 3:

In this situation, a suspicion is raised but does not reach the level for initiating risk communication actions. Safety signals are put under active review, but more data do not necessarily help to make a definitive conclusion because of inherent limitations of data or existence of plausible alternative explanations (e.g., confounding). In such situations, investigators may turn to independent datasets for further insights.

9.3 PRIORITIZATION AND RISK ASSESSMENT

The next issue is how to prioritize assessment of the risk. Usually decision about what should be done for the signal of ADR is based on three types of observations.

1. Traditional pharmacovigilance methods including review of individual cases or case series, aggregate analysis of case report data, or literature search and review.

2. Data mining algorithms including Proportional Reporting Ratio (PRR), Multi-item Gamma-Poisson Shrinker (MGPS) or Bayesian Confidence Propagation Neural Network (BCPNN). (See Ch. 16 on Statistical Methods for more information)

3. Safety data to be monitored including non-clinical investigations, clinical trial reports, adverse event reports, published literature, non-interventional studies, periodic safety reports, information on other drugs of the same class, other relevant information coupled with signal detection in spontaneous reporting systems from company data-bases and health-authority monitoring systems.

Information from all these three resources is interpreted in the context of all available safety data, disease knowledge, biological plausibility , alternative aetiologies for the suspected adverse reactions to identify potential risk involved in the event. Based on this information, identification of the risk is prioritized by evaluating the content related to the signal. The signal is evaluated on the basis of pharmacoepidemiologic studies, mechanistic studies, clinical trials, and other types of studies related to detection of adverse reactions to drugs.

9.4 RISK MANAGEMENT

A pharmaceutical company can prepare a risk management plan (RMP) for its products, especially new products.

An RMP includes a summary of important identified risks of the medicine, potential risks, and missing information—this serves as the basis for an action plan for pharmacovigilance and risk minimization activities. This summary incorporates the safety profile of the medicine at that time in its life-cycle, either during preclinical testing, pre-approval clinical development, or pre-approval.

- Data on known and potential safety risks (drawn from preclinical and/or clinical study results for the medicine) are specified;

- The extent and limitations of the safety database (kinds of studies, numbers of subjects, rigor of study designs, exclusions in study protocols etc.) are defined;

- Areas of risk that have not yet been studied or not studied extensively (such as specific [or larger] patient populations; and

- Patients with other medical conditions or in other treatment settings, interactions with other medications) are identified.

Pharmacovigilance and risk management activities that might be included in an RMP fall into two categories: routine activities—which would generally be conducted for any medicine at the same stage of development where no special safety concerns have arisen—and additional activities designed to address identified safety concerns (as highlighted in the summary). Routine pharmacovigilance would include the safety evaluations incorporated in clinical trials and the monitoring and reporting of spontaneous adverse events pre-approval. Routine risk management activities would include ensuring that suitable warnings are included with all product information and careful labelling and packaging of the medicine.

In an RMP, the action plan might include calling for additional pharmacovigilance in the form of:

- Active surveillance (e.g., medical records reviews, patient or physician interviews, prescription event monitoring, data from disease or drug exposure registries).
- Epidemiology studies (retrospective or prospective).
- Further clinical studies (specific safety studies, larger studies over longer periods).
- Drug utilization studies (which describe how a drug is marketed, prescribed, and used in a specified population—often stratified by age, gender, concomitant medications etc. and how these factors influence clinical, social and economic outcomes).

If the action plan specifies additional risk minimization activities, these could include:

- Additional educational material about the medicine and its use (patient information brochures, visual aids, physician prescribing guides/checklists, pharmacist dispensing guides/checklists, health care provider letters).
- Training programs (patient- or physician-oriented).
- Restricted use of the medicine (e.g., for use/dispensing only in hospital, or where specific equipment [e.g., resuscitation equipment] is available; availability only in limited unit sizes).

■■■

Chapter 10...

Drug and Disease Classification

Contents ...

In order to rationalize the system of reporting ADRs, classification of diseases, drugs, names and doses of drugs need to be clearly defined. The approach has to be unambiguous and very clear. Information about these issues is discussed below.

10.1 ANATOMICAL, THERAPEUTIC AND CHEMICAL CLASSIFICATION OF DRUGS

Anatomical classification is based on different systems of the human body. An illustration of the classification is presented below.

- Drugs acting on Nervous system

- Drugs acting on Cardiovascular system

- Drugs acting on Respiratory system

- Drugs acting on Skeletal system

- Drugs acting on Reproductive system

- Drugs acting on Gastrointestinal system

- Drugs acting on Excretory system

- Drugs acting on Endocrine system

Therapeutic classification of drugs is based on clinical uses of the drugs. Drugs used to treat a specific disease are clubbed together. It may overlap several chemical classes of drugs in one basket. An illustration of such classification is presented here.

- Drugs acting on Depression

- Drugs acting on Schizophrenia

- Drugs acting on Anxiety
- Drugs acting on Ulcer
- Drugs acting on Asthma
- Drugs acting on Congestive Cardiac Failure
- Drugs acting on Hypertension
- Drugs acting on Diabetes
- Drugs acting on Infectious diseases: Tuberculosis, Leprosy, Malaria etc.

Chemical classification of drugs is based on the basic chemical class to which the drug belongs. An illustration of the classification is presented here.

- Purines
- Pyrimidines
- Sulfonylureas
- Pyrazolones
- Thiazides
- Steroids

If this kind of classification is to be followed collectively, then the efforts should be International and subjectivity in classification should be removed. Hence WHO is participating in this activity since 1976. The system is called as ATC/DDD system. It classifies every drug into five levels. At every level, a drug is offered an identification number. The identification number offers unique feature to the drug. It is like name of an individual. The five levels and what they indicate is mentioned here. The levels are illustrated with an example of a drug Metformin, which is an anti-diabetic drug.

A	: Alimentary tract and metabolism
	(First level, anatomical main group)
A10	: Drugs used in diabetes
	(Second level, therapeutic subgroup)
A10B	: Blood glucose lowering drugs, excluding insulins
	(Third level, pharmacological subgroup)
A10BA	: Biguanides
	(Fourth level, chemical subgroup)
A10BA02 :	Metformin
	(Fifth level, chemical substance)

Thus, in the ATC system all plain metformin preparations are given the code A10BA02.

The first level classifies a drug by the anatomical system. An illustration is indicated below.

A : Alimentary tract and metabolism system

B : Blood and blood forming system

C : Cardiovascular system

The second level of the code indicates the therapeutic main group and consists of two digits.

Details of Alimentary tract-related drugs are presented here:

A1 : Stomatological preparations

A2 : Drugs for acid related disorders

A3 : Drugs for functional gastrointestinal disorders

A4 : Antiemetics and Antinauseants

A5 : Bile and Liver Therapy

A6 : Drugs for Constipation

A7 : Antidiarrhoeals, Intestinal anti-inflammatory/anti-infective agents

A8 : Anti-obesity preparations, excluding diet products

A9 : Digestives, inclusive enzymes

A10 : Drugs used in diabetics

The third level of the code indicates the therapeutic/pharmacological subgroup and consists of one letter.

A10A : Insulins and Analogues

A10B : Drugs used to lower blood glucose, excluding insulins

The fourth level of the code indicates the chemical/therapeutic/pharmacological subgroup and consists of one letter.

A 10 BA : Biguanides.

A 10 BB : Sulfonamides, Urea derivatives

A 10 BC : Sulfonamides (heterocyclic)

A 10 BD : Combinations of oral blood glucose lowering drugs

A 10 BF : α-glucosidase inhibitors

A 10 BG : Thiazolidinediones

A 10 BH : Dipeptyl peptidase 4 (DPP-4) inhibitors

A 10BX : Other blood glucose lowering drugs, excluding insulins

A 10 X : Other drugs used in diabetes

A 10 XA : Aldose reductase inhibitors

The fifth level of the code indicates the chemical substance and consists of two digits.

A10BA02 : 02 indicate second drug, which is Metformin.

10.2 INTERNATIONAL CLASSIFICATION OF DISEASES

Just like classification of drugs, internationally acceptable classification of diseases has been worked out by WHO. It is outlined below:

The International Classification of Diseases (ICD) is the standard diagnostic tool for epidemiology, health management and clinical purposes. This includes the analysis of the general health situation of population groups. It is used to monitor the incidence and prevalence of diseases and other health problems, proving a picture of the general health situation of countries and populations.

ICD is used by physicians, nurses, other providers, researchers, health information managers and coders, health information technology workers, policy-makers, insurers and patient organizations to classify diseases and other health problems recorded on many types of health and vital records, including death certificates and health records. In addition to enabling the storage and retrieval of diagnostic information for clinical, epidemiological and quality purposes, these records also provide the basis for the compilation of national mortality and morbidity statistics by WHO Member States. Finally, ICD is used for reimbursement and resource allocation decision-making by countries.

The ICD is important because it provides a common language for reporting and monitoring diseases. This allows the world to compare and share data in a consistent and standard way – between hospitals, regions and countries and over periods of time. It facilitates the collection and storage of data for analysis and evidence-based decision-making. Eleventh revision of ICD has been done in 2015. All comments made here are based on tenth revision made in 2010.

For understanding ICD, it is necessary to comprehend the concept of Family of International classification (WHO-FIC) as developed by WHO. The WHO Family is a suite of classification products that may be used in an integrated fashion to compare health information internationally as well as nationally.

Internationally endorsed classifications facilitate the storage, retrieval, analysis, and interpretation of data and their comparison within populations over time and between populations at the same point in time as well as the compilation of internationally consistent data. Populations may be Nations, States and Territories, regions, minority groups or other specified groups.

Definition of WHO-FIC is as follows:

The WHO Family of International Classifications (WHO-FIC) is comprised of classifications that have been endorsed by the World Health Organization to describe various aspects of the health and the health system in a consistent manner. The classifications may be the property of WHO or other groups. The purpose of the Family is to assist the development of reliable statistical systems at local, national and international levels, with the aim of improving health status and health care.

Classification of WHO-FIC:

The classifications in the WHO-FIC and the broader United Nations family of economic and social classifications are of three major types. Fig. 10.1 represents the types of classifications in the WHO-FIC.

The types are as follows:

1. Related Classification.

2. Reference Classifications.

3. Derived Classifications.

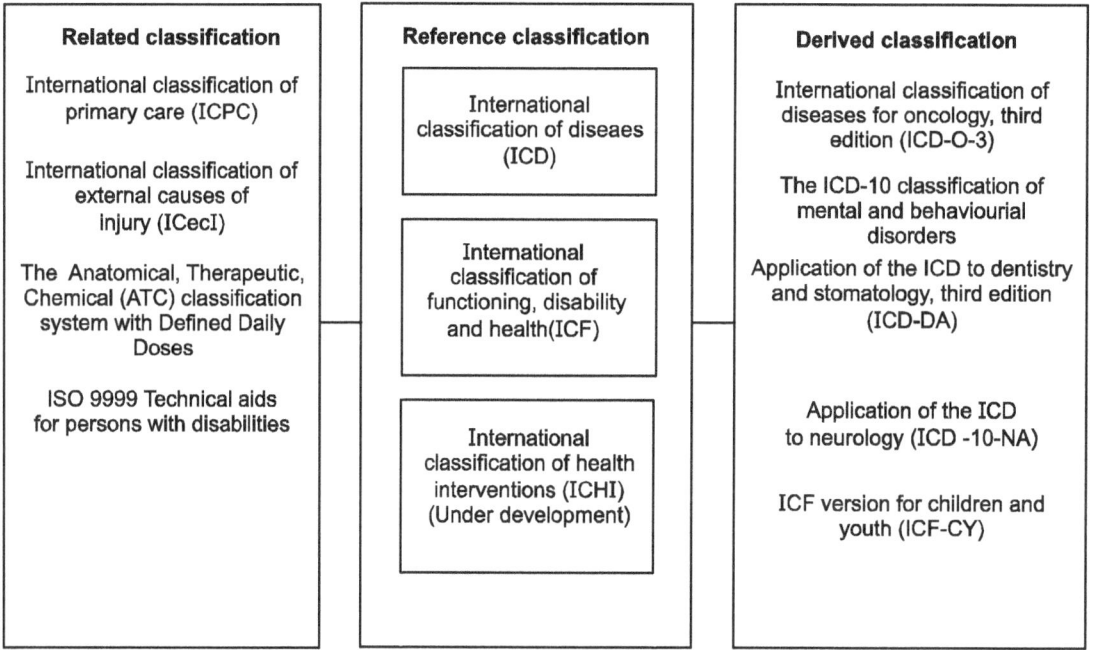

Related classification	Reference classification	Derived classification
International classification of primary care (ICPC)	International classification of diseaes (ICD)	International classification of diseases for oncology, third edition (ICD-O-3)
International classification of external causes of injury (ICecI)	International classification of functioning, disability and health(ICF)	The ICD-10 classification of mental and behaviourial disorders
The Anatomical, Therapeutic, Chemical (ATC) classification system with Defined Daily Doses		Application of the ICD to dentistry and stomatology, third edition (ICD-DA)
ISO 9999 Technical aids for persons with disabilities	International classification of health interventions (ICHI) (Under development)	Application of the ICD to neurology (ICD -10-NA)
		ICF version for children and youth (ICF-CY)

Fig. 10.1: Schematic representation of the WHO-FIC

ICD is one of the Reference classifications, while Anatomical Therapeutic Chemical classification with defined Daily Doses is one of the Related Classifications.

ICD classification divides the diseases into 21 chapters. Each chapter contains sufficient three-character categories to cover its content; not all available codes are used, allowing space for future revision and expansion. Chapters I–XVII relate to diseases and other morbid conditions, and Chapter XIX to injuries, poisoning and certain other consequences of external causes.

The first character of the ICD code is a letter, and each letter is associated with a particular chapter, except for the letter D, which is used in both Chapter II, Neoplasms, and Chapter III, Diseases of the blood and blood-forming organs and certain disorders involving the immune mechanism, and the letter H, which is used in both Chapter VII, Diseases of the eye and adnexa and Chapter VIII, Diseases of the ear and mastoid process. Four chapters (Chapters I, II, XIX and XX) use more than one letter in the first position of their codes. The remaining chapters complete the range of subject matter nowadays included in diagnostic data.

Chapter XVIII covers symptoms, signs and abnormal clinical and laboratory findings, not elsewhere classified. Chapter XX, External causes of morbidity and mortality, was traditionally used to classify causes of injury and poisoning. Finally, Chapter XXI, Factors influencing health status and contact with health services, is intended for the classification of data explaining the reason for contact with health-care services of a person not currently sick, or the circumstances in which the patient is receiving care at that particular time or otherwise having some bearing on that person's care.

As an illustration, classification related to chapter one based on infectious diseases is reproduced below:

CHAPTER I

Certain Infectious and Parasitic Diseases:

(A00-B99)

Includes: Diseases generally recognized as communicable or transmissible.

Use additional code (U82-U84) to identify resistance to antimicrobial drugs.

Excludes: Carrier or suspected carrier of infectious disease, certain localized infections - body system-related chapters, infectious and parasitic diseases:

- Complicating pregnancy, childbirth and the puerperium [except obstetrical tetanus] **(O98)**.

- Specific to the perinatal period [except tetanus neonatorum, congenital syphilis, perinatal gonococcal infection and perinatal human immunodeficiency virus [HIV] disease] influenza and other acute respiratory infections.

This Chapter contains the following blocks:

A00-A09	:	Intestinal infectious diseases
A15-A19	:	Tuberculosis
A20-A28	:	Certain zoonotic bacterial diseases
A30-A49	:	Other bacterial diseases
A50-A64	:	Infections with a predominantly sexual mode of transmission
A65-A69	:	Other spirochetal diseases
A70-A74	:	Other diseases caused by chlamydia
A75-A79	:	Rickettsioses

A80-A89	:	Viral infections of the central nervous system
A90-A99	:	Arthropod-borne viral fevers and viral hemorrhagic fevers
B00-B09	:	Viral infections characterized by skin and mucous membrane lesions
B15-B19	:	Viral hepatitis
B24-B24	:	Human immunodeficiency virus [HIV] disease
B25-B34	:	Other viral diseases
B35-B49	:	Mycoses
B50-B64	:	Protozoal diseases
B65-B83	:	Helminthiases
B85-B89	:	Pediculosis, ascariasis and other infestations
B90-B94	:	Sequelae of infectious and parasitic diseases
B95-B97	:	Bacterial, viral and other infectious agents
B99-B99	:	Other infectious diseases

Classification of Section A15-A19 on Tuberculosis is given below as an illustration.

Tuberculosis (A15-A19):

A15	:	Respiratory tuberculosis, bacteriologically and histologically confirmed.
A16	:	Respiratory tuberculosis, not confirmed bacteriologically and histologically.
A17	:	Tuberculosis of nervous system.
A18	:	Tuberculosis of other organs.
A19	:	Miliary tuberculosis.

Miliary tuberculosis is further sub-classified as:

A19.0	:	Acute miliary tuberculosis of a single specified site.
A19.1	:	Acute miliary tuberculosis of multiple sites.
A19.2	:	Acute miliary tuberculosis, unspecified.
A19.3	:	Other miliary tuberculosis.
A19.4	:	Miliary tuberculosis, unspecified.

Similarly other conditions are subclassified.

International Classification of Diseases (ICD) is so relevant in interpretation of ADRs; because it offers a clue to the fact whether what is observed as a ADR is related to the drug itself or is an exacerbation of the disease process itself. At the same time, it confirms that the choice of drug is correct or otherwise.

10.3 DAILY DEFINED DOSES

When daily defined dose of a drug is to be indicated, ATC code of the drug along with its name is necessary. Along with these details, quantum of the drug, its unit and the route of administration are needed. An illustrative list of units and the routes of administration is indicated below:

Units	Route of administration (Adm. R)
g, G = gram	Implant = Implant
mg, Mg = milligram	Inhal = Inhalation
mcg, Mcg = microgram	N = nasal
u, U = unit	Instill = Instillation
TU = thousand units	O = oral
MU = million units	P = parenteral
mmol = millimole	R = rectal
ml, Ml = millilitre (e.g. eye-drops)	SL = sublingual/buccal
	TD = transdermal
	V = vaginal

An illustrative list of drugs along with their DDDs is indicated here.

ATC code	ATC level name (INN/generic name)	DDD	Unit	Administration Route
A07AA11	Rifaximin	0.6	g	O
A07AA12	Fidaxomicin	0.4	g	O
A10BH05	Linagliptin	5	mg	O
A10BX04	Exenatide	0.286	mg	P depot inj
B01AF02	Apixaban	5	mg	O
B02BD10	von Willebrand factor	6	TU	P
J01GB01	Tobramycin	0.112	g	Inhal powder

This is a standardised method to represent daily divided doses of the drug when the issue is related to recording of adverse reactions.

10.4 INTERNATIONAL NON-PROPRIETARY NAMES (INN) FOR DRUGS

The INN system as it exists today was initiated in 1950 by a World Health Assembly Resolution numbered WHA3.11 and began operating in 1953, when the first list of International Non-proprietary Names for pharmaceutical substances was published. The cumulative list of INN is growing every year by some 120-150 new INN.

Since its inception, the aim of the INN system has been to provide health professionals with a unique and universally available designated name to identify each pharmaceutical substance. The existence of an international nomenclature for pharmaceutical substances, in the form of INN, is important for the clear identification, safe prescription and dispensing of medicines to patients, and for communication and exchange of information among health professionals and scientists worldwide.

As unique names, INN has to be distinctive in sound and spelling, and should not be liable to confusion with other names in common use. To make INN universally available they are formally placed by WHO in the public domain, hence their designation as "nonproprietary". They can be used without any restriction whatsoever to identify pharmaceutical substances.

Another important feature of the INN system is that the names of pharmacologically-related substances demonstrate their relationship by using a common "stem". By the use of common stems the medical practitioner, the pharmacist, or anyone dealing with pharmaceutical products can recognize that the substance belongs to a group of substances having similar pharmacological activity.

The extent of INN utilization is expanding with the increase in the number of names. Its wide application and global recognition are also due to close collaboration in the process of INN selection with numerous national drug nomenclature bodies. The increasing coverage of the drug-name area by INN has led to the situation whereby the majority of pharmaceutical substances used today in medical practice are designated by an INN. The use of INN is already common in research and clinical documentation, while their importance is growing further due to expanding use of generic names for pharmaceutical products.

Use of INN:

Nonproprietary names are intended for use in pharmacopoeias, labelling, product information, advertising and other promotional material, drug regulation and scientific literature, and as a basis for product names, e.g. for generics. Their use is normally required by national or, as in the case of the European Community, by international legislation. As a result of ongoing collaboration, national names such as British Approved Names (BAN), Denominations Communes Françaises (DCF), Japanese Adopted Names (JAN) and United States Adopted Names (USAN) are nowadays, with rare exceptions, identical to the INN.

Some countries have defined the minimum size of characters in which the generic nonproprietary name must be printed under the trade-mark labelling and advertising. In several countries the generic name must appear prominently in type at least half the size of that used for the proprietary or brand-name. In some countries, it has to appear larger than the trade-mark name. Certain countries have even gone so far as to abolish trade-marks within the public sector.

To avoid confusion, which could jeopardize the safety of patients, trade-marks cannot be derived from INN and, in particular, must not include their common stems. As already mentioned, the selection of further names within a series will be seriously hindered by the use of a common stem in a brand-name.

Selection of INN:

The names which are given the status of an INN are selected by the World Health Organization on the advice of experts from the WHO Expert Advisory Panel on the International Pharmacopoeia and Pharmaceutical Preparations.

The process of INN selection follows three main steps:

- A request/application is made by the manufacturer or inventor;
- After a review of the request a proposed INN is selected and published for comments;
- After a time-period for objections has lapsed, the name will obtain the status of a recommended INN and will be published as such if no objection has been raised.

INNs are selected in principle only for a single, well-defined substance that can be unequivocally characterized by a chemical name (or formula). It is the policy of the INN program not to select names for mixtures of substances, while substances that are not fully characterized are included in the INN system in exceptional cases only. INNs are not selected for herbal substances (vegetable drugs) or for homoeopathic products. It is also the policy of the INN program not to select names for those substances that have a long history of use for medical purposes under well-established names such as those of alkaloids (e.g. morphine, codeine), or trivial chemical names (e.g. acetic acid).

An INN is usually designated for the active part of the molecule only, to avoid the multiplication of entries in cases where several salts, esters etc. are actually used. In such cases, the user of the INN has to create a modified INN (INNM) himself; mepyramine maleate (a salt of mepyramine with maleic acid) is an example of an INNM. When the creation of an INNM would require the use of a long or inconvenient name for the radical part of the INNM, the INN program will select a short name for such a radical (e.g. mesilate for methanesulfonate).

In the process of INN selection, the rights of existing trade-mark owners are fully protected. If in the period of four months following the publication of a proposed INN, a formal objection is filed by an interested person who considers that the proposed INN is in conflict with an existing trade-mark, WHO will actively pursue an arrangement to obtain a withdrawal of such an objection or will reconsider the proposed name. As long as the objection exists, WHO will not publish it as a recommended INN.

The selection of a new INN relies on a strict procedure. Upon receipt of an INN request form, the WHO Secretariat examines the suggested names for conformity with the general rules, for similarities with published INN and potential conflicts with existing names, including published INN and trade-marks. A note summarizing the result of these checks is added and the request is subsequently forwarded to the INN experts for comments. Once all experts agree upon one name, the applicant is informed of the selected name.

Newly selected, proposed INNs are then published in WHO Drug Information, which indicates a deadline for a 4-month objection period. This period is allowed for comments and/or objections to the published names to be raised. The reasons for any objection must be stated clearly and these will be evaluated by the experts for further action. Users are invited to refrain from using the proposed name until it becomes a recommended INN, in order to avoid confusion, should the name be modified. Two lists of proposed INN are published yearly.

The final stage of the selection process is the recommended INN. Once a name has been published as a recommended INN, it will not normally be modified further and is ready for use in labelling, publications, on drug information. It will serve to identify the active pharmaceutical substance during its life-time worldwide. Since the name is available in the public domain it may be used freely. However, it should not be registered as a trade-mark since this would prevent its use by other parties.

Recommended INNs are published in the WHO Drug Information as a consequence of the objection procedure applied to proposed INN. As from 1997, two lists of proposed INN are published yearly and as from list 37 of recommended INN, graphic formulae are also included for better identification of the substances.

The procedure for selecting recommended INN is carried out in accordance with a text adopted by the WHO Executive Board.

Names for Radicals and Groups:

During the 1975 meeting on Nonproprietary Names for Pharmaceutical Substances, the experts discussed the issue of INN for salts and esters and noted that requests had frequently been received for INN for salts, esters, or combination products of substances for which INN already existed. At that time, the experts decided that INN for the simple salt and esters should be devised from the INN in conformity with normal chemical practice.

Some of the radicals and groups involved are, however, of such complex composition that it makes it inconvenient to use the chemical nomenclature. It was thus decided that in such cases, shorter nonproprietary names are selected for these inactive moieties and published in proposed lists under the title "Names for Radicals and Groups". Separate names for salts and esters derived from this procedure are not published. If a "radical and group name" is used in conjunction with an INN, they are referred to as International Nonproprietary Name (Modified) or INNM.

A comprehensive list of radicals and groups may be obtained from WHO's Marketing and Dissemination unit (INNs: Names for radicals and groups combined summary list).

Some of the **general principles used in selecting INN** are presented here.

Primary Principles:

1. INNs should be distinctive in sound and spelling. They should not be inconveniently long and should not be liable for confusion with names in common use.
2. The INN for a substance belonging to a group of pharmacologically active substances should, where appropriate, show this relationship. Names that are likely to convey to a patient an anatomical, physiological, pathological or therapeutic suggestion should be avoided.

Secondary Principles:

1. In devising INN for the first substance in the pharmacological group, consideration should be given to the possibility of devising suitable INN for related substances belonging to the new group.
2. In devising INN for acids, one-word names are preferred; their salts should be named without modifying the acid name. e.g. "Oxacillin" and "Oxacillin Sodium".
3. INN for the substances which are used as salts should in general apply to the active base or the active acid. Names for different salts or esters of the same active substance should differ only in the respect of the name of the inactive acid or the inactive base.

Cumulative list of all INNs is available at WHO site. There are two components in the INN. One part is "stem" which is common to the same categories of drugs. The second part can be a fancy name relevant only to that substance. In case of ACE inhibitors, "pril" is the stem. Thus Captopril, Lisinopril, Ramipril are different ACE inhibitors. In case of one series of sulphonylureas used as antidiabetics "gli" is the stem. Thus we have Glimepiride, Gliclazide, and Glibenclamide as different drugs in the same category. List of various stems and their categories are indicated in one of the WHO guidance documents.

■■■

Chapter 11 ...

Drug Dictionaries and Coding in Pharmacovigilance

Contents ...

For rationalizing terminologies used in Pharmacovigilance, it is necessary that words with same meanings be used. Hence, use of standard texts and dictionaries is recommended. Few standard documents are discussed below.

11.1 WHO ADVERSE REACTION TERMINOLOGIES

Definitions of terms related to adverse reactions as defined in the WHO documents is presented in Appendix 1 of the book.

11.2 MedDRA AND STANDARDISED MedDRA QUERIES

The Medical Dictionary for Regulatory Activities (MedDRA) is a large, hierarchical, multiaxial medical terminology. MedDRA is a registered trademark belonging to the International association of Manufacturers named "International Federation of Pharmaceutical Manufacturers Association" (IFPMA). It is a structured vocabulary of medical and other terms relevant to the development and use of medicines in man. The chronology for development of MedDRA is as follows:

- In 1989, UK MCA identified a need for a single medical terminology to support new computer databases.
- In 1991, a new medical terminology, ADROIT (Adverse Drug reaction Online Information Tracking) was created by UK MCA.
- In January 1993, a need for a medical terminology to support European Community Drug Regulatory System was identified.
- During November 1993 to October 1994, a working group reviewed and amended MCA terminology, and termed it as MedDRA.
- In October 1994, ICH recommended that MedDRA (Medical Dictionary for Drug Regulatory Affairs) version 1.0 should form basis of new medical terminology.
- In February 1996, MedDRA version 1.5 was released for review in US and Japan.

- In July 1997, ICH approved it for international terminology.
- In November 1998, IFPMA, holder of intellectual property selected BDM international as MSSO (Maintenance and Support Services Organisation).
- In March 1999, MedDRA version 2.1 was released.
- By 2014, MedDRA version 16.0 was available.

Users of the system have to pay for the services and get access of rights through licensing from MedDRA Maintenance and Support Service Organization (MSSO) and Japanese Maintenance Organization (JMO). Currently the work of these two bodies is undertaken by Northrop Grumman Mission Systems (for MSSO) and Japanese Pharmacopeia (for JMO). The MSSO and JMO release updated versions of MedDRA every six months either on a CD or through internet. In 2015, annual charges for pharmaceutical companies were $ 190 or $ 82000 depending on revenue of the company. It is free to regulatory authorities and nonprofit organizations.

MedDRA is defined as "a clinically-validated international medical terminology used by regulatory authorities and the regulated biopharmaceutical industry". The terminology is used through the entire regulatory process, from pre-marketing to post-marketing, and for data entry, retrieval, evaluation and presentation.

MedDRA system is organized under five levels as a hierarchy. Their number as per version 16 is indicated in the brackets.

1. Lowest Level Terms (LLT)   [71,326]
2. Preferred Terms (PT)   [20,057]
3. High Level Terms (HLT)   [1,717]
4. High Level Group Terms (HLGT)   [334]
5. System Organ Class (SOC)   [26]

LLT is defined as, "the lowest level of terminology, related to a single PT as a synonym, lexical variant or a quasi-synonym" (It is to be noted that all PTs have identical LLTs).

PT represents a single medical concept.

HLT, a subordinate of HLGT, superordinate grouping for one or more PTs.

HLGT, a subordinate to SOC, superordinate grouping for one or more HLTs.

SOC is the highest level of terminology representing an anatomical or physiological system, ethology or purpose.

The list of 26 SOCs have been constant for a long time. It is presented below:

1. Blood and lymphatic system disorders.
2. Cardiac disorders.
3. Congenital, familial and genetic disorders.
4. Ear and labyrinth disorders.
5. Endocrine disorders.
6. Eye disorders.
7. Gastrointestinal disorders.
8. General disorders and administration site conditions.
9. Hepatobiliary disorders.
10. Immune system disorders.

11. Infections and infestations.
12. Injury, poisoning and procedural complications.
13. Investigations.
14. Metabolism and nutrition disorders.
15. Musculoskeletal and connective tissue disorders.
16. Neoplasms benign, malignant and unspecified.
17. Nervous system disorders.
18. Pregnancy, puerperium and perinatal conditions.
19. Psychiatric disorders.
20. Renal and urinary disorders.
21. Reproductive system and breast disorders.
22. Respiratory, thoracic and mediastinal disorders.
23. Skin and subcutaneous tissue disorders.
24. Social circumstances.
25. Surgical and medical procedures.
26. Vascular disorders.

As an illustration, take the case of arrhythmia for consideration. The SOC for arrhythmia is Cardiac disorder (No. 2) from the list. HLGT for this condition is Cardiac arrhythmias. HLT for this condition is Rate and rhythm disorders NEC. PT for this condition is Arrhythmia. LLTs for similar conditions are Arrhythmia NOS, Arrhythmia, Dysrhythmias, and other specified cardiac dysrhythmias. Thus for any specific clinical condition, appropriate LLT, PT, HLT, HGLT and SOC is to be identified. Knowledge of pathological background can help in identifying correct classification group to which the condition belongs. Each MedDRA term is assigned an 8-digit numeric code. It is necessary to know the scope of MedDRA. It refers to medical conditions, indications; investigations (tests, results); medical and surgical procedures; medical, social and family history; medication errors; product-quality issues; device-related issues; pharmacogenetic terms; toxicological issues; and standardized queries. It does not refer to patient demographic terms; clinical trial design terms; severity descriptors; numerical values for results; and frequency qualifiers. MedDRA is not a drug dictionary; it is not equipment, device or a diagnostic product dictionary.

The website www.meddramsso.com offers necessary details about MedDRA.

11.3 WHO DRUG DICTIONARY

WHO Adverse Reaction Terminology (WHOART) is a dictionary meant to serve as a basis for rational coding of adverse reaction terms. The system is maintained by the Uppsala Monitoring Centre (UMC), the World Health Organization Collaborating Centre for International Drug Monitoring. It is structured as follows.

- 32 System-organ classes body organ groups.
- 180 High level terms for grouping preferred terms.
- 2085 Preferred terms/principal terms for describing adverse reactions.
- 3445 Included terms/synonyms to preferred terms.

The information is compiled in the database termed "Vigibase" and all health professionals like physicians, nurses, pharmacists can contribute to the database. Unlike MedDRA, it is not a subscribed database. A standard form, depicting details of the patient, drug(s) consumed by the patients, case history and outcome of the adverse reaction is to be filled by a health-professional. It is a global program supported by pharmacovigilance program of a country at national level and by Upssala Monitoring Centre by support of World Health Organization at a global level.

11.4 EUDRAVIGILANCE MEDICINAL PRODUCT DICTIONARY

Eudravigilance is the European Union pharmacovigilance database and data-processing network (the 'Eudravigilance database'). It supports the secure exchange, processing and evaluation of Individual Case Safety Reports (ICSRs) related to medicinal products authorized in the European Union (EU) and investigational medicinal products (IMPs) studied in clinical trials authorized in the EU, Signal detection, evaluation and management, proactive release of information on adverse reactions in compliance with personal data protection legislation in the EU, Electronic submission of information of medicinal products authorized in EU.

There is a provision of information on IMPs by the sponsor before completing a clinical trials application in the EU.

The Eudravigilance web application (EVWEB) is an interactive data entry tool to allow for message and acknowledgement message generation and administration by a user via a web interface, called EVWEB.

EVWEB can be used by any marketing authorization holder or sponsor of a clinical trial with reporting or submission obligations in the EU but has been specifically designed for Small and Medium Size Enterprises (SMEs), which do not have the necessary IT in-house tools available.

System users have access to controlled vocabularies and terminologies. EVWEB requires an Internet connection and Internet Explorer browser v. 5.5 or higher. The electronic submission of information on medicinal products is secure. Security is achieved in a first instance by a username/password combination to access the registered user restricted area of the Eudravigilance website, and in a second instance by the use of a HTTPS(SSL) protocol. Secure Sockets Layer (SSL) provides security by the use of a public key to encrypt data that is then transferred over the SSL connection. In HTTP (S-HTTP), SSL creates a secure connection between a client and a server, through which any amount of data can be sent securely. SSL and SHTTP, therefore, are complementary technologies.

The specialty of Eudravigilance is the ability to upload ICSRs directly into the web. It provides chance to offer details of the products, country of origin, and details of the adverse reaction. It has a linkage with MedDRA for browsing. The latest version of the user manual provides adequate details as to how entry in the Eudravigilance related website is to be made.

■■■

Chapter 12 ...

Communication in Pharmacovigilance

Contents ...

12.1 EFFECTIVE COMMUNICATION IN PHARMACOVIGILANCE

Communication amongst various professionals is the key factor in improving reporting of adverse reactions. It is vital when safety of patients is relevant in the form of a serious reaction. There are set norms identified by regulatory authorities towards manufacturers of drugs and associated individuals. In all these communications, the doctor under whose supervision, the patient has consumed the drugs is of central importance because details of patients and associated conditions are best known to him/her. All related factors are discussed here.

Interaction and the Communications Loop:

A complete, effective communication is a message which:

- has been tailored to its audiences.

- has been sent out and received.

- has had the desired effect (change or action of some kind).

- has generated feedback of some kind about the process.

- has contributed to the refinement of future messages.

Simple transmission of a message in one direction (usually outwards from the center) is not a communication; it is essentially a random and irresponsible gesture with low probability of success. Communication is an interactive, reciprocal, continuous process.

In the cycle of effective communications, there are some of the questions which need asking and answering:

- Who exactly are my audiences and what are their needs?
- What are the best methods for reaching these audiences?
- How can I check that the message has been received?
- How can I find out what effect the message had?
- How can I establish some kind of useful interaction with my audiences?
- How can I learn to communicate more effectively next time?

Empathy:

This quality is at the heart of all good communications.

Empathy is the ability to grasp, understand and feel what it is like to be someone else:

- Their thoughts and priorities.
- Their worries and problems.
- Their view of the world.

If we have a message for anybody at all (a child, an elderly person, doctors or pharmacists,), then we must know who they are, their circumstances when they receive our message, the ways in which they are likely to perceive and react to our message. They must feel that we understand them; that our communication recognizes who they are.

Empathy is essentially an act of mature emotional and imaginative reaching out. It comes from listening and observation, and, of course, from research, but also from a disposition of humility: my urgent needs to communicate are secondary to, and must be determined by, my understanding of the nature of my audience and what they need.

Audiences:

Every audience has different characteristics and needs. Communications must be tailored, shaped, focused for a particular audience. It is obvious that a message for pediatricians is going to be very different from the message for the parents of sick children. But within the target group of parents, for example, there will also be many different groups with different needs; amongst them, parents who are:

- Blind or partially sighted
- Illiterate or semi-literate
- Foreign language speakers
- Literate and educated
- Poorly motivated or lacking trust

Obviously printed materials are not of much use for blind or partially sighted people; language which is suitable for educated people may mean nothing to those with poor literacy skills; a country's mother tongue may be useless for substantial groups of immigrants. So, one message, in one form, delivered by one method, is likely to miss very large number of other people, who have different needs than the targeted group.

You might think that an audience category like 'doctor' or 'nurse' would be simpler to deal with, but even here there will be large differences in the characteristics of individuals. Some of these include:

- Level of education and literacy
- Seniority and experience
- Specialty and interests
- Motivation and morale
- Working conditions
- Organizational commitment to (for example) patient safety

So, a highly motivated health professional, committed to advancing knowledge and career, will respond very differently from someone who is tired and demoralized and struggling against great pressure. They require different approaches, or approaches which implicitly acknowledge and respond to the differences.

Segmenting the Audience:

So, if one has a communication about new contraindications or adverse reactions relating to a medicine, one has to review his/her entire audience, segment it, and break it down, rationally and realistically:

- Who are the people we wish to reach or influence with this message?
- How many major groups are there with our audience?
- How many sub-groups exist within those larger groups?
- What are the differing needs of the groups and sub-groups we have identified?
- How many versions of the message does this analysis suggest we need?
- For such a communication, we might identify:
  o All health professionals
  o Patients who are using the medicine now or may use it in the future
  o Ministry of health
  o Manufacturers
  o Media

All five of those groups require a different formulation of the message (and different methods), but within each of the major groups are several sub-groups who also require different versions of the message.

What is the common, great failing in much official communication?

It is simply that officials tend to sit in offices and transmit messages from the center, conveying their wishes and priorities, without any serious consideration of their audiences, usually employing the 'one size fits all' approach. This is a largely futile waste of time, because the impact of communication is almost entirely random, instead of being researched, targeted and carefully calculated.

How do one find out what audiences need?

Simple in theory, but difficult to achieve is audience research. Every organization with ambitions for success may not conduct audience research, work with commercial enterprises, political parties. If they do not know their audiences intimately, they would not sell their products or get the vote. In pharmacovigilance and patient safety, we must be ambitious for success, and follow the example of those who know what they are doing.

So, what should one must do?

- Talking, asking questions, listening continuously.
- Meeting representative groups of our target audiences.
- Commissioning audience research.
- Conducting surveys.
- Assessing the impact of our communications.

This is profoundly relevant to spontaneous reporting systems, safety warnings, information about benefit and harm – in fact, everything one does. For those who say, 'We do not have the time or resources' we have to ask, if going through ineffective routines is a better use of resources than doing the job well.

This interaction with our audiences applies especially when we are planning new forms or leaflets or communications of any kind at all: test the material with people who will be receiving it (not with your colleagues or family members – they are not reliable witnesses). Discuss, listen and take the advice you hear; shape your materials in line with what your audience tells you or on which point they will pay attention to. Such consultation also applies to the planning of communication methods.

Methods:

In the twenty-first century, the printed word is not the primary medium through which the world's population gets its information or forms its opinions. Yet, in regulation and pharmacovigilance we are still highly dependent on the printed word, thus dramatically reducing the potential impact of our communications.

When we know our audiences intimately, we shall have a very clear idea of the media which will be most accessible and attractive to them. They will include:

- Mobile phone programs and apps

- Personal digital assistants (PDAs)

- Social media (Twitter, Facebook etc.)

- Internet, emails, RSS feeds

- Professional or general interest journals or publications

- TV, radio

- Printed leaflets

- Posters

- Advertising

- Peer-to-peer activities (e.g. disease-specific organizations, village meetings)

- Colloquia or training programs

- One-to-one detailing or consultation

And what is the most powerful way of communicating with anyone and influencing them? It is, of course, one-to-one contact. The closer the individual contact (even in small groups), then it is more likely that communication will be successful. Contact to remote audience can create uncertain messages.

Ask your audiences about their habits and preferences in communications. Take notice of what they say and follow their guidance.

Repetition and Variety:

In order to reach and influence even one small segment of an audience, we may need to use several channels, and repeat the message over a long period of time. *One communication is no communication.* How often, first time round, do we miss the details of something someone is telling us, or find our minds wandering when we are reading? Repetition is essential.

To reach and influence people, we must be creative and varied in the methods we use and continue communicating until we are sure that the message has been effective. Even then, we need to keep reminding people of the message, because once you stop communicating, the message fades. (This is most obvious in public health campaigns, like safe sex: while a campaign is active, behaviour changes and sexually-transmitted infections fall; once it stops, behaviour reverts and infections rise again). Repeating the same message in the same format over a long period of time results in audience weariness and inattention, of course, so the message has to be constantly refreshed and renewed. It is true in case of ADR reporting also.

Presentation and Design:

The world is full of striking, often memorable and beautiful design, being promoted through every imaginable medium. We see it in every aspect of life: advertising, furniture, clothes, magazines, logos, TV programs, electronic gadgets, cars. Everywhere, much of the enormous investment in design is calculated to attract our attention and to influence our choices in a crazily competitive and noisy environment.

How do communications in pharmacovigilance and safety compare with the competing messages in this vivid and exciting environment? There is no comparison. They are generally pathetic: dull, uncreative, bureaucratic.

We need to make our messages and materials credible and visible, effective and competitive. We do not have the resources for huge investment in design consultancy or extravagant production, but we can do far, far better with little or no extra expense. Most documents and forms coming from official sources look much the same all over the world: big slabs of text or endless boxes, usually in the default typeface, designed, structured and written badly; without pictures or graphics – without flair or originality needs improvement.

Creative energy may be found in an existing employee or may be bought modestly from a local design house. The addition of pictures and graphics costs nothing. The internet is crammed full of advice about design for every imaginable kind of document, and beautiful samples, models, pictures and images to use. Look at how commercial companies project their message and design their forms.

How our messages are presented will have a determining effect on how they are perceived and on how much impact they have. We must pay attention to how things look and make sure they are perfect for the tastes and needs of our audiences.

There are some simple principles for making text look pleasant and readable on a page:

- Leave wide margins and plenty of white (empty) space; do not cram everything together.
- Use an attractive and appropriate typeface (font).
- Use a font size which is easy to read and does not require perfect vision or a magnifying glass (nothing less than about 12 point is really attractive or easy to read for people with normal vision).
- Use a larger font size for the priority aspects of the message and, overall, for elderly or visually handicapped people.
- Give the page structure with bold headings and sub-headings.
- Use graphics, charts, illustrations or photographs wherever possible and appropriate.
- Test your ideas and materials with your specific audiences.

Structure, Content and Language:

Many official communications, no less in pharmacovigilance than in other areas, are too dense, long and complicated. The main point is often buried in the midst of details, much of which may be irrelevant to most of the audience.

There are some very simple rules for making text as effective as possible:

- State the main purpose of the document in the title and first paragraph.

- If you want recipients to do something (change their prescribing habits, for example) say so, at the beginning.

- If there are several messages (e.g. in a patient information leaflet), summarize the most important minimum briefly and clearly ('If you read nothing else, read this').

- Provide such supporting or explanatory detail as is absolutely essential.

- Demote non-essential evidence or detail or further information to the end of the document, where those who want to read it can, but those who do not, would not miss out on critical information

You need to take a very skeptical view of recipients' commitment to spending time on your communication. Assume they will give you a couple of minutes and make sure they get the essence of what you have to say in that very short period. If you manage to hook their attention in that period, they may spend more time – but if their first impression is negative, they may not give you even two minutes.

What may seem terribly important to you (not least, your wish to cover every possible angle of the topic) may be of little or no interest to your audience: you must ask yourself (in an act of empathy): How will my reader feel about this material and how I'm presenting it? What is important for them?

12.2 COMMUNICATION IN DRUG SAFETY CRISIS MANAGEMENT

Crisis in drug safety issues can occur if observed adverse drug reaction is of serious nature. Corrective action during such serious adverse reactions is vital. If the nature of such reaction and its possible cause is known, then adequate care can be taken either to prevent it, or to treat it appropriately. For this reason, communication about serious adverse reactions is so important. In 1997, Upssala monitoring centre of WHO conducted a conference about importance of communication in pharmacovigilance. The outcome of the conference has relevance to drug safety crisis management. It is published in the form of "Erice Declaration". The gist of the declaration is reproduced below.

Preamble:

Monitoring, evaluating and communicating drug safety is a public-health activity with profound implications that depend on the integrity and collective responsibility of all parties - consumers, health professionals, researchers, academia, media, pharmaceutical industry, drug regulators, governments and international organizations - working together. High scientific, ethical and professional standards and a moral code should govern this activity. The inherent uncertainty of the risks and benefits of drugs needs to be acknowledged and explained. Decisions and actions that are based on this uncertainty should be informed by scientific and clinical considerations and should take into account social realities and circumstances.

Declaration:

Flaws in drug safety communication at all levels of society can lead to mistrust, misinformation and misguided actions resulting in harm and the creation of a climate where drug safety data may be hidden, withheld, or ignored.

Fact should be distinguished from speculation and hypothesis, and actions taken should reflect the needs of those affected and the care they require. These actions call for systems and legislation, nationally and internationally, that ensure full and open exchange of information, and effective standards of evaluation. These standards will ensure that risks and benefits can be assessed, explained and acted upon openly and in a spirit that promotes general confidence and trust. The following statements set forth the basic requirements for this to happen, and were agreed upon by all participants at Erice:

1. Drug safety information must serve the health of the public. Such information should be ethically and effectively communicated in terms of both content and method. Facts, hypotheses and conclusions should be distinguished, uncertainty acknowledged, and information provided in ways that meet both general and individual needs.

2. Education in the appropriate use of drugs, including interpretation of safety information, is essential for the public at large, as well as for patients and health-care providers. Such education requires special commitment and resources. Drug information directed to the public in whatever form should be balanced with respect to risks and benefits.

3. All the evidence needed to assess and understand risks and benefits must be openly available. Constraints on communication parties, which hinder their ability to meet this goal must be recognized and overcome.

4. Every country needs a system with independent expertise to ensure that safety information on all available drugs is adequately collected, impartially evaluated, and made accessible to all. Adequate non-partisan financing must be available to support the system. Exchange of data and evaluations among countries must be encouraged and supported.

5. A strong basis for drug safety monitoring has been laid over a long period, although sometimes in response to disasters. Innovation in this field now needs to ensure that emergent problems are promptly recognized and efficiently dealt with, and that information and solutions are effectively communicated.

12.3 COMMUNICATING WITH REGULATORY AGENCIES, BUSINESS PARTNERS, HEALTHCARE FACILITIES AND MEDIA

Communication with regulatory authorities, business partners, health-care facilities and media are important in order to disseminate necessary information. Regulatory authorities have provided guidance documents about information to be supplied to them and details regarding who will submit what, how and when. All serious adverse reactions should be communicated to regulatory authorities within 2 weeks as per US FDA guidance report.

ICHE2F refers to development of safety update report. Summary of important risks like hepatotoxicity, renal toxicity and information about underlying conditions have to be given. There is also a guidance document on FDA's communication to public about safety of the drug. USFDA provided first guideline for post-marketing reporting of adverse drug experiences in 1992.

Enhanced Communications: Earlier and more useful communication about drug safety:

Since 2007, USFDA has substantially restructured its drug safety communication program to provide earlier, more consistent, and more useful information to patients and physicians about drug safety risks as they emerge. These changes reflect feedback from the public, which indicated a desire for USFDA to make information available about potential drug risks as early as possible.

As part of its re-evaluation of drug safety communications. USFDA has created a systematic approach to providing the public with information about possible new drug risks and how USFDA is addressing them.

Important Changes made by USFDA

With this goal in mind, USFDA has made several important changes:

*   USFDA's new default position is to communicate a safety issue to the public as early as possible, unless there is a strong rationale for not communicating;
*   There is now a single format for communicating drug safety issues, called a Drug Safety Communication (DSC), as opposed to the multiple formats used in the past;
*   USFDA is undertaking studies of the most effective methods of communicating drug safety issues, from understanding what platforms are most useful for different types of communications (e.g., website postings, social media, press releases) to understanding what information different audiences need and in what form;

- USFDA publishes articles in medical journals to explain the evidence and analyses used by FDA to make its benefit-risk assessments for specific drugs; and

- USFDA regularly seeks advice from its internal Drug Safety Oversight Board, comprised of representatives of the Agency's federal partners (Centers for Disease Control and Prevention, Veterans Administration, Centers for Medicare and Medicaid Services, Department of Defense, Indian Health Service, Agency for Healthcare Research and Quality, and National Institutes of Health) and its Risk Communication Advisory Committee of outside experts, created by FDAAA, on how to communicate drug risks.

- USFDA has carried through with its commitment to communicate early and often about new drug safety issues. In 2011, USFDA issued 68 DSCs, up from 39 DSCs issued in 2010. These communications reflect the Agency's ongoing commitment to communicating post market safety Issues. The DSC webpage 28 has now become one of the most visited pages on USFDA's website, receiving more than 8 million page views in 2011.

- Recently, USFDA issued an update to the draft guidance "Drug Safety Information, FDA's Communication to the Public", which provides the Agency's current thinking on how FDA develops and disseminates information to the public on important drug safety issues, including emerging drug safety information.

12.4 DEAR DOCTOR LETTERS TO HEALTHCARE PROFESSIONALS

There are situations which warrant communication between the drug-manufacturer and regulatory authorities to the health-professionals directly. The communication is termed as Dear Health Care Provider (DHCP) letters. DHCP letters are correspondence — often in the form of a mass mailing from the manufacturer or distributor of a human drug or biologic or from FDA — and are intended to alert physicians and other health care providers about important new or updated information regarding a human drug or biologic (hereafter "drug" and "product" refer to both biologic and small molecule drug products). DHCP letters may also be distributed by email and are often made available on the Internet (e.g., on company web sites or through patient advocacy groups). USFDA has provided guidance about such communications. This guidance provides recommendations on:

1. When to issue a DHCP letter,
2. The types of information to be included in a DHCP letter,
3. How to organize that information so that it is communicated effectively to health care providers, and
4. Formatting techniques to make the information more accessible.

USFDA believes that effective communication of important new information in DHCP letters can best be accomplished if USFDA and the manufacturer work together to determine:

- Whether a DHCP letter should be used to convey new information
- How to present the new information in the DHCP letter
- The target audience for the information in the DHCP letter
- The time frame for distributing the DHCP letter

Target audience needs to be identified. Certain information should reach only to the physicians. Observation of a new adverse reaction to the existing drug is an example. Some information may be relevant only to pharmacists. Change in packaging can be an example. The means by which communication is to be done should also be worked out. Mass mailing through internet can be one of the effective manners. In addition, publication of a newsletter for a professional group can be another alternative.

The planned time frame for distributing the letter to the target audience should be determined through discussion between the manufacturer and the FDA review division so that the intended audience receives the information promptly, as appropriate to the issue being communicated.

The next issue is when a DHCP letter is needed?

In general, a DHCP letter is used to notify health care providers about important new or updated information about a drug. In most cases, the information relates to an important safety concern that could affect the decision to use a drug or require some change in behaviour by health care providers, patients, or caregivers to reduce the potential for harm from a drug. Some DHCP letters are written as part of Risk Evaluation and Mitigation Strategies (REMS) communication programs to inform intended target audiences about the implementation of a new or modified REMS or to present additional required safety information about the product. In some cases, a DHCP letter provides information on how to improve the effectiveness of a drug or information about drug shortage issues. A DHCP letter also may be needed to correct misleading information in advertising or other types of prescription drug promotion.

Three types of DHCP letters are specifically described in FDA regulations (21 CFR 200.5):

1. Important Drug Warning Letters,
2. Important Prescribing Information Letters, and
3. Important Correction of Drug Information Letters.

As described earlier, DHCP letters relating to other topics (e.g., REMS, drug shortages) may use the concepts and recommendations from this guidance.

1. **Important Drug Warning Letters are recommended in one of the following situations:**
   - Previously unknown serious or life-threatening adverse reactions.
   - Clinically important new information about a known adverse reaction.
   - Identification of a subpopulation at greater risk in whom the drug should be used with added caution (e.g., patients with renal or hepatic failure, HIV+ patients).
   - Identification of a subpopulation in which the drug is contraindicated.
   - A drug interaction or medication error that may result in a serious or life-threatening adverse reaction.
   - Implementation of a new or modified REMS.

2. **Important Prescribing Information Letters are recommended in one of the following situations:**
   - Change in the INDICATIONS AND USAGE section intended to minimize risk, improve effectiveness, or convey a limitation of the indications.
   - Change of the dose or dosage regimen intended to minimize risk or improve effectiveness.
   - Change in the supply of the drug to address a drug shortage issue.

   It is to be emphasized that a DHCP letter should not be used merely to add a new indication.

   Further, if the new information results in the addition of serious risk information to the BOXED WARNINGS, CONTRAINDICATIONS, or WARNINGS AND PRECAUTIONS sections of the prescribing information, in addition to changes to the INDICATIONS AND USAGE or DOSAGE AND ADMINISTRATION sections, the letter should be elevated to an Important Drug Warning letter.

3. **Important Corrections of Drug Information Letters should be done as per actual prevailing situation:**

   Important Corrections of Drug Information letters (21 CFR 200.5(c)(3)) are intended to correct false or misleading information or other misinformation in prescription drug promotional labeling and advertising that is the subject of a Warning Letter or other Agency action.

   (Sample letters to the intended purpose are shown in the appendix 10).

   In order to maintain uniformity, the content and format of such letters is also described in the guidance document.

   European Union has also taken up the issue and provided their thinking in draft guideline.

Key principles about public communication by means of DHCP letters are mentioned as follows:

- Provision of information about the safe and effective use of medicinal products supports their appropriate use and must be considered as a public health responsibility.
- Communication of such information needs to be considered throughout the risk management process.
- It is essential that such information is communicated to Healthcare Professionals and relevant partners including Patient and Healthcare Professional Organizations, learned societies and pharmaceutical wholesalers.
- In principle, new or emerging information should be brought to the attention of Healthcare Professionals before the general public, in order to enable them to take action and respond to patients adequately and promptly. The important function of Healthcare Professionals in disseminating such information to Patients and the general public is recognized and should be supported.
- The overriding principle should be to ensure that the right message is delivered to the right persons at the right time.
- Communication on safe and effective use of medicinal products is authorized in the European Union (EU) needs.
- Co-operation of all partners.
- Co-ordination between relevant partners, within and, if possible, outside the EU; and a strategy which meets the requirements resulting from the urgency to communicate and the expected public health impact of the information.
- Usually a DHPC should not be released before the corresponding regulatory procedure has been completed, but exceptionally there might be need to disseminate a DHPC prior to completion of the procedure.
- In general, an agreement between the Marketing Authorization Holder and the national Competent Authority(ies)/the Agency (and other partners as appropriate) is needed on the format and content of the information, recipients and the timetable. The agreed timetable for release of the information should be fully respected by all partners.

Situations where a Direct Health-care Professional Communication should be considered are indicated as follows:

- Suspension, withdrawal or revocation of a marketing authorization with recall of the medicinal product from the market for safety reasons; or important changes to the Summary of Product Characteristics (SPC), for instance those introduced by means of an urgent safety restriction (e.g. introduction of new contraindications, warnings, reduction in the recommended dose, restriction in the indications, restriction in the availability of the medicinal product); or completion of a referral procedure triggered for safety concerns; or in other situations relevant to the safe and effective use of the medicinal product upon request of a Competent Authority or, in the case of centrally authorized product, upon request of the Agency or European Commission.

Other situations where the dissemination of a DHPC may be appropriate include:

- A change in the outcome of the evaluation of the risk-benefit balance;
- Data, in particular from spontaneous reporting or from studies (e.g. clinical trials or epidemiological studies), indicative of a previously unknown risk or of a change in the frequency or severity of a known risk; or
- New data on risk factors and/or on how adverse reactions may be prevented; or
- Knowledge that the efficacy of a medicinal product is not established as assumed to date; or
- Evidence that the risks of a particular product are greater than those of alternatives with similar efficacy; or
- Availability of new recommendations for treating adverse reactions; or
- ongoing assessment of a possible significant risk, but data are insufficient at this stage to take any regulatory action (in this case, the DHCP will encourage close monitoring of this safety concern in clinical practice and encourage reporting, or provide information about means to minimize the potential risk); or
- Need for communication of other important information, in particular where this has been / is expected to be covered by the media.

A DHPC should not be used to provide safety information which does not require urgent communication, such as changes to the SPC which do not impact on the conditions of appropriate use of the medicinal product.

Key Principles for the Texts of Direct Healthcare Professional Communications have also been indicated:

- The message of the DHPC should be clear and concise with regard to the safety concern. It should not exceed two pages.
- The reason for dissemination of a DHPC at this particular point in time should be explained.
- The safety concern should be placed in the context of the overall benefit of the treatment and not be presented stand-alone.
- Recommendations to Healthcare Professionals on how to minimize the risk should be provided if known.
- The Marketing Authorization Holder should ensure that pharmacovigilance information to the general public (this includes Healthcare Professionals) is presented objectively and is not misleading. For centrally authorized products, this requirement is legally binding as per Article 24(5) Regulation (EC) No. 726/2004

and for nationally authorized products, including those authorized through the mutual recognition or decentralized procedures, as per Article 104(9) of Directive 2001/83/EC.· Public communication of the safety information issued to any target population by other.

Competent Authorities and other public bodies, ideally within and outside the EU, should be taken into account.

- The DHPC should include a reminder on the need to report adverse reactions in accordance with the national spontaneous reporting system.
- The time schedule for follow-up action, if any, by the national Competent Authority(ies)/the Agency or the Marketing Authorization Holder should be provided.
- A list of contact points for further information, including website address(es), telephone numbers and a postal address to write to, should be provided at the end of the DHPC.
- A list of literature references should be annexed, when relevant.
- The DHPC may include a statement indicating that the DHPC has been agreed with the national Competent Authority/the Agency.
- In order to allow Healthcare Professionals to prepare their answers to questions from Patients, the DHPC should also include the content of the information communicated to the general public. In case of suspension, withdrawal or revocation of a marketing authorization, the DHPC should detail the type and procedure of recall of the medicinal product(s) from the market (e.g. pharmacy or patient level, date of recall).
- In general, the texts of DHPCs should be reviewed by, or if the timetable allows, tested among representatives of the targeted Healthcare Professionals in order to assess the perception of the risk and expected adherence to the recommendations provided in the DHPC. Alternatively, standard phrases may be tested and subsequently be used, as appropriate, particularly in urgent situations.

Roles and responsibilities of Marketing Authorization Holder, Competent Authority and the agency have also been narrated in the draft.

Some important issues related to DHCP letters have been identified.

1. DHCP letters appear to be more effective when they are disseminated with greater surrounding publicity––including notification on the FDA website and when followed up by direct intervention at the pharmacy level.
2. The important role of pharmacists should not be overlooked by pharmaceutical manufacturers when disseminating DHCP letters. Pharmacists can identify potentially dangerous drug combinations for patients who receive multiple-refill prescriptions without direct physician involvement or for patients who have

multiple physicians writing prescriptions for them. Despite the importance of the pharmacist, in a 2008 survey of more than 2,000 licensed pharmacists, 18% reported never having received a DHCP letter.

3. When the DHCP letter is intended to warn about drug-drug interactions, the use of specific drug names is more effective in decreasing co-administration than the use of drug class names or characterizations such as "certain drugs".

4. The content, organization and formatting of a DHCP letter can favourably affect prescriber comprehension of the message and prescriber behaviour.

5. Recommendations based on a study of DHCP letters rated by physicians include:

    (a) Place the most important information early and prominently.

    (b) Eliminate or reduce non-critical information.

    (c) Keep the letter as brief as possible without compromising clarity.

    (d) Clearly indicate what risk information and recommendations are new.

    (e) Note the consequences of non-compliance with the new warning early and prominently in the letter (e.g., provide explicit information on possible adverse effects).

    (f) Use special formatting (such as headers, bolding, etc.) to draw attention to key information.

6. Individual intervention letters from hospitals or a state-level drug utilization reviewers sent to prescribers who have been identified as prescribing inappropriately can be effective in altering practice.

■■■

Chapter 13 ...

Tools used in Pharmacovigilance

Contents ...

13.1 Introduction to Argus

13.2 Introduction to ARISg Pharmacovigilance and Safety

The work related to pharmacovigilance involves a large number of drugs, diseases and patients spread all over the world. Various pharmaceutical companies are involved in marketing the drugs. As a result of this, the quantum of information is huge. It is humanly impossible for anybody to keep a track of all information; hence different computer-based programs have been developed to compile and process the information generated from different sources. Information about such tools, used in pharmacovigilance is presented here.

Argus and Aris are two major international software resources used in different pharmaceutical companies. Information about them is presented here. In addition, information about other softwares is outlined.

13.1 INTRODUCTION TO ARGUS

Argus is developed by Oracle. It is a web-based, off-the shelf system for pharmacovigilance. It provides a comprehensive foundation for case-management and reporting. It helps the user in managing the data from multiple sources, meets strict global compliance guidelines, and accesses a flexible drug safety database. As a part of a fully integrated safety system, it offers scalability and high performance for even largest pharmaceutical companies. With Oracle Argus safety, one can improve drug safety by implementing a comprehensive software solution which enables integrated safety and risk management.

Oracle Argus Safety is such an integrated system. It provides the most comprehensive case data management and regulatory reporting in the pharmaceutical industry. Leading pharmaceutical companies use Oracle Argus Safety to provide complete global regulatory compliance, adverse events management, streamlined electronic business process workflow, and data exchange within a scalable, high-performing and cost-effective architecture.

With Oracle Argus Safety, companies realize productivity gains through streamlined business processes. For example, rapid deployment is enabled via an integrated flexible workflow engine that can be configured in the user interface. The built-in MedDRA bowser allows for full auto-encoding capability. In addition, Oracle Argus can integrate with central coding applications via an Oracle Argus API.

Oracle Argus Safety provides a rich native integrated querying environment for unified regulatory and management reporting. Global annual safety reports for clinical and post marketing surveillance are automatically generated. Case quality is managed through logical quality control checks as well as full source document integration. In addition, Oracle Drug Safety complies with all major regulatory reporting guidelines- including those from the European Medicines Agency (EMEA), the U.S. Federal Drug Administration (USFDA), and Japan's Pharmaceutical and Medical Devices Agency (PMDA). Oracle's proactive approach to monitoring global guidance ensures consistent and updated regulatory compliance.

Oracle Argus Safety is fully compliant with the International Conference on Harmonisation's guidelines for transmitting data elements in individual case safety reports (ICH:E2B), enabling the company to electronically exchange information with partners and regulators. Finally, Oracle Argus Safety enables your product to be reported as a drug in one market and as a device or a vaccine in another market—based on how a product is interpreted by local regulatory authorities.

Flexible Drug Safety Database and Drug Dictionary Access:

Oracle Argus Safety is a single global database allowing instant availability of a case, regardless of where in the world the case is originated. The steps involved in processing individual case reports can be configured to match any unique business process—whether centralized or decentralized. Oracle Argus Safety's ability to support any global workflow model makes it the comprehensive pharmacovigilance solution.

In addition, Oracle Argus Safety fully supports all standard dictionaries, including:

(i)   Medical Dictionary for Regulatory Activities (MedDRA).

(ii) Coding Symbols for a Thesaurus of Adverse Reaction Terms (CoSTART).

(iii) World Health Organization Adverse Reactions Terminology (WHO-ART).

(iv) World Health Organization Drug Dictionary (WHO-DRUG).

(v)   International Classification of Diseases, Ninth Revision, Clinical Modification (ICD-9-CM).

Scalability and High Performance:

Oracle Argus Safety is a proven fourth-generation, Web-based system used by the most-demanding and largest pharmaceutical companies. As a commercial, off-the-shelf, Web-based system, it eliminates the risk and expense associated with custom-built safety solutions and frees your IT resources to focus on more-strategic projects. This centralized and easy-to-use system delivers simplified rollout and deployment, low long-term maintenance costs, and effortless upgrades.

Fully Integrated Safety System:

Oracle Argus Safety seamlessly integrates with other products within the Oracle Argus product family, so pharmaceutical companies have the option of adding further functionality. The following products can be integrated with Oracle Argus Safety:

Oracle Argus Insight and Oracle Argus Perceptive, which deliver powerful risk management analysis tools to ensure comprehensive product stewardship. Oracle Argus Interchange, which enables electronic exchange with partners and regulators to meet demanding global safety regulations and to integrate with partners .

Oracle Argus Affiliate, which integrates affiliates and remote sites into the global workflow Oracle Argus Safety Japan, which provides a full Japanese interface to each function in Oracle Argus Safety and includes specific compliance capabilities.

Oracle Argus Dossier, which provides a collaboration platform to support the document writing process for periodic reports.

Oracle Argus Reconciliation, which enables efficient reconciliation of data between clinical data systems and Oracle Argus Safety.

It has following features and benefits.

Features:

- Electronic submission manager.
- Signal generation, crisis management, and configurable workflow.
- Intuitive graphical interface.
- Affiliate support module.
- Automated report scheduling.
- Reconciliation with clinical systems.
- Compliance and productivity dashboards.
- Auto narratives and letter generation.
- MedDRA browser with full hierarchy, compliant with current MedDRA versions.
- 21 CFR Part 11 compliance.
- ICH:E2B electronic data submission.
- ICH:E2C periodic safety update report (PSUR).
- ICH clinical trial periodic report and EUSAR.
- IND and NDA periodic report.
- CIOMS II line listing and CIOMS V.
- EMEA/CPMP reporting.
- Integrations with ds Navigator, Oracle Thesaurus Management System, and WHO drug dictionary.

Benefits:

- Collects, monitors, and analyses safety data across clinical trials, postmarket surveillance and patient care.
- Provides a complete and integrated view of reported adverse events, clinical studies and medical data.
- Identifies risks early for lower clinical development costs.
- Expedites reporting for drugs, devices and vaccines.
- Enables early detection of pre- and post-market safety issues.

Complete Argus Software is available for download for educational purpose. One can acquaint with it before purchase.

13.2 INTRODUCTION TO ARISg PHARMACOVIGILANCE AND SAFETY

ARISg is SAP-certified software with following features:

ARISg is the world's leading pharmacovigilance and clinical safety system, with more than 300 companies maintaining their critical drug safety data in ARISg worldwide. ARISg provides all the functionality required to manage adverse event reporting and adverse reaction requirements of different authorities around the world, from case entry to automatic generation of submission ready adverse event (AE) reports including CIOMS I, MedWatch 3500A and many more.

ARISg forms the core component of an integrated pharmacovigilance and risk management system, enabling companies to monitor their products and identify safety risks proactively. ARISg helps speed up management of adverse drug reactions with the use of its configurable workflow and advanced automation features. Users can set up a system that meets their business process and standard operating procedure (SOP) requirements more efficiently by automating the routing of cases as defined in their workflow rules.

As with all Aris global products, ARISg is available on premise or on demand (SaaS).

Flexible Adverse Event and Reaction Reporting Software:

ARISg offers capabilities for reporting adverse events not just for drugs but also for vaccines, biologics, devices and combination products. Flexible and fully scalable, ARISg can be used by both small companies in the early stages of clinical trials for reporting serious adverse events (SAEs) and large organizations with worldwide pharmacovigilance operations.

Other Features include:

- Single global database for supporting the drug safety requirements of multiple regions, including Europe (EMA), US (FDA CDER and CBER), Canada (Health Canada), Japan (MHLW/PMDA) and other countries following ICH standards.
- Flexible configuration that can mirror practically any business process.
- Integrated ICH E2B submission support (using agXchange ESM).
- Integrated MedDRA browser.

- User-configurable interactive views on the homepage for visibility to basic case processing metrics.
- Extensive support for binding and unbinding.
- Integrated communications module.
- Advanced query and ad hoc reporting capability.

Advanced Capabilities for Managing Adverse Event Reporting:

Used in conjunction with the other components of Aris global's Total Safety suite, ARISg provides a powerful platform for developing a comprehensive pharmacovigilance and risk management strategy.

Key Benefits that ARISg Delivers:

The following are just a few of the key benefits that ARISg delivers:

- Ensures compliance with international regulatory obligations for reporting adverse events and adverse reactions,
- Automation of case processing and report distribution with configurable workflows,
- Shortens data entry, medical review and coding processes,
- Meets a company's pharmacovigilance and clinical safety needs with a proven configurable solution.

Leading pharmaceutical companies and industry experts recognize ArisGlobal as offering the most comprehensive suite of solutions that enhance the collection, assessment and evaluation of adverse event and adverse reaction data.

ArisGlobal enables life science organizations to implement effective domestic and global pharmacovigilance, clinical safety and risk management programs. Each software solution in the Total Safety suite supports case management, report preparation, electronic submissions (using ICH E2B) as well as benefit and risk management in accordance with international guidelines set forth by ICH, FDA, EMA and other national authorities.

Each application in the Total Safety suite can be deployed independently. When deployed together, they offer a comprehensive solution for global pharmacovigilance and clinical safety that is compliant with the legal and ethical responsibilities of both sponsors and marketing authorization holders (MAHs).

Modules for the Purpose of Pharmacovigilance:

Following modules are available for the purpose of pharmacovigilance:

- ARISgagSignals
- ARISj
- agXchange ESM
- agXchange IRT
- agXchange OST
- agSignals
- agEncoder
- agHub

Uses of Modules:

The use of modules is indicated below:

Total Safety is the only software suite that covers the full spectrum of safety case processing needs. The suite is comprised of the following software:

ARISg: Drug safety solution that provides all the functionality required to meet global safety reporting obligations, from clinical trial serious adverse events (SAEs) to post marketing adverse event reporting.

ARISj: ARISj (Japanese version) provides all the functionality required to meet Japanese MHLW/PMDA regulatory obligations with respect to expedited reporting and periodic reporting.

agXchange: Modules for extended electronic exchange across company safety offices and with partners and regulators ESM – E2B Submissions Module –secure exchange of electronic drug safety data in ICH E2B format with authorities to ensure compliance and more efficient collaboration with partners.

SIR: Safety-to-Investigator Reporting – Automate and track safety alert notifications to clinical investigators and ethics committees.

IRT: Inbound Receipt and Triage – harmonize processes for safety data collection across all local and regional offices using a common platform that supports different formats and media (web form, fax, email, paper).

OST: Outbound Submissions Tacking – manage all outgoing case data reports to regulators and partners at the local level.

agSignals: System focused on user-friendly signal detection and analysis, with workflow and other tools for structured issue and signal management.

agComposer: Workflow-guided comprehensive periodic reporting system that schedules, creates and tracks a full range of submission-ready, ICH-approved periodic reports, including PSURs, Risk Management Plans (RMPs), bridging reports and other annual reports such as the ASR. The innate flexibility of agComposer allows customers to address new and emerging needs, such as the PBRER.

agEncoder: Web-based centralized coding and dictionary management system that codes verbatim terms (VTs) from different systems and maintains dictionaries (including MedDRA and WHO drug dictionary) at a central location. agEncoder also helps assess the impact and manages the process of MedDRA upgrades.

agHub: A safety data warehouse offering dimensional models for supporting efficient data analysis and metrics reporting; signaling (using agSignals); and aggregate listings (for agComposer).

Chapter 14 ...

Drug Informatics

Contents ...

Information on pharmacovigilance of drugs needs to be stored in a standardized format so that necessary content is provided to all stake-holders. USFDA has generated a guidance document in 2006 for this purpose. It is entitled as "Adverse Reactions Section on Labelling for Human Prescription Drug and Biological Products – Content and Format". European agency also has provided advice in this context. The content refers to what should be included in labelling and the brochure to be provided to all stake holders. A gist of both regulatory contents is presented below:

14.1 BASIC PRESCRIBING INFORMATION (BPI) LABELLING

USFDA guidance on labelling indicates following primary purposes:

1. Characterising adverse reactions selected for inclusion.
2. Organising and presenting the information within the section.
3. Updating adverse drug reaction information.

It is expected that USFDA reviewers and applicants should access such factors as seriousness, severity, frequency and strength of causal association in determining which adverse reactions are to be included in the section and also in characterising those reactions. In general, the adverse reaction section includes only information that would be useful to health care practitioners making treatment decisions and monitoring and advising patients. Exhaustive lists of every reported event, including those that are infrequent and minor, commonly observed in the absence of drug therapy or possibly related/not related to drug therapy should be avoided.

14.1.1 Content and Format

The adverse reaction section is required to list the adverse reactions which occur with the drug and with drugs in the same pharmacologically active and chemically related class, if applicable. Separate lists are required for adverse reactions identified from clinical trials and those identified from spontaneous reports during post marketing stage of the drug.

(A) Clinically Important Information:

Clinically important adverse reactions can have varying clinical significance ranging from serious nature to minor one. Beginning of this section should identify the most clinically significant adverse reactions and direct practitioners for getting more detailed information about these reactions, if any.

Following advice has been provided by the USFDA guidance document:

- Identify and cross-refer to all serious and otherwise important adverse reactions described in greater detail in other labelling sections, specially boxed warnings / and precautions.
- Identify the most commonly occurring adverse reactions (ADRs), which are more than 10 % or twice that of placebo group.
- Identify adverse reactions, if any, which result in a significant rate of discontinuation or other clinical interventions like dose adjustments in clinical trials.

(B) Adverse Reactions from Clinical Trials:

The adverse reactions from clinical trials should include a listing of all such reactions which occurred at or above a specified rate which is appropriate to the drug's safety data base. A separate listing of those adverse reactions which occurred below the specified rate, but for which there is some basis to believe that there is a causal relationship between the drug and the event should be made. While listing all such ADRs nature, frequency, severity, duration, dose-response, and demographic characteristics should be included.

Following organisation is suggested for the purpose:

1. Description of Data Sources.
2. Statement on the Significance of Adverse Reaction Data Obtained From Clinical Trials.
3. Presentation of Common Adverse Reactions.
4. Presentation of Less Common Adverse Reactions.
5. Commentary on Listing of Common and Less Common Adverse Reactions.

Additional information on Nature, Frequency, and Severity including details like concomitant therapy and time course of the reaction should be provided. In addition, steps which can diminish the likelihood or severity of, or prevent adverse reactions should be indicated. Changes in adverse reaction rates as a function of duration of therapy should also be detailed. Dose response relationship, information about demographic and other sub-groups if any, presence of multiple indications and use of multiple formulations should be provided.

(C) Adverse Reactions from Spontaneous Reports:

Spontaneous reports from domestic and foreign sources should be collected and listed. This listing should be separate from the listing of adverse reactions in clinical trials. To help practitioners interpret the significance of data obtained from post marketing spontaneous reports, additional statement should be preceded. "The following adverse reactions have been identified during post approval use of the drug. Because these reactions are reported voluntarily from a population of uncertain size, it is not always possible to reliably estimate their frequency or establish a causal relationship to drug exposure." Inclusion of information from spontaneous reports in the final label depends on some factors as listed below:

1. Seriousness of the event.

2. Number of reports.

3. Strength of causal relationship to the drug.

14.1.2 General Principles for Selecting and Characterising Data in Adverse Reaction Section

General principles for selecting and characterising data in the Adverse Reaction section are as follows:

(A) Selecting Adverse Events for Inclusion:

Decision about causal relationship between a drug and ADR are based on:

1. The frequency of reporting.

2. Whether the adverse event rate for the drug exceeds the placebo rate.

3. The extent of dose-response relationship.

4. The extent to which the adverse event is consistent with the pharmacology of the drug.

5. The timing of the event relative to the time of exposure.

6. Existence of challenge and dechallenge experience, and

7. Whether the adverse event is known to be caused by related drugs.

(B) Rare, Serious Reactions:

For serious and rare adverse reactions like liver failure, agranulocytosis, rhabdomyolysis, which are unusual in the absence of drug therapy, there is a basis to believe that there exists a causal relationship between the event and the drug, even if the rate of occurrence is low.

(C) Determining Adverse Reaction Rates:

The rate of ADRs is ordinarily derived from all reported adverse events of that type in the database used.

(D) Avoiding Non-specific Terms:

Non-specific terms like well-tolerated, rare, infrequent, or frequent should be avoided. Instead, specific frequency range like less than 1 in 1,000 be used.

(E) Comparative Safety Claims:

Comparative safety claims for drugs in terms of frequency, severity, or character of adverse reaction be based on data from adequate and well controlled studies. Details of studies, on which the claims of comparative safety are based, are discussed in the clinical section of the labelling.

(F) Negative findings:

A negative finding can be reported if the absence of reaction is convincingly demonstrated in a trial of adequate design and power.

14.1.3 General Principles for Presenting ADR Data

In addition, the guidance document also provides general principles for presenting ADR data in a table or a list.

(A) Pooling Data:

If there are no major study-to-study differences in study design, study population, and adverse reaction rates, an overall pooling of safety data from multiple studies may increase the precision of adverse reaction rates and provide a more clinically useful representation of a drug's adverse reaction profile.

(B) Classifying Adverse Reactions:

Adverse reactions should be classified as per convenient sub-grouping; e.g. sedation, drowsiness and somnolence can be grouped together. Similarly, allergic reactions of all types can be grouped together.

(C) Categorising Adverse Reactions:

Within a listing, adverse reactions must be categorised by body system, by severity of reaction, in order of decreasing frequency, or by a combination of these factors, as appropriate.

(D) Frequency cut-off:

The frequency cut-off for the listing of common adverse reactions identified from clinical trials must be appropriate to the safety database. Factors that could influence selection of frequency cut-off include the size of the safety database, the designs of trials in the database, and the nature of indication. The frequency cut-off should be noted as a footer or header of the table.

(E) Quantitative Data:

For quantitative data like abnormal laboratory values, vital signs, it is usually preferable to present rates of abnormal values and to specify the cut-off value for the inclusion e.g. it is preferable to report laboratory values as say "three times more than the upper limit of normal".

(F) Denominator:

The denominator N indicates total number of patients. It should be provided for each column in a table or listing, except for the listing of adverse reactions identified from post marketing spontaneous reports.

(G) Sub-group Rates:

The rates for reactions which are specific to a sub-group, e.g. gender-specific sub-group or ethnicity- sub-group, should be determined using appropriate denominator, and that denominator should be identified in a foot-note.

(H) Percentages:

Adverse reaction rates expressed in percentages should ordinarily be rounded to the nearest integer. Only in cases of serious adverse reactions like stroke, agranulocytosis, occurring at low rates in a larger study, fractions of percentage may be meaningful.

(I) Adverse Reaction Rates for Drug Less Than That for Placebo:

Adverse reactions having incidence less than that of placebo should be included only when there is some compelling factor suggestive of causal relation with the drug. In that case, the adverse reaction should be discussed in the commentary following the table.

(J) Significance Testing:

Results of significant testing should be normally omitted unless they provide useful information and are based on a specified hypothesis in an adequately designed and powered study.

14.1.4 Updating of ADRs

Adverse reactions are being continuously updated, especially during post marketing phase of the drug. While updating adverse reactions following points should be considered.

(A) Sources of Information:

Sources of information to be considered while updating adverse reactions should include controlled trials or epidemiological studies conducted after marketing approval, manufacturer's safety-related labelling supplements, and other analyses of post marketing adverse events, including single cases or case series from the literature or from spontaneous reporting.

(B) New or Outdated Information:

Animal update of adverse reactions is expected. Based on newly acquired information from controlled trials or spontaneous reports, the labelling should be updated in an consistent manner. In case the observed adverse reaction is new and inconsistent to the existing information, then outdated information can be deleted from all affected sections of labelling. Enough care should be taken that labelling is not inaccurate, false, or misleading.

14.2 EMEA LABELLING

Three points need consideration while designing the content of label. They are as follows:

1. Readability of the label and the package leaflet.
2. Label format and
3. Leaflet format.

1. **In readability of the label, following subpoints and suggested guidelines are indicated:**

   1.1 Print size and type: Labels should be printed in characters of atleast 7 points Didot (the words should be atleast 1.4 mm in height), leaving a space between lines of atleast 3 mm.

   Leaflets should be printed in characters of atleast 8 points Didots, leaving a space between lines of atleast 3 mm.

   Words in full capitals/upper case be avoided. The print should be legible.

   1.2 Print colour

   1.3 Syntax: Overlong sentences exceeding 20 words be avoided. Lines of length exceeding 70 characters are not used. A group of bullet points should be introduced. Abbreviations should be avoided.

   1.4 Braile

   1.5 Paper

2. In label format following points are suggested:

   1. Name of the medicinal product:

   1.1 INN name; common name; scientific name.

   1.2 Strength of pharmaceutical form along with trade name e.g. (Trade name) 'X' mg tablets (Generic name).

   1.3 In case of medicinal product, containing one active substance, if it is a new product, invented name be followed by common name or INN.

   2. Active substance:

   The active substance should be stated using the common name [the international nonproprietary name (INN) or the usual common name].

   3. Quantitative declaration of the active substance:

   3.1 The quantity of the active substance should be expressed in one of the following ways:

   - per dosage unit

   - per unit of volume, if appropriate for the dose form

   - per unit of weight, if appropriate for the dose form

3.2 A novel active substance present in the form of a compound or derivative (e.g. a salt or ester) should preferably be expressed in terms of the quantity of the active moiety/entity. For example, as for Fareston : *"60 mg Toremifene (as citrate)"*.

All subsequently authorised products containing this active substance should express the quantity of the active substance as the quantity of the active moiety/entity, followed by the name (the INN or the usual common name), but not the quantity, of the form in which it is present (e.g. Toremifene citrate).

An active substance which forms a salt *in situ* should be expressed in terms of the quantity of the active moiety/entity plus '*in situ formation of* ... (the salt).

3.3 Different strengths of the same product should be stated in the same way, for example tablets 250 mg, 500 mg, 750 mg (mg should be used from 1 mg to 999 mg). Micrograms should be always spelled out in full rather than abbreviated, for safety reasons. However, in certain instances where this poses a practical problem which cannot be solved by using a smaller point size (≤7 points Didot) then abbreviated forms may be used, if they are justified and there are no safety concerns. The use of decimal points should be avoided where these can be easily removed (i.e. 250 mg is acceptable whereas 0.25 g is not). For biological products I.U. should be used where relevant.

3.4 Parenterals:

For single dose parenterals the quantity of active substance(s) should be stated per ml and per total volume. For multi-dose and large volume parenterals the quantity of active substance(s) should be stated per ml, per 100 ml, per 1000 ml etc....as appropriate. For large volume parenterals containing inorganic salts, the quantity of these salts should also be indicated in millimoles.

3.4.1 Concentrates for parenteral use: When the active substance is presented in a concentrate (e.g. a concentrated solution) the label should state the total content of the active substance and the content of the active substance per ml. There should be a clear statement concerning dilution, such as: 'must be diluted before use - see leaflet'. The label should state:-

- the total content of active substance in the concentrate.
- the total content of the active substance per ml of the concentrate.
- 'provides X mg per ml of active substance when diluted as recommended, unless there are several means of diluting which result in different final concentrations.

3.4.2 Powder for reconstitution prior to parenteral administration:
When the active substance is present as a powder for reconstitution, the label should state:

- the total content of active substance in the container provides X mg per ml of active substance when 'reconstituted as recommended' unless there are several means of reconstituting which result in different final concentrations.

There should be a clear statement to consult the leaflet for information on reconstitution.

3.4.3 Diluents provided for either the reconstitution of a powder (as in 3.4.2 above) or the dilution of a concentrate (as in 3.4.1 above), should be labelled with the extractable volume.

3.5 Transdermal patches:
- the content of active substance(s) present in each patch,
- the mean dose delivered to the patient (that means the dose absorbed) per unit time (hour, day ...),
- the adherence surface.

Each of these numbers should be presented clearly and separately so that they can be distinguished from one another, otherwise they could cause confusion at dispensing level.

3.6 Multidose solid or semi-solid products in the form of powders, granules, creams and ointments. The quantity of active substance should be stated, where possible per unit dose, otherwise per gram or percentage.

3.7 Implants and intrauterine devices, (classified as medicinal products), the quantity of the active substance should be expressed in the following way:
- the content of active substance(s) present in each one,
- the mean dose delivered to the patient (that means the dose released and absorbed) per unit time (hour, day ...),
- the total duration (hours, days ...) during which this mean dose is expected to be delivered.

4. Pharmaceutical form and contents:

The European Pharmacopoeia (Ph. Eur.) List of Standard Terms should be used. The list of standard terms contains short terms for some pharmaceutical forms, but these short terms should only be used if there is insufficient space on the label to print the full standard term in 7 points Didot. e.g. on blisters and small packs. The contents should be specified by weight, volume, number of doses (number of doses of a solution, number of puffs of inhalers etc.), number of units of administration, pack size – as appropriate.

5. **Certain excipients:**

See specific guidelines on the excipients in the label and package leaflet of medicinal products for human use in the Rules governing Medicinal Products in the European Community. Guidelines for parenteral products, topical products, ophthalmic products and products used for inhalation – all of the excipients should be stated on the label.

6. **The method of administration and, if necessary, the route of administration:**

The Ph. Eur. List of Standard Terms, for the route of administration, should be used. Some information on the method of administration is particularly necessary if the product is available without a medical prescription.

7. **Keep out of the reach of children:**

A warning to keep out of the reach and sight of children should appear on the label.

8. **Special warnings (if necessary):**

Specific guidelines on the formulation of certain specific warnings for certain categories of medicinal products may be elaborated in the future.

9. **Expiry date:**

9.1 Expression of expiry date

(Article 2.1h) of Directive 92/27/EEC specifies that the format for the expression of the expiry date should be in clear terms and should include month/year. The expiry date printed on medicinal products stating month and year should be taken to mean the last day of that month. Expiry dates should be expressed with the month given as 2 digits or at least 3 characters and the year as 4 digits, as illustrated in the following examples: February-2001, Feb-2001, 02-2001.

9.2 In-use shelf life

In the case of preparations with reduced stability following dilution, reconstitution or after the container has been opened, the maximum in-use shelf life should be stated. If however the maximum in-use shelf life for the reconstituted product varies, depending on how, or with what, it is reconstituted, then there should be a statement on the label, such as: 'read the leaflet for the shelf life of the reconstituted product'.

For certain products such as radiopharmaceuticals and some vaccines it may be necessary to state the expiry date and the shelf life following dilution, reconstitution or after the container has been opened, in detail: time, day, month and year.

10. Storage precautions:

If the product is stable up to 30°C, no storage temperature is necessary. However, this does not preclude mentioning 30°C as the maximum storage temperature if a company wishes to do so. The storage precautions should be in accordance with the summary of product characteristics (SPC).

The following are the storage precautions which should be used:
- Do not store above 25°C/30°C
- Store at 2°C - 8°C (in a refrigerator)
- Store in a freezer
- Do not refrigerate/freeze
- Store in the original package
- Store in the original container
- Keep the container in the outer carton
- Keep the container tightly closed
- There are no special storage instructions

An additional short explanation of the storage statements, in consumer understandable language should be included when appropriate, e.g. 'in order to protect from light/moisture'. Where appropriate, there should be a warning about certain visible signs of deterioration.

11. Special precautions:

For the disposal of materials, if relevant.

12. Name and address of the marketing authorisation holder:

The marketing authorisation holder must be within the EU/EEA.

13. Marketing authorisation number.

14. Manufacturer's batch number:

The Commission will examine the possibility of harmonising the batch number. The holder of the authorisation, on behalf of whom the qualified person has performed the specific obligations laid down in Article 22 of that Directive; i.e. the manufacturer responsible for the release of each batch onto the EU/EEA market.

15. Instructions for use:

If necessary and particularly if the product is for self medication.

Section C - Leaflet Format

1. Content of the leaflet:

The information contained in the leaflet must be in accordance with the Summary of Product Characteristics (SPC) but the text must be phrased so that it is readily understandable for the patient. Where a scientific or specialised term is used, an explanation should be given. The European Pharmacopoeia (Ph. Eur.) List of Standard Terms should be used. In addition, it may be necessary to explain the standard terms used in consumer understandable language.

2. Headings

Headings and sub-headings should be made conspicuous; if different colours are used for the print they should be reserved for headings. Repetition of information can sometimes be avoided by cross referring to information which is under another heading. Therefore the headings should be numbered, for ease of reference. More than two levels of headings may impair readability.

3. Style

3.1 An active and direct style should be used, by placing the verb at the beginning of the sentence, for example:-

- 'take 1 tablet' instead of '1 tablet should be taken'.

- 'you should … ' is the better than 'it is recommended…'.

This principle should be adapted as;. for example, in the case of 'If … then' instructions, such as: 'If you feel ill, tell your doctor'.

This guidance on style may not be appropriate in all languages.

3.2 Where possible reasons should be given for the recommended measures.

3.3 Pictograms may be used as an additional measure if they make the message clearer to the patient but excluding any element of a promotional nature.

3.4 Reserve red colour print for very important warnings only.

3.5 Avoid indiscriminate use of capitals because they detract from the readability. However capitals may be useful for emphasis.

3.6 Where explanations are given for instructions, the instructions should come first. For example: 'take care with X if you have asthma – it may bring on an attack'.

4. Order of items

The Commission has been made aware that placing the statements for excipients, marketing authorisation holder and manufacturer towards the end of the leaflet would make the leaflet more readable. Nevertheless, this guideline cannot be in conflict with the current legislation and therefore the order of the items will not change until the legislation is amended. The commission will propose a modification of Directive 92/27/EEC to allow for this change.

5. Product ranges

There should, in principle, be a separate leaflet for each product of different quantitative strength and pharmaceutical form. In certain circumstances it may be useful to include information on the different strengths and pharmaceutical forms available; e.g. where achieving a recommended dose necessitates a combination of different strengths, or the dose varies from day to day depending on the clinical response. In such circumstances, other strengths and pharmaceutical forms with the same name can be included in the leaflet, provided that these other products have each of the following:

- the same indication(s),
- the same posology,
- the same route of administration,
- the same contraindications, precautions, warnings and side-effects.

In the case of medicinal products available without prescription, it may also be useful to refer to other pharmaceutical forms; e.g. in the leaflet of a tablet, (which is unsuitable for children) to explain that there is an oral solution for children.

6. Products not for self-administration

6.1 For a product administered in hospital additional package leaflets may also be provided separately from the product package; e.g. a pad of tear-off leaflets supplied to the hospital for distribution to patients, as required. In this case, the SPC (e.g. for the hospital staff) could be provided in the product package. When the package leaflet is provided separately, the MA holder should take appropriate measures to enable the hospital staff to provide the patient with the current version of the package leaflet.

6.2 For a product administered by a health professional, information from the SPC for the health professional (e.g. the instructions for use, inter alia) could be included at the end of the patient leaflet in a tear-off portion, to be removed prior to giving the leaflet to the patient.

7. Further information

Further information which is compatible with the SPC and useful for health education may be included, provided it is not of a promotional nature.

8. Model leaflet in the annexure

An example of a model leaflet is presented in Appendix 7, containing headings and text which should be used together with examples of text formulated in consumer understandable language. Further guidance on how to present the leaflet text in a readable way is given in Appendix 8. The model leaflet should be followed in so far as the resulting leaflet complies with Directive 92/27/EEC and upon evaluation, by applicants for a Marketing Authorization (MA), is shown to be clearly understandable to the patient/consumer. For the purpose of presenting this model leaflet, the following tools are used:

- **bold type** for the headings;
- *italics* for text which is usually relevant and is not a heading;
- 'text' with inverted commas for examples of text relevant in certain circumstances;
- normal type for the comments on the text and how it should be formulated.

All of the headings are numbered in this model however, for certain products, they may not all be relevant. In this case, the irrelevant headings should be dropped and the numbering of the remaining headings should be altered accordingly, while maintaining their sequence.

Black Inverted Triangle (▼):

In European Union, some drugs are monitored in a special manner. Such drugs have a specific manner of labelling. List of drugs which are monitored closely are provided by EU separately.

The European Union (EU) has introduced a new process to label medicines that are being monitored particularly closely by regulatory authorities. These medicines are described as being under 'additional monitoring'.

Medicines under additional monitoring have a black inverted triangle (▼) displayed in their package leaflet and in the information for healthcare professionals called the summary of product characteristics, together with a short sentence explaining what the triangle means:

This medicinal product is subject to additional monitoring.

The black triangle will be used in all EU Member States to identify medicines under additional monitoring. It has started appearing in the package leaflets of the medicines concerned from the autumn of 2013. It does not appear on the outer packaging or labelling of medicines.

Additional monitoring status is always applied to a medicine in the following cases:

- It contains a new active substance authorized in the EU after 1 January 2011;

- It is a biological medicine, such as a vaccine or a medicine derived from plasma (blood), for which there is limited post-marketing experience;

- It has been given a conditional approval (where the company that markets the medicine must provide more data about it) or approved under exceptional circumstances (where there are specific reasons why the company cannot provide a comprehensive set of data);

- The company that markets the medicine is required to carry out additional studies, for instance, to provide more data on long-term use of the medicine or on a rare side effect seen during clinical trials.

The black triangle makes it possible to quickly identify medicines that are subject to additional monitoring. Patients and healthcare professionals are strongly encouraged to report any suspected side effects with medicines displaying the black triangle, so that any new emerging information can be analyzed efficiently.

14.3 INVESTIGATOR'S BROCHURE (IB) LABELLING

Double blind studies should be labelled the same, and supplied in child-proof containers.

The 'Global' requirements for labelling of such materials are covered by the EEC directive and should include the following information:

- Contents and dosage form.
- Treatment/drug name or code.
- Other pharmacologically active ingredients.
- Strength.
- Patient number.
- Visit reference.
- Method and route of administration.
- Dosage instructions.
- Warnings.
- Storage conditions.
- If necessary, special destruction instructions.
- Batch number.
- Expiry date.
- Sponsors name and address.
- Name of investigator.

SOP for creating and maintaining 'IB' is included in the Appendix 12.

■■■

Chapter 15...

Seriousness Assessment Criteria

Contents ...

There is a need that serious adverse reactions should be assessed on priority. This is primarily to know the cause so that the reason can be corrected if possible. If the reason cannot be corrected, then precautionary measures can be taken to minimize the impact of adverse reactions. It is for this reason that, criteria for assessment of serious adverse reactions should be well defined. One of the issues is verbatim identification of the adverse reaction by the investigator. The second issue is following CTCEA guidelines. The issues are discussed below.

15.1 EVENT VERBATIM

An investigator examining a patient may report an adverse reaction as it is observed. This reporting is termed as verbatim reporting. However due to clinical interpretations, the verbatim event has to be rightly reported in the context of actual clinical situation, its relation to the drug and their medically meaningful grouping in such a way that it can be reviewed, analysed and communicated to the regulatory authorities in an effective manner. It is necessary that accurate, unbiased and consistent classification of verbatim reports be made for proper documentation of the adverse reactions. Various dictionaries are useful in this context. MedDRA is commonly used for the purpose.

Let us consider an example of the observation of headache. A verbatim report may identify it as a "Headache" or "Pressure Headache" or "Throbbing Headache". In order to report it for regulatory purpose, correct medical term as applicable to clinical situation, causal relation to the drug and the appropriate dictionary, say MedDRA, is to be identified. The name of the drug is to be mentioned as International Non-proprietary Name (INN). Right term for the adverse reaction terminology of MedDRA is to be used.

Verbatim text of the Adverse Event (AE) or Serious Adverse Reaction (SAE) is to be obtained from the Case Report Form (CRF), available either in the paper or electronic form.

A Synonym List can be used to encode the verbatim term into more efficient and consistent term. Whenever auto-coding is not possible or successful then manual coding is done by a competent person having comprehension of the clinical term. In case of any doubt, a query can be made to the principal investigator for clarification of any ambiguity. In addition, auto encoded terms are manually checked for correctness. In manual coding also, while one analyst codes, another analyst checks/ approves the coding. Further to this, clinical trial team checks all coded items in relation to verbatim reports. All these actions help in quality assurance of the process.

15.2 CTCAE GUIDELINES

A Common Terminology Criteria for Adverse Events (CTCAE) has been developed by US Department of Health and Human Services. It is being updated from time to time. Fourth version has been published in 2009. CTCAE guidelines are elaborate to define every term and give its gradation in five types.

In CTCAE, the NCI Common Terminology Criteria for Adverse Events is used. It is a descriptive terminology which can be utilised for reporting Adverse Events (AE). Each term is further graded into five grades as indicated below.

SOC: It refers to System Organ Class. It is the highest level of the MedDRA hierarchy, identified by anatomical or physiological system, ethology or purpose. CTCAE terms are grouped by MedDRA primary SOCs. Within each SOC, AEs are listed and accompanied by descriptions of severity in five grades. (See grading indicated below).

CTCAE Terms: An Adverse Event (AE) is any unfavourable and unintended sign, including an abnormal finding, symptom, or disease temporarily associated with the use of medical treatment or procedure that may or may not be considered related to the medical treatment or procedure. An AE is a term that is a unique representation of a specific event used for medical documentation and specific analysis. (Each CTCAE term v4.0 term is a MedDRA LLT term. See Section on MedDRA for details).

Definitions: A brief definition is provided to clarify the meaning of each AE term.

Grades: Each grade refers to the severity of AE. The CTCAE displays five grades as indicated below. Each grade provides unique clinical descriptions of severity for every AE.

- **Grade 1:** Mild; asymptomatic or mild symptoms; clinical or diagnostic observations only; intervention not indicated.

- **Grade 2:** Moderate; minimal, local or non-invasive intervention indicated; limiting age-appropriate instrumental ADL (Activities of Daily Living) refers to preparing meals, shopping for groceries or clothes, using the telephone, managing money, etc.).

- **Grade 3:** Severe or medically significant but not immediately life-threatening; hospitalisation or prolongation of hospitalisation indicated; disabling; limiting self-care ADL (refers to bathing, dressing and undressing, feeding self, using the toilet, taking medications, and not bedridden.)

- **Grade 4:** Life-threatening consequences; urgent intervention indicated.

- **Grade 5:** Death related to AE.

Not all grades are appropriate for all AEs. Therefore, some AEs are listed with fewer than five options for grade selection. It is to be specially noted that grade 5 is not appropriate for every AE and therefore it may not be treated as an option. A semi-colon indicates "or" within the description of the grade. A single dash (-) indicates that a grade is not available.

As an illustration, gradation of drug-induced anaemia is indicated below:

Title of AE: Anaemia.

Definition: A disorder characterised by a reduction in the amount of haemoglobin in 100 ml of blood. Signs and symptoms of anaemia may include pallor of the skin and mucus membranes, shortness of breath, palpitations of the heart, soft systolic murmurs, lethargy, and fatigability.

For anaemia, gradations are as follows:

- **Grade 1:** Haemoglobin (Hgb) < 10.0 g/dl; < 6.2 mmol/ L; < 100 g/L.

- **Grade 2:** Hgb < 10.0-8.0 g/dl; < 6.2-4.9 mmol/L; < 100-80 g/L.

- **Grade 3:** Hgb < 8.0-6.5 g/dl; < 4.9-4.0 mmol/ L; < 80-65 g/L; transfusion indicated.

- **Grade 4:** Life-threatening consequences; urgent intervention indicated.

- **Grade 5:** Death.

Anaemia is one of the adverse events under the SOC: "blood and lymphatic system disorders". In addition to anaemia other AEs under the SOC are:

1. Bone marrow hypocellular.
2. Disseminated intravascular coagulation.
3. Febrile neutropenia.
4. Haemolysis.
5. Haemolytic uremic syndrome.
6. Leucocytosis.
7. Lymph node pain.
8. Spleen disorder.
9. Thrombotic thrombocytopenic purpura.
10. Others: specify.

For every AE, explanation of five grades in the qualitative or quantitative grades is provided in CTCAC guidelines. Just like "blood and lymphatic system disorders" other SOCs are listed below:

1. Cardiac disorders.
2. Congenital, familial and genetic disorders.
3. Ear and labyrinth disorders.
4. Endocrine disorders.
5. Eye disorders.
6. Gastrointestinal disorders.
7. General disorders and administration site conditions.
8. Hepatobiliary disorders.
9. Immune system disorders.
10. Infections and infestations.
11. Injury, poisoning and procedural complications.
12. Investigations.
13. Metabolism and nutrition disorders.
14. Musculoskeletal and connective tissue disorder.
15. Neoplasms benign, malignant and unspecified (including cysts and polyps).
16. Nervous system disorders.
17. Pregnancy, puerperium and perinatal conditions.
18. Psychiatric disorders.
19. Renal and urinary disorders.
20. Reproductive systems and breast disorders.
21. Respiratory, thoracic and mediastinal disorders.
22. Skin and subcutaneous tissue disorders.
23. Social circumstances.
24. Surgical and medical procedures.
25. Vascular disorders.

■■■

Chapter 16...

Statistical Methods for Evaluating Medication Safety Data

Evaluation of safety data of a drug depends on continuous flow of information. The assessment of safety has to be done on a quantitative basis based on objective information. There are three possibilities which can be assessed in the form of outcome. First possibility is of continued safety of the drug without any inhibitions. Second possibility is of instructions related to safety which are added as the new information is collected. Third possibility is of withdrawal of the drug due to severe adverse effects. Second and third possibility involves statistical evaluation of all observations related to safety of the drug. It is in this context that the statistical methods used for evaluation of the observed safety data are to be understood.

There are two relevant terms in statistical methods for evaluation of adverse drug reactions. The terms are signal detection and data mining. The word signal recognition has origin in Electrical Engineering where a signal is accompanied by noise in the background. While signal is desirable, noise co-exists with it. It is difficult to differentiate between them. One may be recognised as other. Sometimes signal may be detected as noise, while at other times noise may be interpreted as signal. Both are false identifications. Calling noise as signal is a false positive observation, while calling signal as noise is a false negative observation. Both observations have relevance in diagnosis of a disease. The sensitivity of a diagnostic test is high when there is a low false negative rate; the specificity of a diagnostic test is high when there is a low false positive rate. In case of detecting ADRs, the word signal detection is used very often.

While reporting ADRs, there are two levels of diagnosis of causality; first, diagnosis at a single case level; second, at a public health or epidemiological level. When epidemiological perspective is considered, then statistical considerations are of great help. ADRs may initially be reported as a signal. WHO has defined a signal as "Reported information on a possible causal relationship between an adverse event and a drug, the relationship being unknown or completely documented previously". Thus, a signal is of very tentative nature in the beginning. In order to validate it, data mining is necessary. The word "mining" is defined as "A system of excavations made for the extraction of minerals". In essence, data mining should be considered as a term for the application of quantitative methods to analyse large amounts of data in a transparent and unbiased fashion, with the aim of highlighting information worth closer consideration.

In short, statistical methods are useful to identify whether a signal can be causally related to the drug when data mining is done.

Since 1960, Spontaneous Reporting Systems (SRSs) have served as the core data-collection system for post-marketing surveillance. Some of the prominent SRSs are the Adverse Event Reporting System (ARES) maintained by USFDA and the VigiBase managed by the World Health Organization (WHO). The forms which are filled up during SRSs include information on drugs suspected to cause the ADR, concomitant drugs, indications, suspected events, and limited demographic information. Many post-marketing surveillance analyses are based on these reports voluntarily submitted to the national SRSs, which include disproportionality analysis and data mining algorithms.

Disproportionality Analysis:

Disproportionality analysis (DPA) has been the driving force behind most Pharmacovigilance methods involving SRS data. DPA was first used in 1980s for pharmacovigilance. DPA involves frequency analyses of 2×2 contingency tables to quantify the degree to which a drug and ADR co-occurs "disproportionately" compared with what would be expected if there were no association (see table 16.1)

Table 16.1: Contingency table used in DPA

	ADR	No ADR	Total
Drug	a	b	n = a + b
No drug	c	d	c + d
Total	m = a + c	b + d	t = a + b + c + d

Straight forward DPA methods involve the calculation of frequentist metrics. Some of the widely applied frequentist measures (see table 16.2) include the Relative Reporting Ratio (RRR), Proportional Reporting Ratio (PRR), adopted by the Medicines and Healthcare products Regulatory Agency (MHRA) in UK and Reporting Odds Ratio (ROR) adopted by the Netherlands Pharmacovigilance Centre. Hypothesis tests of independence (Chi-square test or Fisher's exact test) are typically used along with the above association estimates as extra precautionary measures.

Table 16.2: Definitions of the frequentist measures of association

Association measures	Definition
Relative Reporting Ratio (RRR)	$\dfrac{(t \times a)}{(m \times n)}$
Proportional Reporting Ratio (PRR)	$\dfrac{[a \times (t - n)]}{(c \times n)}$
Reporting Odds Ratio (ROR)	$\dfrac{(a \times d)}{(c \times b)}$

In addition to the frequentist approaches, more complex algorithms based on Bayesian Statistics have been developed. The examples are Gamma-Poisson Shrinker (GPS), the Multi-item Gamma-Poisson Shrinker (MGPS) and Empirical Bayesian Geometrical Means (EBGMs). The GPS and MGPS methods are currently used by the FDA. In addition, Bayesian Confidence Propagation Neural Network (BCPNN) analysis was proposed based on Bayesian logic where the relation between the prior and posterior probability was expressed as the "information component (IC)". The IC given by the BCPNN is applied by the WHO Uppsala Monitoring Centre (UMC) to monitor safety signals in the SRSs.

Two other methods to analyse spontaneous adverse reactions are as follows:

1. James-Stein type shrinkage estimation strategies and
2. False Discovery Rate (FDR) estimation.

As of now, there is no consensus on which DPA method is better because there is no gold standard data set available to evaluate the performance of the methods.

Data Mining Algorithms:

The above mentioned DPA methods are effective in detecting single Drug-ADR associations, but multi-item ADR associations are also important because they could suggest possible drug-drug interactions. A typical SRS data base contains thousands of drugs and their ADRs; hence it is impractical to enumerate all combinations for statistical analysis. To address this problem, data mining algorithms have been employed.

One investigator has applied the association rule mining algorithm to identify multi-item ADRs. Using a set of 162744 reports submitted to the FDA in 2008, 1167 multi-item ADR associations have been identified. Among these associations, 67% were validated by a domain expert. Later biclustering algorithm was used to identify drug groups which share a common set of ADRs in SRS data. Further one more algorithm has been proposed to mine drug-drug interactions from the adverse event reports by analysing latent signals which indirectly provide evidence for ADRs. Based on this, it was discovered that co-administration of pravastatin and paroxetine had a synergistic effect on blood glucose. In contrast, neither drug individually was found to be associated with such change in the glucose levels.

Multiple regression has also been used in data mining. It computes the strength of a mathematical association between reports of an event and a drug after adjusting for the effects of other potential confounding factors like age group, gender, other drugs etc. These methods are computationally intensive.

There are certain advantages of using statistical algorithms. They provide a safety net for human error; since it is difficult to screen data bases using conventional methods of pharmacovigilance. The value of using these methods is highest when scores of ADRs alert the pharmacovigilance professionals about the unexpected, previously unknown and very rare adverse event.

There are several challenges while using statistical algorithms.

Some of them are as follows:

- Reports with missing information.
- Reporting biases due to unknown reporting mechanism.
- Frequent non-causal associations with indications.
- Co-morbidity.
- Drug naming: Entered drug names may have some inconsistencies in the spelling.
- Duplicate reporting: Same report may be submitted via different channels.

Solutions to these challenges should be obtained while using statistical algorithms.

A background of Bayesian Statistical Methods is presented below:

Bayesian statistics is a subset of the field of **statistics** in which the evidence about the true state of the world is expressed in terms of degrees of belief or, more specifically, **Bayesian probabilities.** Such an interpretation is only one of a number of **interpretations of probability** and there are other statistical techniques that are not based on "degrees of belief". One formulation of the "key ideas of Bayesian statistics" is "that probability is orderly opinion, and that inference from data is nothing other than the revision of such opinion in the light of relevant new information".

In this context, it is necessary to clarify that the real issue in pharmacovigilance is to establish causal relations between the drug and the adverse effect. While establishing intended correlation, many confounding factors coexist. The effects of confounding factors are to be ruled out so that unequivocal relation between the drug and the adverse event is established. Possible correlation with every confounding factor constitute Bayesian probabilities. From these probabilities causal relation is to be established.

The word signal has been defined earlier. Signals are early hints that point at the possibility of novel "unintended drug effects" they need to be causally related to the drug. Crucially signal is considered to be more than just a statistical association. Sometimes the term "Signal of Disproportionate Reporting" (SDR) is used while discussing purely statistical signals without clinical, pharmacological and/or pharmaco-epidemiological context. In reality, most SDRs which emerge from spontaneous report databases in particular represent noise because the reports are associated with treatment indications. There are many confounding factors like indications, co-prescribing patterns, co-morbid illnesses, protopathic bias, channelling bias, or other reporting artefacts. It is also possible that the reported adverse events are already levelled or are medically trivial. In this sense, SDRs generate hypothesis. Confirmation of such hypothesis goes beyond the purview of spontaneous reports and draws on the pharmacoepidemiologist's extensive strength. Longitudinal observational databases can provide a richer context in which safety of the drug can be studied. There, signals that arise from marginal drug-condition associations might reasonably be referred to as SDRs, but more elaborate approaches which adjust for potential confounders, while falling short of definitively establishing causation, could yield "signals".

■■■

Chapter 17 ...

Pharmacogenomics of Adverse Reactions

Adverse drug reactions may be personalized and are dependent on genomic content of the individual. There are two related terms:

1. Pharmacogenomics (PGx) and
2. Pharmacogenetics (PGt).

The terms are defined as follows:

1. **Pharmacogenomics (PGx)** is defined as "the study of variations of DNA and RNA characteristics as related to drug response".
2. **Pharmacogenetics (PGt)** is a subset of Pharmacogenomics (PGx) and is defined as "the study of variations in DNA sequence as related to drug response".

In the following discussion, Pharmacogenomics is of relevance. It can also be defined as "the technology that analyses how the genetic makeup of an individual affects his/her response to drugs". As the word itself indicates, it combines the knowledge of pharmacology and of genomics. It is the technology which deals with the influence of genetic variation on drug response in patients by correlating gene expression or single-nucleotide polymorphisms (SNPs) with a drug's efficacy or toxicity. By doing so, pharmacogenomics aims to develop rational means to optimise drug therapy with respect to the patient's genotype, to ensure maximum efficacy with minimal adverse effects. Such approaches are very near to "personalised medicine"; in which, drugs and drug combinations are optimised for each individual's unique genetic makeup.

Responses to drugs are dependent on genetic variants. There are two kinds of factors on which adverse reactions to a drug are dependent. The factors are intrinsic and extrinsic. Intrinsic factors are age, health and genetics; while the extrinsic factors include diet, use of concomitant drugs which can modify pharmacokinetic and/or pharmacodynamic parameters. Genetic variants which can influence drug response fall into three categories:

1. Single Nucleotide Polymorphisms (SNP): It is a DNA sequence variation occurring when a single nucleotide in the genome, or its complimentary chain, which differs between members of a biological species or paired chromosome in a human.
2. Insertions and deletions of nucleotides.
3. Copy number variations.

Pharmacological responses to drugs depend on following four factors:

1. Genes which are relevant to pharmacokinetic variations of responses to a drug. The parameters are Absorption, Distribution, Metabolism and Excretion (ADME).
2. Genes which encode targets for the drug (intended or unintended). It also includes genes which are associated with pathways in relation to pharmacodynamic responses to the drug. It is to be noted that by and large the targets are proteinous in nature.
3. Genes which influence disease susceptibility or progression.
4. Genes which influence susceptibility to adverse drug reactions.
   European Medical Agency (EMA) has published two types of guidelines:
   1. On pharmacogenomics in drug development and
   2. Pharmacogenomics in pharmacovigilance.

The second guideline is of relevance to the present discussion.

Genetic variations in patients may relate to pharmacokinetics or pharmacodynamics of drugs. As a result, there may be subset of patients with a different benefit/risk profile. Some genomic biomarkers may predict drug exposure or the risk status of a patient related to adverse drug reactions (ADRs). Genomic factors may play a role in pathogenesis of both predictable and unpredictable ADRs as well as in clinical progression of diseases.

In spite of advances in the understanding of inter-individual differences and their genetic basis, the occurrence of rare but serious ADRs or lack of efficacy / effectiveness are identified at a late stage of drug development or long after drug approval. Knowledge and awareness of the presence or absence of a genetic variant may permit estimation of the likelihood of occurrence of ADRs or of effectiveness with the use of genetic information or tests. Currently, there is limited information on utilisation of a genomic biomarker during post-marketing phase or on the effect of labelling with genomic information.

Guidelines in the Context of Pharmacogenomics Genome for the Occurrence of ADRs:

Following guidelines are given in the context of pharmacogenomics genome for the occurrence of ADRs:

1. Systematic consideration of pharmacogenomic effects and the implications of genomic biomarker use in the target population in the risk management plan (RMP) is needed for
   (a) Suspected/ identified lack of efficacy/effectiveness of a relevant medicinal product related to the use of a genomic biomarker.
   (b) Safety concerns of a relevant medicinal product related to the use of a genomic biomarker.
2. Early consideration of, when post authorisation genomic data may need to be mentioned or collected to confirm appropriate dose and co-medications, as well as to provide information or advice based on identified genomic markers.

3. Collection and storage of genomic material like DNA or other, during clinical trials and upon the occurrence of serious ADR, lack of effectiveness during post authorisation phase or unexpected worsening of the condition.

4. Methodologies for post authorisation safety studies and post authorisation efficacy/ effectiveness studies regarding pharmacogenomics and biomarker related issues (for ADRs and for lack of effectiveness) in the post marketing phase.

5. Consideration of the level and type of evidence for identification of signals, and how to report to the competent authorities. It involves documents like Risk Management Plan (RMP) updates, Periodic Safety Update Reports (PSURs), published literature etc.

6. Consideration of risk minimisation measures depending upon the importance of the possible clinical implications.

7. Following issues about labelling should be considered:

   (a) What pharmacogenomics information is to be included in the Product Information (PI) and in which sections.

   (b) Assessing the impact of information contained in PI on the use of the medicinal products.

   (c) Consideration of monitoring the effectiveness of genomic biomarker use in a clinical setting if there are requirements or recommendations in the PI on the use of genomic biomarkers.

■■■

Chapter 18 ...

Hemovigilance

Biovigilance is a comprehensive and integrated national patient safety programme to collect, analyse and report on the outcomes of collection and transfusion and/or transplantation of blood components and derivatives, tissues, organs and cellular therapies. Haemovigilance is a subset of biovigilance. Haemovigilance is defined as "a continuous process of data collection and analyses of transfusion-related adverse reactions in order to investigate their causes and outcomes, and prevent their occurrence or recurrence". It includes the identification, reporting, investigation and analyses of adverse reactions and events in recipients and blood donors as well as incidents in manufacturing processes and eventually errors and "near-misses".

Haemovigilance is of relatively recent origin. Milestones during development of haemovigilance are mentioned below.

- In 1993, French haemovigilance system was established by Transfusion Safety Act.
- In 1996, United Kingdom formally established the SHOT scheme.
- In 2002, European Haemovigilance network was established.
- In 2005, European Union's directive number 2005/61 announced formal requirement for haemovigilance schemes in member states.
- In 2008, Biovigilance Initiative was announced by USFDA.
- In 2009, International Haemovigilance Network (IHN) has been established. European Haemovigilance Network, initially founded in 2002 in France was renamed as IHN in 2009 with 28 member countries.

Objectives of IHN:

The **objectives of IHN** are as follows:

1. Exchange of valid information between members.
2. Encourage educational activities between members.
3. Undertake educational activities in relation to haemovigilance.
4. IHN provides a global forum for sharing best practices and benchmarking of haemovigilance data.

There are several reasons why haemovigilance is practiced. Some of them are discussed below:

- During treatment with blood and blood products an important issue is quality of the product. If there are any additional components, even in traces as impurities/ contaminants, they may be responsible for adverse reactions.

(18.1)

- Even with a pure product, blood transfusion is not without risk. It may imply potential dangers like immunological reactions, viral infections and transfusion-associated death.
- Reporting of adverse drug reactions with blood products is a complex issue. It depends on collaboration between blood banks, blood transfusion services, clinicians and hospitals.
- Avoidable transfusion-related adverse events continue to be a serious cause of injury and death.
- In a pharmacovigilance centre, there are special issues related to the safety of blood products.

Haemovigilance Programme in India:

Being sensitised by international developments in Europe and USA, activities were initiated in 2012 about Haemovigilance in India. First meeting of Haemovigilance advisory committee was held on 29 Nov. 2012 at National Institute of Biologicals(NIB), Noida. Subsequently, the programme was launched in Dec 2012 in collaboration with NIB. It is desired that Indian programme becomes a part of IHN.

The haemovigilance programme in India has following organogram:

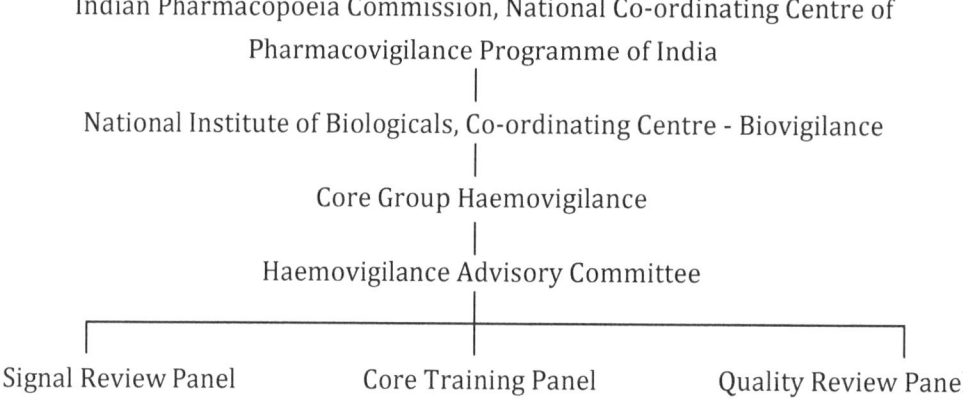

Indian Pharmacopoeia Commission, National Co-ordinating Centre of Pharmacovigilance Programme of India
|
National Institute of Biologicals, Co-ordinating Centre - Biovigilance
|
Core Group Haemovigilance
|
Haemovigilance Advisory Committee
|
Signal Review Panel   Core Training Panel   Quality Review Panel

Medical Colleges (Technical Associate):

While reporting adverse events each one is assessed for following parameters:

- Type of the event: It involves description of nature of the event.
- Severity of the event: It involves impact, if any, on the patient. If the event is serious, its description and the consequences are desirable.
- Imputability of the event: It involves how strong is the causative link between the administered blood product and the observed adverse event.

The data of all adverse events is useful to provide reliable source of information about untoward effects of transfusion to clinical community. It helps to warn hospitals and blood services about adverse events like problems with blood bags, solutions/ blood processing etc. The information is used to make required changes in the transfusion policies, improve transfusion standards and assist in the formulation of transfusion guidelines. It helps to increase the safety and quality of the entire transfusion process. Reporting of suspected adverse reactions in a timely manner facilitates effective risk management.

Following sequence of events is followed in reporting serious adverse reactions related to blood transfusion:

1. In the medical ward, adverse reactions are noted by the physician/ pharmacist/ nurse.
2. The event is documented in Form No. 1. (See Appendix 9 for format)
3. Subsequently Form No. 2 (See Appendix 9 for format) is filled up and forwarded to the department of transfusion medicine along with blood bag, transfusion set, post transfusion sample for further investigation including repeat ABO and Rh (D) grouping, repeat antibody screen and cross match, direct antiglobulin test etc.
4. Now EDTA and citrated blood sample and urine sample of the patient are sent to haematology lab for complete blood count (CBC), plasma haemoglobin, urine haemoglobin, coagulation screen.
5. The clotted blood sample is sent to biochemistry lab for renal function tests (urea, creatinine and electrolytes), liver function tests (bilirubin, ALT and AST).
6. The post transfusion blood is taken in special blood culture bottles to microbiology lab.
7. In the department of transfusion medicine, further investigation about the transfusion reaction is done as per the transfusion reaction work-up form. The findings are documented; the reports are compiled, if necessary from other departments. Finally results and inferences are reported to the respective medical ward.
8. The imputability level of the transfusion reaction is assessed in co-ordination with the attending physician of the respective medical ward.
9. The details are entered in the transfusion reaction-traceability document and intimate the technical associate of pharmacovigilance programme (PvPI).
10. The technical associate of the PvPI enters the information as per the transfusion reaction reporting form for blood and blood products and submit it to the Haemovigilance Centre, NIB.

It is to be noted that first six events are in medical ward; the next three points are in the department of transfusion medicine and the last point is in the haemovigilance centre, NIB.

Responsibilities of Haemovigilance Centre, NIB:

- Collection, collation and analysis of haemovigilance data and forwarding it to Indian Pharmacopeia Commission (IPC).
- Compilation of data and flagging major issues for delivery by Haemovigilance Advisory Committee (HAC).
- Monitor functioning of the ADR monitoring centres of pharmacovigilance programme.
- Review completeness, quality check and causality assessment.
- Preparation of SOPs, guidance documents and training manuals.
- Training and feedback to medical colleges.
- Publication of Haemovigilance news letter.
- Communicate recommendations of HAC to National Co-ordinating Centre, IPC, Ghaziabad.

The PvPi National Co-ordinating Centre, IPC is supposed to forward recommendations of HAC to the Drug Controller General of India (DCGI). Based on the recommendations of HAC, DCGI formulates safety-related regulatory decisions. All such decisions related to safety of blood and blood-products are communicated to stake-holders by Central Drug Standard Control Organization (CDSCO).

Assessment of Imputability:

The assessment of imputability of adverse reactions is made on following basis:

1. **Definite (Certain):** It refers to availability of conclusive evidence.
2. **Probable (Likely):** It refers to availability of evidence clearly in favour of attributing the adverse reaction to the transfusion.
3. **Possible:** It refers to availability of evidence which is indeterminate for attributing the adverse reaction to the transfusion or alternate cause.
4. **Unlikely (Doubtful):** It refers to availability of evidence clearly in favour of attributing the adverse reaction to causes other than the transfusion.
5. **Excluded:** It refers to conclusive evidence beyond reasonable doubt that the adverse reaction can be attributed to causes other than transfusion.

Grading of Severity: The adverse reactions related to transfusion are graded as follows:

1. **Grade 1 (Non-severe):** It involves mere symptomatic treatment through medical intervention.
2. **Grade 2 (Severe):** The event involves in-patient hospitalisation and/or persistent or significant disability or incapacity. It may require medical or surgical intervention to preclude permanent damage or impairment of a body function.

3. **Grade 3 (Life-threatening):** The recipient is required to have a major intervention in the form of use of vasopressors, intubation, transfer to intensive care etc. All these interventions are with an objective of preventing death.

4. **Grade 4 (Death):** The recipient dies as a consequence of an adverse transfusion reaction.

Application of Pharmacovigilance to Biological Products:

Similar to synthetic drugs, pharmacovigilance is also applicable to drugs of biological origin. The drugs are special in having variation in their structures. Few hundred drugs of biological origin have entered international market. Broadly they can be classified as follows:

1. Recombinant products.
2. Monoclonal antibodies.
3. Recombinant vaccines.

Many of the safety problems of these drugs are identified only during post marketing surveillance. Animal studies are not much relevant for determining adverse reactions. There is species-specific action for immunological properties in animals. A recent example is worth citing. A product TGN 1412 (CD28 agonist monoclonal antibody) exhibited serious adverse events in healthy human volunteers. These adverse reactions have never been observed during pre-clinical studies of TGN 1412.

The production and purification process of drugs of biological origin are more complex involving many steps. As a result, characteristics of end products may vary because of experimental variations at any single step in the production cascade. Such variations can be responsible in adverse reactions to few individuals. The incidence of pure red cell aplasia with recombinant human epoetin, was elevated in patients taking one particular formation of recombinant human epoetin in which human serum albumin was replaced with polysorbit 80 and glycine.

In some cases structural variations can lead to immunogenicity or loss of efficacy or even auto immunity.

Pharmacovigilance of immunosuppressants or immunomodulators is of special importance. Mechanism of immunosuppression/ immunomodulation may vary from one agent to another. There is a possibility of opportunistic information for malignancy which may raise challenges for pharmacovigilance systems. Thus, when clinicians and pharmacovigilance experts review serious adverse events in patients receiving biological products, they must consider immunogenicity and immune-mediated reactions as causes of the adverse events.

IPC with NIB has launched a Biovigilance program (BvPi) including Haemovigilance across the country under its Pharmacovigilance Program of India (PvPI) with following terms of reference;

1. To track adverse reactions/events and incidences associated with biologicals, blood transfusion and blood product administration (Haemovigilance) as well as tissue, organ and cell therapy transplantation.

2. To help identify trends, recommended best practices and interventions required to improve patient care and safety while reducing overall cost of the healthcare systems.

Hence Pharmacovigilance centres would have to consider special issues related to safety of these products. Efficient regulations of these products are crucial in order to avoid potential harm due to sub standard manufacture, improper transportation and storage of imported vaccines and biologicals. It is also necessary that careful post-approval safety monitoring with special attention to immune mediated adverse events, infusion reactions etc. should be carefully noted.

■■■

Chapter 19...

Pharmacovigilance of Herbal Drugs

It is widely believed that, since herbal drugs are of natural origin, they do not cause any harm to human body. This is far away from truth. Many plants are known to be poisonous. In fact, it is argued that it is the dose which decides whether a substance can act as a poison, drug or food. Poison is dangerous even in small quantity; while food can be taken in large quantity. Drugs are intermediate. The statement is true both for synthetic as well as herbal drugs. Irrespective of origin, any substance, including drugs, when not used in appropriate quantity or route of administration can cause harm to human body. Therefore pharmacovigilance is an equally important issue even for herbal drugs.

There is one common issue with most of the herbal drugs which makes pharmacovigilance difficult with them. The issue is of polypharmacy, indicating the fact that many of them are given as combination drugs. Thus, whenever an adverse reaction is observed with a combination of drugs, it is difficult to identify which of the component or a combination of products is responsible for the observed adverse effect. Hence, establishing a causal relation between an adverse reaction and a herbal ingredient is difficult. In addition, every plant itself is a combination of several components with variation in seasonal and geographic origin. Still there are several publications and books on the subject. The clue lies in clinical observations of careful clinical practitioners followed by appropriate documentation. It may also be accompanied by knowledge of association between several phytoconstituents and their interrelation with toxicity in experimental animals.

In spite of these uncertainties, credible efforts have been made by few agencies to record and classify adverse reactions with herbal drugs. Efforts made by Uppsala monitoring center are noteworthy. One of the important issue is identification of the plant, its correct botanical name, name of the part used and the name of the manufacturer.

Uppsala Monitoring Centre (UMC) has undertaken a project with the aim of attaining global standardization of herbal medicines. The scope was to standardize information about herbal medicines, including their scientific names and therapeutic implications, which can vary widely between countries. The structure of the ATC-system, developed for classification of orthodox medicines, was used as a basis for the Herbal ATC structure. UMC has published a system with the title, Herbal ATC Classification. The UMC collaborates with the Department of Botany, Uppsala University and the Royal Botanical Gardens at Kew in the UK, and with other international experts.

The UMC is carrying out research on Traditional Chinese Medicine to identify acceptable scientific names. An example of a multi-ingredient herbal preparation is Yi Xian Wan which shows herbal ingredients, elements of animal origin and minerals, all of which require accurate identification.

In the WHO database, as of December 2010, there were 12,679 suspected/interacting case reports where only herbal substances were involved and 21,951 reports which included both herbal and non-herbal substances.

Table 19.1: The most commonly reported critical terms for adverse drug reactions on herbal drugs

Drug abuse	630
Drug dependence	274
Hepatitis	263
Death	176
Angioedema	169
Coma	162
Face edema	160
Anaphylactic shock	151
Cardiac arrest	150
Thrombocytopenia	118
Anaphylactoid reaction	116
Hallucination	115
Asthma	111
Respiratory depression	105
Purpura	103
Prothrombin decreased	92
Aggressive reaction	89
Epistaxis	89
Hepatitis cholestatic	83
Bronchospasm	79
Circulatory failure	77
Edema mouth	77

Table 19.2: The most commonly reported herbals

Cannabis sativa L.	1057
Ginkgo biloba L.	960
Hypericumper foratum L.	713
Herbal pollen extract	690
Senna alexandrina mill	435
Herbal extract	331
Cimicifugaracemosa (L.) Nutt.	312
Echinacea purpurea (L.) Moench	302
Plantagoovata Forssk	287
Serenoarepens (Bartram) Small	284
Glycine max (L.) Merr.	276
Oenotherabiennis L.	274
Vitis vinifera L.	206
Mentha piperita L.	205
Citrus paradisi Macfad	195
Valeriana officinalis L.	192
Silybummarianum (L.) Gaertn	174
Viscum album L.	172
Allium sativum L.	162
Vitexagnus-castus L.	142
Pelargonium reniforme, Curtis	130
Digitalis purpurea L.	129
Ginseng	125

In 1998, De Smet proposed a system for ATC classification of herbal remedies which is fully Compatible with the regular system. With a few modifications this system has now been adopted and is given in the guidelines.

The Herbal ATC Index lists Herbal ATC (HATC) codes per substance, while the Guidelines for Herbal ATC Classification help to assign HATC codes to herbal remedies. In both the ATC and Herbal ATC systems remedies are divided into groups according to their therapeutic use. Whenever possible, the level 1-4 codes in the herbal system are equal to the levels in the regular ATC system.

Two publications of UMC, Herbal ATC index and Guidelines for herbal ATC classification provide adequate information about the entire system.

Issues related to Pharmacovigilance of Herbal Drugs:

There are several issues related to Pharmacovigilance of herbal drugs. Prominent issues are raised here.

- The issue whether herbal combinations are to be treated as drugs needs debate. Different regulatory agencies can have differing opinion about the nomenclature; However whenever any entity is claimed as a drug then, on one hand composition needs to be standardized and on the other hand therapeutic claims have to be justified. On both fronts enough justifications have to be provided in order to validate the claims.

- Standardization of herbal components involves two important points. Physicochemical and Biological issues need to be considered thoroughly. Since plants originate from biological resources, there are possible variations in geographical sources, climatic conditions, chemistry of soils, temperature, humidity, light. All such variables can influence chemical composition of the plant material. In turn, there can be wide variation in biological properties depending on chemical constituents. The problem is more severe when more than one plant is combined. As many as ten or more herbs may be present in one formulation. Presence of every herbal component adds to the issue of physicochemical and biological standardization.

- Safety of herbal components is the most important point for Pharmacovigilance. Herbal components can either be from wild origin or they may be cultivated. During cultivation, pesticides may be added. Presence of pesticidal residues in cultivated herbs and their concentration is an issue of concern. Higher amounts of pesticides above permissible limits have been reported even in bottled water; hence there has to be a mechanism of estimating pesticidal residues whenever herbal components are used. The issue may be of importance even if a wild variety of herb is used because of accidental contamination.

- Presence of metal components depending on soil chemistry is another issue of concern. This is true of either wild or cultivated variety of the herb. Few metallic components like Lead, Mercury, Arsenic, Tin above permissible limits have been detected even in vegetables. Ensuring that herbal components contain metallic contamination below permissible limits is an issue related to safety of herbals.

- There is a possibility of herbal component(s) influencing effect of synthetic drug(s). Literature reports justify the observation. An epileptic patient stabilized on Phenytoin has been shown to get destabilized after consumption of an herbal drug. It is further reported that the patient was stabilized after discontinuation of the herbal drug. Consumption of Grape-fruit juice destabilizing concentration of Calcium-channel-blocker like Verapamil is another example which indicates herbal components can influence therapeutic concentration of a synthetic drug. The issues are of concern for pharmacovigilance.

- There is a need that, all herbal drugs in Indian market should be scrutinized for observation of safety in parameters related to hepatic and renal functioning. Objective parameters like effect on cytochrome enzymes, creatinine clearance rates should be worked out experimentally. Safety towards mutagenicity, carcinogenicity and teratogenicity need to be established. Safety for pediatric and geriatric consumption needs to be established. Safety during special physiological situations like Pregnancy and Lactation also should be worked out. Appropriate protocols for establishing safety in these parameters should be worked out. Information about case studies in human beings needs to be compiled in a sustained manner. Manufacturers of Herbal products in India should be involved as stakeholders in this matter. Whenever scientific information of herbal products in this matter is compiled, it will not only be a progressive step in Pharmacovigilance of herbal products, but can boost confidence of international community and can help in promoting export of Herbal products in a big way. The activity can be linked to Good Agricultural Practices (GAP). This action can favour fortune of farmers in an effective manner. It is to be emphasized that absence of documentation about an old product regarding adverse reaction is not a guarantee for its safety. Safety of herbal products is a pro-active issue which needs to be established by the manufacturers.

- It is in the interest of manufacturers of herbal products that issues related to standardization of extracts, stability and shelf life of therapeutically active ingredients, fingerprinting of active ingredients, following Good Manufacturing Process (GMP) in large scale production along with information about safety of products will go a long way in promoting fortune of herbal products in International Market in an effective manner.

- There is no harm if herbal products are developed as Nutraceuticals. Nomenclature is of less importance. What matters for a consumer is safety of the product. Once the safety of product is established, then international marketing of the products cannot be a problem.

■■■

Chapter 20...

Job Opportunities and Responsibilities in Pharmacovigilance

The companies offering job opportunities for Pharmacovigilance in India are as follows:

- Cognizant Technology Solutions.
- Tata Consultancy Services.
- Sciformix.
- BMS.
- Pfizer.
- Accenture.
- Novatis.
- Quintiles.
- Lupin.
- Clintec International.
- IGATE Clinical Research.
- Siro Pharma.
- Roche India.
- Reliance Life Sciences.
- Alembic.
- Parexel.
- Neeman Medical.

The titles/positions available may be any one of the following:

- Drug Safety Associate.
- Drug Safety Scientist.
- Drug Safety Physician.
- Aggregate Report Scientist.
- Safety Processing Expert.
- Data Management.
- Business Processing.

The job responsibilities are related to the titles with possible variations as per actual need of the company.

■■■

- **Absolute Risk:** It is defined as 'the number of people in a group who experience an adverse effect divided by the number in that group who could not experience that adverse effect'.

- **Abuse of a Medicinal Product:** Persistent or sporadic, intentional excessive use of medicinal products which is accompanied by harmful physical or psychological effects.

- **Advanced Therapy Medicinal Product (ATMP):** A medicinal product for human use that is either a gene therapy medicinal product, a somatic cell therapy product or a tissue engineered products as defined in Regulation.

- **Adverse Event/Adverse Experience (AE):** Any untoward medical occurrence in a patient or clinical trial subject administered to a medicinal product and which does not necessarily have a causal relationship with this treatment.

- **Adverse Reaction/Adverse Drug Reaction (ADR), Suspected Adverse (drug) Reaction, Adverse Effect, Undesirable Effect:** A response to a medicinal product which is noxious and unintended. Response in this context means that a causal relationship between a medicinal product and an adverse event is at least a reasonable possibility.

- **Audit:** A systematic, disciplined, independent and documented process for obtaining audit evidence and evaluating it objectively to determine the extent to which the audit criteria are fulfilled .

- **Audit Finding(s):** Results of the evaluation of the collected audit evidence against audit criteria. Audit evidence is necessary to support the auditor's results of the evaluation, i.e. the auditor's opinion and report. It is cumulative in nature and is primarily obtained from audit procedures performed during the course of the audit.

- **Audit Plan:** Description of activities and arrangement for an individual audit.

- **Audit Programme:** Set of one or more audits planned for a specific timeframe and directed towards a specific purpose.

- **Audit Recommendation:** Audit Recommendation describes the course of action management might considered to rectify conditions that have gone awry, and to mitigate weaknesses in systems of management control.

- **Benefit:** It refers to a gain (+ result) for an individual or a population "expected" or The improvement attributable to the drug, in terms of human heath, health related quality of life, and/ or economic benefit to the individual or group.

- **Case Report Form (CRF):** It is a printed, optical, or electronic document designed to record all of the protocol-required information to be reported to the sponsor on each trial subject.

- **Clinical Trial:** Any investigation in human subjects intended to discover or verify the clinical, pharmacological and/or other pharmacodynamic effects of one or more investigational medicinal product(s), and/or to identify any adverse reactions to one or more investigational medicinal product(s) and/or to study absorption, distribution, metabolism and excretion of one or more investigational medicinal product(s) with the objective of ascertaining its (their) safety and/or efficacy.

- **Closed Signal:** In periodic benefit-risk evaluation reports, a signal for which an evaluation was completed during the reporting interval. This definition is also applicable to periodic safety update reports.

- **Company Core Data Sheet (CCDS):** For medicinal products, a document prepared by the marketing authorisation holder containing, in addition to safety information, material related to indications, dosing, pharmacology and other information concerning the product.

- **Company Core Safety Information (CCSI):** It refers to all relevant safety information contained in the company core data sheet prepared by the MAH and that the MAH requires to be listed in all countries where the company markets the drug, except when the local regulatory authority specifically requires a modification.

- **Compassionate Use of a Medicinal Product:** Making a medicinal product available for compassionate reasons to a group of patients with a chronically or seriously debilitating disease or whose disease is considered to be life-threatening, and who cannot be treated satisfactorily by an authorised medicinal product.

- **Completed Clinical Trial:** Study for which a final clinical study report is available.

- **Consumer:** For the purpose of reporting cases of suspected adverse reactions, a person who is not a healthcare professional such as a patient, lawyer, friend or relative/parent/child of a patient.

- **Contract Research Organization (CRO):** It is a scientific organization (commercial, academic or other) to which a sponsor may transfer some of its tasks and obligations, defined in writing.

- **Crisis:** A crisis is defined as, "a situation where, after assessment of the associated risks, urgent and co-ordinated action is required to manage and control the situation".

- **Data Lock Point:** "The date upto which information about safety of a drug is to be included" is called data lock point.

- **Development Core Safety Information (DCSI):** It is an independent section of an Investigator's Brochure (IB) identical in structure to the CCSI, that contains a summary of all relevant safety information that is described in more detail within the main body of the IB.

- **Development International Birth Date (DIBD):** Date of first approval (or authorisation) for conducting an interventional clinical trial in any country.

- **Development Pharmacovigilance and Risk Management Plan**: It is a plan to conduct activities relating to the detection, assessment, understanding, reporting and prevention of adverse effects of medicines during clinical trials. This plan should be initiated early and modified as necessary throughout the development process for a new drug or drug-use.

- **Development Safety Update Report (DSUR):** It is a periodic summary of safety information for regulators, including any changes in the benefit-risk relationship, for a drug, biologic or vaccine under development, prepared by the sponsor of all clinical trials.

- **Direct Healthcare Professional Communication (DHPC):** A communication intervention by which important information is delivered directly to individual healthcare professionals by a marketing authorisation holder or by a competent authority, to inform them of the need to take certain actions or adapt their practices in relation to a medicinal product.

- **Dominant Risk**: It is defined as 'the risk that is considered to be major contributor to the overall risk profile'.

- **Effectiveness:** It is a major of the effect of a medicine (or medical technology) purported, or represented, to have under conditions for the use prescribed, recommended or labelled.

- **Efficacy:** It is the ability of a medicine or medical technology to bring about the intended beneficial effect on individuals in a defined population with a given medical problem, under the ideal conditions of use.

- **EU Reference Date/Union Reference Date:** For medicinal products containing the same active substance or the same combination of active substances, the date of the first marketing authorisation in the EU of a medicinal product containing that active substance or that combination of active substances.

- **Expected and Unexpected Adverse Drug Reaction**: An unexpected ADR is defined as "an adverse reaction, the nature of severity of which is not consistent with the applicable product information".

- **Failure to Vaccinate:** An indicated vaccine was not administered appropriately for any reason. For interpreting what is appropriate, consider the explanatory note for Immunisation error-related reaction.

- **False Negative:** When a test result is negative in someone who actually does have the disease, it is called as false negative. It is also applied to statistical test results where a non-significant test result is found, whereas the null hypothesis (that there is no difference) is in fact false.

- **False Positive:** When a test result is positive in someone who does not have the disease, it is called as false positive. It is also applied to statistical test results where a significant test result occurs but the null hypothesis (no real difference) is in fact true.

- **Generic Medicinal Product:** A medicinal product which has the same qualitative and quantitative composition in active substances and the same pharmaceutical form as the reference medicinal product, and whose bioequivalence with the reference medicinal product has been demonstrated by appropriate bioavailability studies.

- **Good Pharmacovigilance Practices (GVP) for the European Union:** A set of guidelines for the conduct of pharmacovigilance in the EU, drawn up based on Article 108a of Directive 2001/83/EC, by the European Medicines Agency in co-operation with competent authorities in Member States and interested parties, and applying to marketing authorisation holders in the EU, the Agency and competent authorities in Member States.

- **Hazard:** It is a situation that under particular circumstances leads to harm. It is a source of danger.

- **Healthcare Professional:** For the purposes of reporting suspected adverse reactions, healthcare professionals are defined as, "medically qualified persons, such as physicians, dentists, pharmacists, nurses and coroners".

- **Herbal Medicinal Product:** Any medicinal product, exclusively containing as active ingredients one or more herbal substances or one or more herbal preparations, or one or more such herbal substances in combination with one or more such herbal preparations.

  Herbal preparations are preparations obtained by subjecting herbal substances to treatments such as extraction, distillation, expression, fractionation, purification, concentration or fermentation. These include comminuted or powered herbal substances, tinctures, extracts, essential oils, expressed juices and processed exudates.

- **Homeopathic Medicinal Product:** Any medicinal product prepared from substances called homeopathic stocks in accordance with a homeopathic manufacturing procedure described by the European Pharmacopoeia or, in the absence thereof, by the pharmacopoeias currently used officially in the Member States.

- **Identified Risk:** An untoward occurrence for which there is adequate evidence of an association with the medicinal product of interest.

  In a clinical trial, the comparator may be placebo, an active substance or non-exposure.

- **Immunisation:** The process of making a person immune. For the context of considerations P.I, immunisation refers to the process of making a person immune to an infection.

- **Immunisation Anxiety-related Reaction:** An adverse event following immunisation arising from anxiety about the immunization. In this definition, immunisation means, "the usage (handling, prescribing and administration) of a vaccine for the purpose of immunising individuals", which in the EU is preferably referred to as vaccination.

- **Immunisation Error-related Reaction:** An adverse event following immunisation that is caused by inappropriate vaccine handling, prescribing or administration and thus by its nature is preventable. In this definition, immunisation means "the usage (handling, prescribing and administration) of a vaccine for the purpose of immunising individuals, which in the EU is preferably referred to as vaccination".

- **Immunological Medicinal Product:** Any medicinal product consisting of vaccines, toxins, serums or allergen products.

- **Important Identified Risk and Important Potential Risk:** Any risk that is likely to be included in the contraindications or warnings and precautions section of the product information should be considered important.

- **Incident:** A situation where an event occurs or new information arises, irrespective of whether this is in the public domain or not, in relation to (an) authorised medicinal product(s) which could have a serious impact on public health.

- **Independent Data-Monitoring Committee (IDMC), Data and Safety Monitoring Board (DSMB), Monitoring Committee, Data Monitoring Committee:** It is an independent data-monitoring committee that may be established by the sponsor to assess at intervals the progress of a clinical trial, the safety data, and the critical efficacy end points, and to recommend to the sponsor whether to continue, modify, or stop a trial.

- **Independent Ethics Committee (IEC):** It is an independent body (a review board or a committee, institutional, regional, national, or supra national), constituted of medical/scientific professionals and non-medical/non-scientific members, whose responsibility is to ensure the protection of the rights, safety and well-being of human subjects involved in a trial and to provide public assurance of that protection, by among other things, reviewing and approving/providing favourable opinion on the trial protocol, the suitability of the investigator(s), facilities and the methods and material to be used in obtaining and investigator's documenting informed consent of the trial subject.

- **Individual Case Safety Report (ICSR)/Adverse (Drug) Reaction Report:** Format and content for the reporting of one or several suspected adverse reactions to a medicinal product that occur in a single patient at a specific point of time.

- **Institutional Review Board (IRB):** It is an independent body constituted of medical, scientific and non-scientific members, whose responsibility is to ensure the protection of the rights, safety and well-being of human subjects involved in a trial by, among other things, reviewing, approving and providing continuing review of trial protocol and amendments and of the methods and materials to be used in obtaining and documenting informed consent of the trial subjects.

- **International Birth Date (IBD):** The date of the first marketing authorisation for any product containing the active substance granted to any company in any country in the world.

- **Investigational drug:** Experimental product under study or development. This term is more Specific than investigational medicinal product, which includes comparators and placebos.

- **Investigational Medicinal Product:** An investigational medicinal product is a pharmaceutical form of an active substance or placebo being tested or used as a reference in a clinical trial, including products already with a marketing authorisation but used or assembled (formulated or packaged) in a way different from the authorised form, or when used for an unauthorised indication, or when used to gain further information about the authorised form.

- **Labelling:** Information on the immediate or outer packaging.

- **Marketing Authorization Holder (MAH):** Marketing authorization holder is a legal entity, identified after finalizing a document called Marketing authorization by competent authority of the nation. Marketing authorization involves licencing, registration, approval of the product.

- **Medicinal Product Derived from Human Blood or Human Plasma:** Any medicinal product based on blood constituents which is prepared industrially by a public or private establishment, such as a medicinal product including, in particular, albumin, coagulating factor(s) and immunoglobulin(s) of human origin.

- **Medicinal Product:** Any substance or combination of substances,
  - presented as having properties for treating or preventing disease in human beings; or
  - which may be used in or administered to human beings either with a view to restoring, correcting or modifying physiological functions by exerting a pharmacological, immunological or metabolic action, or for making a medical diagnosis.

- **Minimum Criteria for Reporting:** For the purpose of reporting cases of suspected adverse reactions, the minimum data elements for a case are: an identifiable reporter, an identifiable patient, an adverse reaction and a suspect medicinal product.

- **Missing Information:** Gaps in knowledge about a medicinal product, related to safety or use in particular patient populations, which could be clinically significant. It is noted that there is an ICH definition for important missing information, which is: critical gaps in knowledge for specific safety issues or populations that use the marketed product.

- **Misuse of a Medicinal Product for Illegal Purposes:** Misuse for illegal purposes is misuse with the additional connotation of an intention of misusing the medicinal product to cause an effect in another person. This includes, amongst others: the sale, to other people, of medicines for recreational purposes and use of a medicinal product to facilitate assault.

- **Misuse of a Medicinal Product:** Situations where the medicinal product is intentionally and inappropriately used not in accordance with the authorised product information.

- **Name of the Medicinal Product:** The name which may be either an invented name not liable to confusion with the common name, or a common or scientific name accompanied by a trade mark or the name of the marketing authorisation holder. The common name is the international non-proprietary name (INN).

- **Newly Identified Signal:** In periodic benefit-risk evaluation reports, a signal first identified during the reporting interval, prompting further actions or evaluation.

- **Non-Interventional Trial/Non-interventional Study:** A study where the medicinal product(s) is (are) prescribed in the usual manner in accordance with the terms of the marketing authorisation.

  Thus, a trial is non-interventional if the following requirements are cumulatively fulfilled:

  o the medicinal product is prescribed in the usual manner in accordance with the terms of the marketing authorisation;

  o the assignment of the patient to a particular therapeutic strategy is not decided in advance by a trial protocol but falls within current practice and the prescription of the medicine is clearly separated from the decision to include the patient in the study; and

  o no additional diagnostic or monitoring procedures are applied to the patients and epidemiological methods are used for the analysis of collected data.

- **Occupational Exposure to a Medicinal Product:** For the purpose of reporting cases of suspected adverse reactions, an exposure to a medicinal product as a result of one's professional or non-professional occupation.

- **Off-label Use:** Situations where a medicinal product is intentionally used for a medical purpose not in accordance with the authorised product information. Off-label use includes use in non-authorised paediatric age categories.

- **Ongoing Clinical Trial:** Trial where enrolment has begun, whether a hold is in place or analysis is complete, but for which a final clinical study report is not available.

- **Ongoing Signal:** In periodic benefit-risk evaluation reports, a signal that remains under evaluation at the data lock point. This definition is also applicable to periodic safety update reports.

- **Overdose:** Administration of a quantity of a medicinal product given per administration or cumulatively which is above the maximum recommended dose according to the authorised product information. Clinical judgement should always be applied.

- **Package Leaflet:** A leaflet containing information for the user which accompanies the medicinal product.

- **Periodic Safety Update Report (PSUR):** Format and content for providing an evaluation of the risk-benefit balance of a medicinal product for submission by the marketing authorisation holder at defined time points during the post-authorisation phase.

- **Pharmacovigilance System Master File (PSMF):** A detailed description of the pharmacovigilance system used by the marketing authorisation holder with respect to one or more authorised medicinal products.

- **Pharmacovigilance:** Science and activities relating to the detection, assessment, understanding and prevention of adverse effects or any other medicine-related problem. In line with this general definition, underlying objectives of pharmacovigilance in accordance with the applicable EU legislation are:

  o preventing harm from adverse reactions in humans arising from the use of authorised medicinal products within or outside the terms of marketing authorisation or from occupational exposure; and

  o promoting the safe and effective use of medicinal products, in particular through providing timely information about the safety of medicinal products to patients, healthcare professionals and the public.

- **Pharmacovigilance System:** A system used by the marketing authorisation holder and by Member States to fulfil the tasks and responsibilities listed in Title IX of Directive 2001/83/EC and designed to monitor the safety of authorised medicinal products and detect any change to their risk-benefit balance.

- **Post-Authorisation Safety Study (PASS):** Any study relating to an authorised medicinal product conducted with the aim of identifying, characterising or quantifying a safety hazard, confirming the safety profile of the medicinal product, or of measuring the effectiveness of risk management measures. A post-authorisation safety study may be an interventional clinical trial or may follow an observational, non-interventional study design.

- **Potential Risk:** An untoward occurrence for which there is some basis for suspicion of an association with the medicinal product of interest but where this association has not been confirmed.

- **Quality Adherence:** Carrying out tasks and responsibilities in accordance with quality requirements.

- **Quality Control and Assurance:** Monitoring and evaluating how effectively the structures and processes have been established and how effectively the processes are being carried out. This applies for the purpose of fulfilling quality requirements.

- **Quality Improvements:** Correcting and improving the structures and processes where necessary. This applies for the purpose of fulfilling quality requirements.

- **Quality of a Pharmacovigilance System:** All characteristics of the pharmacovigilance system which are considered to produce, according to estimated likelihoods, outcomes relevant to the objectives of pharmacovigilance.

- **Quality Planning:** Establishing structures and planning integrated and consistent processes. This applies for the purpose of fulfilling quality requirements.

- **Quality Requirements:** Those characteristics of a system that are likely to produce the desired outcome, or quality objectives.

- **Quality System of a Pharmacovigilance System:** The organisational structure, responsibilities, procedures, processes and resources of the pharmacovigilance system as well as appropriate resource management, compliance management and record management. The quality system is part of the pharmacovigilance system.

- **Reference Safety Information:** In periodic benefit-risk evaluation reports for medicinal products, all relevant safety information contained in the reference product information (e.g. the company core data sheet) prepared by the marketing authorisation holder and which the marketing authorisation holder requires to be listed in all countries where it markets the product, except when the local regulatory authority specifically requires a modification.

- **Registry:** An organised system that uses observational methods to collect uniform data on specified outcomes in a population defined by a particular disease, condition or exposure.

- **Relative Risk:** It is 'the ratio of the incidence rate of an outcome (event), in an exposed group to the incidence rate of the outcome (event) in an unexposed group'.

- **Risk Assessment:** It is defined as 'the integrated analysis of the risks inherent in a product, system or plant and their significance in an appropriate context'.

- **Risk Estimation:** It includes, the identification of outcomes, the estimation of the magnitude of the associated consequences of these outcomes and the estimation of the probabilities of these outcomes.

- **Risk Evaluation:** It is the complex process of determining the significance or value of the identified hazards and estimated risks to those concerned with or affected by the process.

- **Risk Management Plan (RMP):** It is a detailed description of the risk management system. It must identify or characterise the safety profile of the medicinal product(s) concerned, indicate how to characterise further the safety profile of the medicinal product(s) concerned, document measures to prevent or minimise the risks associated with the medicinal product, including an assessment of the effectiveness of those interventions and document post-authorisation obligations that have been imposed as a condition of the marketing authorisation.

- **Risk:** It is 'the simple, standard, epidemiological definition stating the probability that something will happen'.

- **Risk Management:** It is the making of decisions concerning risks, or action to reduce the consequences or probability of occurrence.

- **Risk Management System:** It is a set of pharmacovigilance activities and interventions designed to identify, characterise, prevent or minimise risks relating to a medicinal product, including the assessment of the effectiveness of those interventions.

- **Risk Minimisation Activity/Risk Minimisation Measure:** An intervention intended to prevent or reduce the probability of the occurrence of an adverse reaction associated with the exposure to a medicine, or to reduce its severity should it occur.

- **Risk-benefit Balance:** An evaluation of the positive therapeutic effects of the medicinal product in relation to the risks, i.e. any risk relating to the quality, safety or efficacy of the medicinal product as regards patients' health or public health.

- **Risks Related to Use of a Medicinal Product:** Any risk relating to the quality, safety or efficacy of the medicinal product as regards patients' health or public health and any risk of undesirable effects on the environment.

- **Safety Concern:** An important identified risk, important potential risk or missing information.

- **Serious Adverse Event (Experience/Reaction):** It is any untoward medical occurrence that, at any dose results in death; is life-threatening; requires inpatient hospitalization or prolongation of hospitalization; results in persistent or significant disability/incapacity; or is a congenital anomaly/birth defect.

- **Serious Adverse Reaction:** An adverse reaction which results in death, is life-threatening, requires in-patient hospitalisation or prolongation of existing hospitalisation, results in persistent or significant disability or incapacity, or is a congenital anomaly/birth defect.

- **Severe/Severity:** It is a term used to describe the intensity/severity of a specific event; e.g. mild, moderate or severe.

- **Signal Management Process:** It includes the following activities: signal detection, signal validation, signal confirmation, signal analysis and prioritisation, signal assessment and recommendation for action.

- **Signal Validation:** Process of evaluating the data supporting a detected signal in order to verify that the available documentation contains sufficient evidence demonstrating the existence of a new potentially causal association, or a new aspect of a known association, and therefore justifies further analysis of the signal.

- **Signal:** It is a report of an event that may have a causal relationship to one or more drugs; it alerts health professionals and should be explored further.

- **Solicited Sources of Individual Case Safety Reports:** Organised data collection systems, which include clinical trials, registries, post-authorisation named patients use programmes, other patient support and disease management programmes, surveys of patients or healthcare providers or information gathering on efficacy or patient compliance.

- **Sponsor:** An individual, company, institution, or organization which takes responsibility for the initiation, management, and/or financing of a clinical trial is identified as a sponsor.

- **Spontaneous Report/Spontaneous Notification:** An unsolicited communication by a healthcare professional or consumer to a company, regulatory authority or other organization that describes one or more adverse reactions in a patient who was given one or more medicinal products and that does not derive from a study or any organised data collection scheme.

- **Substance:** Any matter irrespective of origin which may be human (e.g. human blood and human blood products), animal (e.g. micro-organisms, whole animals, parts of organs, animal secretions, toxins, extracts, blood products), vegetable (e.g. micro-organisms, plants, part of plants, vegetable secretions, extracts), chemical (e.g. elements, naturally occurring chemical materials and chemical products obtained by chemical change or synthesis).

- **Summary of Product Characteristics (SmPC):** Part of the marketing authorisation of a medicinal product setting out the agreed position of the product as distilled during the course of the assessment process which includes the information.

- **Suspected Unexpected Serious Adverse Reaction (SUSAR):** Any serious adverse reaction which is unexpected but may have causal relation to the drug is termed as SUSAR.

- **Target Population (treatment)/Treatment Target Population:** The patients who might be treated with the medicinal product in accordance with the indication(s) and contraindications in the authorised product information.

- **Target Population (Vaccine)/Vaccine Target Population:** Persons who might be vaccinated in accordance with the indication(s) and contraindications in the authorised product information and official recommendations for vaccinations.

- **Traditional Herbal Medicinal Product:** A herbal medicinal product that fulfils the following conditions:

  (a) it has (an) indication(s) exclusively appropriate to traditional herbal medicinal products which, by virtue of their composition and purpose, are intended and designed for use without the supervision of a medical practitioner for diagnostic purposes or for prescription or monitoring of treatment;

  (b) it is exclusively for administration in accordance with a specified strength and posology;

  (c) it is an oral, external and/or inhalation preparation;

  (d) the period of traditional use as laid down in Article 16c(1)(c) has elapsed;

  (e) the data on the traditional use of the medicinal product are sufficient; in particular, the product proves not to be harmful in the specified conditions of use and the pharmacological effects or efficacy of the medicinal product are plausible on the basis of long-standing use and experience.

- **Unexpected Adverse Reaction:** Unexpected adverse reaction is 'an adverse reaction, the nature, severity or outcome of which is not consistent with the summary of product characteristics'.

- **Upper Management:** Upper management is, "the group of persons in charge of the highest executive management of an organisation". Membership of this group is determined by the governance structure of the organisation.

- **Vaccination:** 'The administration of a vaccine with the aim to produce immune response' is vaccination.

- **Vaccination Failure:** Vaccination failure is due to actual vaccine failure or failure to vaccinate. Vaccination failure may be defined based on clinical endpoints or immunological criteria, where correlates or surrogate markers for disease protection exist.

- **Vaccine failure:** Confirmed or suspected vaccine failure.

  The four types of vaccine failure are:

  - **Confirmed Clinical Vaccine Failure:** Occurrence of the specific vaccine-preventable disease in a person who is appropriately and fully vaccinated taking into account the incubation period and the normal delay for the protection to be acquired as a result of immunization.

  - **Suspected Clinical Vaccine Failure:** Occurrence of disease in an appropriately and fully vaccinated person, but the disease is not confirmed to be the specific vaccine-preventable disease, e.g. disease of unknown serotype in a fully vaccinated person.

  - **Confirmed Immunological Vaccine Failure:** Failure of the vaccinated person to develop the accepted marker of protective immune response after being fully and appropriately vaccinated, as demonstrated by having tested or examined the vaccinated person at an appropriate time interval after completion of immunisation.

  - **Suspected Immunological Vaccine Failure:** Failure of the vaccinated person to develop the accepted marker of protective immune response after being fully and appropriately vaccinated, but with the testing or examination of the vaccinated person done at an inappropriate time interval after completion of immunisation.

- **Vaccine Pharmacovigilance:** The science and activities relating to the detection, assessment, understanding and communication of adverse events following immunisation and other vaccine- or immunisation- related issues, and to the prevention of untoward effects of the vaccine or immunisation.

- **Vaccine Product-related Reaction:** An adverse event following immunisation that is caused or precipitated by a vaccine due to one or more of the inherent properties of the vaccine product.

- **Vaccine Quality defect-related Reaction:** An adverse event following immunisation that is caused or precipitated by a vaccine that is due to one or more quality defects of the vaccine product including its administration device as provided by the manufacturer.

- **Validated Signal:** A signal where the signal validation process of evaluating the data supporting the detected signal has verified that the available documentation contains sufficient evidence demonstrating the existence of a new potentially causal association, or a new aspect of a known association, and therefore justifies further analysis of the signal.

■■■

APPENDIX 2

S.O.P. No. 1

Standard Operating Procedure to fill ADR form

TITLE OF THE INSTITUTION	
Title : Standard Operating Procedure to Fill ADR Form	
SOP No. :	Page 1 of 5
Department :	Version and Date :
Effective Date :	Review Date :

Standard Operating Procedure to Fill ADR Form

DESCRIPTION OF CHANGE				
Type of Document Change	☐ Administrative	☐ Minor	☐ Major	☐ N/A
Training	☐ Required	☐ Not required	☐ N/A	
Document Effectivity	☐ 30 Days	☐ 15 Days	☐ 0 Days	
Implementation Date	Date :			

CHANGE HISTORY			
Change Number	Issue Date	Request Number	Reason for Change

REVIEW HISTORY	
Review date	
Reviewed by	
Approved by	
Review date	
Reviewed by	
Approved by	

	Prepared by	Verified by	Approved by
Signature			
Name			
Designation			

(A.15)

TITLE OF THE INSTITUTION	
Title : Standard Operating Procedure to Fill ADR Form	
SOP No. :	Page 2 of 5
Department :	Version and Date :
Effective Date :	Review Date :

Standard Operating Procedure to Fill in ADR Form

1.0 Purpose

To describe the procedures for filling the adverse drug reaction forms.

2.0 Scope/Applicability:

This SOP/procedure is applicable to all those personnel working in the National Coordination Centre at IPC, ADR Monitoring Centres under PvPI and the healthcare professionals reporting the ADE.

3.0 Related SOPs:

3.1 Processing and reporting of ADR

3.2 Causality assessment

3.3 Quality Assurance

4.0 Reference Documents

4.1 Good Clinical Practice: Standard Operating Procedures for Clinical Researchers by Josef Koffman.

4.2 The use of the WHO-UMC system for standardised case causality assessment by WHO-UMC.

4.3 Glossary of terms used in Pharmacovigilance by WHO-UMC.

	Prepared by	Verified by	Approved by
Signature			
Name			
Designation			

TITLE OF THE INSTITUTION	
Title : Standard Operating Procedure to Fill ADR Form	
SOP No. :	Page 3 of 5
Department :	Version and Date :
Effective Date :	Review Date :

5.0 Definitions

Term	Definition
ADE	Any untoward medical occurrence that may present during treatment with a pharmaceutical product but which does not necessarily have a causal relationship with this treatment.
ADR	A response to a drug which is noxious and unintended, and which occurs at doses normally used in man for the prophylaxis, diagnosis, or therapy of disease, or for the modification of physiological function.
Causality Assessment	The evaluation of the likelihood that a medicine was the causative agent of an observed adverse reaction. Causality assessment is usually made according to established algorithms.
Dechallenge	The withdrawal of a drug from a patient; the point at which the continuity, reduction or disappearance of adverse effects may be observed.
Rechallenge	The point at which a drug is again given to a patient after its previous withdrawal.

Standard Operating Procedure to Fill in ADR Form

6.0 Procedures:

1. Write the patient's initials (No.: 1), age, gender and weight. This information should be as complete as possible as they are used to identify duplicate reports.

2. Mention the date of adverse event started (No.: 5) and date of recovery of the event.

3. Provide maximum information to describe the nature of the event (No.: 7), its localization, severity and characteristics of the event. Mention, if any diagnostic tests/lab reports as well as the treatment was given for the management of ADR. DO NOT use single word description of the event.

4. Mention the patient's details including disease condition (i.e., the primary diagnosis), brief drug history of intake of all medications in the recent past.

	Prepared by	Verified by	Approved by
Signature			
Name			
Designation			

TITLE OF THE INSTITUTION	
Title : Standard Operating Procedure to Fill ADR Form	
SOP No. :	Page 4 of 5
Department :	Version and Date :
Effective Date :	Review Date :

5. Provide generic as well as brand name of the suspected drug(s) (No.: 8) as latter is essential for entry into VigiFlow.

6. Carefully tick in the items no. 09, 10 (Dechallenge/Rechallenge).

7. Write the details of concomitant medications (No.: 11) as this information is required in causal analysis of the event.

8. Fill all the required information in the specified columns.

9. Mention the causality assessment category in the item no. 17 of ADR form (The causality assessment will be done by the AMC personnel as well as by the NCC personnel).

10. Wherever appropriate please write the case sheet no. / hospital numbers/OPD numbers in the lop (left hand side) of the ADR forms. This will help in verification / crosschecking the report by co-ordinator as well as the Quality review panel.

11. Check the Essentially Required Items (ERI) no. 1, 5, 7, 8, 11, 15, 16 and 18 are filled appropriately (Failure to fill even one item in ERI will be considered as Invalid report/form).

12. Ensure all the items in the form are filled appropriately and legibly.

13. All the ADR forms generated at the AMCs should be checked for completeness and signed by AMC Co-ordinator before entering into VigiFlow.

	Prepared by	Verified by	Approved by
Signature			
Name			
Designation			

TITLE OF THE INSTITUTION	
Title : Standard Operating Procedure to Fill ADR Form	
SOP No. :	Page 5 of 5
Department :	Version and Date :
Effective Date :	Review Date :

14. Write the AMC report no. in ascending order based on date of reporting (No. 18) and worldwide unique no. generated by VigiFlow in the top right corner of ADR forms in box provided.

Important Note:

1. All the duly filled ADR Forms should be archived at the ADR Monitoring Centre.

2. For multiple ADRs suspected to be caused by the same drug that are not overtly related to each other (as in a syndrome), use separate forms to record them. So long they are manifestations of the same problem/reaction; they should be recorded in the same form.

3. For multiple ADRs caused by different drugs taken concomitantly by a given patient, use separate forms to capture them.

	Prepared by	Verified by	Approved by
Signature			
Name			
Designation			

Standard Operating Procedure for Quality Assurance of ADR Reports

S.O.P. No. 2

TITLE OF THE INSTITUTION	
Title : Standard Operating Procedure for Quality Assurance of ADR Reports	
SOP No. :	Page 1 of 4
Department :	Version and Date :
Effective Date :	Review Date :

Standard Operating Procedure for Quality Assurance of ADR Reports

DESCRIPTION OF CHANGE				
Type of Document Change	☐ Administrative	☐ Minor	☐ Major	☐ N/A
Training	☐ Required	☐ Not required	☐ N/A	
Document Effectivity	☐ 30 Days	☐ 15 Days	☐ 0 Days	
Implementation Dating	Implementation Date :			

CHANGE HISTORY			
Change Number	Issue Date	Request Number	Reason for Change

REVIEW HISTORY	
Review date	
Reviewed by	
Approved by	
Review date	
Reviewed by	
Approved by	

	Prepared by	Verified by	Approved by
Signature			
Name			
Designation			

TITLE OF THE INSTITUTION	
Title : Standard Operating Procedure for Quality Assurance of ADR Reports	
SOP No. :	Page 2 of 4
Department :	Version and Date :
Effective Date :	Review Date :

1.0 Purpose

The purpose of this procedure is to define a process for quality assurance of ADR reports.

2.0 Applicability

This procedure is applicable to those working at the National Coordinating Centre. IPC Ghaziabad.

Standard Operating Procedure for Quality Assurance of ADR Reports

3.0 Related SOPS:

3.1 Guidelines for filling of ADR forms

3.2 Processing and reporting of ADR

3.3 Causality assessment

3.4 Quality control

4.0 Source Doucments

4.1 Reference:

5.0 Definitions:

Term	Definition

	Prepared by	Verified by	Approved by
Signature			
Name			
Designation			

TITLE OF THE INSTITUTION	
Title : Standard Operating Procedure for Quality Assurance of ADR Reports	
SOP No. :	Page 3 of 4
Department :	Version and Date :
Effective Date :	Review Date :

PROCEDURES:

1. The quality assurance of ADR reports will be performed by the NCC staff in accordance with a checklist prepared and approved by the QA Panel.

2. The quality check of the ADR data sent by the ADR Monitoring Centre (AMC) through vigiflow shall be carried out every month or as and when required by the quality review panel.

3. Quality assurance activity will be monitored by the Quality Review Panel.

STEP 1:

4. The quality control process includes the following procedures:

5. Open the VigiFlow website: https://adr.who-umc.org

   Login with the user id and password

6. Open the 'LIST OF REPORTS' section in VIGIFLOW. Generate the list of "all REPORTS" by selecting the appropriate drop down at the bottom of the page. Generate the list for only one centre at a time, by selecting the desired centre.

Standard Operating Procedure for Quality Assurance of ADR Reports

STEP 2:

7. Select all the report details and paste it in a excel sheet (Keep destination formatting).

8. Retain report ids (World Unique No:) in the excel sheet and remove all other columns.

STEP 3:

9. Remove the bank rows by selecting sort "A to Z" Lowest to Highest.

	Prepared by	Verified by	Approved by
Signature			
Name			
Designation			

TITLE OF THE INSTITUTION	
Title : Standard Operating Procedure for Quality Assurance of ADR Reports	
SOP No. :	Page 4 of 4
Department :	Version and Date :
Effective Date :	Review Date :

STEP 4:

10. Paste all the report ids in column B.

11. Use simple randomization procedure to randomize the report IDs.

12. Highlight the blank cells A1: A(N) where N is the total number of report ids in the excel sheet.

13. Enter the formula = RAND( ) and hit Ctrl + Enter. This will enter the formula in all (N) cells at once.

14. The list of random numbers has been generated and assigned to each row.

15. You could sort by column B and calculate the desired percentage of sample to be picked up either from top or bottom of the list, whichever preferred.

    For example: If 30% has to be picked up then pick up the top 30% of N numbers from the column B.

16. Take a print of the randomized ADR reports through VigiFlow (Internal Reports).

STEP 5:

17. Each report will be checked for the quality parameters as mentioned in essentials required items of the SOP for Filling up of ADR forms.

18. The percentile score of individual parameters will be calculated.

19. Cumulative minimum score of 75% is needed to pass through quality control process for the first three months after induction into the programme

NOTE:

- After the first three months of induction period, the AMCs have to report 100% compliance to the quality control and assurance process. A deviation of 5 % is allowed twice in a year.

- If the reports found to be incomplete, it will be sent back to AMC for completion along with a note.

- In case of repetitive noncompliance, warning letter will be issued by the NCC.

	Prepared by	Verified by	Approved by
Signature			
Name			
Designation			

Standard Operating Procedure for Causality Assessment of ADR Reports

S.O.P. No. 3

TITLE OF THE INSTITUTION	
Title : Standard Operating Procedure for Causality Assessment of ADR Reports	
SOP No. :	Page 1 of 3
Department :	Version and Date :
Effective Date :	Review Date :

Standard Operating Procedure for Causality Assessment of ADR Reports

DESCRIPTION OF CHANGE				
Type of Document Change	☐ Administrative	☐ Minor	☐ Major	☐ N/A
Training	☐ Required	☐ Not required	☐ N/A	
Document Effectivity	☐ 30 Days	☐ 15 Days	☐ 0 Days	
Implementation Dating	Implementation Date :			

CHANGE HISTORY			
Change Number	Issue Date	Request Number	Reason for Change

REVIEW HISTORY	
Review date	
Reviewed by	
Approved by	
Review date	
Reviewed by	
Approved by	

	Prepared by	Verified by	Approved by
Signature			
Name			
Designation			

TITLE OF THE INSTITUTION	
Title : Standard Operating Procedure for Causality Assessment of ADR Reports	
SOP No. :	Page 2 of 3
Department :	Version and Date :
Effective Date :	Review Date :

Standard Operating Procedure for Causality Assessment of ADR Reports

1.0 Purpose

The purpose of this procedure is to define a process for causality assessment of ADR reports.

2.0 Applicability

This procedure is applicable to those working at the ADR Monitoring Centre and National Coordinating Centre. IPC Ghaziabad

3.0 Related SOPs:

3.1 Guidelines for filling of ADR forms,

3.2 Processing and reporting of ADR

4.0 Source Documents

4.1 Reference

5.0 Definitions

Term	Definition
Causality analysis	The evaluation of the likelihood that a medicine was the causative agent of an observed adverse reaction. Causality assessment is usually made according to the established algorithms.
WHO-UMC Scale	The WHO-UMC system has been developed in consultation with the National Centres participating in the Programme for International Drug Monitoring and is meant as a practical tool for the assessment of case reports. It is basically a combined assessment taking into account the clinical-pharmacological aspects of the case history and the quality of the documentation of the observation. Since Pharmacovigilance is particularly concerned with the detection of unknown and unexpected adverse reactions, other criteria such as previous knowledge and statistical chance play a less prominent role in the system. It is recognised that the semantics of the definitions are critical and that individual judgements may therefore differ. This method gives guidance to the general arguments which should be used to select one category over another.
Suspected ADR	An adverse drug reaction, contrary to an adverse event, is characterized by the suspicion of a causal relationship between the drug exposure and the occurrence, i.e. judged as being at least possibly related to treatment by the reporting or a reviewing health professional.

	Prepared by	Verified by	Approved by
Signature			
Name			
Designation			

TITLE OF THE INSTITUTION	
Title : Standard Operating Procedure for Causality Assessment of ADR Reports	
SOP No. :	Page 3 of 3
Department :	Version and Date :
Effective Date :	Review Date :

Standard Operating Procedure for Causality Assessment of ADR Reports

Process/Procedures:

5.1 The causality analysis shall be performed by using WHO-UMC scale.

5.2 The AMC coordinator shall perform causality analysis of the suspected ADR.

5.3 In absence of coordinator, the designated sub-coordinator along with technical associate or any healthcare professionals associated with the AMCs/NCC can also perform causal analysis of the suspected ADR.

5.4 Ensure that the form has all the essentially required items as per SOP for filling of ADR forms before causality analysis.

5.5 Perform causality assessment for all serious, unexpected, suspected and expected adverse events reported for the established medicines/well known medicines/and new drugs.

5.6 The serious adverse events should contain all the essentially required items. The reporter/PvPI personnel involved in collection of the particular reports should attempt to acquire all the information for an individual case safety report immediately upon receipt of the suspected event.

5.7 Finally after causality analysis, AMC coordinator will mention the causal relationship category in item no. 17 of ADR form and put his signature in the form.

5.8 These analyzed reports should be sent to the NCC within 10 calendar days through VigiFlow.

5.9 For all serious adverse events the reports should reach the NCC within 7 calendar days.
Mention SAR in the report title when it is entered in VigiFlow.

5.10 Verification of the causality assessment done by AMC is carried out at random at NCC.

Note: In case, if coordinator is not able to arrive at any consensus regarding the causality assessment of a particular case, he/she can consult either the reporting physician or physician from the speciality.

	Prepared by	Verified by	Approved by
Signature			
Name			
Designation			

Standard Operating Procedure for Processing and Reporting of ADR Reports

S.O.P. No. 4

TITLE OF THE INSTITUTION	
Title : Standard Operating Procedure for Processing and Reporting of ADR Reports	
SOP No. :	Page 1 of 4
Department :	Version and Date :
Effective Date :	Review Date :

Standard Operating Procedure for Processing and Reporting of ADR Reports

DESCRIPTION OF CHANGE				
Type of Document Change	☐ Administrative	☐ Minor	☐ Major	☐ N/A
Training	☐ Required	☐ Not required	☐ N/A	
Document Effectivity	☐ 30 Days	☐ 15 Days	☐ 0 Days	
Implementation Date	Date :			

CHANGE HISTORY			
Change Number	Issue Date	Request Number	Reason for Change

REVIEW HISTORY	
Review date	
Reviewed by	
Approved by	

	Prepared by	Verified by	Approved by
Signature			
Name			
Designation			

TITLE OF THE INSTITUTION	
Title : Standard Operating Procedure for Processing and Reporting of ADR Reports	
SOP No. :	Page 2 of 4
Department :	Version and Date :
Effective Date :	Review Date :

1.0 Purpose:

The purpose of this procedure is to define a process for processing and reporting of ADR reports.

2.0 Applicability:

This procedure is applicable to those working at the AMC/NCC.

Standard Operating Procedure for Processing and Reporting of ADR Reports

3.0 Related SOPs:

3.1 Guidelines for filling of ADR forms

3.2 Causality assessment of ADR reports

4.0 Source Documents

4.1 Reference:

5.   Process/Procedures:

5.1 All healthcare professionals (Consultant/junior resident) senior resident/ paramedical professionals) can report ADP's to AMC/NCC.

5.2 Report coming from the patients should be medically confirmed and reported through the healthcare professionals.

5.3 The ADR/s reported from the public health programmes can be reported to the nearest AMC or to NCC by any healthcare professionals associated with programme.

5.4 The coordinator/technical associate or any healthcare professionals associated with the AMCs/NCC are responsible for recording the ADR.

5.5 The ADR reporting form currently uploaded on the CDSCO website MUST be used.

	Prepared by	Verified by	Approved by
Signature			
Name			
Designation			

TITLE OF THE INSTITUTION	
Title : Standard Operating Procedure for Processing and Reporting of ADR Reports	
SOP No. :	Page 3 of 4
Department :	Version and Date :
Effective Date :	Review Date :

5.6   The AMC/NICC personnel will perform adequate follow up to obtain as much information as possible to complete the form, to ensure effective evaluation of the case. The follow up information will be also reported in VigiFlow.

5.7   Every attempt made to follow up will be documented by the AMC.

5.8   A valid case report should have EIGHT minimum fields as stated in the ADR reporting form guidance. Check the essentially required items (ERI) no. 1, 5, 7, 8, 11, 15, 16 and 18 are filled appropriately (Failure to fill even one item in ERI will be considered as invalid report/form). A case which does not meet the criteria of minimum reporting shall not be entered in VigiFlow.

5.9   Kindly follow the SOP for filling of ADR form. Record all the mandatory fields.

5.10   Check the filled ADR form for the mandatory fields for completeness.

5.11   The Centre Coordinator/Deputy Coordinator will ensure completion and quality of every report.

5.12   Causality Assessment will be performed and authorized by the Centre Coordinator/Deputy Coordinator (As per SOP for Causality assessment of ADR reports). This activity should not be delegated to the Technical Associate.

5.13   The technical associate enters the ADR case in the VigiFlow after the above mandatory checks.

5.14   These ADR data obtained through the public health programme (PHP) shall be entered in VigiFlow with mention in report title as "PHP".

5.15   Case processing in VigiFlow will be done in accordance with the user manual provided by WHO-UMC.

5.18   After entry of ADR data in VigiFlow, check for completeness of required fields and check in the report for central assessment to NCC.

	Prepared by	Verified by	Approved by
Signature			
Name			
Designation			

TITLE OF THE INSTITUTION	
Title : Standard Operating Procedure for Processing and Reporting of ADR Reports	
SOP No. :	Page 4 of 4
Department :	Version and Date :
Effective Date :	Review Date :

Standard Operating Procedure for Processing and Reporting of ADR Reports

5.17 For each ADR entry generate an internal report in VigiFlow following submission of report for central assessment and store the electronic copy.

5.18 Make an entry in log book for every VigiFlow entry and note the auto-generated WORLDWIDE UNIQUE NUMBER.

5.19 The original hard copy of the ADR form entered will be maintained by the AMC/NCC. The ADR form can be scanned and stored as an electronic copy. This is highly recommended to be done especially for all serious adverse events reported.

5.20 All the hard copy of ADR forms reported will be entered in VigiFlow after causal assessment should be stored in cabinets. The access for these cabinets should be restricted to coordinator, sub-coordinator and technical associate.

5.21 The copy of ADRs shall be sent to NCG.

NOTE:

- After the completion of ADR entry in VigiFlow, check in the search and statistics column (Pooled ADR data) with WORLDWIDE UNIQUE NUMBER for reports entered at AMC under central assessment.

- If the report is not available in pooled ADR data, contact your NCC/AMC to check-in the report in VigiFlow.

	Prepared by	Verified by	Approved by
Signature			
Name			
Designation			

Standard Operating Procedure for Training of PvPI Personnel

S.O.P. No. 5

TITLE OF THE INSTITUTION	
Title : Standard Operating Procedure for Training of PvPI Personnel	
SOP No. :	Page 1 of 4
Department :	Version and Date :
Effective Date :	Review Date :

Standard Operating Procedure for Training of PvPI Personnel

DESCRIPTION OF CHANGE				
Type of Document Change	☐ Administrative	☐ Minor	☐ Major	☐ N/A
Training	☐ Required	☐ Not required	☐ N/A	
Document Effectivity	☐ 30 Days	☐ 15 Days	☐ 0 Days	
Implementation Dating	Implementation Date :			

CHANGE HISTORY			
Change Number	Issue Date	Request Number	Reason for Change

REVIEW HISTORY	
Review date	
Reviewed by	
Approved by	
Review date	
Reviewed by	
Approved by	

	Prepared by	Verified by	Approved by
Signature			
Name			
Designation			

TITLE OF THE INSTITUTION	
Title : Standard Operating Procedure for Training of PvPI Personnel	
SOP No. :	Page 2 of 4
Department :	Version and Date :
Effective Date :	Review Date :

1.0 Purpose

The purpose of this procedure is to define a process for Training of PvPI personnel.

2.0 Applicability

This procedure is applicable to those working at the AMC/NCC.

3.0 Related SOPs

Roles and Responsibilities of PvPI Personnel

Standard Operating Procedure for Training of PvPI Personnel

4.0 Source Documents

Reference:

5.0 Definitions:

Time	Definition

6. Process/Procedures:

6.1 The AMC Coordinator/ Sub-coordinator/Technical Associate/s shall participate in training session.

6.2 The training shall be provided by NCC in association with WHO-UMC collaborating centre personnel/ trainers at NCC.

6.3 The technical associate will be trained within three months of joining to the ADR monitoring centre at NCC.

	Prepared by	Verified by	Approved by
Signature			
Name			
Designation			

TITLE OF THE INSTITUTION	
Title : Standard Operating Procedure for Training of PvPI Personnel	
SOP No. :	Page 3 of 4
Department :	Version and Date :
Effective Date :	Review Date :

6.4   The training workshop session will be organized at NCC or in collaboration with the AMC at respective region/s.

6.5   The trained PvPI personnel at NCC/AMC will undertake advanced training provided by WHO-UMC personnel.

6.6   The trained personnel with adequate knowledge and experience as recommended by Core Training Panel will be deputed as trainers.

6.7   These deputed trainers will train all newly joined/ existing AMC PvPI personnel as and when required.

6.8   The training modules and materials will be standardized and authorized by the Core Training Panel.

6.9   The funding for the training workshop will be provided by CDSCO.

6.10 There will be two workshop modules.

6.10.1   Orientation Workshop

6.10.2   Advanced Training Workshop

	Prepared by	Verified by	Approved by
Signature			
Name			
Designation			

TITLE OF THE INSTITUTION	
Title : Standard Operating Procedure for Training of PvPI Personnel	
SOP No. :	Page 4 of 4
Department :	Version and Date :
Effective Date :	Review Date :

Standard Operating Procedure for Training of PvPI Personnel

6.10.1   Orientation Workshop:

Objective: Orientation and sensitization

- The workshop shall provide basic information to AMC/NCC PvPI personnel about ADRs, how to report ADRs, how to fill the ADR reporting form, hands on online training of ADR data entry in VigiFlow, monthly reporting to NCC and inform about obtaining quality ADR data.

- The training will present a general overview on pharmacovigilance, terminologies used in PvPI, hands on training to fill, evaluate, assess, validate and report an ADR cases as well as to sensitize them towards causality assessment.

6.10.2   Advanced Training Workshop:

Objective: To provide training in VigiFlow, Causality assessment and on SOPs

- The AMC/NCC PvPI personnel will receive the advance training in VigiFlow in search and statistics, ADR terminologies usage and listing of reports.

- The AMC/NCC PvPI personnel will receive hands on training to perform causality assessment of ADR reports using WHO-UMC scale.

- Training related to all Standard Operating Procedures associated with PvPI will be imparted by qualified personnel deputed by the NCC.

Note:

1. Pre-and post training assessment are mandatory for training workshop.

2. A standardized feedback form designed by the Core Training Panel will be used for this purpose.

3. Feedback regarding the quality of training from the trainees will be shared with the trainer and Core Training Panel.

	Prepared by	Verified by	Approved by
Signature			
Name			
Designation			

Standard Operating Procedure for Roles and Responsibilities of PvPI Personnel

S.O.P. No. 6

TITLE OF THE INSTITUTION	
Title : Standard Operating Procedure for Roles and Responsibilities of PvPI Personnel	
SOP No. :	Page 1 of 4
Department :	Version and Date :
Effective Date :	Review Date :

Standard Operating Procedure for Roles and Responsibilities of PvPI Personnel

DESCRIPTION OF CHANGE				
Type of Document Change	☐ Administrative	☐ Minor	☐ Major	☐ N/A
Training	☐ Required	☐ Not required	☐ N/A	
Document Effectivity	☐ 30 Days	☐ 15 Days	☐ 0 Days	
Implementation Dating	Implementation Date:			

CHANGE HISTORY			
Change Number	Issue Date	Request Number	Reason for Change

REVIEW HISTORY	
Review date	
Reviewed by	
Approved by	
Review date	
Reviewed by	
Approved by	

	Prepared by	Verified by	Approved by
Signature			
Name			
Designation			

TITLE OF THE INSTITUTION	
Title : Standard Operating Procedure for Roles and Responsibilities of PvPI Personnel	
SOP No. :	Page 2 of 4
Department :	Version and Date :
Effective Date :	Review Date :

Standard Operating Procedure for Roles & Responsibilities of PvPI Personnel

1.0 Purpose:

The purpose of this procedure is to define the roles and responsibilities of PvPI personnel.

2.0 Applicability:

This procedure is applicable to those working at the AMCs/NCC.

3.0 Related SOPs:

Communication in PvPI.

4.0 Source Documents:

Reference

5.0 Definitions:

Time	Definition
DTAR	
CCSR	
NCAR	
DTAB	

	Prepared by	Verified by	Approved by
Signature			
Name			
Designation			

TITLE OF THE INSTITUTION	
Title : Standard Operating Procedure for Roles and Responsibilities of PvPI Personnel	
SOP No. :	Page 3 of 4
Department :	Version and Date :
Effective Date :	Review Date :

6.0 Process/Procedures:

ADR Monitoring Centre (AMC)

1. At PVPI - AMC, the designated Centre Coordinator is responsible for the proper functioning of AMC. In absence of the coordinator, the designated Sub-coordinator is responsible for the smooth functioning of the centre.

2. The technical associate appointed will be responsible for the collection of ADR reports, which have to be reported to the AMC coordinator.

3. Collection and follow up of ADR reports has to be done by technical associate.

4. Collation, checking completeness for a valid case, causality assessment and scrutinizing the ADR reports received will be done as per SOPs by Centre Coordinator/ Sub-Coordinator.

Standard Operating Procedure for Roles and Responsibilities of PvPI Personnel

5. All the scrutinized and signed ADR reports should be entered in VigiFlow by technical associate. Every report has to be sent to the central assessment at NCC.

6. The centre coordinator is responsible for sending the monthly reports of their AMC to NCC.

7. Sensitization of the physicians/ healthcare professionals/ students/ patients of the catchment hospital for spontaneous ADR reporting by various mode (Lectures on ADR reporting, Email, telephone, pamphlet and newsletter) should be undertaken by the center coordinator.

8. Feedback to all healthcare professionals involved in reporting, should be sent by the AMC Centre Coordinators.

National Coordinating Centre (NCC)

1. The NCC personnel will be responsible for review completeness of ADR reports, to perform quality checks, causality assessment and commit ADR reports sent by AMC to WHO-UMC.

	Prepared by	Verified by	Approved by
Signature			
Name			
Designation			

TITLE OF THE INSTITUTION	
Title : Standard Operating Procedure for Roles and Responsibilities of PvPI Personnel	
SOP No. :	Page 4 of 4
Department :	Version and Date :
Effective Date :	Review Date :

2. Monitoring of number of ADR reports entered in VigiFlow by AMCs and the Day-To-day Activity Report (DTAR) will be sent to them on weekly basis.

3. Cumulative Centre wise Status Report (CCSR) will be sent to AMCs on monthly basis.

4. Organizing training workshop/s for ADR Monitoring Centres personnel to train on ADR reporting, data entry in VigiFlow, Causality assessment and on SOPs would be undertaken by NCC on a continuing basis.

5. Generation of reports at periodic intervals or as and when required by the Signal Review Panel and Steering Committee.

6. Review the list of drugs for focused ADR Monitoring suggested by the Strategic Advisory Committee or CDSCO and designates the focused drug monitoring to AMCs.

7. Signal detection and reporting to Signal Review Committee.

8. Publication of SAFETY NEWSLETTER on bi-annual basis.

9. Reporting to CDSCO about the functional status of AMCs.

Zonal CDSCO Offices

1. Zonal CDSCO Offices will provide administrative support to the ADR Monitoring Centres and report to CDSCO HQ.

2. The disbursement of funds towards the conduct of workshop, office expenditures incurred by AMCs.

Standard Operating Procedure for Roles & Responsibilities of PvPI Personnel

CDSCO HEAD QUATER

1. The yearly budget and expansion plan for PvPI will be formulated by the CDSCO.

2. The decision of the steering committee on NCC reports will be forwarded to CDSCO.

3. The CDSCO will report to DTAB (Ministry of Health & Family Welfare).

4. The CDSCO is responsible for formulate and communicate safety related regulatory decisions for medicines.

	Prepared by	Verified by	Approved by
Signature			
Name			
Designation			

Standard Operating Procedure for Communication in PvPI

S.O.P. No. 7

TITLE OF THE INSTITUTION	
Title : Standard Operating Procedure for Communication in PvPI	
SOP No. :	Page 1 of 3
Department :	Version and Date :
Effective Date :	Review Date :

Standard Operating Procedure for Communication in PvPI

DESCRIPTION OF CHANGE				
Type of Document Change	☐ Administrative	☐ Minor	☐ Major	☐ N/A
Training	☐ Required	☐ Not required	☐ N/A	
Document Effectivity	☐ 30 Days	☐ 15 Days	☐ 0 Days	
Implementation Dating	Implementation Date:			

CHANGE HISTORY			
Change Number	Issue Date	Request Number	Reason for Change

REVIEW HISTORY	
Review date	
Reviewed by	
Approved by	
Review date	
Reviewed by	
Approved by	

	Prepared by	Verified by	Approved by
Signature			
Name			
Designation			

TITLE OF THE INSTITUTION	
Title : Standard Operating Procedure for Communication in PvPI	
SOP No. :	Page 2 of 3
Department :	Version and Date :
Effective Date :	Review Date :

1.0 Purpose

The purpose of this procedure is to define the roles and responsibilities of PvPI personnel.

2.0 Applicability

This procedure is applicable to those working at the AMCs/NCC.

3.0 Related SOPs:

Standard Operating Procedure for Communication in PvPI

4.0 Source Documents
Reference:

5.0 Process/Procedures:

1. All PVPI - AMCs must route a copy of all communication/s to CDSCO/ Zonal CDSCO through NCC.

2. The monthly report will be submitted to NCC and a copy to Zonal CDSCO Office by the 2nd day of every month.

3. The standardized reporting format sent by NCC should be used for this purpose.

4. NCC will send a Centrewise Cumulative Status Report (CCSR) on functional status and performance of the participating AMCs on monthly basis and a copy to all CDSCO HQ/Zonal offices before the end of the respective month.

5. The AMC can use manual, print, electronic and digital mode of communication/s to create awareness among healthcare professionals and public upon prior permission from NCC/CDSCO.

	Prepared by	Verified by	Approved by
Signature			
Name			
Designation			

TITLE OF THE INSTITUTION	
Title : Standard Operating Procedure for Communication in PvPI	
SOP No. :	Page 3 of 3
Department :	Version and Date :
Effective Date :	Review Date :

6. Representation in all kind of conferences/workshops/society under the capacity of Centre Coordinator/PvPI personnel must require permission from NCC/CDSCO.

7. Any kind of communication (manual or print or electronic or digital) in order to educate/create awareness in lay public can be released by the AMCs/NCC with prior permission from CDSCO.

8. Media communications regarding the program progress and any updates will be handled by the NCC or CDSCO as appropriate.

9. Any query regarding VigiFlow database should be forwarded to NCC and not directly WHO-UMC.

10. All communication with the WHO-UMC Collaborating Centre, (with copy to WHO India will be managed by NCC and CDSCO HQ as appropriate).

11. All communication with WHO-HQ, WHO-India Country office will be managed by NC and CDSCO HQ, as appropriate.

	Prepared by	Verified by	Approved by
Signature			
Name			
Designation			

Standard Operating Procedure for ADR Report Entry in VigiFlow

S.O.P. No. 8

TITLE OF THE INSTITUTION	
Title : Standard Operating Procedure for ADR Report Entry in VigiFlow	
SOP No. :	Page 1 of 8
Department :	Version and Date :
Effective Date :	Review Date :

Standard Operating Procedure for ADR Report Entry in VigiFlow

DESCRIPTION OF CHANGE				
Type of Document Change	☐ Administrative	☐ Minor	☐ Major	☐ N/A
Training	☐ Required	☐ Not required	☐ N/A	
Document Effectivity	☐ 30 Days	☐ 15 Days	☐ 0 Days	
Implementation Dating	Implementation Date:			

CHANGE HISTORY			
Change Number	Issue Date	Request Number	Reason for Change

REVIEW HISTORY	
Review date	
Reviewed by	
Approved by	
Review date	
Reviewed by	
Approved by	

	Prepared by	Verified by	Approved by
Signature			
Name			
Designation			

TITLE OF THE INSTITUTION	
Title : Standard Operating Procedure for ADR Report Entry in VigiFlow	
SOP No. :	Page 2 of 8
Department :	Version and Date :
Effective Date :	Review Date :

Standard Operating Procedure for ADR Report Entry in VigiFlow

1. Purpose:

To describe the procedure for converting raw data on paper forms to VigiFlow data sets.

2. Applicability:

This procedure is applicable to those working at the ADR Monitoring Centre (AMC) and National Coordinating Centre (NCC).

3. Related SOPs:

3.1   Processing and reporting of ADR

3.2   Causality assessment

3.3   Quality Assurance

4. Reference Documents:

Data Elements for Transmission of Individual Case Safety Reports, European Medicines Agency, 2005 available from-

http://www.ema.europa.eu/docs/en GB/document_library/Scientific guideline/2009/09/WC50000276 7.pdf

	Prepared by	Verified by	Approved by
Signature			
Name			
Designation			

TITLE OF THE INSTITUTION	
Title : Standard Operating Procedure for ADR Report Entry in VigiFlow	
SOP No. :	Page 3 of 8
Department :	Version and Date :
Effective Date :	Review Date :

5. Definitions:

Term	Definition

Procedure:

1. **Report information**
   - Type of report e.g. Spontaneous/literature reference should be captured in the structured test fields.
   - Seriousness criteria of reaction should be given e.g. Death, life-threatening, disabling, hospitalization, congenital-anomaly or other medically important condition.

   Standard Operating Procedure for ADR Report Entry In VigiFlow
   - Information about the organization sending the report and name of sender should be given in relevance tag.
   - Worldwide unique number column should be left blank it will be automatically filled with report number.
   - The primary source(s) of the information is the person who reports the facts. This should be distinguished from senders (secondary sources) who are transmitting the information.
   - Reporter identifier (name or initials) should be captured in the structured test field.

2. **Patient characteristics**
   - The patient initial field can be populated with the patients initials, UNKNOWN or PRIVACY. Entries such as XXX and N/A are not acceptable.

	Prepared by	Verified by	Approved by
Signature			
Name			
Designation			

TITLE OF THE INSTITUTION	
Title : Standard Operating Procedure for ADR Report Entry in VigiFlow	
SOP No. :	Page 4 of 8
Department :	Version and Date :
Effective Date :	Review Date :

- Date of birth/age of patient should be populated in relevance field.
- If the patient initial tag is populated as 'UNKNOWN', then one of the other criteria for patient characteristics should be populated in order for the report to be considered valid e.g., age group, weight, height and sex.
- If a reaction is fatal then the Information on patient death, death date, death cause and autopsy information should be given.

3. Tests and procedures

All tests relevant to the ADR should be captured in the structured test fields.

4. Drug information

This section covers coding on suspect drugs, vaccines and concomitant medication.

4.1 Suspect drug(s)

The drug(s) suspected of causing the reaction should be listed as the suspect drug(s).

Standard Operating Procedure for ADR Report Entry in VigiFlow

4.2 Concomitant medication

Any drug(s) that are not suspected of causing the reaction and that are administered to the patient at the time the case is reported or all drugs discontinued within 3 months prior to the reaction should be listed as concomitant medication.

	Prepared by	Verified by	Approved by
Signature			
Name			
Designation			

TITLE OF THE INSTITUTION	
Title : Standard Operating Procedure for ADR Report Entry in VigiFlow	
SOP No. :	Page 5 of 8
Department :	Version and Date :
Effective Date :	Review Date :

4.3 Patient past drug therapy

All drugs that were completed/discontinued before the start of the treatment with the suspect(ed) drugs should be included in the relevant section (Unless it was recently discontinued prior to the reaction and therefore coded as concomitant medication).

4.4 Additional drug information

- All the drug dosage information should be captured in the structured fields.
- The pharmaceutical form of the drug should be entered in the relevant field.
- The route of administration should be populated as a code using the WHO Code list as per anrexure-1.
- The indication of the drug should be captured in the drug indication field.
- If a drug has more than one indication, then the drug entry should be repeated for the second indication to be entered.
- If the indication of the drug is unknown, this field can be left blank or populated with Drug use for unknown indication.

4.5 Dates

The start and stop dates should all be captured in the structured date fields within the drug tags.

4.6 Action taken with drug

The action taken with the drug as a result of the reaction should be captured in the action drug field.

	Prepared by	Verified by	Approved by
Signature			
Name			
Designation			

TITLE OF THE INSTITUTION	
Title : Standard Operating Procedure for ADR Report Entry in VigiFlow	
SOP No. :	Page 6 of 8
Department :	Version and Date :
Effective Date :	Review Date :

Standard Operating Procedure for ADR Report Entry in VigiFlow

- This field should be populated with 'unknown' rather than left blank if the action taken is unknown.

- A separate drug entry should not be entered for any changes to the dosage as a result of the reaction.

- The rechallenge fields should be used when identical symptoms are experienced on both exposures to the suspect drug. A separate drug entry should not be populated for the rechallenge information.

5. **Reaction Information**

- It is required to code reaction using the medical dictionary terminology.

- Reaction terms should be classified accurately reflects the reporter's wording of the reaction.

- Medical judgment should be used if an exact match cannot be found and the most appropriate existing term should be selected.

	Prepared by	Verified by	Approved by
Signature			
Name			
Designation			

TITLE OF THE INSTITUTION	
Title : Standard Operating Procedure for ADR Report Entry in VigiFlow	
SOP No. :	Page 7 of 8
Department :	Version and Date :
Effective Date :	Review Date :

- Terms should be selected for every ADR reported. Reports that are ambiguous or confusing should be followed up for clarification.

- Pre-existing medical conditions that have not changed should generally be classified as medical history, Pre-existing medical conditions that have changed should be classified using the most specific term.

5.1 Reaction outcomes

It requires all reactions to have an outcome populated. If the outcome is unknown then the outcome field should be populated with 'unknown' and not left blank.

The data entered in Vigiflow by the AMCs will be sent by the AMCs to the NCC. The NCC will review the data in accordance with the SOP on Quality assurance of ADR reports and commit the data to Vigibase database.

This data will then be analyzed at an appropriate stage for any alerts/signals by the signal review committee.

Standard Operating Procedure for ADR Report Entry in VigiFlow

The NCC will also communicate the findings of this review and also the metrics related to data to the CDSCO HQ through a monthly report.

	Prepared by	Verified by	Approved by
Signature			
Name			
Designation			

TITLE OF THE INSTITUTION	
Title : Standard Operating Procedure for ADR Report Entry in VigiFlow	
SOP No. :	Page 8 of 8
Department :	Version and Date :
Effective Date :	Review Date :

Annexure 1

Routes	Codes	Routes	Codes
Buccal	BU	Intrathecal	IT
Conjuctival	CO	Intratracheal	TR
Dental	DE	Intrauterine	IU
Implant	MP	Intravenous	IV
Inhalation	IH	Intravesical	IB
Insufflation	IS	Per oral	PO
Intra-arterial	IA	Per rectal	PR
Intra-articular	IR	Subcutaneous	SC
Intra-cardiac	IC	Sublingual	SL
Intradermal	ID	Systemic (if route is not	
Intramuscular	IM	specified)	SY
Intranasal	IN	Topical (external)	TO
Intraperitoneal	IP	Transmammary transfer	TM
Intrapleural	IL	Urethral	UR
		Vaginal	VA

Source: WHO

	Prepared by	Verified by	Approved by
Signature			
Name			
Designation			

Standard Operating Procedure for the Recruitment of Technical Associate for PvPI

S.O.P. No. 9

TITLE OF THE INSTITUTION	
Title : Standard Operating Procedure for the Recruitment of Technical Associate for PvPI	
SOP No. :	Page 1 of 3
Department :	Version and Date :
Effective Date :	Review Date :

DESCRIPTION OF CHANGE				
Type of Document Change	☐ Administrative	☐ Minor	☐ Major	☐ N/A
Training	☐ Required	☐ Not required	☐ N/A	
Document Effectivity	☐ 30 Days	☐ 15 Days	☐ 0 Days	
Implementation Dating	Implementation Date:			

CHANGE HISTORY			
Change Number	Issue Date	Request Number	Reason for Change

REVIEW HISTORY	
Review date	
Reviewed by	
Approved by	
Review date	
Reviewed by	
Approved by	

	Prepared by	Verified by	Approved by
Signature			
Name			
Designation			

TITLE OF THE INSTITUTION	
Title : Standard Operating Procedure for the Recruitment of Technical Associate for PvPI	
SOP No. :	Page 2 of 3
Department :	Version and Date :
Effective Date :	Review Date :

Standard Operating Procedures for the Recruitment of Technical Associate for PvPI

Technical Associate's for the ADR's monitoring centres under PvPI may be selected from their region. Applications may be received from the candidates with the qualification mentioned under.

Medical Qualification:

M.B.B.S/M.D. in Biochemistry/ Microbiology/Pharmacology

OR

Non Medical Qualification:

Post Graduate in Biochemistry/Microbiology/Biotechnology/Pharmacy

Experience: Minimum one year in relevant field

Emoluments:

Job Description:

1. Collection of ADRs report.

2. Follow up with the complainant to check completeness as per SOP's.

3. Data entry in VigiFlow.

4. Reporting to National Coordination Centre through VigiFlow with the source data attached with each ADRs case.

5. Training/sensitization/feed back to physician through newsletter circulated by the NCC.

6. Other activities as assigned from time to time by CDSCO/NCC.

	Prepared by	Verified by	Approved by
Signature			
Name			
Designation			

TITLE OF THE INSTITUTION	
Title : Standard Operating Procedures for the Recruitment of Technical Associate for PvPI	
SOP No. :	Page 3 of 3
Department :	Version and Date :
Effective Date :	Review Date :

Desirable Qualification/Skills: The applicants are required to be proficient with use of computer and Internet.

The interview to be conducted by a panel of experts as follows:

1. Medical Superintendent or his nominee - Chairman.

2. Nominee of NCC/CDSCO zonal office - Member.

3. The Coordinator of respective ADR's Monitoring Centre - Member.

4. One of the senior Professor of the respective institute - Member.

	Prepared by	Verified by	Approved by
Signature			
Name			
Designation			

Standard Operating Procedure for the Recruitment of Technical Associate for PvPI

S.O.P. No. 10

TITLE OF THE INSTITUTION	
Title : Standard Operating Procedures for the Recruitment of Technical Associate for PvPI	
SOP No. :	Page 1 of 3
Department :	Version and Date :
Effective Date :	Review Date :

DESCRIPTION OF CHANGE				
Type of Document Change	☐ Administrative	☐ Minor	☐ Major	☐ N/A
Training	☐ Required	☐ Not required	☐ N/A	
Document Effectivity	☐ 30 Days	☐ 15 Days	☐ 0 Days	
Implementation Dating	Implementation Date:			
CHANGE HISTORY				
Change Number	Issue Date	Request Number	Reason for Change	

REVIEW HISTORY	
Review date	
Reviewed by	
Approved by	
Review date	
Reviewed by	
Approved by	

	Prepared by	Verified by	Approved by
Signature			
Name			
Designation			

TITLE OF THE INSTITUTION	
Title : Standard Operating Procedures for the Recruitment of Technical Associate for PvPI	
SOP No. :	Page 2 of 3
Department :	Version and Date :
Effective Date :	Review Date :

Standard Operating Procedures for the Recruitment of Technical Associate for PvPI

Technical Associate's for the ADR's monitoring centres under PvPI may be selected from their region. Applications may be received from the candidates with the qualification mentioned under

Qualification: Minimum qualification should be MBBS/BDS/M. Pharm/Pharm D.

OR

Candidates with any other qualification having experience in Pharmacovigilance Programme of India.

Candidates with proficiency in computer application will be preferred.

Composition of Selection Committee:

- IPC nominee will be the Chairman.
- (IPC may nominate from the CDSCO or State Drugs Control or Other source).
- Head of the Institution (ADRs monitoring Centre) - Member.
- Coordinator of the respective ADR Monitoring Centre - Member.

Emoluments:

	Prepared by	Verified by	Approved by
Signature			
Name			
Designation			

TITLE OF THE INSTITUTION	
Title : Standard Operating Procedures for the Recruitment of Technical Associate for PvPI	
SOP No. :	Page 3 of 3
Department :	Version and Date :
Effective Date :	Review Date :

Job Description:

- Collection of ADRs report.

- Follow up with the complainant to check completeness as per SOP's.

- Data entry in VigiFlow.

- Reporting to National Coordination Centre through VigiFlow with the source data attached with each ADRs case.

- Training/sensitization/feed back to physician through newsletter circulated by the NCC.

- Other activities as assigned from time to time by competent authority.

	Prepared by	Verified by	Approved by
Signature			
Name			
Designation			

Note: All SOP's are illustrative only.

■■■

ADR Form

SUSPECTED ADVERSE DRUG REACTION REPORTING FORM

For VOLUNTARY reporting of Adverse Drug Reactions by healthcare professionals

INDIAN PHARMACOPOEIA COMMISSION (National Coordinating Centre-Pharmacovigilance Programme of India) Ministry of Health & Family Welfare Government of India Sector-23, Raj Nagar, Ghaziabad-201002 www.ipc.nic.in	(AMC/ NCC Use only) AMC Report No. Worldwide Unique

A. PATIENT INFORMATION

1. Patient Initials	2. Age at time of Event or date of birth _____	3. Sex ☐ M ☐ F 4. Weight _____ Kgs	12. Relevant tests / laboratory data with dates

B. SUSPECTED ADVERSE REACTION

5. Date of reaction started (dd/mm/yyyy)

6. Date of recovery (dd/mm/yyyy)

7. Describe reaction or problem

13. Other relevant history including pre-existing medical conditions (e.g. allergies, race, pregnancy, smoking, alcohol use, hepatic/ renal dysfunction etc)

14. Seriousness of the reaction

☐ Death (dd/mm/yyyy)
☐ Life threatening
☐ Hospitalization/prolonged
☐ Disability

☐ Congenital-anomaly
☐ Required intervention to prevent permanent impairment / damage
☐ Other (specify)

15. Outcomes

☐ Fatal
☐ Continuing

☐ Recovering
☐ Recovered

☐ Unknown
☐ Other (specify)

C. SUSPECTED MEDICATION(S)

S.No	8. Name (brand and /or generic name)	Manufacturer (if known)	Batch No./ Lot No. (if known)	Exp. Date (if known))	Dose used	Route used	Frequency	Therapy dates (if known, give duration) Date started	Date stopped	Reason for use of prescribed for
i.										
ii.										
iii.										
iv.										

S.No As per C	9. Reaction abated after drug stopped or dose reduced					10. Reaction reappeared after reintroduction				
	Yes	No	Unknown	NA	Reduced dose	Yes	No	Unknown	NA	If reintroduced dose
i.										
ii.										
iii.										
iv.										

11. Concomitant medical product including self medication and herbal remedies with therapy dates (exclude those used to treat reaction)	**D. REPORTER (see confidentiality section on first page)** 16. Name and Professional Address :_____ Pin code: _____ E-mail _____ Tel. No. (with STD code): _____ Occupation _____ Signature _____

	17. Causality Assessment	18. Date of this report (dd/mm/yyyy)

ADVICE ABOUT REPORTING

Report Adverse Experiences with Medications

➢ **Report serious adverse reactions. A reaction is serious when the patient outcome is:**
- death
- life-threatening (real risk of dying)
- hospitalization (initial or prolonged)
- disability (significant, persistent or permanent)
- congenital anomaly
- required intervention to prevent permanent impairment or damage

➢ **Report even if:**
- You are not certain about the product which has caused adverse reaction.
- You do not have all the details, however, point nos. **1, 5, 7, 8, 11, 15, 16 & 18** (see reverse) are essentially required.

➢ **Who can report:**
- Any health care professional (Doctors including Dentists, Nurses and Pharmacists).

➢ **Where to report:**
- Please return the completed form to the nearest **Adverse drug reaction Monitoring Centre (AMC)** or to **National Co-ordinating Centre.**
- A list of nationwide AMCs is available at: http://ipc.nic.in and also at http://cdsco.nic.in/pharmacovigilance.htm

➢ **What happens to the submitted information:**
- Information provided in this form is handled in strict confidence. The causality assessment is carried out at Adverse Drug Reaction Monitoring Centres (AMCs) by using WHO-UMC scale. The analyzed forms are forwarded to the National Co-ordinating Centre through the ADR database. Finally, the data is analyzed and forwarded to the Global Pharmacovigilance Database managed by WHO Uppsala Monitoring Center in Sweden.
- The reports are periodically reviewed by the National Co-ordinating Centre (PvPI). The information generated on the basis of these reports helps in continuous assessment of the benefit-risk ratio of medicines.
- The information is submitted to the Steering Committee of PvPI constituted by the Ministry of Health and Family Welfare. The Committee is entrusted with the responsibility to review the data and suggest any interventions that may be required.

APPENDIX 4

	National Co-ordinating Centre (NCC)	
1.	Department of Pharmacology, All India Institute of Medical Sciences, New Delhi.	National Co-ordinator

	ADR Monitoring Centres (AMC)		
1.	Department of Pharmacology, Therapeutics & Toxicology, Govt. Medical College, Bakshi Nagar, Jammu.	2.	Department of Pharmacology, PGIMER, Chandigarh
3.	Department of Pharmacology, R. G. Kar Medical College, Kolkatta	4.	Department of Pharmacology, Lady Hardinge Medical College, New Delhi
5.	Department of Clinical Pharmacology, Seth G. S. Medical College & KEM Hospital, Parel, Mumbai	6.	Department of Clinical & Experimental Pharmacology, School of Tropical Medicine, Chittaranjan Avenue, Kolkata
7.	Department of Pharmacology, JIPMER, Pondicherry	8.	Department of Clinical Pharmacy, JSS Medical College Hospital, Karnataka
9.	Department of Pharmacology, Medical College, Guwahati. Assam	10.	Institute of Pharmacology, Madras Medical College, Chennai
11.	Department of Pharmacology, SAIMS Medical College, Indore, Ujjain	12.	Department of Pharmacology, GSVM Medical College, Swaroop Nagar, Kanpur, U.P.
13.	Department of Pharmacology, Pandit Bhagwat Dayal Sharma, Post Graduate Institute of Medical Sciences, Rohtak, Haryana.	14.	Department of Pharmacology, Dayanand Medical College and Hospital, Ludhiana, Punjab
15.	Department of Clinical Pharmacology, Sher-i-Kashmir Institute of Medical Sciences, Srinagar, J&K.	16.	Himalayan Institute of Medical Sciences, Dehradun, Uttrakhand
17.	Department of Pharmacology, Santosh Medical University, Santosh Nagar, Ghaziabad	18.	Department of Pharmacology, SMS Medical College, Jaipur
19.	Department of Clinical Pharmacology, Christian Medical College, Vellore, Tamil Nadu		

LIST OF ADR MONITORING CENTRES UNDER PHARMACOVIGILANCE PROGRAMME OF INDIA (PVPI) Phase 1

Sr. No.	AMC Address	Govt/ Non-Govt.	Co-ordinator's Name
	NORTH ZONE		
1.	All India Institute of Medical Sciences, New Delhi	G	National Co-ordinator Department of Pharmacology
2.	Lady Hardinge Medical College, New Delhi	G	Prof. and Head, Department of Pharmacology
3.	University College of Medical Sciences Dilshad Garden, New Delhi	G	Head, Department of Pharmacology
4.	Indraprastha Apollo Hospitals, New Delhi	NG	Clinical Pharmacologist, Apollo Phamacovigilance Centre, AHEL
5.	Medanta-The Medicity Sector-38, Gurgaon, Haryana -122 001	NG	Medical Director, Medanta Hospital
6.	Pandit Bhagwat Dayal Sharma, Post Graduate Institute of Medical Sciences, Rohtak, Haryana	G	Prof. and Head, Department of Pharmacology
7.	Santosh Medical University, Santosh Nagar, Ghaziabad	NG	Prof. and Head, Department of Pharmacology
8.	U.P. Rural Institute of Medical Sciences and Research, Safai, Etwah, U.P.	G	Prof. and Head, Department of Pharmacology
9.	GSVM Medical College, Swaroop Nagar, Kanpur, U.P.	G	Prof. and Head, Department of Pharmacology
10.	JN Medical College, Aligarh Muslim University, Aligarh-202002	G	Prof. and Head, Department of Pharmacology
11.	Institute of Medical Sciences, Banaras Hindu University Varanasi, U.P.	G	Prof. and Head, Department of Pharmacology
12	Dayanand Medical College and Hospital, Ludhiana, Punjab	G	Prof. and Head, Department of Pharmacology

contd. ...

Sr. No.	AMC Address	Govt/ Non-Govt.	Co-ordinator's Name
13.	PGIMER, Chandigarh	G	Prof. and Head, Department of Pharmacology
14.	SMS Medical College, Jaipur	G	Prof. and Head, Department of Pharmacology
15.	Himalayan Institute of Medical Sciences, Dehradun, Uttrakhand	NG	Prof. and Head, Department of Pharmacology
16.	Govt. Medical College, Haldwani, Uttarakhand	G	Prof. and Head, Department of Pharmacology
17.	Govt. Medical College, Bakshi Nagar, Jammu	G	Prof. and Head, Department of Pharmacology, Therapeutics & Toxicology
18.	Sher-i-Kashmir Institute of Medical Sciences, Srinagar, J&K	G	Prof. and Head, Department of Clinical Pharmacology
19.	Sardar Patel Medical College, Bikaner- 334001, Rajasthan	G	Senior Prof. & Head, Department of Pharmacology
20.	Vallabhbhai Patel Chest Institute, University of Delhi, New Delhi – 110 007	G	Head, Department of Pharmacology
21.	VMMC & Safdarjung Hospital, New Delhi – 110029	G	Prof. and Head, Department of Pharmacology
22.	M. L. N. Medical College, Near Company Bag, Allahabad-211001, U.P.	G	Prof. and Head, Department of Pharmacology
23.	M. L. B. Medical College, Jhansi, U.P.	G	Head, Department of Pharmacology
24.	B. R. D Medical College & Nehru Hospital, Gorokhpur – 273013, U.P.	G	Prof. & Head, Dept. of Pharmacology
25.	Govt. Medical College Patiala, Patiala-147001, Punjab	G	Prof. & Head, Department of Pharmacology, Government Medical College, Patiala

contd. ...

Sr. No.	AMC Address	Govt/ Non-Govt.	Co-ordinator's Name
26.	Veer Chandra Singh Garhwali Medical Science and Research Institute, Srinagar, Uttarakhand	G	Prof & Head, Department of Pharmacology
27.	Gandhi Medical College, Sulfania Road, Bhopal-462001, MP	G	Prof & Head, Department of Pharmacology
28.	Christian Medical College and Hospital, Brown Road, Ludhiana-141008, Punjab	NG	Prof. & Head, Department of Pharmacology
SOUTH ZONE			
29.	Nizam Institute of Medical Sciences, Hyderabad	G	Prof., Department of Pharmacology
30.	St. John's Medical College Benguluru , 560034	NG	Prof., Department of Pharmacology
31.	Bangalore Medical College and Research Institute, Benguluru	G	Prof. & Head, Department of Pharmacology
32.	Kasturba Medical College, Manipal, Karnataka	NG	Prof. & Head, Department of Pharmacology
33.	Vydehi Institute of Medical Sciences and Research Centre, Whitefield, Benguluru	G	Prof. & Head, Department of Pharmacology
34.	SDS Tuberculosis Research Centre & Rajiv Gandhi Institute of Chest Disease, Benguluru	G	Prof. & Head, Department of Pulmonology & Director
35.	JSS Medical College Hospital, Karnataka	NG	Prof. & Head, Department of Clinical Pharmacy
36.	Belgaum Institute of Medical Sciences, Belgaum, Karnataka	NG	Prof. & Head, Department of Pharmacology
37.	Department of Clinical Pharmacology, Christian Medical College, Vellore, Tamil Nadu	G	Prof. & Head, CMC

contd. ...

Sr. No.	AMC Address	Govt/ Non-Govt.	Co-ordinator's Name
38.	Institute of Pharmacology, Madras Medical College, Chennai	G	Prof. & Head, Department of Pharmacology
39.	Govt. Kilpauk Medical College, Chennai-600 010	G	Prof., Department of Pharmacology
40.	PSG Institute of Medical Sciences & Research, Coimbatore, Tamil Nadu	NG	Prof. & Head, Department of Pharmacology
41.	JIPMER, Pondicherry	G	Prof. & Head, Department of Pharmacology
42.	SRM Medical College Hospital & Research Centre, Kattankulathur, Chennai	NG	Prof. & Head, Department of Pharmacology
43.	Pushpagiri Institute of Medical Sciences and Research centre, Pushpagiri Medical College Hospital, Tiruvalla-689101, Kerala	NG	Prof. & Head, Department of Pharmacology
44.	Karnataka Institute of Medical Sciences Hubli-580022 Karnataka	G	Associate Professor, Department of Pharmacology
45.	Vijaynagar Institute of Medical Sciences, Bellary-583104, Karnataka	G	Prof. & Head, Professor of Pharmacology
46.	Mandya Institute of Medical Sciences (MIMS), District Hospital Campus, Mandya - 571401, Karnataka	G	Professor & Head Department of Pharmacology
47.	Govt. Medical College Kozhikode-673008, Kerala	G	Prof. & HOD Pharmacology
48.	Bidar Institute of Medical Sciences, Bidar, – 585401 Karnataka	G	Prof. & HOD Pharmacology

contd. ...

Sr. No.	AMC Address	Govt/ Non-Govt.	Co-ordinator's Name
49.	Andhra Medical College, King George Hospital (KGH), Visakhapatnam-530002, Andhra Pradesh	G	Prof & Head of Pharmacology
50.	Govt. Medical College, Kottayam-686008, Kerala	G	Prof. & HOD Pharmacology
51.	Indira Gandhi Medical College & Research Institute, Pondicerry, Vazhudavur Road, Kadirkamam Puducherry-605009	G	Prof of Pharmacology
52.	Guntur Medical College, Guntur-522004, Andhra Pradesh	G	Prof & HOD of Pharmacology Dr. Meena Kumari Prof, Dept. of Pharmacology
53.	Kakatiya Medical College, Warangal-506007 Andhra Pradesh	G	Professor, Dept. of Pharmacology
EAST ZONE			
54.	Rajendra Institute of Medical Sciences (RIMS), Ranchi	NG	Prof. & Head, Department of Pharmacology
55.	SCB Medical College and Hospital Cuttack, Odisha	G	Deputy Co-ordinator, Department of Pharmacology
56.	Department of Pharmacology VSS Medical College Burla, Odisha	G	Prof. & Head, Department of Pharmacology
57.	M. K. C. G Medical College, Berhampur, Orissa	G	Prof. & Head, Department of Pharmacology
58.	School of Tropical Medicine, Chittaranjan Avenue, Kolkata	G	Department of Clinical & Experimental Pharmacology
59.	R.G. Kar Medical College, Kolkatta	G	Prof. & Head, Department of Pharmacology
60.	Calcutta National Medical College, Kolkata	G	Prof. & Head, Department of Pharmacology
61.	Institute of Postgraduate Medical Education & Research, Kolkata	G	Prof. & Head, Department of Pharmacology
62.	Burdwan Medical College, Burdwan, West Bengal	G	Prof. & Head, Department of Pharmacology

contd. ...

Sr. No.	AMC Address	Govt/ Non-Govt.	Co-ordinator's Name
63.	Department of Pharmacology, Govt. Medical College, Guwahati, Assam	G	Prof. & Head, Department of Pharmacology
64.	Sikkim Manipal Institute of Medical Sciences 5th Mile, Tadong Gangtok - 737 102, Sikkim	G	Prof. & Head, Department of Pharmacology
65.	Agartala Govt. Medical College, Agartala Tripura-799006	G	Prof. & Head, Department of Pharmacology
66.	Bankura Sammilani Medical College, Bankura, West Bengal-722101	G	Professor and Head, Department of Pharmacology
67.	Tripura Medical College & Dr. BRAM Teaching Hospitals, Hapania, Agartala-799006, Tripura	G	Professor & Head, Department of Pharmacology
68.	Nilratan Sircar Medical College, Acharya Jagdish Chandra Bose Road, Kolkata - 700014, West Bengal	G	Prof. & Head, Department of Pharmacology
69.	Silchar Medical College & Hospital, Ghungoor, Silchar, Assam-788014	G	Associate Professor, Department of Pharmacology
70.	Indira Gandhi Institute of Medical Sciences, Shekhpura, Patna, Bihar-800014	G	Prof. & Head, Department of Pharmacology
	WEST ZONE		
71.	SAIMS Medical College, Indore - Ujjain	NG	Prof. & Head, Department of Pharmacology
72.	RD Gardi Medical College, Ujjain, MP	NG	Professor and Head, Department of Pharmacology
73.	Government Medical College, Bhavnagar	G	Prof. & Head, Department of Pharmacology
74.	SMT NHL Municipal Medical College, Ahmedabad, Gujarat	G	Prof. & Head, Department of Pharmacology

contd. ...

Sr. No.	AMC Address	Govt/ Non-Govt.	Co-ordinator's Name
75.	BJ Medical College, Ahmadabad	NG	Prof. & Head, Department of Pharmacology
76.	MGM Medical College and Hospital, Kalamboli, Navi Mumbai, Maharashtra	NG	Prof. & Head, Department of Pharmacology
77.	Grant medical college & Sir JJ Group of Hospital, Mumbai	G	Prof. & Head, Department of Pharmacology
78.	Seth GS Medical College & KEM Hospital, Parel, Mumbai	G	Prof. & Head, Department of Clinical Pharmacology
79.	Lokmanya Tilak Municipal Medical College & General Hospital, Mumbai	G	Prof. & Head, Department of Pharmacology
80.	BJ Medical College & Sassoon General Hospital, Pune	NG	Prof. & Head, Department of Pharmacology
81.	Indira Gandhi Government Medical College, Nagpur	G	Prof. & Head, Department of Pharmacology
82.	Mahatma Gandhi Institute of Medical Sciences, Nagpur	NG	Prof. & Head, Department of Pharmacology
83.	Swami Ramanand Teerth Rural Govt. Medical College, Ambajogai, Dist. Beed, Maharashtra-431517	G	Prof & Head, Department of Pharmacology
84.	Pd. Dr. D. Y. Patil Medical College, Pimpri, Pune-411 018	NG	Prof & Head, Department of Pharmacology
85.	Goa Medical College & Hospital, Bambolim	G	Prof. & Head, Department of Pharmacology
86.	PDU Medical College, Rajkot – 360001, Gujrat	G	Professor and Head, Department of Pharmacology
87.	Government Medical College & Hospital, Nagpur -440003, Maharashtra	G	Prof. of Dept. Pharmacology

contd. ...

88.	M.P. Shah Medical College, Jamnagar-361008, Gujrat	G	Prof. & Head, Dept. of Pharmacology
89.	TN Medical College & Byl Nair Hospital, Dr. AL Nair Road, Mumbai Central, Mumbai-400008	G	Prof. & Incharge, Dept. of Clinical Pharmacology
90.	Surat Municipal Institute of Medical Education & Research, Surat-395010, Gujrat	G	Prof. & Head Department of Pharmacology

- **South Zone** : 25 AMCs
- **North Zone** : 28 AMCs
- **West Zone** : 20 AMCs
- **East Zone** : 17 AMCs

■■■

The Erice Declaration on Communicating Drug Safety Information:

The following declaration was drawn up at the International Conference on Developing Effective Communications in Pharmacovigilance, Erice, Sicily, 24-27 September 1997.It was attended by health professionals, researchers, academics, media writers, representatives of the pharmaceutical industry, drug regulators, patients, lawyers, consumers and international health organizations.

Preamble:

Monitoring, evaluating and communicating drug safety is a public health activity with profound implications that depend on the integrity and collective responsibility of all parties — consumers, health professionals, researchers, academia, media, pharmaceutical industry, drug regulators, governments and international organizations — working together. High scientific, ethical and professional standards and amoral code should govern this activity. The inherent uncertainty of the risks and benefits of drugs needs to be acknowledged and explained. Decisions and actions that are based on this uncertainty should be informed by scientific and clinical considerations and should take into account social realities and circumstances.

Flaws in drug safety communication at all levels of society can lead to mistrust, misinformation and misguided actions resulting in harm and the creation of a climate where drug safety data may be hidden, withheld or ignored.

Fact should be distinguished from speculation and hypothesis, and actions taken should reflect the needs of those affected and the care they require. These actions call for systems and legislation, nationally and internationally, that ensure full and open exchange of information, and effective standards of evaluation. These standards will ensure that risks and benefits can be assessed, explained and acted upon openly and in a spirit that promotes general confidence and trust.

The following statements set forth the basic requirements for this to happen, and were agreed upon by all participants, from 30 countries at Erice:

1. Drug safety information must serve the health of the public. Such information should be ethically and effectively communicated in terms of both content and method. Facts, hypotheses and conclusions should be distinguished, uncertainty acknowledged, and information provided in ways that meet both general and individual needs.

2. Education in the appropriate use of drugs, including interpretation of safety information, is essential for the public at large, as well as for patients and health-care providers. Such education requires special commitment and resources. Drug information directed to the public in whatever form should be balanced with respect to risks and benefits.

3. All the evidence needed to assess and understand risks and benefits must be openly available. Constraints on communication parties, which hinder their ability to meet this goal, must be recognized and overcome.

4. Every country needs a system with independent expertise to ensure that safety information on all available drugs is adequately collected, impartially evaluated, and made accessible to all. Adequate non-partisan financing must be available to support the system. Exchange of data and evaluations among countries must be encouraged and supported.

5. A strong basis for drug safety monitoring has been laid over a long period, although sometimes in response to disasters. Innovation in this field now needs to ensure that emergent problems are promptly recognized and efficiently dealt with, and that information and solutions are effectively communicated.

These ideals are achievable and the participants at the conference commit themselves accordingly. Details of what might be done to give effect to this declaration have been considered at the conference and form the substance of the conference report.

■■■

Available Bibliographic Databases Suitable for Identifying Reports of Adverse Drug Reactions

Introduction

There is a wide variety of bibliographic databases suitable for identifying reports of adverse drug reactions. Perhaps the two most widely used general biomedical databases for this purpose are Medline and Embase. In addition, there are several more general biological and scientific databases such as SciSearch, Biosis, and the Derwent Drug File. SEDBASE is a specialist database derived from Meyler's Side Effect of Drugs, which specialises in drug reactions and interactions. There are also specialized databases which deal with specific disease areas (such as CancerLit and AidsLine), or with the toxicological effects of drugs (ToxLine). All these databases are available on major online hosts such as Dialog, and many are available in other formats such as CD-ROM or magnetic tape. Several are available for free searching on the World Wide Web.

Further details on the databases mentioned above are given below.

1. **Medline**

    Medline is a vast source of medical information, covering the whole field of medicine including dentistry, veterinary medicine and medical psychology. The database covers clinical medicine, anatomy, pharmacology, toxicology, genetics, microbiology, pathology, environmental health, occupational medicine, psychology, and biomedical technology etc. The database corresponds to the printed publications: Index Medicus, Indexto Dental Literature, International Nursing Index and various bibliographies. Over 3,900 journals from more than 70 countries are regularly indexed.

    Producer:

    National Library of Medicine (NLM),

    8600, Rockville Pike,

    Bethesda, Maryland 20894,

    USA.

    http://www.nlm.nih.gov/databases/medline.html

    It is available on most major online hosts such as Dialog, and in various CD-ROM and tape formats. It is also available in many manifestations on the World Wide Web, several of which are free to use. One of the best is the official NLM Internet version called PubMed at http://www.ncbi.nlm.nih.gov/PubMed/

2. **EMBASE**

EMBASE, the Excerpta Medica database, is a current and comprehensive pharmacological and biomedical database containing over 7.5 million documents from 1974 to date, with approximately 415,000 records added annually. It features unique international journal coverage and includes many important journals from Europe and Asia not found in other biomedical database; overall coverage is approximately 4,000 journals published in 70 countries. EMBASE covers the whole world's biomedical literature whilst concentrating in particular on European sources. The emphasis of the database is on the pharmacological effects of drugs and chemicals. Over 40% of current data are drug-related. Additional areas of coverage are human medicine and biological sciences relevant to human medicine, health affairs (occupational and environmental health, health economics, policy and management), drug and alcohol dependence, psychiatry, forensic science, pollution control, biotechnology, medical devices and alternative medicine.

Producer:

Elsevier Science B.V.

Secondary Publishing Division

Molenwerf 1

1014 AG Amsterdam

The Netherlands

http://www.elsevier.nl/inca/publications/store/5/2/3/3/2/8/index.htt

It is available on most major online hosts such as Dialog, and in various CD-ROM and tape formats.

3. **SciSearch**

SciSearcht: (Cited Reference Science Database) is an international, multi-disciplinary index to the literature of science, technology, biomedicine and related disciplines produced by the Institute for Scientific Information (ISI). It indexes all significant items (articles, review papers, meeting abstracts, letters, editorials, book reviews, correction notices etc.) from approximately 4,500 major scientific and technical journals. Some 3,800 of these journals are further indexed by the references cited within each article, allowing for citation searching. An additional 700 journals indexed have been drawn from ISI Current Contents series of publications.

Producer:

Institute for Scientific Information (ISI)

3501, Market Street,

Philadelphia, PA 19104.

http://www.isinet.com/products/citation/citsci.html

It is available on most major online hosts such as Dialog, and in various CD-ROM and tape formats. SciSearch is also available directly from ISI on the World Wide Web, where it is marketed as the Web of Sciencet.

4. **Biosis Previews**

BIOSIS Previews is the electronic format of the respected print publications, Biological Abstract and Biological Abstracts/RRMt (Reports, Reviews, Meetings). BIOSIS Previews supplies comprehensive coverage of international life science journal and meeting literature. BIOSIS Previews covers approximately 5,500 life science journals, 1,500 international meetings, as well as review articles, books and monographs.

Producer:

BIOSIS

2100, Arch Street,

Philadelphia, PA 19103-1399

http://www.biosis.org/htmls/common/bp.html

It is available on most major online hosts such as Dialog, and in various CD-ROM and tape formats.

5. **Derwent Drug File**

The Derwent Drug File (DDF) presents information on all aspects of drug research and usage. It selectively covers the worldwide pharmaceutical literature; papers chosen may cover the chemistry, analysis, pharmaceutics, pharmacology, metabolism, biochemistry, interactions, therapeutic effects and toxicity of a drug. Each document in DDF contains a detailed abstract written by a Derwent subject specialist and is accompanied by extensive drug oriented indexing allowing highly specific retrieval. Papers from over 1,150 scientific and medical journals and conference proceedings are included.

Producer:

Derwent Information Ltd.,

Derwent House,

14, Great Queen Street,

London, WC2B 5DF,

UK.

http://www.derwent.com/prodserv/pharm/drug_file.html

It is available on many major online hosts such as Dialog, and in CD-ROM and tape formats.

6. **SEDBASE**

SEDBASE — derived from Meyler's Side Effects of Drugs — contains synopses of relevant drug reactions and interactions. Each year approximately 9,000 articles on adverse drug reactions are published in the scientific literature. These are identified and collected for SEDBASE from over 3,500 journals published in 110 countries, using the resources of the Excerpta Medica database, EMBASE. All articles are sent to recognised authorities who critically assess the information and distil the key elements for inclusion. Speculative or unsubstantiated statements on the side effects of ethical drugs are not included.

Producer:

Elsevier Science B.V.

Secondary Publishing Division,

Molenwerf 1,

1014, AG Amsterdam,

The Netherlands.

http://www.elsevier.nl/

It is available on many major online hosts such as Dialog.

7. **CancerLit**

CANCERLITt is produced by the International Cancer Research Data Bank Branch (ICRDB) of the U.S. National Cancer Institute. The database consists of bibliographic records referencing cancer research publications dating from 1963 to the present. CANCERLIT includes indexing for articles from more than 3,500 journals; approximately 200 core journals contribute a large percentage of the citations. Selected records are taken from the MEDLINE database beginning in June 1983. In addition, proceedings of meetings, government reports, symposia reports, selected monographs, and theses are also abstracted for inclusion in the database.

Producer

CANCERLIT is produced by the U.S. National Cancer Institute (NCI):

http://cancernet.nci.nih.gov/nci.htm. Questions concerning file content should be directed to:

National Library of Medicine,

8600, Rockville Pike,

Bethesda, MD 20894.

http://www.nlm.nih.gov/

It is available on many major online hosts such as Dialog, and directly on the World Wide Web from the National Cancer Institute at http://cnetdb.nci.nih.gov/cancerlit.shtml

8. **AidsLine**

AIDSLINEt, produced by the U.S. National Library of Medicine (NLM), contains citations to literature covering research, clinical aspects, and health policy issues concerning AIDS (Acquired Immunodeficiency Syndrome). The citations are derived from Medline, CancerLit and HealthStar. In addition, the file includes the meeting abstracts from the International Conferences on AIDS, the Symposia on Non-human Primate Modes of AIDS, and AIDS-related abstracts from the Annual Meetings of the American Society of Microbiology.

Producer:

National Library of Medicine,

8600, Rockville Pike,

Bethesda, MD 20894.

http://www.nlm.nih.gov/

It is available on many major online hosts such as Dialog, and directly on the WorldWideWeb via Internet GratefulMed (IGM): http://igm.nlm.nih.gov/

9. **ToxLine**

TOXLINE covers the toxicological, pharmacological, biochemical and physiological effects of drugs and other chemicals. It is composed of a number of sub-files, several of which are unique to TOXLINE. TOXLINE includes primarily English-language items with international coverage of journal articles, monographs, technical reports, theses, letters, meeting abstracts, papers, reports, research project summaries, and unpublished material.

Producer:

National Library of Medicine,

8600, Rockville Pike,

Bethesda, MD 20894.

http://www.nlm.nih.gov/

It is available on many major online hosts such as Dialog, and directly on the World Wide Web via Internet Grateful Med (IGM).http://igm.nlm.nih.gov/

■■■

An Example of a Model Leaflet

For medicinal products available only with a prescription:

Read all of this leaflet carefully before you start taking/using this medicine.

- Keep this leaflet. You may need to read it again.
- If you have further questions, please ask your doctor or your pharmacist.
- This medicine has been prescribed for you personally and you should not pass it on to others. It may harm them, even if their symptoms are the same as yours.

For medicinal products available without a prescription:

Read all of this leaflet carefully because it contains important information for you.

This medicine is available without prescription, for you to treat a mild illness without a doctor's help. Nevertheless, You still need to use X carefully to get the best results from it.

- Keep this leaflet. You may need to read it again.
- Ask your pharmacist if you need more information or advice.
- You must see a doctor if your symptoms worsen or do not improve after ... days.

In this leaflet:

1. What X is and what it is used for.
2. Before you take/use X.
3. How to take/use X.
4. Possible side effects.
5. Storing X.

The (trade) name (referred to as X throughout this document) strength and pharmaceutical form of the medicinal product should be stated here.

- The active substance is
- Other ingredients ....

Marketing authorisation holder: 'ABC Ltd. at address...'

Manufacturer: 'DEF Ltd. at address..'

1. What X is and what it is used for

The following should be stated here in consumer understandable language:

- The pharmaceutical form and contents and the pharmaco therapeutic group or type of activity;
- The contents by weight, volume, number of doses, pack size;
- The therapeutic indications (e.g. 'lowers temperature, 'eases pain' etc.); If appropriate, specify that the medicinal product is for diagnostic use only.

2. Before you take/use X

Do not take/use X ...

- 'If you have a stomach ulcer (peptic ulcer) or used to have one.'

Contraindications should be stated here in consumer understandable language, including contraindications due to interactions with other medicines.

Take special care with X...

- 'If you have asthma (or used to), because X can bring on an attack.'

Precautions, special warnings and interactions with other medicines, should be stated here in consumer understandable language.

- 'If you are over 60/80....'
- 'If X is given to children....'
- 'X may make you feel sleepy'

'Please consult your doctor, even if these statements were applicable to you at any time in the past'.

Taking/using X with food and drink

Pregnancy

Ask your doctor or pharmacist for advice before taking any medicine.

Breast-feeding

Ask your doctor or pharmacist for advice before taking any medicine.

Driving and using machines:

- 'X may make you feel sleepy'
- 'Do not drive because X could stop you driving safely'
- 'Do not operate any tools or machines'

Important information about some of the ingredients of X

If appropriate, provide information on those excipients, knowledge of which is important for the safe and effective use of the medicinal product. Please refer to the Guideline on Excipients in the Label and Package Leaflet of Medicinal Products for Human Use.

Taking/using other medicines

'Please note that these statements may also apply to products used some time ago or at some time in the future'.

'Please inform your doctor or pharmacist if you are taking, or have recently taken, any other medicine - even those not prescribed.'

3. How to take/use X

The instructions for proper use and the dosage should be stated here, together with the route and method of administration.

'... one or two tablets (500 to 1000 mg of Paracetamol) three times a day, this means a daily maximum of six tablets (3000 mg of Paracetamol)'

'... in the morning, at lunchtime, immediately before meals, with food, after food'

'Do not swallow'

'Do not chew'

'Shake well before use'

'Dissolve the effervescent tablet in one glass of water. Then drink the whole contents of the glass'.

'Take the tablets with a sufficient quantity of liquid (e.g. one glass of water)'.

'Proceed as follows to obtain the solution you wish to take/use: Fill the bottle upto the mark (white line) with tap water. Shake the bottle until all of the dry powder is moist with water. Then the foam will settle. Refill the bottle up to the mark (white line) with tap water and shake it vigorously. You will obtain 100 ml of the ready-for-use solution'.

'Take X once a day, every day, at about the same time each day'.

'Taking your tablets at the same time each day will have the best effect on your blood pressure. It will also help you remember when to take the tablets.'

'Follow these instructions unless your doctor gave you different advice'.

'Remember to take your medicine'

'Your doctor will tell you how long your treatment with X will last. Do not stop treatment early because ...'.

If you have the impression that the effect of X is too strong or too weak, talk to your doctor or pharmacist.

If you take/use more X than you should:

If you may have taken/used more X than you should, talk to a doctor or pharmacist immediately.

If you forget to take X:

Do not take a double dose to make up for forgotten individual doses.

Effects when treatment with X is stopped:

4. Possible side effects

Begin this section with:- Like all medicines, X can have side effects.

Here is an example of side effects grouped according to seriousness:

'If any of the following happen, stop taking X and tell your doctor immediately or go to the casualty department at your nearest hospital':

- 'swelling of the hands, feet, ankles, face, lips, mouth, or throat which may cause difficulty in swallowing or breathing',
- 'hives',
- 'fainting',
- 'yellowing of the skin and eyes, also called jaundice'.

'These are all very serious side effects. If you have them, you may have had a serious allergic reaction to X. You may need urgent medical attention or hospitalisation'. 'All of these very serious side effects are very rare'.

'Tell your doctor immediately or go to the casualty department at your nearest hospital if you notice any of the following':

- 'chest pain',
- 'angina',
- 'changes in the way your heart beats, for example, if you notice it beating faster',
- 'difficulty breathing',
- 'signs of frequent infections such as fever or sore throat',
- 'less urine than is normal for you',

'These are all serious side effects. You may need urgent medical attention'.

'Serious side effects are rare'.

'Tell your doctor if you notice any of the following':

- 'nausea (feeling sick)',
- 'abdominal cramps or stomach pains',
- 'headache',
- 'dizziness',
- 'fatigue',
- 'light-headedness',
- 'dry cough',
- 'muscle cramps',
- 'flatulence or wind',
- 'diarrhoea',
- 'loss of appetite'.

'These are all mild, side effects of X'.

If the consumer needs to seek help urgently, use the term 'immediately'. For less urgent conditions use the phrase 'as soon as possible'.

Close this section with:- If you notice any side effects not mentioned in this leaflet, please inform your doctor or pharmacist.

5. Storing X

Keep X out of the reach and sight of children.

'Do not store above 25°C/30°C'

'Store at 2°C - 8°C (in a refrigerator)'

'Store in a freezer'

'Do not refrigerate/freeze'

'Store in the original package'

'Store in the original container'

'Keep the container in the outer carton'

'Keep the container tightly closed'

'There are no special storage instructions'

An additional short explanation of the storage statements, in consumer understandable language should be included when appropriate, e.g. 'in order to protect from light/moisture'.

Use by date: Do not use X after the expiry/use before date on the label/carton/bottle.

Where appropriate, there should be a warning about certain visible signs of deterioration.

'Do not use X if you notice …'

This leaflet was approved … Month and year when this leaflet was last approved.

■■■

Further Guidance on the Content of a Model Leaflet

    (i)   **The name of the product:** At the beginning of the leaflet, the (trade) name of the medicinal product (referred to as X throughout this document) should be stated in bold, together with the strength and pharmaceutical form. This should be followed by the INN or common name of the active substance (as stated on the label), which may be written on the line below. The statements of the active substance and of the excipients should be identified as such. The full qualitative composition of all the excipients should be given here.

    (ii)   **The marketing authorisation holder:** The marketing authorisation holder must be established.

    (iii)   **The manufacturer:** The manufacturer is as defined in appropriate legal documents, on behalf of whom the qualified person has performed the specific obligations laid down in regulatory document. The manufacturer is responsible for the release of each batch.

1. What X is and what it is used for

The pharmaceutical form and contents and the pharmaco-therapeutic group, or type of activity, should be stated here, in accordance with the SPC. The pharmaceutical form should be stated according to the European Pharmacopoeia Standard Terms. In addition, it may be necessary to explain the pharmaceutical form in consumer understandable language.

The contents should be stated here as weight, volume, number of doses, pack size. A physical description may be included e.g. shape, colour, texture, imprint.

The therapeutic indications should be stated here, using consumer understandable language.

2. Before you take/use X

This section should take into account the particular condition of certain categories of users, e.g. children, the elderly and special patient populations such as patients with renal or hepatic impairment. When specifying the age range; for children please refer to CPMP. Note for Guidance on Clinical Investigation of Medicinal Products in Children.

Do not take/use X ...

The information here should be strictly limited to real contraindications, including those due to interaction with other medicines. Other precautions and special warnings should be given in next section. Duplication of information is to be avoided.

Care must be taken to ensure that complex details are not omitted. It is not acceptable to state only the common or major contraindications. Belief that a patient cannot understand a contraindication is not a reason for omitting it.

Contraindications due to excipients should be mentioned in the guideline on the excipients in the label and package leaflet of medicinal products for human use.

Take special care with X ...

Information on precautions, special warnings and interactions, including those due to interaction with other medicines, should be provided here. Care must be taken to ensure that complex details are not omitted and that they are expressed in a way that consumers can understand. It is not acceptable to state only the common or major precautions. Belief that a patient cannot understand a precaution is not a reason for omitting it.

Specific guidelines on the formulation of certain specific warnings for certain categories of medicinal products may be elaborated in the future.

A precaution should be presented as implying the action a patient should take, rather than as factual information which describes a medical condition.

The influence of the drug on the patient's behaviour should be described. A differentiation should be made between the influence on cognitive abilities, reactivity and judgement.

Also describe in what cases (if any) the consumer should only use X after consultation with a physician.

Include, (as appropriate and if not mentioned in the previous section), reference to chronic accompanying diseases (renal insufficiency, liver insufficiency diabetes and other metabolic diseases).

Give the information on necessary checks which may be carried out by the physician prior to, or during, the therapy, for example tests carried out in order to exclude contra-indications.

Give information (if there is any) about important symptoms which may be masked by the product or if the product influences laboratory values. If relevant, reference should be made here to possibilities for intolerance to various materials (e.g. disposable plastic syringes) which must be used as part of this product.

Refer to the need for the avoidance of external influences, such as sunlight after the use of phytotoxic drugs. Other warnings concerning for example other diseases and the influence of the product on behaviour should be described. Statements should also include for example, reference to discolorations of underwear as a result of changes in the colour of urine and stool.

Taking/using X with food and drink

Interactions not related to medicinal products should be mentioned here. For example, patients should not consume milk in combination with tetracyclines and no alcohol should be consumed during treatment with benzodiazepines.

Important information about some of the ingredients of X

Information on intolerances to excipients should be indicated in guideline on the excipients in the label and package leaflet of medicinal products for human use.

Taking/using other medicines

Describe the effects of other products on the product in question and vice versa. Reference should be made to the intensification/weakening and the extension/shortening of effects.

3. How to take/use X

The instructions for proper use and the intended dosage ranges (individual and daily doses separately), as well as the maximum daily dose, the frequency, method, route of administration and the duration of treatment, should be stated if relevant.

The route of administration should be stated according to the European Pharmacopoeia Standard Terms. In addition, it may be necessary to explain the route of administration in consumer understandable language.

For products containing one active substance the number of dosage units should be stated first, followed directly by the quantity of the active constituent in brackets; e.g. 'one or two tablets (50 mg to 100 mg of 'active' - the name of the active ingredient should be given) twice daily, this means a daily maximum of four tablets (200 mg of 'active').

In addition, the times for administration should be stated (frequency of administration).

The text should be structured according to indication, age and sex, taking into account organic disorders.

Reference should also be made here to a dosage reduction in case of renal insufficiency and/or liver insufficiency.

Instructions should:
- be used to tell people what to do. They should not be used to justify or explain an action.
- be described in a practical way.
- tell consumers how to use a product properly.
- be positive rather than negative, whenever possible. Negative instructions should only be used when the consumer should avoid specific actions.
- be given as separate instructions when the consumer is to carry out two separate actions. Separate actions should not be compressed into a single sentence.
- be numbered and put into the exact order which the consumer should follow.
- usually be understandable without explanations, so as not to overburden consumers with information.

Explanations should be used to expand on the reasons for instructions and not to give further information. Instructions may be presented in bold type with explanations in plain type, so as to give consumers a guide as to the importance of the information.

Explanations should be placed immediately after the instructions when:

- an instruction is contrary to expected behaviour,
- the reasons for an instruction are not self-evident,
- an instruction can be made more memorable by using an explanation.

An instruction and its related explanation should be kept on the same side of the leaflet. Also, related groups of instructions and explanations should be on the same side of the leaflet.

When applicable, there should be descriptions (if useful with illustrations) of opening techniques for child-resistant containers and other containers to be opened in an unusual way.

Specific instructions for administration may be important, for example: Take the tablets with a sufficient quantity of liquid - one glass of water.

If appropriate, precise statements should be included on:

- the usual duration of the therapy;
- the maximum duration of the therapy;
- the intervals with no treatment;
- the cases in which the duration of treatment should be limited.

In particular and if at all possible, for products available without prescription, precise statements should be included on the usual duration of the therapy, the maximum duration of the therapy and intervals with no treatment, together with clear guidance on when to consult a doctor. For medicinal products available only with a prescription a statement such as the following should be included:

'your doctor will tell you how long your treatment with X will last. Do not stop treatment early because ...'.

If you take/use more X than you should:

Describe how to recognise if someone has taken an overdose and what to do.

If you forget to take X:

Make clear to consumers what they should/should not do if one or more doses have been missed.

Effects when treatment with X is stopped:

These should be described.

4. Possible side effects

The information given on undesirable/side effects should be in accordance with the SPC.

Side effects should be subdivided according to seriousness and frequency, or according to symptom type. Wherever possible, for all undesirable effects the frequency with which they occur is to be mentioned in the package leaflet to allow patients to know the risk. If exact data are available, numbers can be given in per cent. Within the different groups of frequency, undesirable effects should be listed in a decreasing order of seriousness if possible. Irrespective of their frequency, very serious, typical, undesirable effects of the product should be mentioned first or specially emphasised. This applies in particular to undesirable effects where there is an urgent need to take action.

The estimated frequency is currently subdivided:

- very common 10%+, (more than 1 per 10);
- common > 1% and < 10%, (less than 1 per 10 but more than 1 per 100);
- uncommon 0.1% to 1%, (less than 1 per 100 but more than 1 per 1000);
- rare 0.01% to 0.1%, (less than 1 per 1000);
- very rare upto 0.01%, (less than 1 per 10,000).

A structure based on organic systems is also possible.

Should there be undesirable effects that occur mostly at the beginning of the treatment and then subside or that only occur after prolonged treatment, these are to be mentioned here.

The measures to be taken to remedy or at least alleviate the undesirable effects should be mentioned here, if relevant. If the consumer needs to seek help urgently, use the term 'immediately'. For less urgent conditions use the phrase 'as soon as possible'. The consumer should be expressly invited to communicate any undesirable effect, especially if it is not mentioned in the leaflet, to a doctor or pharmacist.

5. Storing X

Please refer to Note for Guidance on Declaration of Storage Conditions for Medicinal Products in the Product Particulars.

In the case of products with reduced stability following reconstitution, or after the container has been opened, the maximum in-use shelf life should be stated together with the storage conditions. Please refer to Note for Guidance on Maximum Shelf Life for Sterile Products for Human Use after First Opening or Following Reconstitution".

Where appropriate, there should be a warning about certain visible signs of deterioration.

■■■

Haemovigilance Forms

Form No. 1
Whole Blood/Blood Component/Blood Product
(Compatibility Report)

(Name of hospital _____)

(To be retained in patient's file)

1.0 PATIENT DETAILS

DTM S. No. _____ Date _____

Name of Pt. _____

Age/Sex _____

C.R.No. _____

Blood Group _____ Rh _____

Hosp. _____ Wd _____ Bed _____

2.0 PRODUCT DETAILS

2.1 BLOOD/COMPONENTS

1. WB
2. PRBC
3. LPRBC
4. PC
5. PRP
6. FFP
7. Cyro Poor Plasma
8. Cryo Precipitate
9. Blood Product (Name) _____
    Batch No. _____ Manufacturer
    _____ Expiry _____

Bag No(s)   Date   Blood
Bank
1.
2.
3.
4.

Doctor

Form No. 2
Whole Blood/Blood Component/Blood Product
TRANSFUSION REACTION FORM
(Name of hospital _____)
(To be sent to Department of Transfusion Medicine after transfusion)

DTM S. No. _____ Date _____

Name of Patient _____

C.R. No. _____ Group _____ Rh _____

Hospital _____ Ward _____ Bed No. _____

Donor Unit

Blood Bag No(s).

1.

2.

3.

4.

BLOOD/COMPONENTS/PRODUCTS
1. WB
2. PRBC
3. LPRBC
4. PC
5. PRP
6. FFP
7. Cyro Poor Plasma
8. Cryo Precipitate
9. Blood Product (Name) _____
Batch No. _____
Expiry _____
Manufacturer _____

Transfusion started at _____ completed at ____.

Rate of Transfusion _____ drops per minute.

Actual quantity of blood transferred ____ (ml).

Clinical Observation:

General condition	Pre Transfusion	During Transfusion	Post Transfusion
Pulse			
Resp.			
Temp.			
B.P.			
Rigor			
Chills			
Myalgia			
Uiticaria			
Other Observation			

Doctor/Nurse

Note: In any case of transfusion reaction, inform the blood bank staff immediately. Send blood bag, transfusion set, post-transfusion sample (EDTA).

Transfusion Reaction Work-Up Form | Sr. No. |
(Name of the Hospital _____)

Name: _____   Hospital _____

CR No _____   Ward/Bed No. _____

Age. Sex: _____   Unit In-charge _____

Diagnosis: _____

Indication for Transfusion: _____

Clinical Status of Patient:

    Respiratory system: Renal:

    CVS: GIT:

    CNS: Liver:

    H/o Previous Transfusion Pregnancy, Transplantation:

    _____

    H/o Drug intake: _____

    _____

    Any otter infusion through. B.T. set: _____

    Reaction details: _____

    _____

    _____

    _____

    _____

    _____

Received:

Reaction from (duly filled): _____

Blood Bag/Bags along with transfusion set: _____

Post transfusion sample: _____

Date/time at which Blood/Blood component was transfused: _____

Date/time at which reaction occurred: _____

Date/time at which sample/reaction form were sent to blood bank: _____

Transfusion Reaction Work-Up Form | Sr. No. |

(Name of the Hospital _____)

Blood/Blood Component unit No.: _____

Amount of Blood/Blood Component transfused: _____

Investigation:

Identification of Patient:

Rechecking of Records:

Cross matchfile _____

Issue Register _____

Blood Group Register _____

Visual Examination of bag/transfusion set: _____

_____

Supernatant of Sample:

PreTx Sample: _____

PostTx Sample: _____

Bag Sample _____

Blood Group:

PreTx Sample: _____

PostTx Sample: _____

Bag Sample _____

Direct Coombs Test (DCT):

PostTx Sample: _____

PreTx Sample: _____

Repeat cross match of Blood Bag Sample with:

	Major (RT)	Major (37th) AHG phase	Minor (RT)
PreTx Sample			
PostTx Sample			

Transfusion Reaction Work-Up Form　　　| Sr. No. |

(Name of the Hospital _____)

Evidence of Hemolysis:

Plasma Haemoglobin: _____　Haemoglobin: Pre Tx _____

Serum Bilirubin: _____ Post Tx: _____

Urine Haemoglobin: _____

Urine Haemosidrin: _____

Coagulation status:

PTI: _____

Platelet count: _____

Blood Culture (Date/time at which culture was sent):

Blood Bag: _____

Patient: _____

Peripheral Blood smear (Patient sample/Blood Bag sample):

Leishman stain: _____

_____

Gram stain: _____

_____

Unstained smear: _____

Blood Bag Details

Type of Blood Bag: _____

Lot No.: _____　Date of collection: _____

Tube No.: _____　Date of Expiry: _____

Cross match details

Date of Cx-match: _____

Emergency/Routine: _____

Name of Technical Staff who cross matched the unit: _____

Date/time of Issue: _____

Interval between issue and transfusion: _____

Were was blood kept dining that interval: _____

Was blood warmed before transfusion, if yes; by what method: _____

Transfusion Reaction Work-Up Form

(Name of the Hospital _____)

Sr. No.

If Blood bag has been previously Cx-matched/issued:

Date of Cx Match	Date/time of Issue	Date of Receive Back

Donor Details:

Name: _____ Age/Sex: _____

Address: _____

Phone: _____

Date of Collection: _____ Place of Collection _____

Name of Phlebotomist/Assistant: _____

Type of Donor VD/RD _____

Any special investigation _____

_____

Inference:

_____

_____

_____

Signature of Consultant/Senior Resident   Signature of Junior Resident

■■■

Artemisin Combination Therapy

Pharmacovigilance of Antimalarial Medicines - Adverse Event Report Form - ACT Cohort Event Monitoring

Pre-treatment Questionnaire - Side A

Health facility: ....

1. **Patient Details:**

   First name: .... Family name: .... Patient Identification Number: ....

   Date of birth: ..../..../....   Age: ..... years; For children < 1 year:.....months

   Gender: Male □ Female □   Weight (kg): .... Height (cm): ....

   Pregnant: No □ Uncertain □ Yes □ if yes specify: 1st □ 2nd □ 3rd □ trimester

   Address: ....

   Nearest contact person for patient follow-up:..

2. **Signs and symptoms at presentation:**

   ....
   ....

3. **Malaria laboratory tests results (Blank row is for additional tests)**

Test	Date	Result	Test	Date	Result
Microscopy	... / ... / ...		Rapid Diagnostic Test	... / ... / ...	
Hb/Ht Level	... / ... / ...				

4. **Medicines taken during previous two weeks:**

Name of medicine	Indication	Dose & Frequency	Date started	Date stopped
			... / ... / ...	... / ... / ...
			... / ... / ...	... / ... / ...
			... / ... / ...	... / ... / ...

   4.1 Traditional herbal medicines taken during previous two weeks: No □ Yes □

5. **All clinical events in the last 5 days :**

Conditions	Date

6. **Present or past medical conditions :**

Conditions	Present	Past

7. **Medicines prescribed at this visit**

Name	Dose and Frequency	Date started	Expected completion
Act (specify brand)		... / ... / ...	... / ... / ...
		... / ... / ...	... / ... / ...
		... / ... / ...	... / ... / ...

8. **Date of planned follow-up visit in heath facility:** ... / ... / ...

9. **Reporter:**

    Name .... Signature .... Date ... / ... / ...

    Cell Phone number ....

Post treatment Questionnaire - Side B

10. **Type of follow-up**

    Attendance at health center / clinic   □   Date ... / ... / ...

    Visit at home   □   Date ... / ... / ...

    Other (specify) ....   Date ... / ... / ...

    Follow-up visit at home by: Name .... Signature ....

11. **All medicines taken at any time during ACT treatment (days 0-3)**

Name	Indication	Dose & frequency	Date started	Date stopped
Act (specify brand)			... / ... / ...	... / ... / ...
			... / ... / ...	... / ... / ...
			... / ... / ...	... / ... / ...

12. **Outcomes noted at post-treatment visit**

Outcome	Tick	Outcome	Tick
Adhered to complete treatment		Incomplete adherence to treatment	
Improvement of clinical condition		Deterioration of clinical condition	
No change in clinical condition		New clinical event	
No referral to health center/ hospital		Referral to health center/hospital	
Lost to follow-up		Reasons for referral:	

13. **In case of incomplete adherence to ACT treatment**

Record reasons given by patient or caretaker for not completing treatment as prescribed.

14. **Describe new events or worsening problems after starting ACT treatment**

Description of event	Date event started	Date event stopped	Suspect Medicine	Outcome * (A, B, C etc.)
1.	... / ... / ...	... / ... / ...		
2.	... / ... / ...	... / ... / ...		
3.	... / ... / ...	... / ... / ...		
* Outcome A - recovered B - improved C - unchanged D - life threatening E - caused or prolonged hospitalization F - persistent incapacity or disability G - death (... / ... / ...) O - Other (describe)				

15. **Abnormal laboratory tests results after starting ACT treatment**

Test	Date	Result	Test	Date	Result
	... / ... / ...			... / ... / ...	

16. **Reporter:**

Name ....   Signature ....   Date ... / ... / ...

Mobile phone number ....

PLEASE SEND THIS FORM TO:

....

....

The report should be sent immediately if the outcome of the adverse event is: death, life-threatening, persistent incapacity or disability, caused or prolonged hospitalization.

Please note: Completion of this form is not an admission of causation by, or contribution to, the suspected adverse event by the suspected medicine(s) or by the reporting professionals. This information will be analysed and will contribute to promoting the safe use of antimalarials.

Coding sheet - Sample from the IMMP (Intensive Medicines Monitoring Program)

Name   Source   Report No.

Monitored Medicine

Dose   Indication

Event		Sev	Rel	Pnt	Duration	
					Onset	Event
1						
2						
3						
4						
5						

Outcome

A   Recovered without seq

B   Recovered with seq

F   Not yet recovered

D   Died - due to AR

C   Died - med may be contributory

N   Died - unrelated to mud

O   Died - cause unknown

U   Unknown

Seriousness ☐

Category ☐ ☐ ☐ ☐ ☐

Dechallenge

1   Definite improvement

2   No improvement

3   Med continued

4   Unknown

Rechallenge

1   Recurrence

2   No recurrence

3   No rechallenge

4.   Unknown

Dose Reduced ☐   **Withdrawn** ☐   **Died** ☐

Abbreviations:

Sev = severity

Rel = relationship

Pnt = print-code

'Category' refers to the major Clinical Category in which the event should be classified.

Antiretroviral therapy : Cohort Event Monitoring
Baseline Questionnaire

Treatment centre/Clinic: .... **Contact person:** ....

A.   **Patient:** Name: .... Clinic number ....

                 Contact details: ....

                 Date of birth: ... / ... / ...   Sex: Male ☐   Female ☐

                 Weight: ....   Height: ....

B.   **HIV/AIDS:** Stage at first screening* ....

C.   **Current medicines**

D.   **Laboratory Tests** *(Blank row is for other tests)*

Test	Date	Result	Test	Date	Result
CD4 count			Cholesterol		
Viral load			Triglyceride		
ALT			Glucose		
FBC					

E.   **Current conditions** (background morbidity) *(Blank spaces for "other")*

Problem	Tick	Problem	Tick	Problem	Tick
Malnutrition		Depression		Heart disease	
Anaemia		Tuberculosis		Hepatomegaly	
Alcohol abuse		Renal disease		Splenomegaly	
Substance abuse		Liver disease		Significant bacterial infection	

F.   **Past conditions of significance** *(Might include some of above problems, but not currently present)*

Date	Event(s)

Continue on other side of form if necessary

(PLEASE SEND THIS FORM TO: ....)

Recorder: Name .... Signature: .... Date ... / ... / ...

Pre-treatment Questionnaire

Treatment centre/Clinic: .... **Contact person:** ....

A.   **Patient:**   Name: .... Clinic number: ....

                  Contact details: ....

                  Date of birth: ... / ... / ...   Sex: Male ☐   Female ☐

B.   **HIV/AIDS:** Stage at current reivew ....

C.   **Medicines**

ARV medicines	Daily dose	Date begun	Date stopped
1.			
2.			
3.			
4.			
Reason(s) for stopping ARV medicines Poor compliance ☐; lost to follow-up ☐; death ☐ (given date and cause below in Section E); Suspected adverse reaction ☐ (describe in E); lack of effect ☐; other ☐ (describe) Comment on efficacy:			
Other medicines (in review period)			

D.   **Laboratory Tests** *(Blank row is for other tests)*

Test	Date	Result	Test	Date	Result
CD4 count			Cholesterol		
Viral load			Triglyceride		
ALT			Glucose		
FBC					

E.   **Any new events or worsening problems over the period since last seen**

Date	Event(s)

Continue on other side of form if necessary

G.   **Has the patient become pregnant?** Yes ☐   No ☐   If yes, complete pregnancy questionnaire

       PLEASE SEND THIS FORM TO: ....

       Recorder: Name .... Signature: .... Date ... / ... / ...

Pregnancy Questionnaire

Treatment centre/Clinic: .... **Contact person:** ....

A. **Women's details:**

Name: .... Clinic number ....

Contact details: ....

Date of birth: ... / ... / ...

B. **Stage of pregnancy at exposure**

LMP if known: ... / ... / ... Estimated weeks of pregnancy at current examination: .... weeks.

At what stage was she exposed to the antiretrovirals? (Tick all if applicable, or as many as necessary).

1st trimester □; 2nd trimester □; 3rd trimester □; at term □

Was she on treatment when she became pregnant?   Yes □; No □

Was treatment withdrawn when pregnancy was diagnosed?   Yes □; No □

Date of withdrawal ... / ... / ...

C. **Outcome of pregnancy**

Date of birth □;   Not yet born □

1. Abnormalities of pregnancy: None □   Don't know □   Miscarriage □

Date : ... / ... / ...   Therapeutic abortion □

Date	Description

2. Abnormalities of labour (describe)   None □   Don't know □

3. Abnormalities of fetus or infant   Don't know □   Fetal death □   Date ... / ... / ...

None identified at birth □; None identified at 3 months □;

None identified at 1 year □

Date identified	Description of any abnormalities

D. **Breastfeeding**

1. Did the mother breastfeed the infant while on treatment? Yes □; No □; Don't know □

2. If yes, when was the baby first exposed with the mother on treatment? From birth □; From age ....; Don't know □

3. Was there any effect on the infant? Yes □; No □; Don't known □

4. If yes, please describe:

PLEASE SEND THIS FORM TO : ...

Recorder: Name .... Signature: .... Date ... / ... / ...

Adverse Event Form for
Anti-Retroviral Medicines.

Please complete as much as possible, regardless of any missing details

PATIENT DETAILS

Folder Number:		Patient initials:		Sex: [M] [F]

Residential Address:
District

Town/City:
Region:

Date of birth /___/	Age: years months	Weight (kg):

Type of Treatment   ❑ HAART   ❑ PMTCT   ❑ PEP

DRUG DETAILS

	Drug 1	Drug 2	Drug 3	Drug 4
1st Line Drugs	Combivir / Nevirapine Dose: Date Started: ___/___/___	Combivir / Efavirenz Dose: Date Started: ___/___/___	Stavudine / Lamivudine /Nevirapine Dose: Date Started: ___/___/___	Stavudine / Lamivudine /Efavirenz Dose: Date Started: ___/___/___
2nd Line Drugs	Abacavir/ Didanosine/ Nelfinavir Dose: Date Started: ___/___/___	Abacavir/ Didanosine/ Kaletra Dose: Date Started: ___/___/___		
CONCOMITANT DRUG	Co-trimoxazole prophylaxis Dose: Date Started: ___/___/___	Drug: Dose: Date Started: ___/___/___	Drug: Dose: Date Started: ___/___/___	Drug: Dose: Date Started: ___/___/___

DETAILS OF ADVERSE EVENT

Date event started:____/____/____   Date event stopped:____/____/____

Adverse reaction observed (*please tick all that apply*)
❑Vomiting   ❑Nausea   ❑Itching   ❑Skin rashes   ❑Diarrhoea   ❑Headache   ❑Mouth sores   ❑Abdominal pains
❑Dizziness   ❑Insomnia   ❑Dark-coloured urine   ❑Other (please specify):

Description of event (*Continue on back page if necessary*):

Treatment or action taken (*Continue on back page if necessary*):

Outcome (please tick all that apply)
❑Change of therapy   ❑ Recovered without change of therapy   ❑Death
❑Required / prolonged hospitalisation   ❑Ongoing   ❑ Other outcome (please specify)

REPORTER DETAILS

Profession	❑Doctor ❑Pharmacist ❑Nurse ❑Other (please specify)	
Last Name:	Other Name(s):	Title
Address:	Tel No. Email:	
Signature	Date:	

This SOP is illustrative only.

Direct Health Care Professional Communication on the association of interferon-Beta with the risk of Thrombotic Microangiopathy and nephrotic syndrome

Dear Healthcare Professional,

This letter has been distributed by "Marketing Authorization Holders (MAHs) for products containing Interferon-Beta" to inform you of important safety information regarding interferon beta products used in the treatment of multiple sclerosis.

Summary

- Cases of thrombotic microangiopathy (TMA) including fatal cases have been reported during treatment of multiple sclerosis with interferon beta products. Most TMA cases presented as thrombotic thrombocytopenic purpura or haemolytic uraemic syndrome.

- Cases of nephrotic syndrome with different underlying nephropathies have also been reported.

- Both TMA and nephrotic syndrome may develop several weeks to several years after starting treatment with interferon beta.

- Be vigilant for the development of these conditions and manage them promptly if they occur, in line with the advice below.

Advice regarding TMA:

- Clinical features of TMA include thrombocytopenia, new onset hypertension, fever, central nervous system symptoms (e.g. confusion and paresis) and impaired renal function. If you observe clinical features of TMA, test blood platelet levels, serum lactate dehydrogenase levels and renal function. Also test for red blood cell fragments on a blood film.

- If TMA is diagnosed, prompt treatment (considering plasma exchange) is required and immediate discontinuation of interferon beta is recommended.

Advice regarding nephrotic syndrome:

Monitor renal function periodically and be vigilant for early signs or symptoms of nephritic syndrome such as edema, proteinuria and impaired renal function especially in patients at high risk of renal disease. If nephrotic syndrome occurs, treat promptly and consider stopping treatment with interferon beta.

Further information

This communication follows a review by European drug regulatory agencies after reports of TMA and nephrotic syndrome were received in association with use of interferon beta products for the treatment of multiple sclerosis. The review could not rule out a causal association between interferon beta products and nephrotic syndrome or between interferon beta products and TMA.

More information on the conditions:

TMA is a serious condition characterized by occlusive microvascular thrombosis and secondary haemolysis. Early clinical features include thrombocytopenia, new onset hypertension and impaired renal function. Laboratory findings suggestive of TMA include decreased platelet counts, increased serum lactate dehydrogenase (LDH) and schistocytes (erythrocyte fragmentation) on a blood film.

Nephrotic syndrome is a nonspecific kidney disorder characterized by proteinuria, impaired renal function and edema.

The following interferon beta products are authorized for the treatment of multiple sclerosis:

- Avonex® (interferon beta-1a) - Biogen Idec Ltd
- Rebif® (interferon beta 1a) - Merck Serono Europe Ltd
- Betaferon® (interferon beta-1b) - Bayer Pharma AG

■■■

Standard Operating Procedure for Creating and Maintaining and Investigator's Brochure (IB) for Development Products

SOP ID Number :	Effective Date :
Version Number & Date of Authorisation :	Review Date :
eDocument Kept:	

Revision Chronology:

SOP ID Number :	Effective Date :	Reason for Change :	Author :

Acronyms:

ATIMP	Advanced Therapy Investigational Medicinal Products
CI	Chief Investigator
CTC	Cancer Research UK and UCL Cancer Trials Centre (UCL affiliated Clinical Trials Unit)
GCP	Good Clinical Practice
IB	Investigator's Brochure
ICH	International Conference of Harmonisation of Technical Requirements for Registration of Pharmaceuticals for Human Use
IMP	Investigational Medicinal Product
IP	Intellectual Property
JRO	Joint Research Office
SOP	Standard Operating Procedure
TMF	Trial Master File
UCL	University College London

Standard Operating Procedure for Creating and Maintaining and Investigator's Brochure

1. PURPOSE

This Standard Operating Procedure (SOP) describes the purpose, minimum content, creation and maintenance of an Investigator's Brochure (IB) for the products used in clinical trials of Investigational Medicinal Products and managed by the Joint Research Office (JRO) or by an affiliated Clinical Trials Unit.

2. JOINT RESEARCH OFFICE POLICY

All Joint Research Office (JRO) SOPs will be produced, reviewed and approved in accordance with the JRO SOP on SOPs.

The JRO acts as the representative of the Sponsor and will be the official name used on all SOPs.

3. BACKGROUND

All SOPs are written in accordance with applicable GCP requirements as outlined in Directives 2001/20/EC and 2005/28/EC (in the UK, these Directives were transposed into UK law by SI 2004/1031, SI 2006/1928) and subsequent amendments and where applicable incorporates elements of ICH GCP tripartite guidelines (E6).

The IB is a compilation of the clinical and non-clinical data on the Investigational Medicinal Products IMP(s) that are relevant to the study of the product(s) in human subjects as per Section 7.1 of ICH E6. The requirement for an IB is implemented into law through Article 2(g) of Directive 2001/20/EC and Article 8 of Directive 2005/28/EC in the European Union and Regulation 2 of SI 2004/1031 in the UK.

The Amended Regulations (SI 2006/1928) state that the Sponsor of a clinical trial is responsible for the IB and shall ensure that the trial IB presents the information it contains in a concise, simple, objective, balanced and non-promotional form that enables a clinician or potential investigator to understand it and make an unbiased risk-benefit assessment of the appropriateness of the proposed clinical trial; and shall validate and update the IB at least once a year.

The IB provides the investigators and others involved in the trial with the information to facilitate their understanding of the rationale for and their compliance with many key features of the protocol, such as the dose, dose frequency/interval, methods of administration and safety monitoring procedures. The IB also provides insight to support the clinical management of the study subjects during the course of the clinical trial.

The Detailed Guidance on the collection, verification and presentation of adverse event/reaction reports arising from clinical trials on medicinal products for human use (CT-3) declares that the IB contains the Reference Safety Information (RSI) for the IMP against which the expectedness of an adverse reaction is determined.

4. SCOPE OF THIS SOP

This SOP relates to products that don't have a Marketing Authorisation and are used as IMPs in trials.

This SOP does not apply where another organisation is responsible for creating and maintaining the IB.

5. RESPONSIBLE PERSONNEL

	Responsibility	Undertaken by	Procedure
5.1	Sponsor	JRO Clinical Operations Manager or CTC Tumour Group Lead (TGL)	Assigning a responsible individual to ensure oversight of creation, regulatory approval and on-going maintenance of the IB, such as for example a JRO Sponsor Regulatory Advisor or CTC Trial Coordinator.
5.2	Responsible individual	Chief Investigator (CI)	Creating and maintaining IB as per regulatory requirements and SOP. Reviewing the IB at least annually to ensure the clinical and non-clinical content of the IB is up-to-date and appropriate for the IMP in question.
5.3	Sponsor	Responsible individual	Coordinating internal reviews and sign off of the IB. Submitting the IB for regulatory approval as per applicable JRO/CTC SOP for approvals (Associated SOP 1) Distribution of the approved IB to applicable parties as per local procedures, such as to the CI or directly to the trial sites.

6. PROCEDURE

6.1	Content of the IB
6.1.1	Refer to ICH GCP E6 (R1), section 7, for guidance on the minimum information that should be included in an IB and suggestions for its layout. See also **Associated Document 1** for guidance on information that should be included on the title page of an IB and for a suggested Table of Contents.

contd. …

6.1.2	In addition, for CTMPs with Advanced Therapy Investigational Medicinal Products (ATIMPs) the following should be considered in relation to the content of the IB (as per European Commission Detailed guidelines on good clinical practice specific to advanced therapy medicinal products):
	(a) A description of the scope and sufficiency of existing information and its limitations;
	(b) Information obtained from on-going risk analysis based on existing knowledge of the type of product and its intended use including risk associated with the application method (e.g. surgery, concomitant medication, associated devices);
	(c) Information on the risk management plan (for marketed products);
	(d) Information on the risks due to product failure;
	(e) Information on the product safety handling, containment and disposal;
	(f) Information on short and long term safety issues particular to ATIMPs such as infections, immunogenicity/immunosuppression and malignant transformation as well as those related to medical devices for combined ATIMPs.
6.2	**Finalisation of IB**

	Responsibility	**Undertaken by**	**Procedure**
	Sponsor	CI	Creating and finalizing the IB
6.2.1	Sponsor	Responsible individual	Reviewing the IB to ensure inclusion of the required sections.
6.2.2	Responsible individual	JRO/CTC Pharmacovigilance Manager/Coordinator	Evidenced review of safety section of IB to ensure it contains expected side effects and is appropriate with regards to SUSAR evaluation and DSUR line listing evaluation. Acknowledgement, communication and filing of review as per local JRO/CTC procedures.
6.2.3	Responsible individual	Regulatory Manager for Advanced Therapy Trials	Evidenced review of IB for CTMPs with ATIMP to ensure the additional information has been appropriately addressed. Acknowledgement, communication and filing of review as per local JRO/CTC procedures.

contd. ...

6.2.4	Sponsor	Responsible individual (as per 5.1)	Submission of IB for Regulatory approval for use within the trial as per applicable JRO/CTC SOP for approvals (Associated SOP 1). Filing and distribution of the approved IB to applicable parties as per local procedures, such as to the CI or directly to the trial sites.
6.3	**Updates to IB**		
	Responsibility	**Undertaken by**	**Procedure**
6.3.1	Responsible individual	Chief Investigator	Annual review, and if applicable, revision of IB using Associated Document 2 to evidence review. More frequent revision may be appropriate depending on the stage of development and the generation of relevant new information. However, in accordance with Good Clinical Practice, relevant new information may be so important that it should be communicated to the investigators, and possibly the Ethics Committee(s) and/or Regulatory Authority/ies before it is included in a revised IB. The timing of the annual review may be in line with the development International Birth Date (DIBD) of the IMP development safety update reports (DSURs), since the IB is submitted to the MHRA as an Appendix alongside the DSUR. The new version of the IB must contain a revision history indicating the changes that were made to the document.
6.3.2	Responsible individual	Pharmacovigilance Manager/Coordinator	Review of revised and amended safety sections of the IB before release of new version. Acknowledgement, communication and filing of review as per local JRO/CTC procedures.

contd. ...

	Responsible individual	Regulatory Manager for Advance Therapy Trials	For CTIMPS with ATIMP review of revised and amended IB before release of new version. Acknowledgement, communication and filing of review as per local JRO/CTC procedures.
6.3.4	Sponsor	Responsible individual	Submission of the revised and amended IB for regulatory approval, as required. For further guidance see applicable JRO/CTC SOP for submissions of amendments (Associated SOP 2). Filing of the revised and amended IB in the Trial Master File (TMF) (and for CTIMP managed by JRO CTIMPs team, also in the Sponsor Trial File). Filing of the completed and signed Associated Document 2 as well as other, internal, evidence of reviews in the TMF (and for CTIMP managed by JRO CTIMPs team, also in the Sponsor Trial File). Distribution of the newly approved version IB to applicable parties as per local, such as CI or directly to the trial sites.

7. ASSOCIATED SOPs

Associated SOPs: JRO/CTC/CTU referenced SOPs for Regulatory Approvals

JRO	JRO/SPON/S29/ Standard Operating Procedure for Obtaining Research Ethics Committee and Clinical Trial Authorisation Approvals for Clinical Trials of Investigational Medicinal Products
CTC	CTC/10/T67/01 Standard Operating Procedure for Obtaining Permissions and Approvals for Clinical Trials

Associated SOP 2: JRO/CTC/CTU referenced SOPs for Amendments

JRO	RO/SPON/S13/03 Standard Operating Procedure for the classification, review and submissions of clinical trial amendments
CTC	CTC/12/T71/01 Standard Operating Procedure for Submitting, Processing and Disseminating Amendments

8. ASSOCITATED DOCUMENTS TO THIS SOP

Associated Document 1:	Guidance on information that should be included on the title page of an IB and a recommended Table of Contents for an IB.
Associated Document 2:	Template letter evidencing IB review by the CI.

9. SOP DISSEMINATION AND TRAINING

SOPs will be distributed to the relevant staff, by the named author on the front page of the SOP. Staff will sign the SOP training log (11. SOP Training Log) which is part of each SOP. The training will constitute of the person reading the SOP and being provided with the opportunity to ask specific questions to the author of the SOP.

At CTC

Where JRO SOPs are in use in the CTC, preparation and use will follow Sponsor requirements. Release of JRO SOPs at CTC will be carried out as per local CTC procedures.

10. SIGNATURE PAGE

Author and Job Title:	
Signature :	
Date :	

Authorised by: Name and Job Title	
Signature :	
Date :	

11. SOP TRAINING LOG

Sr. No.	Name of Staff (Capital Letters)	Job Title: Department:	Training Date	I confirm that I understand and agree to work to this SOP SIGNATURE	Name of Trainer (if training required)	Signature	Date
1.							
2.							
3.							

GLOSSARY

A-CASI	:	Audio Computer-Assisted Self-Interviewing
ACEI	:	Angiotensin Convertase Enzyme Inhibitor
ACK	:	Acknowledgement
ADR	:	Adverse Drug Reaction (preferred term: Adverse reaction)
ADROIT	:	Adverse Drug Reaction On-line Information Tracking
AE	:	Adverse Event
AEFI	:	Adverse Event Following Immunisation
AERS	:	Adverse Event Reporting System (USA)
AESI	:	Adverse Event of Special Interest
AIIMS	:	All India Institute of Medical Sciences
AMCs	:	ADR Monitoring Centers
AR	:	Assessment Report
Art	:	Article
ATCC	:	Anatomical, Therapeutic, Chemical Classification
ATMP	:	Advanced Therapy Medicinal Product
BAN	:	British Approved Name
BCPNN	:	Bayesian Confidence Propagation Neural Network
BvP	:	Biovigilance Program of India
CAP	:	Centrally Authorised Medicinal Product
CBC	:	Complete Blood Count
CCDS	:	Company Core Data Sheet
CCSI	:	Company Core Safety Information
CDC	:	Centers for Disease Control and Prevention (USA)
CDSCO	:	Central Drugs Standard Control Organisation
CEM	:	Cohort Event Monitoring
CHMP	:	Committee for Medicinal Products for Human Use (at the European Medicines Agency)
CIOMS	:	Council for International Organizations of Medical Sciences
CMDh	:	Coordination Group for Mutual Recognition and Decentralised Procedures – Human (at the European Medicines Agency)
COSO	:	Committee of Sponsoring Organizations of the Treadway Commission
CoSTART	:	Coding Symbols for a Thesarus of Adverse Reaction Terms

CRO	:	Contract Research Organization
CTCAE	:	Common Terminology Criteria for Adverse Events
CV	:	Curricular Vitae
DB	:	Database
DCF	:	Denominations Communes Francaises
DCSI	:	Development Core Safety Information
DDPS	:	Detailed Description of the Pharmacovigilance System
DHCP	:	Dear Health-Care Provider
DHPC	:	Direct Healthcare Professional Communication
DIBD	:	Development International Birth Date
DIR	:	Directive 2001/83/EC of the European Parliament and of the Council of 6 November 2001 on the Community code relating to medicinal products for human use as amended
DLP	:	Data Lock Point
DP	:	Decentralised Authorisation Procedure
DPA	:	Disproportionality Analysis
DRESS	:	Drug Rush with Eosinophelia and Systemic Symptoms
DSC	:	Drug Safety Communication
DSMB	:	Data and Safety Monitoring Board
DSUR	:	Development Safety Update Report
DUS	:	Drug Utilisation Study
EBGMs	:	Empirical Bayesian Geometrical Means
EC	:	European Commission
ECDC	:	European Centre for Disease Prevention and Control
ECG	:	Electrocardiogram
eCTD	:	Electronic Common Technical Document
EDTA	:	Ethylene Diamine Tetra Acetate
EEA	:	European Economic Area
EMEA	:	European Medicines Agency

ENCePP	:	European Network of Centres for Pharmacoepidemiology and Pharmacovigilance
ENS	:	Early Notification System
EPAR	:	European Public Assessment Report
EPITT	:	European Pharmacovigilance Issues Tracking Tool
EPPV	:	Early Post-marketing Phase Vigilance (e.g. in Japan)
ePSUR	:	Periodic Safety Update Report in Structured Electronic Format
ERMS FG	:	European Risk Management Strategy Facilitation Group (of the Heads of Medicines Agencies)
ESoP	:	European Society of Pharmacovigilance
ESTRI	:	ICH Electronic Standards for the Transfer of Regulatory Information
EU	:	European Union
EURD	:	EU Reference Date
EV	:	EudraVigilance
EVCTM	:	EudraVigilance Clinical Trial Module
EVDAS	:	EudraVigilance Data Analysis System
EVMPD	:	EudraVigilance Medicinal Product Dictionary
EVPM	:	EudraVigilance Post-Authorisation Module
EVWEB	:	Eudravigilance Web
FDA	:	Food and Drug Administration
FDR	:	False Discovery Rate
GAP	:	Good Agricultural Practices
GCP	:	Good Clinical Practice
GDP	:	Good Distribution Practice
GLP	:	Good Laboratory Practice
GMP	:	Good Manufacturing Practice
GPP	:	ISPE Guidelines for Good Pharmacoepidemiology Practices
GVP	:	Good Pharmacovigilance Practices (for the European Union)
HAC	:	Haemovigilance Advisory Committee
HLA	:	Human Leuckocyte Antigen
HLGT	:	High Level Group Terms

HLT	:	High Level Term (in MedDRA)
HMA	:	Heads of Medicines Agencies
IB	:	Information Brouchure
IBD	:	International Birth Date
ICD	:	International Classification of Diseases
ICD-10	:	International Classification of Mental and Behavioural Disorders
ICD-DA	:	International Classification of Diseases to Dentistry
ICD-NA	:	International Classification of Diseases to Neurology
ICD-O	:	International Classification of Diseases for Oncology
ICecI	:	International Classification of External Causes of Injury
ICF	:	International Classification of Functioning
ICF-CY	:	International Classification of Functions - Version for Children & Youth
ICH	:	International Council on Harmonization (earlier International Conference on Harmonization)
ICHI	:	International Classification of Health Interventions
ICPC	:	International Classification of Primary Care
ICSR	:	Individual Case Safety Report
IDMC	:	Independent Data-Monitoring Committee
IEC	:	Independent Ethics Committee
IFPMA	:	International Federation of Pharmaceutical Manufacturers and Associations
IHN	:	International Haemovigilance Network
IIA	:	Chartered Institute of Internal Auditors
IME	:	Important Medical Event
IMPs	:	Investigational Medicinal Products
INN	:	International Non-proprietary Name
IPC	:	Indian Pharmacopeia Commission
IPC	:	Indian Pharmacopoeia Commission
IR	:	Commission Implementing Regulation (EU) No. 520/2012 on the Performance of Pharmacovigilance Activities Provided for in Regulation (EC) No. 726/2004 and Directive 2001/83/EC

IRB	:	Institutional Review Board
ISO	:	International Organization for Standardization
ISoP	:	International Society of Pharmacovigilance
ISPE	:	International Society for Pharmacoepidemiology
IT	:	Information Technology
IVRS	:	Interactive Voice Response Systems
JAN	:	Japanese Adopted Names
JMO	:	Japanese Maintenance Organisation
LLT	:	Lower Level Term (in MedDRA)
MA	:	Marketing Authorisation
MAH	:	Marketing Authorization Holder
MaxSPRT	:	Maximised Sequential Probability Ratio Test
MedDRA	:	Medical Dictionary for Regulatory Activities
MEs	:	Medication Errors
MGPS	:	Multi-item γ-Poisson Shrinker
MHRA	:	Medicines and Healthcare Products Regulatory Agency (UK)
MR	:	Mutual Recognition Authorisation Procedure
MS	:	Member State
MSSO	:	Maintenance and Support Service Organization (for MedDRA)
NAP	:	Nationally Authorised Medicinal Product
NCA	:	National Competent Authority
NIB	:	National Institute of Biologicals
NIH	:	National Institute of Health (USA)
NIMP	:	Non-Investigational Medicinal Product
NLM	:	National Library of Medicine (USA)
O/E	:	Observed-versus-Expected analysis
P	:	Product- or Population-Specific Considerations (in GVP)
PAES	:	Post-Authorisation Efficacy Study
PAS	:	Post-Authorisation Study
PASS	:	Post-Authorisation Safety Study

PBRER	:	Periodic Benefit-Risk Evaluation Report
PCG	:	Project Co-ordination Group (of the governance structure set up by the European Medicines Agency and national competent authorities for the implementation of the new pharmacovigilance legislation)
PEMS	:	Prescription Event Monitoring System
PGx	:	Pharmacogenomics
PhV DB	:	Pharmacovigilance Database
PhVIWG	:	Pharmacovigilance Inspectors Working Group (at the European Medicines Agency)
PL	:	Package Leaflet
PMDA	:	Japan's Pharmaceutical and Medical Devices Agency
PPC	:	Peripheral Pharmacovigilance Centre
PPP	:	Pregnancy Prevention Programme
PRAC	:	Pharmacovigilance and Risk Assessment Committee (at the European Medicines Agency)
PrAR	:	Preliminary Assessment Report
PRR	:	Proportional Reporting Ratio
PSMF	:	Pharmacovigilance System Master File
PSUR	:	Periodic Safety Update Reports
PT	:	Preferred Term (in MedDRA)
PvPI	:	Pharmacovigilance Program of India
QPPv	:	Qualified Person Responsible for Pharmacovigilance in the EU
QRD	:	Quality Review of Documents (at the European Medicines Agency)
REG	:	Regulation (EC) No. 726/2004 of the European Parliament and of the Council of 31 March 2004 laying down Community procedures for the authorisation and supervision of medicinal products for human and veterinary use and establishing a European Medicines Agency as amended.
REMS	:	Risk Evaluation and Mitigation Strategy
Rev	:	Revision
RGt	:	Pharmacogenetics
RMP	:	Risk Management Plan
ROR	:	Reporting Odds Ratio

RPC	:	Regional Pharmacovigilance Centre
RRR	:	Relative Reporting Ratio
SADR	:	Suspected Adverse Drug Reaction
SAE	:	Serious Adverse Event
SCCS	:	Self-Controlled Case Series Design
SDR	:	Statistic of Disproportionate Reporting
SMEs	:	Small and Medium Size Enterprises
SmPC	:	Summary of Product Characteristics
SMQ	:	Standardized MedDRA Queries
SNPs	:	Single Nucleotide Polymorphisms
SOC	:	System Organ Class (in MedDRA)
SRS	:	Spontaneous Reporting System
SSAR	:	Suspected Serious (or Serious Suspected) Adverse Reaction
SSL	:	Secure Sockets Layer
SUSAR	:	Suspected Unexpected Serious Adverse Reaction
TT	:	Timetable
UMC	:	Uppsala Monitoring Centre (WHO Collaborating Center)
URD	:	Union Reference Date (preferred term: EU reference date)
USAN	:	United States Adopted Names
USFDA	:	United States Food and Drug Administration
WHO	:	World Health Organization
WHO-ART	:	WHO - Adverse Reaction Terminology
WHO-FIC	:	WHO Family of International Classifications
XEVMPD	:	eXtended EudraVigilance Medicinal Product Dictionary
XEVPRM	:	eXtended EudraVvigilance Product Report Message
ZPC	:	Zonal Pharmacovigilance Centre

■■■

REFERENCES

1. GENERAL REFERENCES

1. Pharmacovigilance: A Way for Better Tomorrow; A. Rashmi, K. Ramit, Gill N. S., A. Amit, Rana A. C.; Int. Res. J. Pharm; 2 (12); 43-46; 2011.

2. Experiences With Adverse Drug Reaction Reporting by Patients; F.Hunsel, L. Hramark, Shanthipal, Staen Olsson, K. Grootheest; Drug Saf; 35 (1); 45-60; 2012.

3. Assessing, Managing and Reporting Adverse Drug Reactions may better equip us to minimize medicines related harm; A. R. Cox; Pharmacy in Practice; 57-61; 2008.

4. Data Mining Techniques in Pharmacovigilance: Analysis of the Publicly Accessible FDA Adverse Event Reporting System (AERS); E. Poluzzi, E. Raschi, C. Piccinni, F. De Ponti; INTECH, Chapter 12; 265-302; 2012.

5. Access to New Health Products in Low Income Countries and the Challenge of Pharmacovigilance; P. Lalvani and J. Milstein; PDP Access Stearing Committee; 2011.

6. Pharmacovigilance; Chapter 35 in Management Sciences for Health Part II; 35.1-35.19; 2012.

7. Pharmacovigilance in Emerging Markets; J. McEwen; Drug Delivery; Pharma Asia; 27-29; 2009.

8. Safety Monitoring of Drugs – Where we stand? Palian S., Mishra P., Shankar P. R., Bista D, Almeida R, Kathmandu Uni. Med. J., 4(1), 119-127; 2006.

9. Safety Monitoring in Clinical Trials; B. Yao, L. Zhu, Q. Jiang, H. A. Zia; Pharmaceutics, 5, 94-106, 2013.

10. Pharmacists' Role in Reporting Adverse Drug Reactions in an International Perspective; K. Grootheest, Sten Olsson, M. Couper, L. Berg; Pharmacoepidemiol. Drug Safety; John Wiley and Sons Limited, pp 1-8, 2003.

11. FIP Statement of Policy: The Role of Pharmacist in Pharmacology; FIP 2006.

12. Involvement of Private Players in Pharmacovigilance Program of India: Data Reliability will be Under Question; R. Mahajan; Editorial; National J. Physiol. Pharm. Pharmacol; 3 (2) 102-104; 2013.

13. Need for Uniform Guidelines for Submitting Adverse Event Reports for Publication in Biomedical Journals; V. R. Tandon; Editorial, JK Science 16 (2) 49; 2014.

14. National Pharmacological Program; C. Adithan; Editorial; Indian J Pharmacol. 37 (6) 347; 2005.

15. National Pharmacological Program S. B. Bavdekar, S. Karande, Editorial, Indian Pediatrics, 43 pp27-32; 2006.

16. Pharmacovigilance, R. D. Mann, E. B. Andrews (Eds); John Wiley and Sons Limited, Second Edition; 2007.

17. To Err is Human: Building a Safer Health System, L. T. Kohn, J. M. Corrigan, M. S. Donaldeson (Eds); Committee on Quality of Health Care in America, Institute of Medicine, National Academic Press Washington D. C. 1999.

18. Drug Benefits and Risks: International Text Book of Pharmacology; C. J. Boxtel, B. Santoso, I.R. Edwards (Eds); The Uppsala Monitoring Centre; IOS Press; Second Edition; 2008.

19. A Practical Hand Book on The Pharmacovigilance of Medicines Used in the Treatment of Tuberculosis, Enhancing the Safety of the TB Patient; WHO 2012.

20. ASHP Guidelines on Adverse Drug Reaction Monitoring and Reporting; Medication Misadventures-Guidelines ; Am. J. Health-Syst Pharm. 52: 417-419; 1995.

21. PIPA Guidelines for Signal Management for Small and Medium Sized Pharmaceutical Companies, PIPA Signal Detection Working Party; Pharmaceutical Information and Pharmacovigilance Association (PIPA) 2012.

22. Pharmacovigilance Program of India (PvPI); Pharmacovigilance Tool Kit; Indian Pharmacopoeia Commission; Ministry of Health and Family Welfare, GOI; 2013.

23. National Pharmacovigilance Protocol, Ministry of Health and Family Welfare, GOI;

24. Current Problems and Future Aspects of Pharmacovigilance in India; A. K. Ghosh, A. De and N. N. Bala; Int. J. Pharm Bio Sci.; 2 (1), 15-28; 2011.

25. Importance of Pharmacovigilance in Indian Pharmaceutical Industry; S. S. Shukla, B. Gidwani, R. Pandey, S. P. Rao, V. Singh, A. Vyas; Asian J. Res. Pharm. Sci., 2(1); 04-08; 2012.

26. Pharmacovigilance: An Overview; B. R. Alhat ; Int. J. Res. Pharm. Chem.; 1 (4); 968-974;2011.

27. Pharmacovigilance: A Review; A. Patel, D. Giles, V. Thomas, Gurubasavarajaswamy P.M., R. Patel; Int. J. Pharm. Biol. Arch.; 2(6), 1569-1574; 2011.

28. Adverse Drug Reactions and Their Risk Factors Among Indian Ambulatory Elderly Patients; Mandavi, S. DÇruz, A. Sachdev, P. Tiwari; Indian J. Med. Res., 136; 404-410; 2012.

29. Adverse Drug Reaction Monitoring, V. V. Bhosale, S. P. S. Gaur; Curr. Sci.; 101 (8); 1024-1027; 2011.

30. Indian J. Pharmacol.; Special Issue; P. Biswas (Ed) 40 (S1); S1-S34; 2008.

31. Pharma Times; Special Issue 47 (8); 07-61; 2015.

32. Text Book of Pharmacovigilance; S. K. Gupta (Ed)ICR;, Jaypee Brothers Medical Publishers (P) Ltd., 2011.

33. India; M. Antani, K. Baxi Chapter 9 in Global Pharmacovigilance Laws and Regulations: The Essential Reference ; 151-163; 2008.

34. Adverse Drug Reaction Monitoring in India; V. Dhikav, S. Singh, K. S. Anand; J. Indian Acad. Clin. Med.; 5(1); 27-33; 2004.

2. TOPIC-RELATED REFERENCES

Chapter 5

1. Requirements for Drug Information Centres; FIP Pharmacy Information Section; FIP.
2. Medication Safety in the Community; A Review of the Literature; National Prescribing Service Limited, Sydney, 2009.
3. Literature Review: Medication Safety in Australia; L. Roughhead, S. Semple, E. Rosenfeld; Sanson Institute; University of South Australia; Adelaide; 2013.
4. Ensuring Drug Safety and Effectiveness Through Pharmacovigilance; Risk Sciences International; 2012.
5. Literature Evaluation; P. M. West; Pharmacotherapy Self-Assessment Program; 5th edition; pp 93-114.

Chapter 6

1. Guideline on Good Pharmacovigilance Practices (GVP); Module I-Pharmacovigilance Systems and their Quality Systems; European Medicines Agency; EMA/541760/2011; 2012.
2. SOPs on Filing of ADR forms, Processing and Reporting of ADR Reports, Causality and Assessment of ADR Reports, Quality Assurance of ADR Reports, Roles and Responsibilities of PvPI Personnel, Training of PvPI Personnel, Communications in Pharmacovigilance Program of India; Pharmacovigilance Program of India; National Co-ordinating Centre; AIIMS; New Delhi; 2011.

Chapter 8

1. Guidelines for Submitting Adverse Event Reports for Publication; W. N. Kelly et. al. ISPE Commentary; Pharmacoepidemiol. Drug Safety; 16, 581-587, 2007.

Chapter 9

1. Risk Management Plan; European Regulation (EC) No. 726/2004 and Directive 2001/83/EC.
2. Volume 9 A of the Rules Governing Medicinal Products in the European Union-Guidelines on Pharmacovigilance for Medicinal Products for Human-beings. EMA; 2007.
3. ICH Topic E2E; Guidance on Planning Pharmacovigilance Activities (CPMP/ICH/5716/03).
4. Pharmacovigilance, Signal Detection and Signal Intelligence Overview; A. Shibata; M. Hauben; 14th International Conference on Information Fusion; Chicago; USA ; 2011.
5. Pharmacovigilance and Risk Management; S. Gagnon, P. Schuler, J. (Dachao) Fan; in Global Clinical Trials Play Book; Elsevier Inc.; 141-159; 2012.

6. Enhanced Signal Detection and Management Enables More Effective Pharmacovigilance; K. Chatterjee, V. K. Pannala, P. Chakraborty; Cognizant White Paper; 2008.

7. Core Competencies for Drug Safety/Pharmacovigilance Professionals, E. King; A Master's Paper to the Faculty of University of North Carolina; Chapel Hill; 2011.

Chapter 10

1. Guidelines for ATC classification and DDD assignment; 16th Edition, WHO Collaborating Centre for Drug Statistics Methodology; Noawegian Institute of Public Health; Oslo 2013.

2. A Study on the Use of International Non-proprietary Names in India; K.M. Gopakumar, N. Syam; C.E.N.T.A.D.; 2007.

3. Guidelines on the Use of International Non-proprietary Names (INNs) for Pharmaceutical Substances; The Vision of Drug Management and Policies; WHO 1997.

Chapter 11

1. WHOART; Wikipedia; 2014.

2. COSTART; Wikipedia; 2015.

3. EUDRAVIGILANCE: Pharmacovigilance in the European Economic Area; European Medicines Agency; eXtendedEudra Vigilance Medicinal Product Dictionary (XEVMPD); Data-Entry Tool (EVWEB) User Manual Version 5.0; 2012.

4. Introductory Guide; MedDRA Version 14.0 ; MedDRA Maintenance and Support Services Organization; Virginia; USA, 2011.

5. MedDRA ; Wikipedia; 2015.

6. Adverse Event and Drug Coding in Clinical Research; S. Qureshi; J. Clin. Res. Best Practices; 8 (3); pp: 1-4;2012.

Chapter 12

1. Effective Communication in Pharmacovigilance – The Erice Declaration; Sept. 1997.

2. USFDA Guidance for Industry and FDA Staff; Dear Health Care Provider Letters: Improving Communication of Important Safety Information; Jan. 2014.

3. Communicating Important Drug Safety Messages: the Dear Health Care Provider Letter; Mary Sullivan from regulatoryfocus.org; June 2013.

Chapter 13

1. Oracle Argus Safety; Oracle Data Sheet; pp 1-3; 2009.

2. Aris G Pharmacovigilance and Safety; Total Safety™ The Leading Pharma-covigilance and Clinical Drug Safety Suite; Version 7.1; 2015.

Chapter 14

1. Guideline on the Readability of the Labelling and Package Leaflet of Medicinal Products of Human Use; European Commission; 2009.
2. Guideline on the Packaging Information of Medicinal Products for Human Use Authorized by the Union; European Commission; 2013
3. Quick Response (QR) codes in the labelling and package leaflet of Centrally authorized Medicinal Products; General Principles of Acceptability and Rules of Procedure ; European Medicines Agency; 2015.
4. Investigator's Brochure (IB); Wikipedia; 2013.
5. Standard Operating Procedure for Creating and Maintaining Investigator's Brochure (IB) for UCL Developed Products; Reviewed on October 2015.
6. Adverse Reactions Section of Labelling for Human Prescription Drug and Biological Products - Content and Format; Guidance for Industry; USFDA; CDER/CBER; 2006.

Chapter 15

1. Common Terminology Criteria for Adverse Events (CTCAE) Version 4.0, USDHHS; NIH; NCI; 2010.

Chapter 16

1. Data mining methodologies for Pharmacovigilance; Mei Liu, M. E. Matheny, Yong Hu, HuaXu; SIGKDD Explorations, 14 (1) 35-42; 2013.
2. EMA: Guideline on the statistical signal detection methods in the Eudravigilance Data Analysis Systems June 2008.
3. Novel Statistical Tools for monitoring the safety of marketed drugs; Almenoff et. AL; Clin. Pharmacol. Ther.; May 2007.
4. Application of Data Mining Techniques in Pharmacovigilance; Andrew M. Wilson Etal; BR. J. Clin. Pharmacol 57;2 ; 127-134; 2003.
5. The role of data mining in Pharmacovigilance; HaubenEtal, Expert Opin. Drug Saf.; 4*(5) 929-48; 2005.
6. Disproportionality Analysis using empirical Bayes Data Mining: A tool for the evaluation of drug interaction in the post-marketing setting; AlmenoffEtal, Pharmacoepederminol and drug safety: 12; 517-521; 2003.

Chapter 17

1. Pharmacogenomics and Personalized Medicine; (Ed.) Nadine Cohen; Humana Press; a part of Springer Science; 2008.
2. ICH E 15; Definitions for Genomic Biomarkers, Pharmacogenomics, Pharma-cogenetics, Genomic Data and Sample Coding Categories; Nov. 2007.
3. EMEA Position Paper on Terminology in Pharmacogenetics; (CPMP); Nov. 2002.

Chapter 18

1. Haemovigilance Advisory Committee to DCGI-CDACO; Central Drug Standard Control Organization; New Delhi.

3.   REGULATORY

3.1   ICH

1. E1: The extent of Population exposure to assess clinical safety for drugs intended for long-term treatment of non-life-threatening conditions (Oct. 1994)

2. E2 A: Clinical Safety Data Management: Definition and standards for Expedited Reporting. (March 1995)

3. E2 B:Maintenance of the ICH guideline on Clinical Safety Data Management: Data Elements for Transmission of Individual Case Safety Reports (Feb. 2001)

4. E2 C:Periodic Benefit-Risk Evaluation Report (PBRER) (Dec. 2012)

5. E2 D: Post-Approval Safety Data Management: Definitions and Standards for Expedited Reporting (Nov. 2003)

6. E2 E: Pharmacovigilance Planning (April 2005)

7. E2 F: Development Safety Update Report (DSUR); (Aug. 2010)

8. E3: Structure and content of Clinical Study Reports; (Nov. 1995)

9. E4: Dose-Response Information to support Drug Registration; (Mar. 1994)

10. E5: Ethnic Factors in the Acceptability of Foreign Clinical Data; (Feb. 1998)

11. E6: Guideline for Good Clinical Practice; (June 1996)

12. E7: Studies in Support of Special Populations: Geriatrics; (June 1993)

13. E8: General Considerations for Clinical Trials; (July 1990)

14. E9: Statistical Principles for Clinical Trials; (Feb 1998)

15. E10: Choice of Control Group and Related Issues in Clinical Trials; (July 2000)

16. E11: Clinical Investigation of Medicinal Products in the Pediatric Population (July 2000)

17. E12 A: Principles for Clinical Evaluation of New Antihypertensive Drugs (March 2000)

18. E14: The Clinical Evaluation of QT/QTc Interval Prolongation and Pro-arrhythmic Potential for Non-antiarrhythmic Drugs (May 2005)

19. E15: Definitions for Genomic Bio-markers, Pharmacogenomics, Pharma-cogenetics, Genomic Data and Sample Coding Categories (Nov. 2007)

20. E16: Bio-markers related to Drug or Biotechnology Product Development: Context, Structure and Format for Qualification Submissions (Aug 2010)

21. E17: General Principle on Planning/Designing Multi-Regional Clinical Trials (2014 in process)

22. E18: Genomic Sampling Methodology for Future Use (2014 in process)

3.2   EUROPE

Guidelines on Good Pharmacovigilance Practices (GVP) :

1. Module 1: Pharmacovigilance Systems and their Quality Systems; (June 2012)
2. Module 2: Pharmacovigilance System Master File (Feb. 2012)
3. Module 3: Procedure for Conducting Pharmacovigilance Inspections Requested by the CHMP (Nov. 2007)
4. Module 4: Pharmacovigilance Audits (Dec. 2012)
5. Module 5: Risk Management Systems (April 2014)
6. Module 6: Management and Reporting of Adverse Reactions to Medicinal Products (July 2012)
7. Module 7: Periodic Safety Update Report (PSUR) (July 2012)
8. Module 8: Post-authorization Safety Studies (Jan 2012)
9. Module 9: Signal Management (June 2012)
10. Module 10: Additional Monitoring (April 2013)
11. Module 15: Safety Communication (July 2012)
12. Module 16: Risk Minimization Measures: Selection of Tools and Effectiveness Indicators (March 2013)
13. Modules 11-14 are in preparation.

Guidances:

1. Guideline on the exposure to Medicinal Products during Pregnancy: Need for Post-authorization Data (Nov. 2005)
2. Guideline on Conduct of Pharmacovigilance for Medicines used by the Pediatric Population (Jan. 2007)
3. Detailed Guidance on the Collection, Verification and Presentation of Adverse Reaction Reports arising from Clinical Trials on Medicinal Products for Human Use. (R2 April,2006)
4. Guideline on the use of Statistical Signal Detection Methods in the Eudra-Vigilance Data Analysis System (Nov. 2006)
5. Note for Guidance – EudraVigilance Human – Processing of safety messages and Individual Case Safety Reports (ICSRs) (Oct. 2010)
6. Note for Guidance on Clinical Safety Data Management: Definitions and Standards for Expedited Reporting (June, 1995)(ICH E2 A)
7. Electronic Transmission of Individual Case Safety Reports (ICSRs)-Data Elements and Message Specification - Implementation Guide (Aug. 2015) (ICH E2 B R3)
8. Note for Guidance on Definitions and Standards for Expedited Reporting; Post-approval Safety Data Management (May 2004) (ICH E2 D)

9.   Note for Guidance on Planning Pharmacovigilance Activities (June,2005) (ICH E 2 E)

10. Note on Guidance on Development of Safety Update Report (Sept. 2011) (ICH E 2 F)

11. Note on Guidance on Periodic Benefit-risk Evaluation Report (PBRER) (Jan. 2013) (ICH E 2 C R2)

Directives:

1.   DIRECTIVE 2001/20/EC OF THE EUROPEAN PARLIAMENT AND OF THE COUNCIL of 4 April 2001 on the approximation of the laws, regulations and administrative provisions of the Member States relating to the implementation of good clinical practice in the conduct of clinical trials on medicinal products for human use.

2.   DIRECTIVE 2001/83/EC OF THE EUROPEAN PARLIAMENT AND OF THE COUNCIL OF 6 NOVEMBER 2001 ON THE COMMUNITY CODE RELATING TO MEDICINAL PRODUCTS FOR HUMAN USE; amended by 2002/98/EC; 2004/24/EC; 2004/27/EC

3.   DIRECTIVE 2004/27/EC OF THE EUROPEAN PARLIAMENT AND OF THE COUNCIL of 31st March 2004 amending Directive 2001/83/EC on the Community code relating to medicinal products for human use.

4.   DIRECTIVE 2010/84/EU OF THE EUROPEAN PARLIAMENT AND OF THE COUNCIL of 15 December 2010 amending, as regards pharmacovigilance, Directive 2001/83/EC on the Community code relating to medicinal products for human use.

5.   DIRECTIVE 2012/26/EU OF THE EUROPEAN PARLIAMENT AND OF THE COUNCIL of 25th October 2012 amending Directive 2001/83/EC as regards pharmacovigilance.

Regulations:

1.   REGULATION (EC) No. 726/2004 OF THE EUROPEAN PARLIAMENT AND OF THE COUNCIL of 31st March 2004 laying down Community procedures for the authorization and supervision of medicinal products for human and veterinary use and establishing a European Medicines Agency.

2.   VOLUME 9A of The Rules Governing Medicinal Products in the European Union: Guidelines on Pharmacovigilance for Medicinal Products for Human use; Sept. 2008.

3.   REGULATION (EU) No. 1235/2010 OF THE EUROPEAN PARLIAMENT AND OF THE COUNCIL of 15th December 2010 amending, as regards pharmacovigilance of medicinal products for human use, Regulation (EC) No. 726/2004 laying

down Community procedures for the authorization and supervision of medicinal products for human and veterinary use and establishing a European Medicines Agency, and Regulation (EC) No. 1394/2007 on advanced therapy medicinal products.

4. COMMISSION IMPLEMENTING REGULATION (EU) No. 520/2012 of 19 June 2012 on the performance of pharmacovigilance activities provided for in Regulation (EC) No. 726/2004 of the European Parliament and of the Council and Directive 2001/83/EC of the European Parliament and of the Council.

3.3   USA

Guidances:

1. Guidance for Industry E2C Clinical Safety Data Management: Periodic Safety Update Reports for Marketed Drugs; November 1996.
2. Guidance for Industry E2F Development Safety Update Report; August 2011.
3. Guideline for Industry Clinical Safety Data Management: Definitions and Standards for Expedited Reporting; March 1995.
4. Guidance for Industry E2BM Data Elements for Transmission of Individual Case Safety Reports; April 2002.
5. Guidance for Industry E2E Pharmacovigilance Planning; April 2005.
6. Guidance for Industry Drug-Induced Liver Injury: Premarketing Clinical Evaluation; July 2009.
7. Guidance for Post-marketing Reporting of Adverse Drug Experiences; Feb 1997.
8. Guidance for Industry: Pre-marketing Risk Assessment; March 2005.
9. Guidance for Industry: Development and Use of Risk Minimization Action Plans; March 2005.
10. Guidance for Industry: Good Pharmacovigilance Practices and Pharmacoepidemiologic Assessment; March 2005.
11. Guidance for Industry: FDA's Communication to the public March 2012.

Others:

1. Common Terminology Criteria for Adverse Events (CTCAE)- Version 4 USDHHS September 2009.
2. Advances in FDA's Safety Program for Marketed Drugs; CDER, USFDA, April 2012.
3. MedDRA: Understanding MedDRA (The Medical Dictionary for Regulatory Activity) available on the website: www.meddra.org (accessed on Nov. 2015).
4. MedWatch: The FDA safety information and adverse event reporting program. Available on USFDA website (accessed on Nov. 2015).

CIOMS:

1. Benefit Risk Balance for Marketed Drugs: Evaluating Safety Signals; Report of CIOMS working group IV: CIOMS: Geneva 1998.
2. Current Challenges in Pharmacovigilance: Pragmatic Approaches: Report of CIOMS Working Group V: CIOMS: Geneva 2001.
3. Management of Safety Information from Clinical Trials: Report of CIOMS Working Group VI: CIOMS: Geneva 2005.
4. The Development Safety Update Report: Harmonizing the format and content for periodic safety reporting during clinical trials: Report of CIOMS Working Group VII: CIOMS: Geneva 2006.
5. Definition and applications of terms for vaccines Pharmacovigilance: Report of CIOMS/WHO working group on Vaccine Pharmacovigilance, CIOMS 2012.
6. International Ethical Guidelines for Biomedical Research involving Human Subjects: Report of CIOMS/WHO working group on Vaccine Pharmacovigilance, CIOMS 2002.
7. Reporting Adverse Drug Reactions: Definitions of terms and criteria for their use: CIOMS Geneva 2000.
8. Pharmacogenetics: Towards Improving Treatment with Medicines; CIOMS Geneva 2005.

WHO:

1. A Practical Handbook on Pharmacovigilance on Anti-Retro Viral Medicines, WHO 2009.
2. A practical Handbook on Pharmacovigilance of Anti-Malarial Medicines, WHO 2007.
3. Pharmacovigilance for Anti-Retro Virals in Resource Poor Countries, WHO 2007.
4. Safety Monitoring of Medicinal Products: Guidelines for Setting up and running a Pharmacovigilance center; UPPSALA Monitoring Center/ WHO 2000.
5. The Role of WHO Program on International Drug Monitoring in Co-ordinating World Wide Drug Safety Reports; Sten Olsson; Drug Safety 1998; 19(1)1-10.
6. The Importance of Pharmacovigilance: Safety Monitoring of Medicinal Products; WHO 2002.
7. The Safety of Medicines in Public Health Programs: Pharmacovigilance an Essential tool UPPSALA Monitoring Center; WHO 2006.
8. Safety Monitoring of Medicinal Products: Reporting System for the general public; WHO 2012.
9. International Drug Monitoring: The Role of National Centers WHO TRS No.498 ; WHO Geneva; 1972.
10. Pharmacovigilance Toolkit version 2.0 WHO; Jan 2012.
11. Reporting and Learning Systems for Medication Errors: The Role of Pharmacovigilance Centers; WHO; 2014.
12. Pharmacovigilance: Ensuring Safe Use of Medicines ; WHO Policy Perspectives on Medicines ; WHO; 2004.

■■■

www.ingramcontent.com/pod-product-compliance
Lightning Source LLC
Chambersburg PA
CBHW080954020726
47505CB00009B/2197